"IF YOU KNEW
CAN'T

If one rejection stung, cat-o-nine-tails snapped ders. "I'm not guilty of anything but getting softheaded over a female. You're the one who prances around in trousers, gambles like some kind of fancy cardsharp, and bellies up to the bar like a…like a tart."

"I am not a tart! I like to wear trousers. And I like to ride, shoot, gamble, and cuss. How could you want to marry me if you don't like who I am? That's who I am, and that's who I'll always be."

"No, it isn't! I'll tell you who you are, Katy O'Connell."

She turned her face away, but he was having none of that. Taking her stubborn chin in a firm grasp, he forced her to look at him. "I'll tell you who you are. You're a butterfly just crawling out of her cocoon, with a spirit like the wind. You're strong, smart, and brave—about everything but your heart. You're not afraid of passion. I'll tell you what you're afraid of, Katy O'Connell—you're afraid of me, because with me you feel like a woman."

He bent forward and kissed her hard.

Also by Emily Carmichael

Outcast
Lawless
Visions of the Heart
Touch of Fire

Published by
WARNER BOOKS

Gold Dust

EMILY CARMICHAEL

WARNER BOOKS

A Time Warner Company

WARNER BOOKS EDITION

Cover design by Diane Luger
Cover photograph by Herman Estevez
Hand lettering by Carl Dellacroce

Warner Books, Inc.
1271 Avenue of the Americas
New York, NY 10020

Visit our web site at
http://pathfinder.com/twep

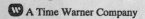 A Time Warner Company

Printed in the United States of America

First Printing: June, 1996

10 9 8 7 6 5 4 3 2 1

CHAPTER 1

Katy O'Connell didn't usually frequent saloons. Not because she couldn't hold her whiskey; Katy had a head for liquor that would have been the envy of any hard-drinking man. And not because she feared for her reputation. The only reputation she truly cared about was her three-year reign as champion of the Willow Bend Fourth of July rifle shoot.

No, the reason Katy avoided saloons was that a saloon was not a ladylike place to rest your bones and wet your whistle, and her stepmother wanted Katy to be a lady, among other expectations. Katy loved her stepmother and most times tried to please her. But not today. Today was a day that deserved whiskey—a drink not to be had in the hotel tearoom up the street. Therefore, she dusted some of the dirt from her baggy shirt, hiked up her trousers over narrow hips, settled her slouch felt hat on her head, and pushed through the batwing doors of the Watering Hole Liquor Emporium.

"Afternoon, Katy," Myrna Jenkins eyed Katy from behind the mahogany bar. The owner's wife looked amazingly like the plump, pink lady who reclined in the mural that decorated one whole wall of the room, the only difference being that Myrna had her clothes on. "Ain't you walkin' through the wrong door, honey?"

"Nope," Katy answered. "Gimme a whiskey."

Myrna snorted.

"Come on, Myrna! I'm parched as a weed in a dry gully."

"You're about as dusty as one, too." She set a glass of pale brown liquid in front of Katy. "What'cha been doin'? Wrasslin' snakes?"

Katy grimaced. "I was chasing that wild mustang and his herd of mares that've been grazing over by our place."

"The mustang won?"

"How'd you guess?"

"Ain't nobody been able to lay a rope on that devil's head, and better'n you have tried, kiddo. Thought your pa warned you off of that horse."

"Pa's not here." Katy took off her hat, scratched at her scalp through the pile of dark braids that were coiled atop her head, and stuck the misshapen hat back on her head. Then she took a deep, grateful gulp of her drink—and sputtered. "This isn't whiskey!"

"Cold tea," Myrna admitted. She swiped at the bar with a rag.

"If I'd wanted tea, I'd be sitting in the hotel tearoom!"

"Not dressed like that, you wouldn't."

Katy's eyes flashed a warning.

"Don't start cussin', kiddo. Don't sound good on a female. You're in a rare pissin' mood today. I ain't seen you like this since you laid out Porky Brinkman for callin' you and your sister squaws. Thought your stepma had finally turned you into a lady."

"I'm rankled, that's all."

"So you bust into town lookin' like a draggletail cowhand?"

"What's wrong with looking like a cowhand?" Katy sighed wistfully and took another gulp of tea. "Pa sure does admire that mustang stallion. Would've been nice if I could've brought it in. He would've been mighty pleased when he and Olivia got back."

"You ain't got enough to do out at your pa's ranch that you got time to run after wild horses?"

"Got nothing to do at the ranch. Ol' Jenkins does the think-ing, and the hands do the work. Damned useless is what I am."

Myrna shook her head as she refilled Katy's glass of tea. "You don't know when you got it good, kiddo. You got a pa who's middlin' rich, a family what loves ya, and ya live on the purtiest piece o' land between here and Bozeman. You been given the world, and all you can do is spit on it."

"Yeah. Well, maybe I don't want to be given the world. Maybe I want to win it like my pa did. Like my stepma Olivia did."

Myrna answered with a scornful grunt as Katy took another deep swig of tea.

"This stuff isn't bad," Katy conceded.

"Better'n the whiskey Carl serves here."

"That's for sure." Katy gazed morosely into the amber depths of the cold tea for a few moments, then glanced around the room. One other customer, a gray-haired, sunken-cheeked oldster she recognized as a lineman for the railroad, shared the long bar with her. One table was occupied by five men playing poker—the two Hackett brothers, Clive Messenger, Corky Stillburn, and a man she didn't recognize.

"Where is everybody?" she asked Myrna. "All the men in this town swear off booze and cards?"

Myrna huffed contemptuously. "All gone off with gold in their eyes."

"Huh?"

"Y'ain't heard? There's gold been discovered up north, up the Yukon river a ways. They're sayin' them streams have more gold in 'em than a henhouse has chicken feed."

She reached beneath the bar and slapped a newspaper down in front of Katy. It was from Bozeman, a week old, and stained with whiskey and coffee. The banner headline blared out the news that gold had been discovered in the Canadian Klondike. Katy scanned the article, which declared that on July 15, 1897, the steamer *Portland* had docked in Seattle car-rying over two tons of gold taken from several tributaries of the Klondike River. A white man, his Indian wife, and her brother had struck gold in their diggings on what was now being called Bonanza Creek. Since then similar strikes had been made on the same creek and others that flowed into the Klondike River and thence into the Yukon.

"A new gold rush," Katy said softly, wonder in her voice.

"Yeah. Every man jack who's got two good legs to carry him up to Dawson is runnin' after that gold. They've been comin' through town on the train all week, and most of Willow Bend has joined 'em. Most of 'em that've stopped in the bar don't know squat about what they need to survive up there. But they all stampede back to the train when the conductor puts out the call."

"Gold!" Katy said wistfully. "Just think. They'll win themselves a fortune."

Myrna snorted. "Most of 'em will win nothing but a place six feet under. Either that or they'll turn back after spendin' their life's savin's on a wild-goose chase. That's a damned rough wilderness they're headed to. My Carl spent a couple 'a summers up there when he was young, and it cured him of any notion of goin' back."

"They're pioneers!"

"Pioneers my ass! Fools is what they are. Know-nothing store clerks, bankers, farmers, schoolteachers. I talked to one fella who was goin' with his brother who's a preacher. His brother wouldn't come in the bar 'cause he don't hold with liquor." She made a rude noise. "Met another fella who's a pot salesman. Can you imagine that? A damned pot salesman!"

Katy grinned. "Bet he won't be selling pots after he stakes his claim!"

"He'll be sellin' 'em at the Pearly Gates if he's not careful," Myrna scoffed. "Then there's that fancy cuss over there at the table."

Katy's gaze moved in the direction of Myrna's nod. For a moment she let her eyes rest on the stranger sitting at the poker table with the Hacketts, Clive, and Corky. He wore a well-tailored broadcloth suit, fancy polished boots, a silk waistcoat with the chain of a pocket watch looping from the pocket. A black derby hat hung from one corner of his chair back. He didn't look flashy enough to be a gambler or cardsharp, but he was much too citified to be from around Willow Bend.

"Who is he?" Katy asked Myrna.

"Says he's a writer. Came in with the train a couple 'a days ago, and he's been askin' everyone who comes in here all sorts o' questions. Even had a chat with me. Called it an interview. Says he's writin' a story about the dyin' Old West for some newspaper Back East."

"No kidding?"

"Heard him tell one fella that Willow Bend's a 'treasure trove of local color,' whatever that means."

Katy took a second look at the stranger. He was clean-shaven with closely trimmed brown hair that sprang from his head in thick waves. Not over thirty, Katy guessed. Maybe younger. Broad shoulders and masculine good looks that explained why Myrna's daughter Ruthie, who served drinks in the bar, was hanging over his shoulder giggling whenever he said anything. But then, Ruthie didn't have the sense God gave a chipmunk. All she thought about was men.

"Handsome piece, ain't he?" Myrna asked.

Suddenly the stranger grinned in a way that lit his eyes with roguish humor. His hand reached over and patted Ruthie's backside in a way that made Katy's face grow hot.

"He looks like a libertine to me. You gonna let him do that to Ruthie?"

Myrna shrugged. "Ruthie's a grown woman. She knows what she wants. Besides, he'll be gone afore long. If he had a head on his shoulders, he'd 'a been gone an hour ago. From what I can see, he don't know a thing about playin' poker against the likes of the Hacketts. They been cleanin' 'im out all mornin'."

The stranger scooped the money on the table into a neat pile in front of him. Ruthie clapped and giggled while the Hacketts scowled.

"Doesn't look like they're cleaning him out now."

"No, it don't, do it?"

Clive Messenger slapped the table and stood up. "That's enough fer me. That's the second big pot in a row you pulled in, friend. When your luck changes, it really changes."

"Changed a bit too fast to my way of thinkin'," Jud Hackett grumbled.

Jud's brother Jacob shuffled the cards and rapped them loudly on the table. "We don't tolerate cheatin' around here, boy."

Katy chuckled into her glass of tea as Jacob's words carried to her ears. The Hacketts didn't tolerate cheating only when they weren't the ones dealing from the bottom of the deck.

"Well now, gents," the stranger said. "If I'd been cheating, I'd have won more than two hands, don't you think?" His grin was placating, his voice reasonable and friendly.

The greenhorn fool, Katy thought. Didn't he know when he was being set up?

Jud turned to Clive, who stood watching with a shuttered look on his face. "I think pretty boy was cheatin'. Whadda ya think, Clive?"

Clive backed off from the table. "Uh . . . maybe. I dunno."

Jacob set down the cards and rolled up his sleeves. "How 'bout you, Corky? You see 'im cheatin'?"

Corky pushed back his chair and got up. "Ain't my fight, boys. Leave me out of it."

"Fight?" the stranger asked. "Nobody's going to fight, gents. We're all civilized men here."

That assumption was a big mistake, Katy mused, holding out her glass for a refill of tea. She was starting to enjoy the show.

"Not only is he a cheat," Jud declared. "He's a pissant yella coward." He reached across to the pile of coins in front of the stranger and pulled the money his way. "He's lucky we don't hang 'im, eh Jacob. Cheatin's a hangin' offense in this town, ain't it?"

"Leastwise it rates a big fine," Jacob agreed with a grin.

"Hold on now, gents. I won that money fair and square. You've got no call to be accusing me of cheating."

Jud stood up. He was big as a bear and smelled twice as bad. The stranger looked uncertain.

"I think we oughta fine 'im, Jacob."

"Maybe we jest oughta hang 'im by his heels and see how much money falls out of those fancy pants of his."

Katy could tell the Hacketts were enjoying themselves. They were like wolves playing with a helpless lamb.

"Wait a minute, boys. This is ridiculous." The city gent got up and pushed his chair back. Katy was surprised that he was almost as tall as Jud. Ruthie faded back and cast an anxious look toward her mother.

"Ooooo!" Jacob cooed. "He's gonna fight us, Jud."

"Just give me what's mine, and we'll call it a day."

Katy wondered if she should fetch the marshal. Probably not. If the law got called in on every barroom brawl in Willow Bend, he'd not have time to eat or sleep.

"You want your money, pretty boy? Come get it. We'll fight you fair and square. One at a time."

The greenhorn's face settled into a hard mask of determination. It was really a very nice looking face, Katy thought. Such a shame the Hacketts were going to mess it up.

"You boys go outside if'n you wanna brawl," Myrna called. "I won't have my place being broke up."

"Hell. Myrna. We're not gonna break up anythin' other than pretty boy, here." Jud pushed aside the table to clear a space. "Come on, pretty boy. Come get your winnings."

The stranger took off his coat, took his pocket watch from his waistcoat and set it aside, and assumed a classic boxing stance. Katy shook her head in pity.

Jud swung. City boy danced nimbly out of range, and was promptly clobbered from behind by Jacob's meaty fist. The greenhorn staggered, shook his head, and—to Katy's amazement—recovered.

"Thought you were going to fight me one at a time," he complained.

"That's right, boy. We'll only hit ya one at a time. Fair enough?"

Jud swung again, and this time connected. The greenhorn had no place to dodge that wasn't in the range of the other Hackett's fists. His own fist lashed out and struck Jud an admirably solid hit on the jaw. Jud staggered back, and Jacob roared forward to wrap the greenhorn in a lethal bear hug. He lifted him off his feet and squeezed. Katy could see the stranger's face growing red as he tried to break Jacob's hold. It was going to be a short fight.

Katy had never cared much for the Hackett brothers. They had sense enough to stay away from her, but several years ago they'd tried to bother her sister Ellen. Katy had come upon the scene and sent the brothers packing with their tails between their legs, and when he'd heard about the incident their pa had made sure the Hacketts didn't dare to bother an O'Connell woman again.

She supposed the Hacketts had their function in the scheme of the world. Like wolves, they picked on the weakest and least fit—witness their cutting out the ignorant tenderfoot like a wolf pack cutting the slowest elk from a herd. Any citified dandy who didn't have the sense to stay away from such trash deserved what he got. Still, the urge to throw her two cents into the brawl was almost irresistible. Katy never had been one who could keep her nose out of other people's business, especially when butting in promised a small bit of adventure.

"Myrna, you got a pistol behind the bar?"

"You know I do."

"Care to loan it to me for a little while?"

"Katy girl, I don't like the look in your eye."

Jacob gave the stranger a final squeeze, then tossed him into the next table, which he hit with enough force to splinter one of the wooden legs. Both brothers grabbed him before he could get up and pulled him roughly to his feet.

"Ah-ah!" Jud scolded Jacob. "One at a time, brother. We promised."

Jacob released his hold on the reeling man's shirt. "Whatever you say, brother. We gotta fight fair."

The greenhorn threw a punch that landed full on Jud's nose. Katy gave the man credit for persistence. He had staying power.

Jud threw the fellow into his brother's arms and cradled his injury. Curses, nasal and bubbling, issued from behind his crimson-smeared hands. "Now you've made me mad, you sonofabitch."

Katy raised an eyebrow at Myrna. "They're going to break up your place. Jud's riled."

With a grimace, Myrna handed over the pistol. "Just try to miss the chandelier," she advised. "It cost Carl three months' profits."

Katy fired into the air. The brawlers froze. Clive and Corky both backed even farther into the corner than they already were. The old lineman at the bar jumped so suddenly he spilled his drink.

Thoroughly enjoying the little drama, Katy blew smoke away from pistol's muzzle.

"You stay outta this . . . !" Jud's mouth formed around the word 'squaw,' but he didn't have the guts to say it out loud.

Katy merely smiled. "You're a poor sort of a man if you can't beat up one lousy tenderfoot without your brother's help. You too, Jacob. Jud, if you go for that gun of yours, I'm gonna shoot it right outta your hand, along with a couple of fingers. You know I can do it."

Jud spit a wad on the plank floor.

Katy turned her scathing smile on the Hacketts' victim. "Stranger, if you have a brain in your head, you'll hightail it outta here now."

The stranger was quick to act on her invitation. He gathered up his money, then grabbed his coat and watch and gave the Hacketts a jaunty farewell salute.

"We'll be seein' ya around," Jud promised.

"Not if I see you first, gents." He made haste toward the batwing doors, throwing a coin toward Myrna for his drinks. "Thank you, friend," he said as he passed Katy.

Katy laughed, tossed the pistol to Myrna with a wave of thanks, and followed the greenhorn out the door. She ran to catch up to him.

"I'd make better time if I were you."

"What?" he said.

The Hacketts charged out of the saloon like a brace of snorting bulls. Katy whooped with joy and grabbed the stranger's arm. "Let's go, greenhorn!"

They ran together down the dusty street, the Hacketts pursuing. People in the street and on the boardwalk stopped and stared, but no one made a move to interfere. In Willow Bend, a man's fights were his own business.

"Where's your horse?" Katy asked between gasps for air.

"Horse?" the man puffed back. "No horse. Train."

"Do you have a gun?"

"Hell no!"

If she hadn't been running so hard, Katy would've kicked herself. She should have kept Myrna's pistol. She hadn't realized the Hacketts were quite this riled. Still, the day hadn't dawned when she couldn't defeat the likes of Jud and Jacob without a gun. They rounded a corner, and she skidded to a stop.

"Hold up!"

"Shit!" The greenhorn bent over and gasped for breath. "They're big suckers, but they're damned fast. They're going to beat the shit out of both of us."

"Nah!" A lamb among wolves, was this one. Not only no brains, but no imagination. Katy untied a coiled rope from the saddle of the nearest horse. "We'll fix 'em. Follow me."

As the Hacketts rounded the corner, she grabbed his arm. They sprinted to increase their lead, then ducked into a shadowed alley that was littered with empty whiskey bottles.

"Keep running down the alley!" Katy told him. "You're gonna be the bait."

Chuckling to herself, Katy made a large slip loop of the rope, laid it across the alley entrance, and faded into the shadows against the wall. Only a dumb Hackett would fall for this trick, she told herself happily.

"They went in there!" she heard Jacob exclaim. "We got the bastard now."

Come on, you stupid jackasses. Katy almost chortled out loud. Her blood sang.

Jud was in the lead as the brothers pelted into the alley. Katy let him pass. Jacob was close behind. When he stepped into the loop of rope, Katy yanked hard. The noose tightened around both his legs. He hollered in surprise before his face hit the dust of the alley. Jud skidded to a stop and sprinted back to aid his brother. He didn't see Katy swing the empty whiskey bottle until too late. It bounced off his skull with a resounding thwack. A split second of surprise sparked in his eyes before they went blank. Katy tapped a slender finger against his shoulder, and he toppled like a felled tree.

"You can come back now," she hollered to the stranger.

The stranger arrived, looking ready to fight. When he saw the two limp Hacketts on the ground, he regarded Katy with amazement. "What did you do to them?"

"Took advantage of how stupid they are," Katy told him with a grin. "If they had a brain between them, I would've had to think of something else."

"You're damned remarkable!"

"Yeah," Katy admitted.

Just then Marshal Fields blustered into the alley. He looked at the greenhorn, at the Hacketts, and at Katy. "You again. Myrna came running over to tell me you was dusting up trouble, and I see she was right." He shook his head, half with amusement, half with disgust.

"Now, Marshal . . ."

Fields held up his hand to cut off the stranger's defense. "I know you aren't the culprit here, son." He nodded in Katy's direction. "Whenever this one comes into town, I can count on some sort of a scuffle to keep the day from becoming dull."

"That's not true," Katy said indignantly.

"Most times it is."

"They were cheating him at cards, then jumped him when he won a pot or two."

"So you led them a merry chase down Main Street and coldcocked them both in an alley?"

"Well, someone had to do something!" Katy declared. "They were bound to beat this poor sucker outta ten years of his life."

"Well, I don't doubt that." Fields pulled thoughtfully at his face. "You got a way out of town, mister?"

"I'm leaving on the train in the morning."

"Well, I can dump these two into a cell and let them cool off overnight. But I'll have to let them go in the morning. I wouldn't be anywhere around here, if I was you. These boys have long, nasty memories."

"I'll be gone. Don't worry."

"See that you are. Now you two can help me haul these carcasses off to jail."

When Jud and Jacob were safely locked away, the greenhorn clapped Katy on the shoulder and offered to buy her a drink in thanks.

"You sure you're old enough to drink?" he asked as they headed toward the saloon.

"Hell yes."

"I'm not going to have your ma or pa collaring me for feeding their kid liquor."

"I'm old enough! Besides, my ma and pa are long gone." Since Katy's parents were on their way to New York with her sister and baby brother, their interference with a little sojourn in the Watering Hole was unlikely.

Myrna greeted them with a raised eyebrow. "You got Hacketts on your tail?"

"Don't worry," Katy said. "They're in jail."

"Yeah, well, who's gonna pay for the damage to my place?"

"How much?" the city gent asked.

"Ten dollars oughta do it."

Katy scoffed. "Five's more like it."

Myrna shrugged. "Worth a try."

Katy chuckled as the stranger laid five silver dollars on the bar. "You don't know diddly, do ya?"

He grinned. "Enough to get by."

She tugged him along to a table. "More of what I was drinking before," she told Myrna. "And he'll have whiskey. Carl's good stuff."

He chuckled as they sat down. "You're a real pistol, aren't you, friend?"

"Have to be if you don't want folks to stomp all over you. Isn't it the same where you come from?"

He grinned engagingly. "Back in Chicago folks are more subtle when they try to skin you, that's all."

"Chicago! You're from Chicago?"

"That's where my family lives."

"You got a wife and kids back there?"

"No. A mother and sister. I'm a writer for the *Chicago Record*—that's a big newspaper. I get sent all over the country to do articles, and that doesn't leave me time for a wife. Isn't fair to leave a woman on her own a lot, you know. A man takes on a wife, he ought to take care of her."

Myrna set their drinks down on the table. "If'n you think that, stranger, you're one of the few men who do. I've not met many men who won't take off and leave their wives behind when the notion strikes 'em. Look at all those fools headed up north lookin' for gold."

"That's why I don't feel the urge to marry. I like to go wherever the good stories are. I'm headed north myself."

Katy was instantly consumed with envy. "You're really headed to the Klondike?"

"Yes indeed. Not looking for gold, but writing about those who are." He flipped a coin at Myrna for the drinks, along with a smile that brought a flutter to the woman's lashes. "Thanks, sweetheart."

Myrna simpered. "You just crook a finger if you want anythin' else."

"I will," he assured her.

Katy snorted. "I figure writing about gold must be about the same as smelling a good steak cooking without getting to eat it."

"Not to me, friend. I'm writing a series of articles on the dying Old West. Might even turn it into a book someday. This new gold rush is right up the line of what I want to write about. Stopped by here to soak up some of the local color. You know, most places out West have gotten pretty tame, settled down to be just as dull and safe as anyplace else. This little town is an absolute treasure of colorful characters and stories, though." He raised his glass in a toast. "The Klondike will be even better."

Katy chuckled. "New to the West, aren't you?"

"I've been out here a couple of months."

Katy's heart beat faster at the very thought of what she was going to do. It would give her stepma a heart attack if she knew, and probably gain her a licking from her pa, even though she was a woman grown. Her parents wouldn't be back for at least two months, though, and after their first surprise, they would understand why she had to jump at this chance. She wasn't needed at the ranch; Clem Jenkins, the ranch manager, had things well in hand. Adventure and freedom beckoned. In the Klondike one could win independence and a fortune with nothing more than guts and hard work. What she could do with such a fortune danced merrily across Katy's mind. She could make her own rules, dependent on no one, not even her father.

She eyed the stranger speculatively. For a greenhorn, he seemed a good enough guy. Lucky man. Katy had decided to do him a favor.

CHAPTER 2

Jonah Armstrong had seen the look a thousand times since joining the great flow of humanity toward Seattle and Tacoma, the launching places for the golden north. Gold fever—a combination of greed, hope, and lust—shone from the eyes of storekeepers, cowboys, drummers, farmers, even doctors, bankers, lawyers, politicians, and preachers. They all wanted a piece of the new gold rush—perhaps the last real gold rush.

Now the fever flamed in this sassy kid. Gold shone bright as the sun in those sparkling green eyes. Jonah could almost see the visions of El Dorado dancing through the kid's mind.

"Ya know," the youngster started. "That's a tough country on the Klondike, and a tough trip to get there. Before this there's not been anybody there but Indians and a few prospectors, and maybe an exploration party or two."

"That's all going to change now," Jonah said.

"It's still a tough country. How you planning to make the trip?"

"Just follow the flow, I guess. Most everybody is sailing from Seattle or Tacoma to a place called Skaguay, which is right below White Pass. I heard someone say it's the easiest, fastest way if you don't want to spend a fortune sailing all the way to St. Michael and from there up the lower Yukon."

"You'd better have more to go on than hearsay," the kid advised.

"There's going to be a highway of humanity headed to Dawson. The trail will be trampled so well a blind man could find it."

"You got money?"

"Enough."

"You know what kind of supplies you need to see you over the trail?"

"I'll figure it out."

The kid made a rude sound. "If you don't mind me saying so, mister, you're sitting on most of your brains. Some of these people are gonna get killed trying to get to the gold. A lot of the others are gonna have to turn back—because they don't know a rat's ass about the outdoors and the wilderness." The sassy little imp's eyes lit with mischief. "It would be a pure cussed shame if you couldn't write your story because you left your bones drying on the trailside."

Jonah took a gulp of his whiskey and banged the glass down in appreciation. "It would at that. But I haven't left my bones out to dry yet, and I've traveled to plenty of tough places. Those brains I'm sitting on haven't failed me up to now."

"Maybe 'cause you haven't asked them to take you to the Klondike before now. Ya know, mister—what you need is a guide."

Jonah had known this was coming. "I don't need a guide," he said with a tolerant grin.

"Yes you do."

"Why?"

"You don't have a gun."

"Don't figure on needing one."

"You fight like some swell from Back East."

"I am a swell from Back East. Well, Chicago isn't really Back East."

"It's far enough east for you to learn to fight like a sissy. That I know for a fact!"

"I was trying to fight those boys clean. That's not sissified."

The kid shook his head. "That's what I mean. Fighting fair just invites a knock on the head, or worse. I'd bet you can't hit the side of a barn with a rifle. You can't skin a rabbit, tell a spavined horse from a sound one . . ."

Jonah listened with amusement as the kid listed the reasons a 'citified greenhorn' couldn't possibly survive a Klondike adventure without a bit of help from a wilderness-wise woodsman. No doubt the woodsman in question was the kid himself. Lord but the boy was a corker! With smooth, blushing cheeks and girlish lashes, he looked no older than twelve, yet he packed more trouble in him than most grown men. No doubt he'd need his spunk as he got older, for he didn't have the build to grow into a bruiser. The kid's hands were delicate beneath the grubbiness of calluses and dirty nails. The bone structure in his face was as fine as a girl's.

". . . and from the looks of it you've not done a hard day's labor in a long time," the kid concluded, taking Jonah's hand and turning it over to reveal a relatively uncallused palm.

"I'm a writer, friend. I don't chop wood for a living."

"Writing's not going to get you to Dawson," the boy said with an all-knowing nod.

Jonah chuckled. "If I hired a guide to take me to the Klondike, what makes you think I'd hire you? You're no bigger than a half-grown girl and you look about as tough as a butterfly."

The kid flushed. "I did all right with the Hacketts! And there've been some others who crossed me and wished they hadn't."

"That so? How old are you? Twelve. Thirteen?"

The flush staining the too-smooth cheeks deepened. "I'm twenty."

Jonah guffawed. "How old are you really?"

"Ask Myrna!" the kid demanded indignantly. "She knows I'm no youngster!"

Jonah raised an eyebrow in Myrna's direction, fully aware the woman had been eavesdropping. She nodded.

"Well, you're mighty small."

"I can shoot the eye out of a squirrel with a rifle, pistol, or rock sling. I can skin a rabbit and have it cooking before your mouth even starts to water. There hasn't been a horse born that I can't ride, nor a mule I can't get to work. I can find dry wood in a rainstorm, and build a shelter outta nothing but what the woods have to offer. What's more, I know how to handle trash like the Hacketts, and you'll be meeting lots of their kind on the way to the goldfields. Hell, mister! Without me, you're gonna be robbed blind, stomped on, chewed up, and spit out before you get halfway to Dawson. If the trash along the trail doesn't do it, then the wilderness will."

"Well now," Jonah said with a smile. "You must be one talented kid."

"I'm not a kid, and I know what I'm doing."

A talented little con man is what the kid was, but what a character—a real throwback to the days of the wild and woolly Old West. The staid bankers and housewives and clerks who read the *Chicago Record* would devour the sketches he could write about the boy. It would add some color to their plodding lives. And if the kid was half as good as he claimed, he could make the trip to Dawson a good deal easier. The big city was a jungle that Jonah could deal with, but wild forests, wilderness mountains, and tough frontier towns were not his element. The kid's proposition was beginning to look attractive.

He gave the boy a sharp look. "You got family that's going to miss you. A pa or ma who needs to give permission?"

"Nope. My family's all gone."

"That's too bad. I'm sorry."

The boy regarded him with a carefully neutral expression. Probably the tough little character didn't want to show any emotion over his family's loss. Jonah decided not to question him any further on it.

"Okay, kid. You want to come? I'll pay you twenty-five cents a day to be my guide up to the goldfields."

The offer met with a rude snort. "A buck a day."

"You're trying to rob me, young'un. Fifty cents and I pay all expenses."

"Done!"

The kid offered his hand for a shake. Jonah took it in a firm grasp and wondered again at the delicacy of the bones in his grip. "Armstrong here. What's your name?"

"O'Connell."

"All right, O'Connell. Be at the train in the morning," Jonah warned, "or I'll go without you. I'll leave you a ticket at the window."

"I'll be there." The kid downed the last of whatever it was he was drinking and slammed the glass onto the table with gusto. "Gotta go. See you in the morning."

Jonah suppressed a laugh as the boy strutted toward the door, full of piss and vinegar and grinning like a virgin who'd just bedded his first wench. He had to admire the kid's spirit and nerve. "O'Connell!" he called as the boy reached the door.

The youngster turned.

"Thanks for your help with the Hacketts."

"Don't mention it."

With a mocking salute, the boy was gone. Jonah saw the sparkle of amusement in Myrna's eyes as she looked on from behind the bar. He shook his head, wondering if he'd just made a big mistake.

The world was still dark when Katy kicked Hunter off her legs, rolled out of her bed, and lit the lamp. The gray wolf gave her a scathing look and yawned a toothy objection.

"Proper wolves spend the night hunting and howling at the moon, not curled up on a bed sleeping."

The wolf jumped back on the bed, curled into a compact circle of thick fur, buried his nose beneath his tail, and regarded her balefully.

"You're no proper wolf, that's for sure." Katy knuckled the plush fur between his ears. "And I'm sure you don't care."

Katy herself yielded to a great, gaping yawn. Dawn was still an hour away, but she hadn't been able to sleep all night for thinking of the fine adventure that lay before her. How things had changed since yesterday, when her life had seemed so useless and dull! Olivia had always told her that things generally looked darkest right before the dawn. Katy had thought her stepma was spouting platitudes, but in this case Olivia had been telling the truth.

The day before, Katy had been dejected about her life. She'd let the mustang stallion slip through her fingers; she wasn't needed on the ranch; she missed her family; and she was smotheringly, overwhelmingly bored. Now, however, a new day had dawned. Frustration, boredom, and uncertainties about her future sloughed off as easily as old skin slipped off a snake, revealing a bright new Katy beneath. Now someone needed her for her own unique skills. Now she had the chance to prove she could make it on her own, without her pa. As much as she loved her pa and her stepma, the time had come for her to be her own person.

Katy dressed carefully. Yesterday, because she was mad at the world, she had let herself slip back into the boyish guise of her younger years. She was still more comfortable in trousers, shirt, and boots than in a dress, but she did know how to dress and speak like a lady. Olivia had taken great pains and exercised great patience to teach her. She slipped into bloomers, chemise, a voluminous skirt that would allow her to ride astride into town, a simple shirtwaist, and a tailored jacket. Examining herself in the mirror with a critical eye, she wondered how Jonah Armstrong would react when he saw her. Twelve years old indeed! She was a woman grown, and a passable looking one at that when she took the trouble to get gussied up. Green eyes, the Irish green she'd inherited from her father, twinkled back at her from the mirror. Smooth olive skin and high cheekbones were the gift of her Blackfoot mother. Thick black hair tumbled to her narrow waist in tangled waves.

She threw back her shoulders and admired the bosom that had finally come in when she was fifteen. It was small, but it was definitely there. When she was younger, Katy had thought she was going to be flat as a boy for the rest of her life. Up until today, she had almost regretted that her womanly assets had bloomed, but now she wondered if the greenhorn would think she was attractive. Men had been ogling her twin sister Ellen for the past six years, and supposedly she and Ellen looked very much alike. Of course, no man in his right mind would ogle Katy. If one had, she would have decked him.

Thinking of the greenhorn made Katy smile. Lucky for the poor fellow that he'd bumped into her. He had no notion what he was about going to the Klondike with his city-bred ignorance. There would be more like him on the trail, she guessed, and the tenderfeet would only make it more dangerous for the rest of them. Mr. Armstrong would get through to the goldfields, though, because he had Katy O'Connell helping him. Lucky for him he wasn't the sort of man who refused to accept help from a woman.

When Katy doused the lamp, took the small valise she had packed, and stumbled her way from her bedroom into the kitchen, Hunter followed. He sat beside her when she propped the note for her parents against the flower arrangement on the dining room table. He pressed against her legs when she cut herself slabs of bread and cheese in the dark kitchen and headed out the door toward the corral and barn. Her gelding, Little Brown, whuffed loudly when Katy opened the corral gate and Hunter followed her in.

"Ssssh!" Katy hissed at the gelding. "You want old Jenkins to know we're taking off?"

The gelding rolled an eye at her as she lifted the saddle to his back.

"Don't worry, you old plowhorse. You're only going as far as Willow Bend. I left a note for Jenkins to pick you up at the livery."

Hunter joined in the conversation with an unwolflike whine. Katy hunkered down and put her arms around the furry body.

"I'll miss you, you old wolf!"

Hunter had been her best friend for eight years, ever since her pa and Olivia had rescued him from a cave where the rest of his litter had been killed by a grizzly bear. Raised with the doting attention of Katy, Ellen, and Olivia, the gray wolf had developed an unstinting devotion toward his adopted pack. Never once had he cast a longing eye into the wild. He was more like a devoted dog than a wolf.

Hunter raised a paw and placed it on Katy's knee.

"Don't do that!" Katy cried. "You're just making this harder!"

The wolf gazed at her from woebegone yellow eyes.

"What would you do in the Klondike—a soft and pudgy old wolf like you?"

Probably the same thing that he'd always done—play with the wind, pounce on rabbits and rodents, play tag with her in the high grass, be her faithful friend.

Katy expelled a huge sigh. "All right. You win, stupid wolf. You can come. We'll manage it somehow."

So Hunter was still beside Katy when she tied the valise onto the back of her saddle, mounted Little Brown, and rode off toward the dawn. A few hundred yards from the barn, she stopped to let her gaze sweep a circle around the valley that was her family's land—the Thunder Creek Ranch. In the muted light of predawn, everything seemed too still for life. The cattle were small black specks dotting the broad gray palette of the valley. The ranch buildings huddled together as if seeking protection from the vast Montana sky. In the distance rose sharp peaks still wearing caps of white in high summer. All together the scene looked like a painting—a somber study in grays and browns.

How long would it be before she saw this scene again? Katy wondered. How angry would her pa be when he read the note explaining why she had to go? How hurt would Olivia feel? Katy shook her head to chase away the doubts. She was doing the right thing. Jonah Armstrong needed her, and she needed to find a place that was her own. Katy O'Connell wasn't a person who could live in someone else's shadow.

Besides, Katy thought as she turned Little Brown and headed away from her home, ranching was dull, and Montana had become much too tame.

Jonah slid up the window beside his seat to let in more air. Already the car was stifling, and the morning was scarcely begun. The noise from the railroad platform flowed in a dissonant crescendo through the open window. The train was almost full, and there were people on the platform who still had to board. A motley crowd it was. Business suits to buckskins and everything in between. Young and old, fat, tall, skinny, short— they were all headed for Puget Sound and a steamer to take them north to their dream of riches. How many of them would get there? he wondered. And of those who reached the gold-fields on the Klondike, how many would strike it rich? A large battleship of a woman followed by two younger versions of herself sailed down the aisle and crowded into one of the few vacant seats in the car. Surely they couldn't be headed for the Klondike! Such a place was certainly no place for females.

Jonah searched through his pocket for the ever-present pencil and notepad. He scrawled a few key words that would recall the color and restlessness of the crowd when he had the time to write in more length. Once the train moved there would be no more taking notes—he'd tried years ago to write on a railcar. Deciphering his jerky scrawl had been impossible.

A large man smelling of stale sweat and cigar smoke started to sit in the seat beside him.

"Sorry," Jonah told him. "This seat's taken."

The man gave him a scowl but moved on. If his urchin guide didn't show up soon, Jonah was going to be lynched by the half dozen people he'd denied the seat. He wondered if the boy was going to come. Maybe the kid had been all show and no substance. He hadn't impressed Jonah that way, and Jonah considered himself a shrewd judge of character. He smiled, thinking of O'Connell's cockiness. He'd probably show up in buckskins and a coonskin cap with scalps dangling from his belt.

"Thank goodness! I thought I was going to miss the train!"

A young woman in a full skirt, tailored jacket, and jaunty flat-brimmed straw hat plopped down next to him. Jonah scarcely was able to grab his hat from the seat before she crushed it beneath her backside. He opened his mouth to object, but when the young lady turned her face toward him, he thought better of it. His grubby little guide, if he showed up at all, could find his own seat on the crowded train. The trip would be much more pleasant sitting next to this young woman. He couldn't very well ask the lady to leave. Besides, she was a fetching creature. In fact, when she smiled, as she did just then, with her green eyes alight and her face beaming pleasure, she was goddamned beautiful.

"How do you do, ma'am." Jonah flashed her his most charming smile.

The fine black wings of her brows drew together briefly in a little frown. Then she smiled again, to devastating effect. "I didn't mean to cut it this fine," she said. "But I had a time of it."

The train lurched, gasped, and lurched again. Slowly the car began to move. They were on their way. Jonah glanced around. There was no sign of young Daniel Boone, unless he had gotten on a different car. All things considered, it was probably for the best. Jonah didn't need the responsibility of dragging a half-wild kid to the Klondike, no matter how interesting a character O'Connell would have been for the *Chicago Record* readers.

"That uppity conductor made me leave my wolf in the baggage car," the lady beside him said. "I told him Hunter was perfectly harmless. There wouldn't have been a peep out of him unless he thought someone was making trouble for me."

Jonah blinked. Had the girl said she had a wolf? He must have misunderstood her. "That's too bad," he commiserated cautiously.

"And before that I had the devil's own time picking up the ticket from the window. The pile of cow shit that passes for a ticket agent couldn't find the ticket." Her eyes widened and she pressed a small hand to her mouth. "Oops! And here I swore I'd talk and act like a lady today. It's just that I was so riled. Thought I was going to miss the train!"

Jonah was beginning to feel like Lewis Carroll's Alice in Wonderland. This conversation was not right. The words coming out of that most attractive mouth didn't quite belong with the high-class appearance. Some of them didn't make sense at all.

She took the pins from her hat and set it in her lap, revealing a shining mass of black braids coiled atop her head. Her face turned toward his with an expectant smile. "Are you excited, greenhorn?"

A small tinkle of alarm went off in Jonah's brain. Did everyone in this dustball of a town label strangers with the name greenhorn? "Uh . . . excited?" The lovely young miss sitting next to him was more than capable of getting him excited, Jonah was sure, but excitement wasn't precisely what she was inspiring at the moment.

She cocked her head at his confusion, then grinned impishly. "I'll bet you thought I wasn't going to show up, didn't you?"

The tinkle of alarm grew to a clanging clamor. Jonah stared at the girl. It couldn't be. He could not have been so flamingly stupid. Yes he could have. The green eyes sparkled with the same mischief. The flawless skin that had been too smooth for a boy of twenty looked perfect on a female. Too damned perfect. The high, delicate cheekbones and fine hands had made his grubby rescuer look effeminate. The same features gave the girl sitting beside him a real claim to beauty.

"Well, I'm here," she said, "so you don't need to worry any longer. I'm going to take good care of you."

Seemingly unaware of Jonah's horror, Katy chattered on like a little magpie. She hoped he didn't mind her bringing the wolf along. He would be a help in hunting, she assured him, and a good camp sentry at night. Though getting him on the steamer was going to be a problem, she admitted. They should see about getting an outfit in Seattle, for supplies there would no doubt be cheaper than at the head of the trail in Alaska, though not much. The demand being what it was, the greedy damned—oops!—storekeepers would take the opportunity to dig into the pockets of those headed for the goldfields. This was going to be a successful trip, she assured him. He shouldn't worry. Others might fall beside the way, but as long as he had Katy O'Connell at his side, he would see the gold-fields and get his story.

Jonah felt his head begin to pound. The longer the girl talked, the more plain it became that what he feared was really true. "You're a woman," he said.

Her chatter cut to silence and she threw him a sharp look.

"I've hired a *woman* to take me to the Klondike."

"Good thing for you that you're not one of those morons who think women can't do anything but sew and cook. Look at the opportunity you would have missed."

"Why didn't you tell me yesterday you were a woman?"

Katy's eyes narrowed suspiciously. "Most of the gents I've met can tell the difference."

"For pity's sake! You were wearing trousers and boots and covered with dust!"

"I'd been out chasing wild horses. You expect me to do that in a dress?"

"And that hat! You looked like you'd been sleeping in alleys and eating out of garbage heaps for two weeks!"

Her face started to grow red. "You thought I was a man?"

"You drink like a man—"

"I was drinking cold tea!"

"You fight like a man, you talk like a man—"

"I can talk like a lady. I'm talking like a lady now!"

"And you looked like a boy. I thought you were small, and young. How was I supposed to know you were a woman under those trousers and dirt?"

"You're a pretty sad case if you can't tell girls from boys, mister!"

"I hired a *woman*!"

"You make it sound like you hired a kangaroo!"

"You're fired. I'm sorry, but I made a stupid mistake. It's my fault. I'll admit it. But you're fired just the same."

"Fired?"

"That's what I said." He stared out the window, unable to meet her eyes. "You're fired."

"You can't fire me! We're on a train to Seattle!"

"You can get off at the first stop. I'll give you money to buy a ticket back to Willow Bend."

"Like hell!"

"You can't come with me."

"Why not?"

"You're a woman. Didn't I make myself clear? A woman cannot make the trip to the Klondike. Especially as a trail guide. For God's sake! What kind of man do you think I am?"

"You're a damned greenhorn who's gonna get himself into trouble without my help! That's the kind of man you are!"

He met the blaze of her eyes and saw the same impetuous fighting spirit that had saved him from a drubbing by the Hackett brothers the day before. How could he have mistaken her for a boy, even dirty and dressed as she had been? There was nothing even remotely masculine about that face and figure.

"Look, Miss O'Connell. I'm sorry to have caused you inconvenience, and I'm sure you can do everything you said you can, but such a thing is entirely unsuitable—"

"Suitable hell! Don't try to make excuses, greenhorn. You're a damned welcher, and no one welches on Katy O'Connell!"

She might be able to pose as a lady, but when her temper was up, her true colors certainly shone through. "I can't be responsible for taking a female into such a harrowing and strenuous situation. Besides, you and I traveling together—a bachelor man and single lady—would not be proper."

She snorted inelegantly. "Proper, my ass! You're just looking for a way to back out. A bargain is a bargain, I say. We shook on it, and out here, a man's hand is as good as a contract. A woman's, too."

"What kind of a woman would contemplate such an outrageous adventure?"

"A damned smart one, that's who. One who can shoot and ride better than most men—"

"And cuss better," Jonah added with a disapproving scowl.

"And has more guts and a better head on her shoulders!"

He pulled a wad of greenbacks from his pocket, separated several, and stuffed them into her hand. "This should get you back to Willow Bend, madam, with enough left over for one day's wages. This discussion is at an end!"

"Don't bet on it!" she shot at him as he rose and brushed past her into the aisle. "You're not getting rid of me that easily!"

All eyes followed Jonah down the aisle as he escaped into the next car. He deserved the amused looks. How could he have been so stupid? He could only hope the little ruffian adventuress didn't follow him and chase him the length of the train to continue the fruitless argument. And to think he had mistaken her for a lady when she had first sat down! That was as wide of the mark as mistaking her for a boy!

CHAPTER 3

Katy returned the curious looks of the other passengers in the car with a glare that could have melted the snowcaps off the Montana mountains, then stared sullenly out the window. To think she'd credited that sissified jackass greenhorn with enough sense to see past the fact that she was a female! Why was it that men thought they were the only ones who could have fun in this world, do interesting things and achieve accomplishments more challenging than batting eyelashes and simpering when some man deigned to take an interest in them? She was beginning to appreciate the fight her stepmother had won in becoming a physician. Even her pa, when he'd first known Olivia, had thought it far more important for her to dedicate herself to loving him than to follow her chosen profession. That she could be both a woman and a doctor hadn't occurred to him until Olivia had hit him over the head with it.

If her pa, who was usually smart, could be such a nincompoop about such things, how much worse were the rest of the men in the world, who didn't have half her pa's brains or good sense—especially a certain brown-haired, blue-eyed, citified, mulehead skunk from Chicago. Unsuitable, indeed! He couldn't take a puny little woman into such a harrowing and strenuous situation! She'd show him harrowing and strenuous!

The damned welcher wouldn't get rid of her so easily! She was more determined than ever to get to the Klondike, even if Armstrong wouldn't live up to their bargain. She would pass him on the trail and thumb her nose at him, and when he had to turn back because he didn't know what the hell he was doing, she would laugh in his face. If he made it as far as the goldfields—an unlikely prospect—she would dangle her bags of gold nuggets in his face and remind him how he'd said a woman should never even think of such an outrageous adventure. Let him write *that* story for his damned Chicago newspaper!

A portly gentleman in a suit and derby hat stopped beside the empty seat next to her. He tipped his hat.

"Afternoon, ma'am! Is this seat available?"

"Help yourself," Katy said.

He dropped down into the seat with enough weight to make the supports groan. "Hot, isn't it?" he commented, taking off his derby and fanning his red face.

Katy looked out the window at the passing scenery, but she felt his eyes on her.

"I'm headed for Seattle. Is that where you're going, too?"

"Yes," she answered shortly.

"Traveling alone all the way to Seattle. My, my. Aren't you a brave little thing."

She shot him a seething glance.

"Myself, I'm bound for the Klondike." He puffed out his chest, which had the effect of also expanding his rotund stomach. "Going to make a fortune in gold."

Katy surveyed his pudgy build with unconcealed contempt. "You plan to haul yourself and a thousand pounds of supplies over White Pass?"

His eyes grew round, his face red. "I beg your pardon?"

"Do you know how steep that pass is?"

"I imagine I know much more about it than you, miss! I've read accounts in the newspapers."

"By someone who's actually done it?"

"Well, no. But someone who knew, nonetheless, that White

Pass is most hospitable to the traveler who wishes to travel overland to the Yukon River, and thence to the Klondike."

Katy shook her head.

"Even if the trail to Dawson presents difficulties, they will be overcome. I wouldn't expect you to understand, miss. You, after all, are a woman."

The look Katy gave him made the man lean away, then get up. He slapped his derby firmly onto his head as his lips pursed in disapproval.

"Good day to you, miss!"

"And a good day to you, fool," Katy muttered to his back as he retreated down the aisle. She felt a twinge of guilt for taking out her ire on an innocent bystander. Today didn't seem to be her day to be a social success.

The train made two stops during the day. During both Katy sat glued to her seat. If Armstrong expected her to get off the train and turn tail back to Willow Bend, he was sorely mistaken. It would take more than a single setback to knock Katy O'Connell from her chosen path. Other passengers left the car and strolled about outside, stretching their legs, while the train took on coal, water, passengers, and mail. Katy almost expected the greenhorn to seek her out at the first station to make sure she followed his orders, but the twenty-minute stop passed without a sign of him. She was relieved and miffed at the same time. He'd forgotten her, the ingrate, dismissed her like some piece of dust he would flick from his sleeve.

An hour after sunset, the train stopped in Missoula, and Katy went to the baggage car to visit Hunter. The wolf was glad to see her, his tail wagging like a dog's, his eyes accusing her of neglect.

"Don't give me that woeful look!" Katy scolded him. "I figure you've been sleeping all day. And that blanket the conductor gave you is a lot more comfortable than the hard seats back in the passenger cars."

Hunter's tail thumped in acknowledgment.

"Bet you'd like a walk, though, huh?"

Nervous that the train would leave without her, Katy took the wolf out only long enough for him to accomplish his business. When she returned to the baggage car, men were unloading baggage under the supervision of the conductor.

"So many people are getting off the train here?" an amazed Katy asked.

"The train's stopping for the night, miss," the conductor said. "There's a mighty steep stretch a ways ahead, and we need to add another engine. It won't be available until tomorrow morning."

"Can't we sleep on the train?"

"I wouldn't advise it, miss. Those seats make a mighty hard bed, and there's riffraff in this part of town. There's a hotel about half a block up that's safe enough for a lady, though."

Katy felt in her pocket for the money Armstrong had given her to get back to Willow Bend. That would be more than enough for a room, and a bed would feel better than the hard seat she'd been sitting on until her backside was numb. She didn't mind sleeping on the ground under the stars; but a wooden seat in a stinky train car was a different prospect altogether.

"I'll take my valise," she told the conductor. "That one there."

He pried it from under the pile and handed it down. "Your dog can stay here, if you like."

Katy shook her head. "He'd better come with me."

"We'll see you in the morning then, miss."

The hotel clerk was polite enough to Katy when she registered for the night, but he eyed Hunter with misgivings.

"Don't worry. He's perfectly housebroken. He's probably cleaner than most of the people you have staying here."

"Uh . . . well, there'll be an extra charge for the dog."

Katy dug into the little reserve of funds she'd brought with her from home—very little. At the time she'd thought Armstrong would be holding to his bargain and paying their expenses. At this rate she wouldn't be having many more meals on the way to Seattle.

She left Hunter in the hotel room with a firm admonish-
ment to behave himself and went down to the dining room for
what probably would be her last meal until she could find
someone willing to take her on as a guide. A waiter met her at
the door with the look that waiters reserve for women who
enter a restaurant alone.

"We do not serve unescorted females, miss."

"I'm a guest at the hotel," she explained.

"Be that as it may, we still do not serve unescorted females.
Sorry."

Katy drew herself up and tried to intimidate the waiter with
silent indignation. She'd seen Olivia do it a time or two to
other doctors who refused to accept her as a professional
equal. Olivia occasionally employed this method on her pa as
well, who wasn't easy to intimidate. It worked slick as spit for
Olivia. For Katy it didn't work at all. The little weasel in a
stuffed shirt simply looked right through her as though she
weren't there.

"If you'll excuse me, miss, I have duties to attend to."

"Wait a minute, mister. Whoa there. If I can't eat here,
where am I supposed to eat?"

If she'd been a pig wallowing in slime he couldn't have regarded her with any more distaste. "I'm sure I don't know,
miss. Perhaps one of the boardinghouses."

"I didn't see any boardinghouses."

"A few miles into town."

"Oh, yeah?" She balled her fists and slammed them onto
her hips. "I'm supposed to walk a few miles into town because I'm not good enough to eat in this damned hog trough
of yours. Like hell I will, you little—"

A familiar voice interrupted her rising temper. "Well, if it
isn't Miss Katy O'Connell! I see you didn't take my advice."

The waiter, whose upper lip was beginning to bead with
nervous sweat, jumped on the opportunity. "Are you with this
lady, sir?"

The greenhorn raised one mocking brow. "I suppose I must be."

"Come this way, if you will."

"After you." Jonah made a sweeping bow to Katy and motioned her forward. She obeyed, because the small concession was the only way she was going to get something to eat.

The waiter deposited them at a table that was none too clean, and the foursome at the next table—men she recognized from the train—had obviously made a quick trip to a saloon before dinner. Their boasts of what they would do with the fortunes of gold from the Klondike were loud and slurred.

"They won't allow an unescorted woman into the place, but they'll serve those blowhards," Katy scoffed.

"Those gentlemen are just savoring a bit of adventure," Jonah said. "As apparently you are, Miss O'Connell. What are you still doing here? I told you to get off at the first stop."

"Well forgive me for not bowing, Your Highness. I didn't know your command was law."

"I gave you money—"

"Which you owed me."

"Dammit, Miss O'Connell. You—"

"Watch your language, buster." She grinned. "You're with a lady."

"A lady, is it? I don't think so. A lady does not offer her services as companion to a single man traveling alone. A lady does not go running off hell-bent for leather on a wild-goose chase to the Alaskan and Canadian wilderness."

"Hell-bent for leather? Very good, Mister Newspaper Writer. Did you use that expression in one of your stories about the Old West?"

Jonah's eyes narrowed. He really could look intimidating when he tried, Katy noted. Usually, his smile and the resident sparkle in those blue eyes drew attention away from the breadth of his shoulders and obvious fitness of his physique.

"What's more," Jonah said through clenched teeth, "a lady does not patronize saloons or brawl with the scum therein."

"I wouldn't go so far as to call you scum, Mr. Armstrong."

"I wasn't talking about me!"

"Oh. That's right. It was you and me against the scum. I pulled your bacon out of the fire. Remember?"

"I remember, Miss O'Connell."

"You can call me Katy."

He seemed to make an effort to control himself. She could see a muscle at the hinge of his jaw flex in rhythmic agitation.

"Your turn," she prompted. "I can call you . . ."

At the expectant lift of her brows, he sighed in resignation. "Jonah."

"Not bad. Better than some other names I could call you."

He rolled his eyes toward the ceiling. "Look, Miss . . . uh . . . Katy, I admit that I'm responsible for the misunderstanding that brought you here. I will accept that you offered your services in good faith."

"I did!" Katy confirmed emphatically.

"And if you say that you had no intent of deceiving me as to your gender, I will believe you."

"Big of you. If I was pretending to be a boy, I'm sure I wouldn't have gotten on the train in this getup." She spread her arms to better display her feminine attire. Jonah's gaze traveled in a single instant from the top of her coiled black braids, over her face, down her neck, and then seemed to hesitate for a split second at each and every brass button on her tailored jacket. He blinked and shook his head slightly. Katy suddenly felt exposed. Heat crawled up her neck and into her cheeks.

A waiter—one other than the fellow who had shown them to their table—chose that moment to ask for their order. "The lamb and beefsteak are both very good tonight."

"The lamb for both of us," Jonah said.

"Nope. I want the beefsteak," Katy insisted. "Rare."

Jonah's mouth drew tight. "And wine. Red." He lifted a brow at Katy. "You do drink wine as well as whiskey, don't you, my dear?"

"I do. But it was cold tea. Not that I don't drink whiskey," she said as the waiter left.

"I'm sure you do," Jonah sighed. "Katy, as I was saying, I admit that this situation is not your fault. And it's not that I have anything personally against you—or . . . or women in general. I'm very fond of women, in fact."

"I'll bet." Katy suffered a sudden and inexplicable vision of Jonah Armstrong's eyes warm with passion, his long, blunt fingers caressing a woman's face, his mouth descending to a woman's waiting lips . . . Her face flamed, and she felt an urge to strike out. "You have the look of a man who has flocks of women clucking around you."

"That's not what I meant!" Jonah denied sharply.

"Then what did you mean?"

"I meant that I respect women. But a gold rush is not a place for a female."

"Horsefeathers!"

"Katy, men are dangerous animals when they run in herds, and they're at their very worst when they're in a herd running after gold. And the goldseekers would be the least of your worries. Think of the natural dangers: wild animals, storms, treacherous rivers, insects, mud. Not to mention the lack of privacy. Natural feminine delicacy requires a certain accommodation, and a rough trail in the wilderness alongside thousands of men is not a place to find it."

Katy snorted her contempt.

"The difficulties are legion!" Jonah insisted. "Only one kind of woman would subject herself to that kind of peril."

"Peril! Hmph! You're the one going to be in peril!"

"We're talking about you, not me. You might shoot like a Wild West show sharpshooter. You might have the courage of a bear and be able to outdo Daniel Boone in the woods, but the Klondike is still no place for a woman. It's not safe. It's not proper. There are things that a woman can do that a man can't do—having babies, for instance. And there are things men can do that women can't."

"Like going to the Klondike to find gold?"

"That's right!"

"That's the biggest load of bullshit—sorry! garbage—I ever did hear, Jonah Armstrong. You're not as smart as you look."

He flashed white teeth in an infuriating grin. "I'm smart enough to dump a load of trouble when I see one."

Katy gave him a sour look, but the waiter came just then with their dinner, so she held her tongue. Not that she conceded the fight. Armstrong's whole line of reasoning—if one could call it reasoning—seemed silly to her. She eyed him speculatively over her plate of beefsteak and beans and wondered if reason was the proper fighting tactic with this man. Her pa had told her once that a woman who knew what she was about could get a man to do just about anything. All the woman had to do was use her natural assets, he'd said with a twinkle in his eye, and not give the poor sucker a chance to think.

He was right, most likely. Katy had seen Olivia twist her pa— who was stubborn as only an Irishman can be stubborn—around her little finger more than once. Katy's twin sister Ellen, too, was gifted in such a way. Katy remembered their second Fourth of July town picnic in Willow Bend, when she and Ellen were fourteen, and Ellen had broken a big jug of lemonade while showing off her slingshot to Toby Riley. She had made sad doe eyes at poor Toby, and the idiot had fallen all over himself taking the blame for her. Of course, Ellen had confessed before Toby had gotten whupped by his pa, but it had been an impressive display of feminine magic if Katy had ever seen one.

Perhaps the same kind of magic would work on Jonah Armstrong. Katy recognized she had a bit of catching up to do if she was going to try it, for her effect on the man so far had been anything but enticing. She might have the same natural assets as Ellen, but she didn't have the same talent or inclination for using them. But hell! Getting to the Klondike was worth the effort.

Katy darted a look at her dinner partner and caught him staring at her while he toyed with his lamb. She offered a tentative smile. He didn't return it.

"Scowling like that isn't good for your digestion," she chided. "Don't be in such a temper, greenhorn. If you insist on firing me, at least we can be civilized about it. It was just a misunderstanding, after all."

Jonah's eyes narrowed suspiciously. "Indeed?"

"Indeed?" she mimicked his dubious tone, then smiled. "I'm tired of arguing. Having food in my stomach has put me in a much better mood. Maybe if you ate some of yours, you'd feel better, too."

He resumed poking at the lamb. Katy watched him. Other than his fancy tailored clothes, he didn't have the appearance of an Easterner—or at least Katy's image of an Easterner. His face looked as though it spent a lot of time in the sun. Fine lines creased the skin around his eyes when he smiled, making the smiles seem to start deep in his eyes instead of his mouth. His shoulders were broad; his hands were large, and though the palms were not horny with calluses, as a ranchhand's would have been, the fingers were long and blunt and looked capable of hard work.

Katy decided that sharpening her womanly wiles against Mr. Jonah Armstrong wouldn't be so bad.

"That must not taste very good," she suggested sympathetically. "Aren't you hungry?"

"This meat is tough as shoe leather."

Katy's instinct was to comment that his fancy Chicago taste just didn't appreciate real food, but realized that such a gibe would hardly be charming. "My beefsteak was good, but maybe we should go someplace where you can get better food."

He shot her a wary glance.

"Besides, I think you owe me a night on the town for all the trouble you've caused me."

"All the trouble *I've* caused?"

She smiled.

"Well, I wouldn't mind getting something else to eat." He pushed away his plate in disgust. "Missoula is scarcely the place I'd choose for a night on the town, but it's the place we are. The hotel clerk told me there's a dance at the Freemasons' lodge just up the street. I'm a Mason, so why don't we go up there and take a look?"

"Why don't we?" Katy said blithely. She looked at the lamb on his plate. "If you don't want that, I know someone who does."

Katy took a few minutes in her hotel room to wash her face, fiddle with her hair, and try vainly to brush the dust from her clothes—the clean clothes in her valise were too wrinkled to wear without being hung out.

"You don't know how lucky you are not to worry about such things," she told Hunter, who was enjoying Jonah's leavings of lamb. She gave a final pat to the braided coil atop her head and sighed, ready to ooze charm as she would ever be. "Don't wait up for me," she advised the wolf. "*I* have a social engagement with a gentleman."

The Freemasons' lodge was an imposing stone structure only five minutes' walk from the hotel. Once Jonah's membership in the fraternity was established, they were made welcome. Tonight was Saturday night, and the Missoula Masons and their wives were enjoying a dance and buffet.

Katy and Jonah enjoyed it as well. Fortunately for them, the dance was not a formal one, though Katy did feel rather out of place wearing the same skirt and jacket that had endured the stifling heat and dust of the train car. She felt the curious glances of the other women—all rosy and bright in their summer ginghams and crisp, freshly ironed shirtwaists, bows decorating their braids, ringlets carefully wrought with a hot iron, hair neatly pinned, tamed, braided, and tied.

The buffet spread on a table along one side of the hall was simple: cold chicken and fancy little sandwiches provided by Mason wives and daughters, who obviously were as at home in a kitchen as Katy was on the back of a horse. Jonah, having donated his roast lamb to Hunter, didn't hesitate to stuff himself. Katy had just consumed a beefsteak at the hotel, but she made room for more. If tonight's strategy didn't work, her next meal might be a long time in coming. After eating two of the delicious little sandwiches and a drumstick of chicken, she felt almost too full to be charmingly feminine.

Jonah gave her the opportunity, however, when he asked her to dance. For the first time in her life, Katy was grateful that Olivia had insisted she learn. Unfortunately, she hadn't learned very well, for the notion of fancy-stepping around a room with a man had seemed quite useless to her at the time. The little band in one corner of the room was playing a Strauss waltz when Jonah led her onto the floor. He was an excellent dancer. He did not step on her toes, or push her this way and that out of time with the music, as did some of the boys she had danced with at Willow Bend's infrequent socials. Katy was not as accomplished, however, and her partner's toes suffered for her lack of practice.

"Sorry," Katy mumbled as she trod on Jonah's feet for the fourth time.

"Don't mention it."

"I'm afraid dancing isn't one of my talents."

"So I gather," he admitted with a smile.

When the waltz ended, Jonah guided her to the punch bowl, where he ladled sarsaparilla punch into two glass teacups and handed her one. She smiled sweetly and thanked him. Ellen would have batted her eyelashes, but Katy couldn't bring herself to go that far.

"How long have you been alone?" Jonah asked.

"Alone?"

"You said your whole family was gone."

"Oh. Yes. Not long. A little over a month." She hadn't bothered to tell him her family was gone only to take her sister to school in New York and then travel on to Paris to visit with some of Olivia's medical school chums.

"Your bereavement is so fresh?" His tone was full of sympathy, but his face and eyes were unreadable as he looked down at her. "You're bearing up rather well."

Unwilling to tell an out-and-out lie, Katy merely lowered her gaze and let her lashes shield her bravely hidden grief. "My family are . . . were . . . the best people in the world. They would want me to meet the world head-on and make my way in it. My pa once dug a fortune out of a hardrock mine above Elkhorn." Katy didn't have to struggle to produce a warm smile as she remembered those good/bad days when her father had been a fugitive—before Olivia had come to them. "Gold and silver in veins of quartz. I helped Pa dig it out. Elkhorn was more than a day's ride away, and the only close neighbor we had was on old rogue grizzly we named Old Bruno. That was one nasty bear. I aimed to kill it someday, but I never did. It killed a whole litter of wolf cubs once just for the hel . . . the heck of it. That's when I got Hunter, my wolf."

"Ah yes," Jonah said with a smile. "The wolf in the baggage car."

"In my hotel room, now. He appreciated the lamb, by the way."

"They're playing another waltz. Shall we dance?"

They danced, and Katy continued the effort to be feminine and appealing, to use those natural assets her pa had told her could make a man's will turn to clay. She recounted stories about the summers that she and Ellen had spent with the Blackfeet, how she had learned to track from Crooked Stick, how Squirrel Woman had taught her to tan hides and build cozy lodges of saplings and brush, and how Shadow on the Moon had taught her the skill of catching trout with her bare hands. While she was charming the man out of his stubbornness, Katy reasoned that reminding him of her talents couldn't hurt.

Before the evening was over, though, Katy began to wonder just who was charming whom. She was working very hard to radiate feminine appeal, but Jonah Armstrong seemed to exude seductiveness with no effort at all. He held her close when they danced—too close, Katy suspected, to be proper. He smelled good, which was amazing for a man who'd been on a hot dusty train all day. The bright electric lights of the Mason hall gleamed in the crisp brown waves of his hair, finding hidden gold that was surely as bright as anything coming out of the Klondike. At this close distance, his eyes were very blue, like a warm summer sky at the end of dusk. Looking at them made her feel oddly dizzy. A horse grazing on locoweed was steadier on its feet than Katy was when Jonah smiled down at her, his eyes smiling, too, his arm holding her close.

When they finally headed back to the hotel, the moon had climbed to its zenith and flooded the street with a romantic, milky light. Jonah held on to Katy's arm as they walked down the slight incline.

"I'm glad I learned something about you tonight, Katy," he said. "You're quite a remarkable woman."

Katy's heart leapt. He was going to tell her she could come! She just knew it! Her feminine allure had softened his objections while reminders of her competence made him realize how much he needed her.

Outside the hotel, in the shadows and out of the streetlight, he swung her around and took her in his arms. "Yes, you are quite a woman, Katy O'Connell."

Her heart thumped in her chest, and a fearful feeling that things were hurtling out of control made her stiffen in his grip. He didn't release her.

"I know exactly what you've been doing all night, my dear. I may be new to the West, but I'm not new to the world."

His mouth captured hers before she could duck away. His lips were as warm as the rest of him—warmer even. When she opened her mouth to object, he took full advantage, plunging his tongue inside in a way that frightened her and at the same time called to something deep within her. When he finally let her go, she didn't know if she wanted to hit him or kiss him again.

"Katy, darlin'," he drawled, smiling his dazzling smile. "You're still fired."

CHAPTER 4

Jonah leaned on the deck railing and looked out over the gray water toward the forested land slipping slowly by. A day and a half after leaving the port of Seattle, their steamer was still in the narrow passage between Vancouver Island and mainland Canada. Vancouver Island looked no different than the mainland, with green, fir-covered slopes rising sharply out of the gunmetal-colored sea. Jonah found it hard to believe it was indeed an island, that the smooth water that slipped under the steamer's bow was the northern Pacific Ocean and not some quiet lake.

Hands braced on the rail beside Jonah, Alan Smith observed the gray scene and growled: "Another foggy day. Lord Almighty! I haven't seen the sun since I crossed the Cascades. Makes a body wonder why the Lord created this here world in color instead of just making everything a muddy gray."

"The captain said last night at dinner that the weather can be sunny this time of year."

"Well it hasn't been sunny since I got here, and I hear from October on the sky closes in like this all the time. I'd wager that once you get into the mountains, it gets cold as a whore's heart. I'm glad to be starting out in August. Those who dilly-dally around and decide to come a month from now will have hell to pay making it to the Yukon before ice blocks the river."

"You're probably right," Jonah agreed.

"Damned right I am. Mr. Hayes told me sometimes the Yukon freezes as early as October—in a bad year. Said that's why we're lucky to be making the trip now."

"I guess Mr. Hayes knows what he's talking about." Jonah smiled wryly. "At least I hope he does. We're paying him enough to be a goddamned genius on the subject of the Klondike."

Alan grinned. "Hell, Jonah. That $500 we all gave him won't amount to a hill of beans once we've made our gold strikes. Besides, the man isn't too far off the mark. I did some asking around. In Seattle, an outfit for one man costs $400. More at the head of the trail. Hayes needs to have a bit left over to pay for his time and services."

"I'd say he's getting plenty for his time and services. The man's going to get richer than the prospectors without ever sinking a shovel into the ground."

"That's where you're wrong. What he's getting is pennies compared to what a man can make in the goldfields. Lord, the stories I've heard! The streams up there are paved with gold. All a man has to do is sink a shovel into the ground and he's rich."

Jonah had heard the stories also. He wondered what would make a man like Alan Smith, a middle-aged postal clerk from Indiana with a wife and five children, believe such obviously exaggerated hyperbole. The suspension of common sense among the goldseekers might make an interesting article for the *Record*, he decided. He'd certainly met a number of prospective gold kings who believed that the trail through the mountains between the sea and the Klondike was nothing more fearsome than a Sunday stroll in the woods. Others drank in accounts that the stream gravels were so loaded with gold that a single day's work on a good claim would make a man's fortune. Most of the eager argonauts dismissed the few stories about arduous passes, dangerous rivers, unpredictable weather, and the blossoming concern that Dawson would not be able to stock enough supplies to support the burgeoning population of goldseekers through the long, isolated winter.

At least the little group of men he had joined seemed more down-to-earth than some. They had hired a guide, a Mr. David Hayes, who seemed to know what he was about. Smith was right. The money they had paid him to buy their outfits and arrange for a pack train to carry it over White Pass was not an unreasonable sum, given the current outrageous prices. Mr. Hayes seemed reliable. He was burly and quiet spoken, and had made the trip over the pass several times before. White Pass was the best route, he'd told them, because unlike Chilkoot Pass, pack animals could make it all the way to the summit. Understandably, the demand for good horses and mules was greater than the supply since the gold strike had been announced, and he had gone ahead to secure their party some sturdy animals. He would meet them at Skaguay.

"Yep," Smith said, staring into the gray water that foamed along the side of the ship. "Just sink a shovel into the ground and get rich. Sure would like to see the sun, though. When I'm rich as Midas, I think I'll pack up Thelma and the kids and buy some land in Arizona Territory. They say the sun always shines down there."

"Sounds like a good plan to me," Jonah said.

Smith pushed back from the rail. "You comin' to supper?"

"In a minute or two. I think I'll stay here a while and think on what I'm going to write about this boat trip. Strangely enough, after furnishing the money to send me up here, my editor expects me to send him material for the newspaper now and then."

Smith puffed out his narrow chest. "That's A-L-A-N H-O-R-A-T-I-O S-M-I-T-H, from Muncie, Indiana. Just in case you want to put me in your newspaper."

"Might be I will, Mr. Smith. Might be I will."

Jonah was grateful for the peace that descended when Smith left. He really did need to think of something riveting to send back to old Hobbs at the *Record*. Hobbs liked colorful adventure and drama, either heartwarming or heartrending. Something to get the readers salivating for more. The most interesting adventure Jonah had experienced so far was a common barroom brawl invited by his own stupidity, and the most colorful character he had met on the way to the Klondike he had fired—fired twice, just to be sure he was rid of her.

He stared out at the scenery. This country was truly an invitation to poetry. Clouds hung low over the land, undecided whether to be clouds or fog, to be one with the sky or belong to the hills and trees. Cool shades of gray mixed with deep, peaceful greens and browns. The hiss of water sweeping past the hull and the cry of seagulls only seemed to add to the silence. Though the world was hemmed in by hills and clouds, Jonah felt the vastness of the land, the isolation, the wild serenity—so different from anywhere else he had been, and he'd traveled to many places. The Northwest was infecting his soul, and he wondered why. He was a city boy, and he had no wish to be anything else. Yet this unspoiled green-and-gray boundary where sea and land intertwined—this was a special place. Special and different.

And thinking along the lines of special and different, he couldn't help wondering what Miss Katy O'Connell was doing right now. He could have written a whole series of articles on that one, but no doubt some of his more proper lady readers would have been mortally shocked and offended. Conventional women certainly didn't want to read about such undecorous females in their husbands' newspapers.

But then, most undecorous females weren't as interesting as Katy O'Connell. Jonah had met his share of adventuresses. Most were cursed with transparent greed that detracted from their allure. They were fortune hunters, con artists, or female libertines who entertained themselves by shocking society. Katy was the first he'd met who pursued her own gold instead of someone else's. And she was the first who could brawl like a Irish stevedore and cuss like a Montana mule skinner.

Jonah had little doubt Katy O'Connell was an adventuress of the boldest cut, though. When bluster and indignation hadn't worked, she'd resorted to the oldest female tricks in the book to lure him into her scheme. He could still see those clear green eyes sparkling up at him as they danced, feel the very feminine curves of her body press against him in practiced temptation. How in hell had he ever believed her to be a boy? Her kiss had come close to melting every bone in his body. How many men had the little con artist sucked in with that artless sensuality of hers?

The fog thickened into a drizzle that persuaded Jonah to take refuge in his cabin. He'd been fortunate to book a cabin with Alan Smith and two other men of their little group. Many passengers steaming from Seattle to the gold trails were forced to settle for space on deck, and even the decks were crowded.

At this hour his cabin mates were in the dining room. Jonah was willing to forgo his dinner for an hour of privacy and quiet. He got out his notebook and pen, reclined on his hard bunk, and wrote a tentative title on the paper: "Klondike Bound." Circles and swirls of ink slowly filled the page as Jonah tried to organize his thoughts. There was enough human interest on the steamer alone to fill several articles, but where to start? He thought of the streetcar driver from Boston he'd met the day before. The man had brought a sectional boat with him, a clever contraption that was transported in small, manageable sections that could be easily assembled into a sturdy craft that would take him into Dawson. Others crossing White or Chilkoot passes would need to stop at Lake Bennett, which was the head of the Yukon River, to build boats to take them downriver to the confluence with the Klondike at Dawson. Farsighted fellow, Jonah mused. Worth mentioning in an article. Others also were worthy of mention. One lady, clearly a modest, proper woman, was accompanying her husband on his gold adventure. Mrs. Burke was young, Jonah guessed, though careworn in appearance, which might be accounted for by the young babe in arms she had with her. Her husband was a strapping Irishman with a ready grin and a fiddle he played at the merest hint of a request. What would possess a man to take a young wife and infant on such a hazardous journey? Jonah wondered. Though she never said a word of complaint, Mrs. Burke did not look happy with the prospect of the toils that lay before them.

Jonah's eyes focused on the doodles that covered the page. He chuckled wryly, tore the page from the book, and wadded it into a ball. In spite of his minimal artistic ability, the doodles had coalesced into an unmistakable rendition of Katy O'Connell's perfect oval face.

"Might as well give in," he muttered as he wrote a new title on a clean page: "Faces of the Old West."

> *The Old West is dead,* he scrawled, *but the deceased has left a few survivors, pariahs who, whether nobly or foolishly—the reader must decide—cling to the anarchy and unchecked freedoms that characterize the frontier. They obey no rules but their own and chafe restlessly in the peace that a new millennium promises to this once-rowdy land.*
>
> *One of these colorful remnants of Chaos came to the aid of your most intrepid correspondent when he was in mortal danger of having his teeth shoved down his throat by two bullies of the sort who inhabit drinking establishments wherever they are found. This bantamweight little cockerel evened the odds by firing a pistol at the ceiling, bringing down splinters of the rafters along with my assailants' hopes of the rousing entertainment of beating me to a pulp.*

A smile spread across Jonah's face as he planned out his narration of the little adventure that followed. He would end the story with Katy's neat disposal of both of the Hacketts, and then reveal that his savior was a woman, of all things. His readers would be delighted at the twist—much more delighted than he had been. To hell with the proper ladies who might be shocked. Most of his readers were men, anyway.

Morning cast a whole new light on their journey. The sun blazed down from a bright blue sky; the breeze was warm and fragrant with the tang of seawater and verdant forests of fir. The northern tip of Vancouver Island was a hump of green rising off their stern, and from the port rail of the steamer to forever, it seemed, stretched the sea, deep green fading to blue in the distance. Sea blended into sky without a perceptible line. Not a cloud relieved the bright expanse of the heavens; not a wisp of fog shadowed the sea.

Jonah wished he had a camera that could do the scene justice, but no camera could do that. How could his readers understand the vast beauty of this changeable land without seeing it for themselves? His words would not be enough.

In the dining room, Jonah found his cabin mates and sat at their table.

"I heard you moving about last night," Toby Walsh, a farm laborer from one of the Carolinas, told him. "Was you sick?"

"No. I got an inspiration in the middle of the night to finish an article I had started, so I got dressed and came up here to work. Sorry if I woke you."

"Didn't bother me much," Toby said. "Went right back to sleep."

"Writers sometimes keep odd hours. I'll try to be more quiet."

"You find a good claim in the goldfields," Alan Smith said, "and you won't need to work in the middle of the night."

"I'm going to Dawson in search of stories, gentlemen. Not gold."

Everyone at the table guffawed their disbelief of that.

"Here comes breakfast, and lookee what's bringin' it," Toby said. "Didn't know they allowed women to work these ships."

"I haven't seen her before," Carl Gundescheim commented in his thick German accent. "I would have remembered that one."

Jonah grew warm all over. As if thinking about her almost the whole night through had somehow conjured her out of thin air, Katy O'Connell stood before the table, a platter of steaming flapjacks in her hands. She grinned at him, seemingly not at all discomfited at seeing him. "Here's your breakfast, gents, still hot from the griddle. Enjoy them, because cook says there's only one platter to a table. No seconds." She leaned across Toby to place the platter in the center of the table. The Carolina man's eyes nearly popped as the material of her blouse strained across a small but shapely bosom. By the time she straightened, every face at the table except Jonah's wore a blissful grin.

"You have butter, syrup, forks—yep. Guess you've got everything. Coffeepot's on the table over there. Just help yourself if you want a refill." She turned the full force of her smile on Jonah. "Morning, Mr. Armstrong. Glad to see you made it this far, at least."

"Katy?"

She turned and walked away with a light, lithe step and saucily swaying hips. Jonah's tablemates regarded him with awe and envy.

"Katy! Come back here!"

His breakfast companions all babbled questions at once, but Jonah didn't stay to answer. He pursued. She wasn't hard to catch, as she had merely returned to the kitchen for another platter of flapjacks. He met her coming out the swinging wooden door. The platter bumped his chest.

"What are you doing here?" he demanded.

"Working my way to Skaguay." She dodged around him, deftly balancing the heavy tray.

He followed. "They don't hire women to work on these steamers."

"They didn't exactly hire me."

"What did you—"

"Excuse me, Jonah." She set the platter on a table and blithely ignored the men who sat there ogling her with curiosity, surprise, and lurid interest. "I have work to do, and you're in my way." She smiled at the diners. "That's your only platter, gents, so enjoy it."

She pushed past Jonah with impishly twinkling green eyes. "You wouldn't want the captain to toss me into the sea, would you?"

"Katy!"

She danced away from his outstretched hand. "He would, you know. Then wouldn't you be sorry you got me into trouble?"

Before he could catch up to her she once again disappeared into the kitchen. Giving up for now, Jonah returned to his own table. The flapjacks had disappeared. This was not an auspicious beginning to a good day.

For Katy, this was an exceptionally good day. The expression on Jonah Armstrong's face when he'd seen her serving breakfast was almost worth getting hauled out of her hiding place in a storage closet and dragged before the steamer's captain. Jonah looked as though he'd seen a ghost, poor man. Poor man, indeed! Every time she recalled how he'd let her make a fool out of herself that night in Missoula she wanted to strangle him. He'd known all along she was trying to manipulate him, and throughout the evening he'd been laughing at her as she masqueraded as a female who actually knew how to be a woman. He deserved every bit of grief she could give him!

Plenty of work remained to be done after the breakfast dishes were washed and the dining room cleaned. The captain of this tub had no sense of humor when it came to people stealing a ride on his ship. He had no soft spot in his heart for women, either, Katy had discovered. If she didn't give him the full value of labor he thought he deserved, she wouldn't put it past the old buzzard to throw her and Hunter overboard and let them swim to shore.

Katy had no desire to test her swimming abilities in the Pacific Ocean, even if the steamer did hug the shore. So she did everything she was told to do by the chief steward, and she did it with energy—cleaned cabins, polished brass fittings, mopped the deck, scrubbed laundry, helped with preparing and serving meals. She didn't mind such tedious work on the steamer nearly as much as she had resented it at home, where it had kept her from being outdoors, working cattle, breaking horses, or hunting. The work she did now propelled her toward the Klondike and a bright future.

As Katy moved about the ship, she delighted in letting her presence grate on Jonah Armstrong's nerves. Every time he saw her, aggravation darkened his face. The more she smiled at him, the darker was his scowl, the more cheerful her greeting, the more surly his response. Therefore, she was as smiling and cheerful as she could be, and when, three days out of Seattle, she spotted Jonah at the rail looking pensively out to sea, she grabbed the opportunity to nettle him.

"Afternoon, Jonah," Katy said as she slipped up to the rail beside him. "Nice afternoon, isn't it?"

A single raised brow lent his smile a dash of the devil. "Katy. You didn't tell me that you include maid-of-all-work among your other accomplishments. I'm surprised you could convince Captain Jefferies to hire on a woman."

Katy grinned. "He didn't exactly have a choice. I stowed away in a storage closet. Bet I could've gone the whole trip without being discovered if Hunter hadn't chosen the wrong time to hang his butt over the water."

"What?"

"You remember Hunter. He needed to go."

"Not that! You stowed away?"

She met his shocked amazement with a proud smile. "I can do anything I need to do to get where I want to be."

"So I gather," he said darkly.

"What's that supposed to mean?"

"That means I was right in my original estimation of your character."

"What's wrong with my character?"

"Nothing that would bother you, I'm sure."

Katy huffed indignantly. "What do you think I am, anyway?"

"What you said yourself—a woman who will do anything to get what she wants. And I mean anything."

Katy wasn't sure she liked her words repeated to her in that tone of voice. Jonah made determination, hard work, and ingenuity sound like something immoral. She struck back. "At least I'll be getting to Dawson. I'm not so sure about you."

"I'll get there," he assured her confidently.

Katy expressed her doubts in a derisive laugh.

"I've taken your advice and hired a guide," he told her. "Along with a party of five other Klondikers."

"Who?"

"A gentleman by the name of David Hayes."

Katy cocked her head and lifted one brow. "Is he on the ship?"

"No. He's meeting us at Skaguay with provisions and a pack train."

"Which you already paid him for, I suppose."

"Naturally. How is he supposed to buy the outfits without money?"

"How much?"

"Five hundred apiece."

Katy shook her head. "You'd have been safer with me, greenhorn. I think Mr. David Hayes just got himself one nice grubstake to go to Dawson and dig himself some gold, and I'd be willing to bet he doesn't take you and your friends with him."

"What makes you so sure?"

"I know a crooked scheme when I hear one. When there's gold to be had, don't let anyone out of sight with your grubstake. Too bad you didn't stick with me. You wouldn't have to worry about someone cheating you."

"And I suppose you're as honest as a midsummer day is long, Miss Stowaway."

"I am honest. That's how my pa raised me."

Jonah made a sound that Katy took as disbelief, but she was enjoying the fresh air and warmth too much to get angry at the slur. She leaned back against the oak rail, arms braced behind her, and arched toward the sun like a cat. She felt Jonah's eyes on her and smiled just to make him mad. Her smiles always seemed to make him mad.

"Katy, why aren't you married with children hanging on to your skirts rather than running with a pack of uncouth men up to the Klondike? Look at you! You're young and pretty enough to find a husband and have him care for you, but instead you run wild as some barefoot rowdy."

"Mmm. I'd like that—to run barefoot through that cold Klondike water and see gold nuggets between my toes." Out of the corner of her eye she saw him flush, as if the image was too much for him. "What's the matter, greenhorn? Haven't you ever waded barefoot and barelegged through a mountain stream? What kind of life have you had?"

"A responsible life lived within the confines of social convention, which I suspect you know very little about."

"Horsefeathers! You talk as if I'm some sort of criminal."

"You ought to get married to some brave man who will take you in hand."

"If marriage is so grand and responsible, why aren't *you* married?"

"I told you before. I don't lead a settled enough life to care for a woman. A woman needs to be sheltered."

"Well, Mr. Responsible, *I* don't need to be cared for, especially by some bossy man who expects a woman to spend her life cooking and cleaning and mopping up after babies."

"Most women enjoy that."

"Some women don't!" She threw his words back in his

face. "Some women want to live a life not settled enough to care for a man. And out here, a greenhorn like you needs to be sheltered."

For a moment his face was a battleground of conflicting expressions. Then he smiled with an unexpected flash of strong white teeth. "You are the most outrageous female I have ever met, Katy O'Connell."

"You don't say!"

"You belong to a world that died a couple of decades ago, do you know that? But I wish you luck."

Katy couldn't help but grin. Jonah was impossible to stay mad at for very long. "I guess I wish you luck, too. Though I don't know why I bother. Generally I figure that someone who doesn't know how to take care of himself deserves what he gets." She walked jauntily away and shot him a knowing smile over her shoulder. "Just remember, I warned you that you need help. Don't blame me when you get taken!"

Jonah told himself that he would be glad to see the last of Katy O'Connell, entertaining as she was. With her free-swinging stride and her open, easy smile, she was disturbing in a way no proper woman should be. Of course, that was because she wasn't even close to being a proper woman.

One would think that on a steamer crowded with 140 passengers, a conglomeration of boats, sleds, wagons, carts, and various types of livestock, avoiding one rather small female would be easy; but it wasn't. She seemed to be everywhere he was, serving, cleaning, polishing, running errands. Jonah suffered an urge to help the little imp when he saw her lifting, scrubbing, and hauling, but sternly reminded himself that she'd gotten herself into this position. She wanted a man's adventure; let her pay a man's price.

The fifth night out of Seattle, north of Mary Island in the tortuous sea channels known as the Inside Passage, Jonah relaxed in the evening cool, leaning against a lifeboat, gazing out upon the calm sea. Katy sat nearby, propped against the deck cabin with her face tilted toward the full moon. Her wolf, a handsome silver-gray animal of intimidating size, sat close against her. Jonah expected the creature to loose a blood-chilling howl toward the sky at any moment, but he merely leaned against his mistress as a child might press close to its mother. Though quite sure Katy knew she was watched from the concealing evening shadows, Jonah began to feel as though he were intruding upon a private moment. He was about to leave when two prospective gold kings came walking along the deck. They had obviously been celebrating their expected gold strikes a bit early, for their steps were uncertain and their voices loud and slurred.

"Lookee here!" one said. "It's our little waiter-girl."

"Waitin' fer us, I'll bet," the other crowed.

"How 'bout comin' with us, missy! We'll have us a time, we will!"

One of the men reached down and grabbed Katy's arm. She slapped him away with the same lack of concern with which she might swat at a pesky fly. "Take your hands and keep them where they won't get you in trouble, friend," she warned.

"Whooo-eeee!" the man said with relish. "She's got as much spit as a she-cat!"

"That's the way I like 'em!" his friend exclaimed. "Come on, missy! We'll show you a fine time. Pay ya, too."

Katy got slowly to her feet. At her side, the wolf regarded the men with bored yellow eyes and yawned. "If you don't want to lose a good number of your ugly yellow teeth, sucker-bait, I'd be on my way."

"The bitch is gettin' nasty," one of the men observed. "I think she needs shakin' down off'n that high horse of hers."

The other agreed, grinning to display the teeth Katy had so disparaged.

Katy sighed with seeming unconcern. Yellow-teeth grabbed at her, but she pushed him away with a strong shove. The other grabbed her from behind. She aimed her foot back-

ward in a kick that would have knocked his feet from beneath
him, but he anticipated her move and jerked her off-balance
while Yellow-teeth moved in with a lecherous chuckle, his
hands reaching toward her breasts.

Jonah needed no more provocation; he burst from the shadows, full of gentlemanly ire, and grabbed the arm of the man
who reached for Katy. The drunk whirled and sent a meaty fist
in Jonah's direction. Jonah ducked and answered with a punch
to the gut that should have sent the man reeling, especially
considering he wasn't very steady on his feet in the first place.
The man hesitated a moment, shook his head, then grinned
and took another shot at caving in Jonah's face. This time he
connected. Jonah staggered back and measured his length
along the deck. A shriek of pure fury split the night air.

Jonah hiked himself up on one elbow and watched dizzily
as Katy sent the point of her elbow into the gut of the wretch
who held her. When he doubled over in pain and turned her
loose, she attacked Jonah's assailant, spun him around, and
landed a small but effective fist in his paunch and an expert
left hook to his jaw. The lecher bounced off the deck cabin
bulkhead and groaned. His groaning buddy backed into a corner created by the cabin and a canvas-covered pile of freight.
He was held at bay there by the wolf, who eyed him with a
quiet ferocity that left no doubt of the creature's ability to
wreak mayhem if he were so inclined.

Jonah looked up into Katy's concerned face. "Are you all
right?" she asked.

He gingerly touched his nose, decided it wasn't broken,
and sighed. "Yes. I'm all right. I should have known that you
of all females didn't need me rushing to your rescue."

"It was very sweet of you." Green eyes twinkled at him.
The woman had no mercy.

She turned back to her chagrined attackers. "Why don't
you fellows go find a corner and sleep it off. Hunter, back
off."

Hunter stepped back, still alert. His charge inched out of the corner.

"Go on now," Katy urged. "Before I tell him to take a piece of your fat backside."

When the two rowdies were gone, Jonah got to his feet. "Jesus! That ape packs a punch."

"What do you expect? He outweighs you by about a hundred pounds."

"You'd think someone that drunk couldn't hit what he was aiming at."

"He didn't. He was aiming at your throat to knock your Adam's apple down your windpipe. Then you wouldn't be hurting at all, would you?"

"No, he wasn't."

"Yes, he was. Whatever made you jump those two gorillas? You know you can't handle yourself in a fight!"

Jonah rubbed his injured nose. He wished his injured pride could be comforted as easily. "I can handle myself in a fight."

"That's why I've had to snatch your bacon out of the fire twice in the short time I've known you?"

"I'll have you know I was middleweight boxing champion at the Smithson School for Young Men in Chicago. I can handle myself in a fight. The odds here weren't fair, you know."

She laughed, a delicious sound that nevertheless made Jonah want to strangle her. "The odds are never fair, and no one ever fights clean, greenhorn. Fighting's serious business. You're going to have to learn to fight dirty."

"There's no reason I should be fighting at all." He wiped his sleeve across his face and grimaced when it came away streaked with blood. "There are not a whole lot of things that are worth getting your teeth knocked out for."

Katy smiled impishly. "Well, Jonah Armstrong, since you were nice enough to consider me one of those things, I guess I'll take the trouble to teach you how to beat the stuffings out of the other guy before he can do it to you."

"Thank you, Katy, but I don't need—"

She punched him lightly in the chest. "Yes you do. Try to punch me."

"Don't be ridiculous. People are going to think I'm assaulting you."

"Nah. Most everyone's drinking beer and playing cards down in the dining room." She danced around him like a pesky mosquito, goading him with stinging shots to his arms, chest, and back. "What's the matter, Jonah? You afraid of a helpless little female—one of those poor creatures who need to be cared for and coddled."

"Katy . . ." He tried to grab her.

Slippery as a little snake, she slid away, whirled, and kicked out. Her foot stopped just short of his groin.

"Katy! For God's sake!"

Her hand whipped up in a chop that ended with a mere touch on his Adam's apple. He grabbed again, but she was hard to capture as air.

Suddenly her foot slipped behind his and pushed. He toppled, hitting the deck hard. "Goddamn it!"

"Tsk, tsk," Katy chided. "No cussing, please. You're in the presence of a lady."

Jonah surged to his feet. Finally managing to grab her, he pushed her back against the deck cabin before she could break free and work more mayhem.

"See?" she chirped. "I could never fight fair against you. You probably weigh twice what I do, and you're almost a foot taller."

"I wasn't trying to fight back."

"You would've been on the floor before you threw your first good punch."

She was right. Even if he had been serious, he never would have touched her had she not permitted it. Fearing another demonstration, he kept her against the cabin bulkhead. She merely smiled up at him.

"The groin, the throat, the eyes." She gently touched each area to demonstrate. The artless intimacy ignited a fire in one of those most vulnerable areas. Jonah cursed to himself. The little hussy was an expert at getting under a man's skin. The scent of her—how could she smell so clean after five days on this wretched steamer?—threatened to overwhelm him. Where his hands grasped her arms, her skin seemed to burn against his.

Katy continued. "The gut is a good spot on some. Not on you, I think." She patted his stomach then punched him—not so lightly—with her closed fist. "Not bad. Pretty hard. On someone with only flab here you can really put them out with a good gut punch."

Abruptly Jonah let her go. If he didn't get away from the damned temptress right now, he would give her something she richly deserved, but that he would be sure to regret.

"Next time you get in a fight," she warned solemnly, "just remember what I said. Don't fight fair. Fight to win."

"As you do," he growled

"Exactly."

With a friendly wave she walked away, hips swinging un-boyishly in that long boyish stride of hers. Jonah combed a hand through his hair and blew out a frustrated sigh. Katy O'Connell could teach most of the world's harlots a thing or two about subtle seduction. What she did to a man ought to be against the law.

CHAPTER 5

Skagua was an Indian word describing a very windy place, a member of the ship's crew had told Katy, and Skaguay, true to its name, was windy on the morning the steamer reached its destination. It was also gray, drizzly, and cold, despite the month still being August. Ice floes had littered the last leg of their journey and now mingled with the ships in Skaguay's harbor. Summer ended early in Alaska, and the air held an ominous promise of autumn.

From Katy's vantage point in the harbor, the town looked unprepossessing. In fact, it didn't even look like a town. Few permanent-looking buildings dignified the settlement. Tents of all sizes and descriptions sat haphazardly on the effluvium deposited at the mouth of the Skaguay River, which flowed along the west side of the town to empty into the Lynn Canal, a north-reaching finger of the sea that had Skaguay at its northern extremity.

Despite its drab appearance, the settlement seemed alive with excitement. Boats small and large crowded the harbor, and more were arriving. Heedless of the danger and waste of good ammunition, high-spirited passengers fired off guns at birds, porpoises, ice floes—anything that they could get in their sights that wasn't human, and sometimes that was. To add to the confusion, lifeboats, log rafts, and dinghies littered the harbor. Passengers, freight, and livestock had to be transported in these fragile vessels about two hundred yards over the rough water from the anchored boats to the beach, for the docking wharf was only half-built. Piles of freight decorated the strand like so much seaweed, and men scurried about with carts and pack animals, moving it to higher ground before the tide could swallow it up.

Their steamer had anchored at midmorning and for the last hour had worked at unloading. Two lifeboats were in use, but Captain Jeffries wouldn't allow livestock to go ashore in his precious boats. Log rafts were floated out from the shore for those passengers who had to transport mules, horses, and the like. One fellow had traveled with a sled and an eight-dog sled team, despite it still being summer. Another had brought a bicycle with him and protested loudly when it wouldn't fit into the lifeboat. Finally, he was forced to endure the passage to shore on an open raft.

Katy waited on the deck with Hunter and her little valise, content to wait her turn on one of the rafts. She wasn't impatient. This experience was worth savoring, despite the wind and the drizzle. Besides, she would just as soon wait until the anxious ones, the ones who overloaded their rafts and didn't take the time to balance their loads, were already on the beach or had dumped themselves into the cold water. Did they believe a few minutes, or even a few hours, would make a difference in them finding gold? Katy wondered.

In the early afternoon she watched Jonah Armstrong and his little group of goldseekers cross in a lifeboat. Their crossing was a rough one. The weather had deteriorated during the day. When the boat tipped dangerously, Jonah was the one who was up and ordering that the weight be redistributed. Katy recognized him from his size—he was as tall as her pa, and that was tall. He didn't seem so tall up close, because he had a masculine broadness that put him nicely in proportion, but next to the others on the lifeboat, he was easy to pick out.

Katy had said a cheerful good-bye to him when she had served his breakfast that morning. She'd even been generous enough to wish him luck. He would need it. There was little chance of him coming to his senses and rehiring her as his guide, even if the much-vaunted Mr. David Hayes turned out to be a crook. Jonah Armstrong had very definite ideas about what women should do and should not do, and what Katy wanted to do certainly didn't fit his picture of what was proper or possible. Too bad. She was beginning to like the fellow, even if he was too citified to be of much use. It would be a shame if he got into trouble.

"Miss O'Connell?" Captain Jeffries' voice boomed from behind her. "I believe the time has come when I can be rid of you. The next raft is the last."

"I appreciate the ride, Captain," Katy said as she picked up her valise.

"Just don't let me catch you on my ship again, young woman."

As she started down the companionway to the lower deck, Hunter at her side, the captain's mouth twitched in what might have been the sparse beginnings of a smile. "And Miss O'Connell . . ."

"Yes, sir."

"You know how to do a day's work. Good luck to you."

Katy smiled. "Thank you, sir."

She would need luck, Katy admitted when the raft finally beached against the sand and she and the other passengers waded through cold, calf-deep water to dry land. Everywhere was confusion: men shouting, dogs barking, mules braying, carts creaking and rumbling. Towering above the tents, noise, and chaos were the mountains the goldseekers had to cross to reach the goldfields. Wrapped in dignified, eternal silence, the great massifs frowned down upon the town that sat so precariously on its little fluvial fan of a beach. Looking at the mountains, Katy almost felt dizzy. Her heart expanded at the awesome splendor.

But less poetic concerns had to be dealt with, such as finding a place to sleep and something to eat—and in the long run, buying the supplies she needed for the trek to the goldfields.

She called Hunter from where he was dodging in and out of the little waves that foamed onto the sand. "Playtime's over," she told him. "Time to go to work." With the possibilities of gainful employment in mind, Katy set out to explore the town.

The exploration did not take much time. The mountains and the sea left little room for civilization to gain more than a toehold on the edge of the land. The Skaguay River flowed out of the mountains to a sandy beach. Perched on that beach and the little river plain behind was the scraggle of tents and hastily constructed shelters that was Alaska's newest boomtown. The streets of the town were muddy paths running between ramshackle structures. The canvas walls of the tents flapped and shivered in the wind and sagged beneath the wet weight of the drippy weather.

Yet, for all its humble appearance, Skaguay teemed with life. The beach was not the only area that was busy. The streets were clogged with humanity as well as mud. Carts bumped their way through muddy ruts, horses stood with heads down in the cold drizzle, dogs barked and wove through the traffic, chasing each other, nosing people and garbage, and generally getting in the way. Katy turned up a street and saw a pig rooting through a heap of refuse behind a large tent. The tent boasted a brightly painted sign that promised a delicious dinner for seventy-five cents. The pig obviously thought the food was delicious, until a pack of three dogs spotted it and set off in pursuit with pork dinner on their minds. The pig ducked into the next tent down the line, a large, dingy gray structure from which lively piano music emerged. The pack of dogs followed. Several bulges in the canvas walls bore evidence of the fracas inside, as did the thumps and curses audible above the piano music, which never faltered. A moment later, all three dogs shot through the tent exit, tails between their legs. The pig stayed.

Katy laughed and scratched Hunter's head with one finger. He looked up at her with a wolfish smile, tongue lolling. "Yes," Katy agreed. "Wolves are much smarter than dogs. There's no denying it. If you had taken out after that pig, it would have been pork chops."

Some town, Katy mused as she wandered on. Every second tent seemed to be a saloon, gambling emporium, or dance hall, and those businesses that didn't hawk liquor or offer card games sold supplies, mining equipment, maps to and of the goldfields. She passed several flimsy structures in which tables of shell games and other sirens of chance relieved the gold kings of their money before they even made it. Outfitters' signs announced having everything from long underwear to shovels. One enterprising fellow sold boats to be carried over the pass and used for transport down the upper Yukon River. A tentmaker hawked tents that could be folded into a neat package to be carried upon the back during the day, then expanded into a "palace of comfort" at night.

Nowhere did Katy find a hotel or a rooming house—there were no houses at all, with the exception of one or two unimpressive log structures. One rather large tent did advertise beds for two dollars a night—an outrageous price that many were willing to pay, apparently, for the sign in front announced that the place was full. People were camped on the beach and in the woods, in tents, under makeshift branch and brush shelters, or with no shelter at all. The prospect of sleeping under the stars didn't disturb Katy. She knew better than most of the inhabitants of Skaguay how to live outdoors. But before she set up camp for herself, she wanted to find work.

The task was harder than one would think in a town so lively. The safest place to seek employment seemed to be one of the groceries that displayed canned goods, fresh meat, sorry-looking vegetables, fresh and dry milk, dried fruits, and huge bins of flour, sugar, salt, and beans. Katy ducked through the canvas entrance of one such business and wandered up and down the rows of shelves. The grocery had a wide variety of goods, all selling at prices twice what they would fetch in the States. But then, where else could the eager goldseekers buy if they hadn't purchased a complete outfit in Seattle and paid to have it hauled north on the steamer? Doubtless all the groceries in Skaguay charged similar prices.

Katy decided that the proprietor could afford to hire on a bit of help with all the money he must be making on his goods. She picked up a box of matches, a half pound of salt, and two bars of bath soap and took them to the counter that ran along the front of the tent.

The proprietor, a balding, slight man in his mid-fifties, regarded her with polite curiosity. "Will that be all, miss?"

"For now. You need any help in the store? I'm looking for a job."

His expression changed immediately from friendly to shuttered. "Don't need any help. I've already got two fellas helping me—one of them living in the back room to watch the place at night. And every day I get at least ten more in looking for work or, worse, a grubstake."

"Oh. Know anyone who's looking for help?"

He shook his head. "For every job in this place, there's five or ten men looking for a way to earn enough to get to Dawson."

With that many men clamoring for work, why would anyone hire a woman? The storekeeper didn't say it, but the implication was in his words. Katy nodded coolly, put her purchases in her valise, and walked out. Hunter waited for her just outside the door.

"No luck there," she told the wolf. "Don't worry though. We can always live off the woods until I think of something."

She inquired at three other groceries with the same result. Two clothing stores turned her down, and the proprietor of the hardware store wasn't even polite. Toward midafternoon she grew desperate enough to peek into a dance hall, which was doing a rousing business even at midday. That sort of place hired women. No doubt about it. A platform of unfinished planks took up one end of the large tent. The sign out front advertised hourly shows, but right then the stage was vacant. Women moved between tables, serving drinks, laughing, chatting, flirting, sitting on laps. A job serving tables in that joint definitely included extra duties that Katy couldn't stomach.

Almost every place in town except the dance halls had a chance to turn Katy down. She almost landed a job as a server in the restaurant whose garbage pile the pig had found so tasty. The owner was a decent, overworked, and tired-looking woman who was sympathetic to Katy's plight. She needed help who could cook as well as serve, though, and Katy was honest about the fact that she was better at chopping wood than mixing up a batch of biscuits. The woman gave her a bowl of stew for herself and a plate of scraps for Hunter, then told her to come back if she couldn't find any work by the end of the day.

Katy's last hope was something she had been reluctant to do, but it would be better than ruining that nice woman's business by trying to cook. She has spotted at least two stables that advertised pack trains for hauling equipment over White Pass. No one could handle horses and mules better than Katy O'Connell, but she knew her chances of landing a job were less than nil if she presented herself as a woman. Disguising herself as a boy and maintaining the disguise would not be hard. Jonah Armstrong had taken her for a boy when she hadn't even been trying to fool him. Katy didn't like the idea, though. She didn't like to lie, and she wasn't ashamed of what she was, even though being female was often inconvenient. Still, she needed the job only long enough to earn a place in one of the numerous high-stakes card games in town. From what she had observed of the games, Katy was sure she could win enough in a few hours of play to get her to the goldfields—if she just could get money enough to ante into one of them. Even her pa wasn't a better poker player than she was.

Tomorrow was soon enough to tackle that problem, though. Katy headed back to the restaurant, planning to wash dishes, clean tables, or anything else she could do—except cook—to earn a meal for herself and Hunter. On the way she passed a saloon where a familiar figure sat at a table near the open tent flap. Katy stopped and gave in to the temptation to do a bit of spying.

Sitting with five others, Jonah Armstrong looked morose and angry at the same time. The men with him were equally down in the mouth. Katy couldn't hear what they were saying over the sound of a banging piano and a singer who passed among the tables sounding more like a scalded cat than a soprano, but a fair amount of fist pounding and arm waving gave a clue to the grim nature of the discussion. Could it be, Katy wondered with a hint of malicious joy, that the renowned Mr. David Hayes, whom Jonah had thought a more suitable guide than her, had stood them up? She tsked to herself, then smiled. Flapping the tent canvas gently, she tried to get Jonah's attention. He didn't turn her way, however.

Katy was not about to pass up this opportunity for a "told-you-so." She ordered Hunter to stay where he was and walked boldly into the tent. Her modest skirt and jacket, dusty and well used as they were, distinguished her as a woman who shouldn't be inside a saloon; she stood out like sparrow among a flock of cardinals. Jonah spotted her about the same time that everyone else did, and the frown he gave her was dark indeed. She didn't care.

"Hello, Jonah!" she said cheerfully. Three of the men at the table half stood, then sat, undecided about the proper etiquette of greeting a lady in such an awkward situation. Two others turned red and stared at the table. Jonah, however, simply stared at her. "Don't tell me you're working here," he growled.

"Of course not! What do you think I am?"

"I'm afraid to explore the subject."

Alan Smith, with whom Katy was slightly acquainted from the steamer, rose hesitantly and offered his seat.

"She's not staying," Jonah told Alan and Katy at the same time.

"I just want a few words with you, Jonah."

"Not here. Katy, this is not Myrna's friendly little saloon in Willow Bend, where everyone knows you."

"Myrna's friendly little saloon wasn't so friendly to you, was it?"

His eyes narrowed at the reminder of his debt to her. "All right. You want to talk about something, let's go where a whole tentful of men aren't staring at us."

"Fine with me."

They walked out into the dusk. Jonah took Katy's arm and guided her down the muddy street. Hunter fell in behind them. The fine drizzle had all but stopped, though by this time, Katy didn't care. She was soaked clear through and was saving the dry parka in her valise for when night came and the temperature dropped.

"What is it?" Jonah asked before they'd gone five steps.

"Goodness! Aren't we cranky today!"

"Katy!"

"Things aren't going so well, Jonah?"

He stopped and pulled her to a stop beside him. Blue eyes looked down at her without their usual glint of humor. "Did you have something to do with this?"

"By 'this' you mean your guide who took a powder?"

"Yes," he snapped.

"It's not my fault you chose the wrong person to trust."

"Then how did you know about it?"

"With you and those other gents moaning and groaning about something in that saloon, your guide not showing up seemed a pretty good guess. I did warn you, you know."

"Is that what you wanted to say? I told you so?"

"Naw," Katy said happily. "But I did tell you so. No guide, huh? No supplies, no pack train. Am I right?"

Jonah abruptly headed back toward the saloon they'd left.

"Wait!" Katy shouted at his broad back. "That's not what I wanted to say!" She caught up to Jonah in a few strides and grabbed his arm. He shook it off. "Don't be so touchy!" she complained.

He stopped and faced her, hands balled into fists on his hips.

"What do you want, Katy?"

She smiled her most engaging smile. "I want you to take me and Hunter to dinner."

He looked at the wolf, then at her. "I might consider taking Hunter, but why should I take you?"

Katy lifted a brow. "Because I'm going to do you a favor. I don't know why I continue to be so nice to you."

"Katy, I'll buy you dinner only if you promise not to do me any favors."

"Don't be any stupider than you have to be, Jonah. You need me." She dragged him toward the restaurant where she'd eaten earlier. "The food's good here, and the woman who runs the place is nice. She gave me lunch, so I owe her some paying business for dinner."

The big tent was full when Katy pulled Jonah through the door, but they managed to grab seats at the end of one long table just as a pair of diners left. Katy waved at the proprietor and winked. The woman smiled and winked in return. In a few minutes she set two bowls of steaming stew before them.

"Is your wolf friend outside?" the woman asked Katy. "You can bring him in. No one here is going to mind. He's probably cleaner and better mannered than most of my two-legged customers."

Thus Hunter had the privilege of lying beneath the table and gulping down table scraps while Katy and Jonah ate and talked, or rather, Katy talked.

"Do you have enough money to put together another outfit?" Katy asked. She believed in getting right to the point. Small talk was for people who were afraid to say what they wanted.

"No," Jonah answered succinctly.

"Can you get more money from your newspaper?"

"Probably."

"How long will it take?"

Jonah sighed and put down his fork, as though he had suddenly lost his appetite. "Katy, is there a point to this interrogation?"

"Yes," she said around a mouthful of stew. "Of course. Have you got any money left?"

"Yes."

"How much?" Katy asked with a sigh. For a writer, the man was as tight with his words as a miser with money.

"About a hundred dollars. A little less."

"How long will it take you to get the rest of the money you need?"

"I don't know exactly. A while."

"A while is too long," she said confidently. "Tomorrow's the first day of September. Winter's around the corner. Every day is going to get colder. Start a lot too late and you won't get to Dawson this season. Start a little too late and you'll get there, but you won't get out."

"Katy . . ."

"Listen to me, Jonah. Do you want to spend the winter in a cabin on the Klondike? There's going to be a lot of people doing it, but I don't think it's going to be any picnic. The ink in your fancy pen might freeze."

"You missed your calling," Jonah told her. His expression had softened a bit, but Katy didn't know if the softening was because the stew was so tasty or because what she said made sense.

"What do you mean, I missed my calling?"

"Pushy as you are, you should have been a salesman, or better yet, a politician."

"Women aren't supposed to do those things, either, remember?"

"In your case maybe an exception could be made."

Katy grinned impishly. "I'll tell you what exception you should make. I'm going to help you get to Dawson on time to write your stories and get back before the winter freezes you in. And you're going to help me, too."

"Katy, even if I were willing to hire you on—something I'm not sure I would do—I don't have money to buy our supplies. Have you been listening, or have you just been spouting questions for the fun of it?" He glanced around him and surreptitiously slipped his empty stew bowl under the table for Hunter to lick.

Katy couldn't help liking a man who would do such a thing. She felt a surge of affection for her greenhorn. "I'm going to get you the money," she announced confidently.

"I'm not going to help you rob a bank," he said, "if that's what you're planning."

"Don't be stupid. I'm not a bank robber."

"God only knows what you are."

"What I am is an absolutely great poker player."

He looked at her blankly for a moment, as if waiting for her to laugh at some joke. When she didn't, he did.

"I mean it," Katy insisted, miffed by his laughter. "Give me the money you have left as a stake so I can ante into a game, and I'll win enough to buy outfits for both of us."

"What kind of fool do you think I am?"

"I've already told you what kind of fool I think you are."

"You also advised me not to let my money out of my sight."

"I won't be out of your sight. Besides, you can trust me. I was talking about other people, like your Mr. David Hayes."

"Oh, I see. Unlike Mr. Hayes, Katy O'Connell is a solid rock of reliability."

"I am."

Katy finished the last of the delicious stew and set her bowl beneath the table for Hunter, along with one of the biscuits.

Those biscuits were better even than her sister Ellen's. She'd really wanted to eat both that were on her plate, but Hunter deserved some dessert along with his scraps.

Jonah's sky blue eyes rested upon her with unnerving intensity. The man had an irksome way of looking at her that set her on edge. He made her go woozy inside for no reason at all. She didn't much like the feeling.

"This place must be making me crazy even to consider such a thing," he finally grumbled.

Katy's heart leapt.

"What makes you think you could even get into one of these games? How many of these gents do you think want to play poker with a woman?"

"They won't see past my money," Katy assured him happily. "I've taken a look at some of the games going on around here—from a distance," she added when Jonah frowned. "A lot of them are run by pros out to make money off these ignorant prospectors. They won't hesitate to fleece a well-heeled woman."

Jonah leaned back against the wall behind his bench, folded his arms across his broad chest, and swept his eyes over her in critical assessment. His inspection made her uncharacteristically aware of her appearance—the damp, wrinkled skirt and jacket, the soiled cuffs of her shirtwaist, the straggling wisps of hair that had escaped her coiled braids. "Katy, my girl," he announced, "even with a wad of money in your hand, you wouldn't come close to looking well-heeled. They'll know something's up."

She merely smiled. "I may not look like a gold-plated easy mark now, but I will."

In two hours' time, she did. For an outrageous amount of five dollars, they purchased from one of the town's clothing shops a used dress that fit Katy well enough that it could pass for tailor-made. The dress was silk, with a high neckline and a row of interminable tiny pearl buttons running from the stiffly laced collar to snug vee waist. The skirt was narrow and very effective in emphasizing Katy's slender figure and youthful grace. It even had a hint of a bustle in the rear. The dress would have been modest enough if not for the color, which was a flamboyant red. The hue set off Katy's coloring in a most spectacular way. When she looked at herself in the clothing shop dressing room mirror, Katy scarcely knew herself.

She called Jonah into the dressing room. "What do you think?" she asked as she pirouetted before him.

His brows shot up, and his eyes widened momentarily. "I'd hardly recognize you."

"Is that good?"

He chuckled. "In this case, I think it is. You look like a woman who might consider a poker game an evening's entertainment. You need to do something with your hair, though. Braids are definitely not the style a sophisticated gambling woman would choose."

Katy stared at her reflection in the mirror. The red dress made her look older. Her eyes looked larger, her hair blacker, her skin smoother. She felt every inch a woman—feminine, powerful in a way she didn't understand. The feeling was disconcerting. "What would rich gambling woman choose?"

"Do you have a comb in that valise?"

"A brush."

"Then I'll show you."

For the next twenty minutes, Katy struggled to tame the heavy waves of her hair into one of the current fashions. Katy had no idea what current fashion was, but Jonah had a sister, he told her, whose primary task in life was to not let the fashion world move an inch without her following. So Jonah assumed the mantle of supervisor to Katy's efforts. The result was less than haute couture, for, unlike Jonah's sister, Katy did not have the advantage of a dressing table full of curling irons and hairpins. They made do with a brush, the few pins she had used to anchor the coils of her braids, and ingenuity. Katy did the work herself, and only permitted Jonah the job of critic. She didn't want him to touch her hair—or, perhaps, Katy admitted to herself, she did want him to touch her hair—for no good reason she could understand. When she had loosed her braids and he'd drawn her brush through the kinked mass that fell to her waist, a vibrant shock had run through her. She didn't like it. Jonah Armstrong could keep his shocks to himself, fashionable sister and all, and she would do her own hair.

Katy managed finally to concoct a style that left a gentle fullness around her face and gathered the rest of her hair into a large, heavy coil at the back of her head. If she relaxed her neck for a single instant, her head would tip back from the weight of her hair and she would spend the rest of the evening staring at the sky, Katy was sure. As soon as this charade was over, her hair was going into braids again.

"Am I presentable?" she asked irritably.

A slow, disconcerting smile crinkled Jonah's eyes. "More than presentable. You're beautiful, Katy O'Connell."

His compliment gave her back some of her confidence, and she forced herself to be nonchalant. "Sure I am."

"A man would have to be blind to pay attention to his cards with you sitting at the same table."

Katy grinned. "If he were blind, he wouldn't be paying much attention to the cards, either, then, would he?"

Jonah smiled in a way that made her heart skip a beat.

"You just remember, Armstrong—once I've won the money, you're going to live up to our bargain. We split fifty-fifty. And we go to Dawson together."

His eyes narrowed slightly. "I remember the fifty-fifty part. I don't remember anything about going to Dawson together."

"It's safer to go with a partner. Besides, without me to keep you out of trouble, you'll never get there. Like I said before, I'm doing you a favor."

"Or you want to continue to annoy me."

She arched a brow. "It could be that, too."

Jonah threw up his hands and laughed. "What do I care? This scheme is impossible in any case. Just don't cheat some cardsharp and get us both shot."

"I never cheat. I just win."

"Someone should write a book about you. Fiction. No one would believe you're real." He leaned forward and pecked her on the cheek. The chaste brush of his lips set fire to her skin. "For luck," he said.

On raw impulse Katy pulled him to her and landed a kiss full upon his mouth, grinding her lips against his in unpracticed enthusiasm. A moment's stiffness instantly melted to heated cooperation as Jonah pulled her more tightly against him. His arms folded around her, gentling her. His tongue traced the seam of her lips, and instinctively she opened to him. He thrust inside, and a bolt of raw sensation shot to the very pit of her belly, just as though Old Bruno the grizzly had opened her up with a claw of raw fire—and the fire felt so good! Jonah's hard, warm body conformed to hers in a disturbingly natural manner. His heart beat against her breasts, and something hard and very male rose to prod her belly.

In sudden panic, Katy peeled herself off of him and pushed back. Unwilling to let him see how profoundly he had affected her, she forced a careless tilt to her chin and a cocky smile to her face. "For luck," she told him.

Jonah looked a bit dazed. "For luck," he repeated.

Katy felt giddy, panicked, and elated at the same time. She felt alarm, wonder, and a touch of guilt wrapped into one soaring excitement. And yes, she did feel very, very lucky.

CHAPTER 6

Finding a poker game was not difficult. Every other tent housed a saloon, and every saloon had at least two or three games going. Katy and Jonah chose the highest class establishment they could find—if such a temporary, canvas-walled business could be called high-class. Unlike some of the other saloons they had looked into, this one had a plank floor covering the dirt. The bar was a magnificent oak counter which, along with the fancy mirror that was its backpiece, must have been shipped up from the States at very great cost. The bartender wore a silk vest and tie. His hands were clean, as well as his clothes, and compared to the average inhabitant of Skaguay, most of the customers were clean as well.

Katy sailed into the saloon on Jonah's arm as if she had every right to be walking into such an establishment. Jonah had spiffed up in a fancy Back East suit and looked every inch the dapper gent who might be expected to accompany such a magnificent specimen of womanhood as herself. They received a few curious looks from the customers and a swift, knowing scrutiny from the bartender, but no one made any objection to Katy's presence.

When they sat down at a table, a man in a clean white apron over an even cleaner white shirt appeared beside their table to ask what they would drink.

"Whiskey," Katy said with an arch voice. "And make sure it's good-quality whiskey."

"We serve only the best, madam."

"Good."

"And you, sir?"

"The same," Jonah said. His face was bland, but when the waiter left, he scowled. "Whiskey, Katy? This isn't a lark, you know."

"Don't worry. I can drink you under the table, then shoot out a knothole at fifty yards."

"I'm not concerned about your aim," he growled. "It's your judgment I'm worried about."

"Believe me, no one in here is going to think some tea-sipping miss is worth playing poker with."

"I don't think there's any danger of anyone in his right mind mistaking you for a tea-sipping miss," Jonah noted under his breath.

"Good." The smoldering look Katy sent Jonah's way was merely practice for the role she was about to play, but the answering snap of his eyes was gratifying just the same.

"Let's get this over with," Jonah urged.

Katy looked around the smoky, canvas-walled room. Poker rivaled drinking for the main activity in the place. Four different games were going on. One table she dismissed immediately. She recognized the cut of the man who sat there with three others. He studied his cards with the eye of a professional. A good professional. There was no sense in stacking the odds against herself.

Another table was occupied by five men who were drinking more than they were playing, and having a very fine time of it. Drunks got riled much too easily, and Katy wanted a nice sober table with men who weren't going to blow up when she taught them how the game was played.

In a far corner was the table she was looking for. The four gentlemen there were prosperous-looking. They seemed more serious about their cards than their drinks, but none had the cool intensity of a sharp. What's more, one of them was picking up his winnings and preparing to leave.

"There it is," Katy said to Jonah.

He closed his eyes and looked as if he were muttering a prayer.

Katy's heart thudded as she threaded her way through the tables and the curious eyes and presented herself to her intended victims. She was more nervous about the role she played than the poker game. She'd never in her life been so aware of male scrutiny. Actually, she'd never in her life felt so female, and thus so vulnerable. It had to be the dress that was making her feel so strange. Or the kiss. That damned stupid kiss.

"You gentlemen have an empty seat," she said smoothly to the men seated around the table. She had rehearsed the words enough that they came out sounding confident and casual.

Three pairs of eyes locked onto her. A few brows lifted. One mouth quirked upward in a tolerant smile.

"It seems we do, ma'am," said the smiler. He was a pleasant-faced man with a middle-aged paunch and a closely trimmed beard. The player to his left had white hair, a beard down to the middle of his chest, and watery blue eyes that regarded her disapprovingly. The other man at the table was young and slender—frail-looking, almost. Sparse brown hair was combed meticulously over the bald spot on top of his head. His face wore a dazzled expression, as though he'd never seen a woman before this moment.

"Would you mind if I make a fourth?"

The room around them grew quiet. The gentlemen at the table were not the only ones taking her measure. Katy felt Jonah's presence at her back, reassuring and yet disconcerting as well.

"This game is for money, ma'am, not for entertainment. The stakes are high."

Katy managed a confident smile. "That's the only kind of game I play, gentlemen."

The smiler looked to the others at the table for approval. One nodded. The other shrugged.

"We'd be honored, ma'am." All three stood. One pulled out the empty chair.

Katy settled herself therein as gracefully, she hoped, as a true sophisticated gambling lady might do. "I appreciate your sociability, gentlemen. This"—she patted the hand that Jonah laid on her shoulder—"is my . . . uh . . . friend, Mr. Armstrong."

"Ah," the smiler said, his expression friendly but cautious. "Would you like to join the game also, sir?"

"Not me," Jonah denied amiably. "My game's whiskey, not cards."

Katy tactfully pried Jonah's hand from her shoulder, where it rested with proprietary firmness. "That's true," she simpered to the other players. "I'm afraid poor Jonah doesn't know a jack from a queen." She couldn't resist the little private dig. She might be dressed like a lady, but she was, after all, still Katy O'Connell. "Why don't you just go up to the bar where you can watch, Jonah." She gave his hand a surreptitious pinch. He gave her shoulder a hard squeeze that could have been mistaken for affection by the other players.

"Whatever you say, my dear."

As Jonah retreated to the bar, the smiler followed him with a contemptuous look that men reserve for their brothers who don't quite measure up to manly standards of conduct. Katy was suddenly eager to put the gentleman in his place. "Shall we play?" she said.

"By all means, ma'am. I'm Caleb Johnson. This here"—he indicated the mousy little man on his right—"is Terrence Gobel, and on my left is Strather Williams."

"Pleased to make your acquaintance, gentlemen. I'm Kathleen O'Connell. You can call me Katy."

"Honored, ma'am. Would you take the deal?"

"Certainly."

She dealt a game of five-card stud, deuces wild. A very

tame game to begin. She lost. That was all right. Win at the beginning and she would scare off the players.

The deal went to the old man. Katy lost with a pair of tens. She won a small pot in the third hand with three jacks, then couldn't get above a single pair and lost two more. Each hand made her more disgusted with herself. A run of bad cards didn't mean she had to lose. Bluff and intimidation were her strong suits, along with reading the other players' faces to decide when to bet and when to fold without undue loss. Obviously her mind wasn't on the game. She was losing money—Jonah's money—hand over foot, letting three mediocre poker players make her look like an amateur.

She won a pot, then lost two more. So far she'd lost four times what she'd won. Jonah's eyes burned the back of her neck. Doubtless he thought her an overblown braggart and was even now plotting ways to take her losses out of her hide. That damned kiss was what was doing this to her, Katy decided. It had muddled her mind and dulled her senses. Or maybe it had sharpened her senses, for her body was still alive with strange feelings, her stomach all fluttery and nervous, her brain fuzzy. She had only herself to blame for her condition, Katy bemoaned silently. What had possessed her to do such a harebrained thing? She didn't go around kissing men. When Gil Eversham had caught her behind his pa's livery in Willow Bend and tried to kiss her, she'd decked him but good. Whenever her pa kissed Olivia, Katy still got embarrassed and turned away. Her pa didn't just peck Olivia on the cheek like most husbands kissed their wives; he always took his time and made a very thorough job of it. Katy had never said so, because she didn't want to hurt her parents' feelings, but she had always thought it was a bit disgusting.

So why had she acted upon that silly impulse to kiss Jonah? And why hadn't she pulled away immediately when he latched onto her like a suckerfish? Of course, Jonah Armstrong was a good deal better looking than any suckerfish, and staying in his arms had just seemed sort of natural. Warm and secure. Spine-tingling. Exhilarating, even.

"Royal flush." Terrence Gobel spread his cards on the table with a satisfied grin. Katy experienced her own flush, but not the royal kind. She should have known the man had a good hand; it was written all over his mousy face. She had only a pair of nines. Why had she bet? If she'd been paying attention, she wouldn't have.

Dismayed, she looked at her dwindling bankroll—only twenty dollars left. Jonah must think she was an idiot. She was surprised he hadn't descended upon her and irately plucked her from the game. The other players must have seen her distress, because Caleb Johnson, who seemed to be the leader of the pack, offered in a condescending voice: "I think we should lower the ante a bit for Miss O'Connell, gentlemen. Don't you agree? After all, the privilege of having such a beautiful lady at our table should be worth something."

That was it! They were treating her as though she were some sort of know-nothing empty-headed female who couldn't tell a spade from a club. Jonah Armstrong no doubt thought so too, the damned greenhorn! He should have known better than to distract her before a poker game. She should have known better as well, but how was she to know that an experimental kiss would turn into such a mind-numbing disaster?

"I don't need any special privileges, gentlemen," Katy said smoothly. "I wouldn't dream of taking advantage of your kind courtesy."

The swollen-headed, puffed-up, blowhards. Let them enjoy their little victories while they could, because the game was going to change as of now, Katy vowed to herself. She would concentrate on winning, because if she lost, she wouldn't get to the Klondike, and neither would Jonah Armstrong.

"Are you sure, Miss O'Connell?" Terrence Gobel asked solicitously. "We wouldn't want to cause you any distress."

"Call me Katy, and don't bother yourself about distress. I can dish it out as well as take it, gents. Be warned."

They laughed politely, and Caleb dealt a hand of five-card draw.

Katy lost that hand, but the loss didn't bother her. Not much money went with it, because she knew when to fold. She was in the swing again; she could feel it. She won the next hand with two pairs—queens and fives—and the next with three aces. The gentlemen were condescendingly happy for her. Strather Williams won the next hand with a straight. He should have won the next as well with three treys, but Katy bluffed him on two pair.

In the next hour the gentlemen's smiles grew thin, their courtesy strained. Katy willed the cards to come to her. In the past, her pa, when he was tired of losing to her, had often accused her of using Blackfoot magic to make the cards fall her way. Sometimes she believed she could really do magic, and now was one of those times. She willed the cards to come, and they came. And when they didn't, she knew when to bluff and when to hold.

At the end of an hour, Terrence Gobel threw in his cards and announced he'd had enough pummeling for one night's play. A slick-looking fellow with a Southern accent grabbed his chair before anyone else could sit down.

"I would be delighted to relieve this beautiful lady of her burden of excess funds," he announced in lazy drawl. "With your permission, ma'am, gentlemen."

Williams and Johnson nodded curtly. Katy smiled. Another goat eager to be milked.

An audience had gathered, and there were plenty of men eager to play. Katy found herself the target for admiring stares and hoots of encouragement. When Caleb Johnson bowed out, a fight ensued as to who would take his place. The fracas was quickly broken up by other spectators eager to watch the play continue.

At the start of the second hour, Katy had a run of bad cards.

It slowed her momentum, but didn't stop it. She knew the cards would fall her way again—felt it in her bones. And they did.

White-bearded Strather Williams, the only one of the original players who hadn't given up his place to someone else, prodded Katy with a half-mocking question. "Little lady, if you weren't so pretty, I'd have to say you were cheating to have such a run of luck."

She had skill, not luck, and being pretty had absolutely nothing to do with it. Katy gave him a smile that was every bit as condescending as the ones he'd given her at the beginning of play. "I never cheat, sir. I'm simply good."

"You're *very* good." Too good, his tone implied.

"My father's Irish," she explained, trying to keep the tone light. "That must explain it. The Irish are very lucky, you know."

She started to gather in the pot she had just won, but Williams put his hand on her arm. "I've not seen anyone, Irish or not, have as much luck as you."

A small rumble began in the onlookers and started to swell. Katy didn't know if the protest was objection to Williams's implied accusation or support of it. She just might be in a bit of trouble.

Jonah's voice broke in, silencing the rumble. "I'm surprised at you, sir, questioning the lady's integrity. You seemed willing enough to win from her at the beginning. Seems those willing to take ought to be equally willing to give."

Katy closed her eyes and wished she'd left Jonah at the hotel. She uttered a silent prayer that he would let her handle this.

"What are you two?" Williams asked with narrowed eyes. "Do you send her into the game to take honest men off guard? What man can watch for dealing under the table or thumbing back an ace when he's watching that." His pale gaze swept contemptuously over Katy's body.

Katy clung to her composure and reminded herself she was

posing as a sophisticated lady. Getting the old goat in a throat lock or yanking his white hair from its roots was probably not something a lady would do. "You are no gentleman, Mr. Williams," she said primly. "What's worse, you're a very poor loser. I believe the game is at an end."

Protests rose from those of the onlookers who had hoped for a chance to end her run of luck.

"Blame Mr. Williams," Katy told them. "Not me." She gathered in her recent winnings and added them to the heap she had already stuffed into her large reticule.

"Nobody cheats me," Williams said nastily. "Especially some whore who thinks all she has to do is bat her eyelashes and—"

"That's enough." Jonah's command rang with a quiet steel Katy had never heard in his voice before. He had taken a gun from his coat and pointed it in the general direction of the troublemaker. A gun? Katy thought with frantic dismay. More like a gunmetal-colored peashooter. The weapon was scarcely bigger than the palm of his hand. Most of the men in this room could have swallowed it whole for a snack.

"What kind of shit-assed con is this?" Williams asked.

"No shit-assed con at all," Jonah said coolly. "The lady's game is honest. I'm just here to help her collect her honest debts."

The crowd began to rumble again, not from protest, but from the sheer enjoyment of the prospect of a fight. Katy had a sudden vision of Jonah and his silly little gun lying on the carpet, Jonah's face caved in from Williams's fist.

"Let's leave, Jonah."

"Don't move!" Jonah warned Williams as he started to get up.

"Let's go!" She grabbed the hand that didn't hold the gun and tugged Jonah along with her. The fool was enjoying his show too much. One could push a man like Williams just so far before getting down to business. It would be a shame if she had to spoil this pretty red dress to come to Jonah's rescue.

"Another time, gentlemen," she said to her gallery just before they ducked out of the tent. "And next time, Mr. Williams, if you can't afford to lose, don't play."

Since both establishments that passed for hotels in Skaguay were full, Katy erected a temporary shelter for them just off the beach in the woods, a locale almost as populous as the town itself. Potential gold kings were living in everything from packing boxes to canvas sheets hung over a tree branch to bona fide tents. Katy went far enough back in the trees to give them some privacy and showed Jonah how to quickly set up a little shelter of saplings, branches, and brush. He caught on fast, for a tenderfoot, and she was able to entrust the task to him while she sought the privacy of a thicket to change out of the uncomfortable boned corset and the red dress. The trousers and flannel shirt that lay wrinkled in her valise tempted her, but she donned the skirt she'd worn on the train, along with a clean gingham blouse and deerhide vest her grandmother Squirrel Woman had made for her one of the summers she and Ellen had lived on the reservation. Katy wasn't quite ready to give up her role as a lady. Not that the role fit her. Nothing was further from what she really was. But she was too old to be dressing in britches, or so Olivia had been telling her for the last five years.

When Katy returned to their campsite, the shelter was nearly done. Having someone tall to spread the spruce branches over the top of the structure was handy. But Jonah's quick aptitude didn't earn him forgiveness for his stupid stunt in the saloon. He was going to get them both killed if he insisted on being a part of the fabled Old West instead of just writing about it.

"I have a few words to say to you," she warned him. "You chuckleheaded idiot! What was the idea behind that stupid little peashooter? Don't you know better than to draw a gun when you don't know how to use it?"

"I know how to use it," he insisted. "I covered Cuba's rebellion against Spain in '95. Learned to shoot there. And I picked up this handy little pistol in Seattle."

"Can you hit the side of a barn?" Katy asked scornfully.

"Yes, as a matter of fact."

"When you're aiming at it?"

"May I remind you that I saved you from getting robbed of your winnings—our winnings? I don't see what you're in such a knot about."

"I could've handled Williams."

Jonah grinned with infuriating mockery. "Don't take to being rescued by a city slicker, eh?"

"Rescued?" She laughed. "With this?" She reached into his coat and brought forth the little gun, which fit neatly into her hand. The barrel wasn't more than three inches long. "If you were lucky, this might have made a dent in Williams's vest. Where did you get this thing, anyway?"

"Trust me, it would've made more than a dent. Sometimes, Katy, the size of a weapon doesn't matter as much as the determination of the man who's wielding it. You seem to think that a man who doesn't punch cows for a living, doesn't fight at the first cross word, and isn't a walking armory can't take care of himself and what's his. That's a stupid mistake to make."

For a moment Katy was fascinated by the snap of his eyes, but then she looked down at the tiny gun in her hand and had to laugh. She tossed it back to him. "Don't shoot yourself. We might not be able to find a bandage small enough for the hole."

Jonah simply smiled.

By the light of a kerosene lantern they counted their winnings, laying out the bills and coins on a freshly cut tree stump. Hunter had joined them after an evening spent terrorizing the local wildlife. He sat beside the stump and regarded each coin with lupine intensity.

"Your wolf looks as though he's expecting a share," Jonah observed.

Katy smiled mischievously. "He's just protecting my share."

Beneath the smile, Katy sweated out the count, afraid that for all her spectacular poker playing, they still wouldn't have enough to get them both to Dawson. Supplies and equipment for the trail did not come cheap.

"One thousand, two hundred, sixty-eight dollars and twenty-two cents," Jonah pronounced finally.

"Yeooww! We made it!"

"Don't think I've ever seen anything like you and those cards tonight. Who taught you to play poker like that?"

"My pa," Katy said with a grin. "On long winter nights in the Montana mountains. I always beat him, though. At chess, too. He always had something else on his mind. Never could concentrate on his game as he should."

Jonah shook his head. "You could be a rich woman if you took up poker for a living."

"Naw," Katy said. "Gambling's no way to live. I want to do something productive."

"Well, you were damned productive tonight, Miss Katy O'Connell."

She basked in his smile. "I was, wasn't I?"

The hour was late, and Katy should have been exhausted, but every beat of her heart pumped more eagerness through her veins. The goldfields were within their reach, and the great adventure awaited. Her mind whirled with things they had yet to do.

"Tomorrow we'll book passage to Dyea," Katy announced. "We'll pick up supplies there and hire some packhorses—"

"Wait a minute!" Jonah interrupted. "Book passage to Dyea?"

"Dyea's at the foot of the trail over Chilkoot Pass."

"I know where it is. We're going over White Pass. It's easier."

"Chilkoot is shorter, and it's been used for years."

"It's steeper and rougher. Packhorses can't make it all the way to the summit."

"People can, though, and from what I hear, the trail up White Pass is in bad condition."

"That's not what I heard."

"Only because you've been talking to the yahoos in Skaguay who are pushing White Pass as if it were some paved path to El Dorado. They just want the Klondikers to spend their money in Skaguay. I heard a man who helps with one of the pack trains talking about what it's really like up there. Horses are going over the edge of the trail; there's already carcasses stinking up the canyon. Some places are so deep in mud that people almost can't get through. I hear the trail might even be shut down while bridges and log walkways are built over the quagmires."

"I didn't hear anything like that."

"You listen to the wrong people. We'll have better luck on the Chilkoot Trail. With any luck, we can be there by noon tomorrow. It's only a few miles up the Lynn Canal."

"Wait a minute." Jonah screwed his eyes shut and shook his head as though he were trying to throw off a dizzy spell. "Katy, I've been making my own decisions since I was eighteen—a good long time ago, and I've gotten accustomed to doing things that way."

Katy arched a brow. "Which is why you ended up in Skaguay with no guide, no provisions, and not much money."

"Yes, well, I realize you have rescued me from my own ignorance—twice now—but I prefer to make my own mistakes. Why don't we just split the money and both get to Dawson our own way? We'll compare experiences at the end of the trail."

Katy suffered a momentary panic. "We travel together!

That was part of our deal! Besides, without me along, you're not likely to reach the end of the trail."

"I'm constantly flattered by your confidence in my abilities."

"Don't take it personally," Katy told him with a roll of her eyes.

"By all means." He refused to meet her eyes, and instead toyed with a coin on the tree stump that served as their table. "Katy, it's not proper, us being together on the trail. Think of our reputations."

"What reputations? What do I care what people think?"

"You may not care what people think, but I have to. Major newspapers don't employ men who go about their assignments flaunting fast women on their arm."

Momentarily entranced with the idea of being thought a fast woman, Katy smiled. Then she realized that Jonah's eyes lacked the devilish twinkle that characterized his teasing. "I'm only fast with cards and guns. Besides, you agreed!"

He shrugged an admission of guilt. "I didn't think you'd win."

A sense of loss washed over Katy. She could get to Dawson without bothering with Jonah Armstrong, but he had somehow become an integral part of the adventure. The journey, the excitement, even the gold, would lose its flavor without him. A childish desire to cry almost conquered her, and she tightened her lips and blinked her eyes to keep tears at bay.

"You're a damned welcher, Jonah Armstrong. That's what you are. A damned lying welcher!"

"Now, Katy—"

"I rescue you from the Hacketts, I win all this money so you can get to Dawson, and what do you do? You call me a fast woman and throw me out of the shelter I taught you how to build, dammit!"

"Katy, I'm not throwing you out, for God's sake—"

"I try to give you advice to keep you out of trouble, and you

say you'd rather make stupid mistakes alone than travel with
me!"

"Katy . . ."

A sudden silence seemed to draw out the faint sounds of the
woods. The night wind sighed in the trees, a small animal rus-
tled in a nearby thicket. Somewhere far away a dog barked, a
man laughed.

I kissed you, Katy told him silently. *You said I was beautiful, and you made it feel almost right to act like a fancy lady.
How could you do that and not want me around?*

As if he heard her silent plea, Jonah looked her full in the
eyes. His straight brows puckered, relaxed, then puckered
again in an uncertain frown. Katy recalled her own pride and
lifted her chin. Wrenching away from the grip of his eyes, she
pressed her lips even more tightly together and began to count
out her half of the winnings.

"All right!" she said. "Katy O'Connell doesn't stay where
she isn't wanted."

"Katy . . ." Jonah sighed. "Don't. I didn't mean to hurt your
feelings."

"I *don't* have hurt feelings. If you want to make your decisions without my help, just go ahead! I'll be out of here as
soon as I've counted out my half."

"All right," he conceded. "All right. I did agree. Those
were the terms. We'll go together."

"No, we won't. I wouldn't want to ruin your precious reputation. I wouldn't make you tarnish your halo by keeping
company with a fast woman."

He grabbed her hand and halted her counting. "Stay, Katy."

"Why?" she asked, eyes narrowed.

"Because that's what we agreed to do."

"You don't have any trouble breaking agreements."

He breathed a long-suffering sigh. "All right. Stay because
I want you to, because I need a guide to keep me from falling
off the trail or getting drowned in the river on the way to
Dawson."

"You don't mean it," she denied stubbornly.

"Yes, I do. I really do."

Katy let her face relax into just the hint of a smile. "Really?"

"I never lie, Katy. Sometimes I change my mind, but I never lie."

Her smile grew. "All right. You're in luck. It just so happens I'm free to take you to Dawson."

"Shake on it," he urged with a grin.

Katy took his hand. The warmth of his flesh pressing against hers felt too good. Some instinct warned her that she'd just dived into water that was deeper and swifter than she knew, but she ignored it. She and Jonah Armstrong were going to Dawson together.

CHAPTER 7

Dyea was a town much like Skaguay, only smaller. Built up around the Healy and Wilson Trading Post—an establishment that long preceded the gold rush—the settlement burgeoned with outfitters, saloons, and purveyors of mining equipment, clothing, food, and every other possible item the Klondikers required or could be persuaded that they required. As in Skaguay, every imaginable way to lose money was offered potential gold kings before they could travel across the mountains to stake their claims—from poker games to prostitutes to shell games and elaborate grubstaking and investment schemes.

Jonah contented himself with absorbing the atmosphere for later regurgitation into a piece for the *Record* and let Katy take care of seeing to the preparations for their trek. He was amazed at the vitality of the place and the people. A gold rush reduced human beings to their rawest elements. Greed abounded. Lust ran unchecked. Professional gamblers, prostitutes, con artists, and crooked outfitters fed upon the gullibility of inexperienced and unwary goldseekers disgorged from every steamer.

Jonah was amazed at how easily Katy fit into the rough-and-ready crowd. Women were not an uncommon sight in town, but the majority of women here were of the sporting sort. They had come to mine the Klondikers, not the Klondike. Katy was mistaken for such a one more than once. Where most women of Jonah's acquaintance would have fainted, or at the very least thrown a hissy fit at such an insult, Katy merely laughed and set the offender straight as to her purpose in town. In bargaining for their provisions, she quickly cut through the outfitters' condescending and obsequious efforts to charge her twice the going price or sell her items that would be useless on the trail. Jonah stood by and watched with amazement as Katy hacked both prices and storekeepers down to size. More than one storekeeper who looked like a cat about to swallow a canary when Katy walked in resembled that same feline with a thoroughly pecked nose by the time she walked out.

By evening they had filled their hired wagon with provisions that included six hundred pounds of flour, fifty pounds of rolled oats, three hundred pounds of bacon, two hundred pounds of beans, fifty pounds of evaporated potatoes, ten pounds of evaporated onions, thirty pounds of jerked beef, and similar quantities of sugar, coffee, condensed milk, soap, baking soda, matches, and dried fruit. In addition Katy had purchased nails, safety pins, boot lacings, thread, and candles.

"Which battalion of the army are we traveling with?" asked Jonah as he loaded the final round of provisions onto their wagon.

"Trust me," Katy said seriously. "We'll need all of this."

"We're going to eat this in just over a month on the trail?"

"The Canadian government is asking everyone going to the Klondike to take enough supplies for the entire winter. Haven't you read the handbills?"

"Yes, I've read the handbills," he said patiently. "But I'm not going for the entire winter."

Katy shrugged and gave him the smile that always transformed her face from simply pretty to radiant. "Suppose the river freezes early this year? Suppose an early storm keeps you in Dawson? You've got to plan ahead, Jonah. If you head back early, you can always sell what you don't need to somebody who doesn't have a 'sister' as smart as I am."

"If they're lucky," Jonah shot back with a wry smile, "they don't have a sister at all."

Katy sent him a mock glare, but didn't take offense. Jonah had persuaded her to accept the pretense that she was his sister—to keep tongues from wagging. She had protested the need; the woman really did seem to be oblivious to any concern of reputation. Every opportunity she poked fun at him about it. How amused his real sister Daphne would be to know that she had just acquired a new sibling who was so extraordinarily improper. Daphne would like Katy; Daphne liked anything and anyone who would outrage their mother's sensibilities, but she would like Katy especially for her straightforward boldness, her unquenchable spirit, her sense of mischief.

Jonah liked Katy also. He liked her a bit too much. Her impulsive kiss before the poker game had nearly undone him. Katy didn't know how close she had come to not making it to that damned saloon. He wondered how in hell he was going to endure five or six weeks in her constant company without doing something that would complicate both of their lives.

As in Skaguay, they set up camp in the woods outside of town, along with a number of others who shared the limited space between the beach and the mountains. If Katy found the forced intimacy of sharing a shelter disconcerting, she didn't let on. Not for Katy O'Connell was maidenly modesty, bruised sensibilities, or any other hesitancy Jonah would have expected from a civilized woman in like circumstances. He wasn't surprised. A woman who frequented saloons and games of chance, cussed like a mule skinner, brawled like a longshoreman, and flirted with the practiced skills of a siren couldn't be expected to blink at cozying up to a man in a primitive shelter beneath the stars. Jonah had little doubt that, in spite of her youth, she had discarded the last remnant of her maidenhood and its attendant demureness long ago. It would be far easier to behave himself with his "sister," Jonah reflected, if she'd been a cringing virgin.

Thus their first night in Dyea, Jonah spent staring in frustration at the top of their new tent while Katy slept soundly and innocently not three feet away. Hunter was stretched out beside her. He had nosed his head beneath her arm to rest upon her ribs, and in so doing, had pushed the blankets off a nightdress-clad arm and a pleated cotton-covered breast. The graceful, bare column of her neck was a smooth curve in the darkness, her face a pale moon surrounded by a sea of dark hair. Jonah had excellent night vision. He could see the details of her sleeping form, and in his imagination feel them as well.

He sighed and turned so that his back, not his face, was toward her. The ploy didn't work. He still felt her lying there, heard her quiet breathing, smelled the faint rose scent of the bar of toilet soap she had indulged herself in. Heaven help him! If he didn't get his base urges under control, this was going to be a very hard trip.

The first five miles of the Chilkoot Trail were a bit of a disappointment to Katy. Stories she had heard about the trek ahead of them led her to expect an arduous journey from the very first steps out of Dyea. Primed to expect a challenge worthy of her talents, Katy found the wagon road they followed much lacking in color and adventure. Still, she supposed they were lucky to have an easy time of it their first day on the trail, though Jonah was holding up much better than she had expected under the full pack he carried. He might be a greenhorn, but he was a fit one. The muscle that filled out his tall frame was certainly not just for show.

She carried a pack as well, though it was a good deal lighter than Jonah's. She wasn't fool enough to think she could compete with him in brute strength. The majority of their goods were not carried upon their backs, however—just a change of clothing and a couple of days' worth of food, matches, and the like. The rest of the provisions followed on the backs of five horses, who would accompany them as far as pack animals could climb, which was a point known as Stone House, just below the final and steepest ascent to the summit. The pack animals came with a driver, one Jack Decker, and the young lad who was his assistant.

Katy had found Jack Decker during her second day in Dyea and hired him after only a few minutes of conversation. She hadn't much choice, as he was just about the only packer in Dyea who had horses available. He had promised her five horses in two days' time, which gave her and Jonah leeway to repair their new tent, in which they had discovered a faulty seam, and purchase some additional clothing and equipment recommended by pamphlets that the Canadian government circulated among those preparing to cross the Alaskan border into Canada.

Still, Katy hadn't thought too highly of Mr. Decker when she had first talked to him, and this first day on the trail was proving her instinct correct. The man himself was dirty. Not that there was any great harm in that. Katy herself had learned to ignore dirt when she was out of reach of soap and water. Decker was dirty with more than just the dirt of honest labor, however. Every crease in his skin seemed to have accumulated several layers of undisturbed grime. His teeth were brown with more than just the stains from the tobacco wad that stuffed his cheek. His hair was stiff with grease and sweat, both old and recent. The man stank so, Katy was surprised his horses let him near them.

Jack Decker's horses were almost as sorry as their owner— sorrier, perhaps, because in addition to being caked with old mud and having burrs and matted tangles in their manes and tails, the poor creatures were bone thin. The same could be said for Decker's assistant, whose ratty shirt and threadbare trousers covered an adolescent physique that looked to be merely skin stretched over bare bone. Apparently Decker fed the lad no better than he fed his horses.

The abundance of company along the trail was as big a disappointment as the lack of difficulty. Katy had been looking forward to a wilderness experience. She had grown up in some of the most isolated places in Montana and had learned to love the silence of the back country. Chipmunks, squirrels, and birds were the best company a person could have. Bears had their place also—at a distance, where one could observe their antics without having to put up with their surly tempers. And wolves, of course, were the very pinnacle of God's creation—well represented by Hunter, who had reverted to puppyhood and was bounding in and out of the trees and thickets in playful pursuit of rabbits and small rodents.

Katy had been looking forward to introducing Jonah to her beloved wilderness, to making him understand through a glimpse of nature's raw and elemental grandeur how petty civilization's conventions actually were. But wherever Alaska was hiding its unsullied magnificence, it wasn't the Chilkoot Trail. The trees and mountains were splendid enough, but the birds, squirrels, and chipmunks were hiding. The awesome wilderness silence was replaced by the talking, laughing, cursing, and jostling of a stream of people trekking their way up the valley. The land already bore the scars of their passage, even though only a little over a month had passed since the gold strike had been announced. Fresh tree stumps still bleeding sap stood out like raw wounds where trees had been cut to construct bridges and shore up difficult parts of the trail. Dust kicked from under hundreds of feet smudged the air. Here and there refuse littered the roadside. Civilization was flooding into Alaska and bringing its messy housekeeping with it.

The parties that accompanied them up the trail impressed Katy with how fortunate she and Jonah were. The next party up, two men about a hundred feet ahead of them, carried packs that Katy estimated to weigh over a hundred pounds apiece. They were among the many who couldn't afford professional packers to carry their provisions over the pass, and to transport enough supplies to get them through an arctic winter, they would probably make twenty-five round-trips from Dyea to where they could load their provisions on a raft at Lake Bennett. They might be starting the journey on the same day as Jonah and Katy, but they would arrive in Dawson weeks after them. Katy hoped they had a freighting sled among their goods, for by the time they made Dawson, the Yukon River, which was the road into gold country, would surely be frozen over.

The group traveling behind Katy and Jonah was a family who had been passengers on the same steamer from Seattle— a redheaded, rather raucous Irishman with his mousy little wife. While Katy couldn't help but admire a wife sharing her husband's adventure, this woman carried courage to an extreme, for in addition to a hefty pack, the woman carried an infant at her breast. The man carried a pack much larger than his wife's, and in addition pulled a loaded two-wheeled cart behind him. He whistled a merry tune as he walked, and Katy found herself marching in time to the snatches she could hear.

Midafternoon they reached Finnigan's Point, a tiny settlement which boasted a ramshackle restaurant, saloon, and blacksmith shop surrounded by a huddle of dilapidated tents. It was a popular resting place for people on the trail, and Katy's little party was no exception. They stopped to water the horses and seek temporary respite from their sweat-soaked packs. The whistling Irishman and his wife stopped also, and almost as soon as they sat down, the husband pulled out a fiddle and started to play the same lilting tune he'd been whistling. Katy remembered his playing on the steamer, where his wife would sometimes dance a little Irish jig on the deck. On one particularly rowdy evening, others had taken up the dance and almost turned it into a free-for-all brawl. The wife was not dancing now, however, She looked almost too tired to move as she escaped from the leather straps of her pack, set the infant to her breast, and modestly covered herself with a shawl.

Katy didn't credit herself with many womanly instincts, but one that she did have was a curiosity about babies. Unable to resist, she left Jonah to help Decker with the pack train and wandered toward the little family.

"A good afternoon to you, Miss Katy O'Connell." The Irishman beamed at her when she introduced herself, but he didn't stop playing his fiddle. "I hear the music of the Old Country in your name, lass."

"My father is Irish."

"Then an even better afternoon to you," he said. "I'm Patrick Burke, and here is my good wife Camilla."

Katy smiled shyly at Camilla. She didn't often feel shy, but in the presence of babies she lost much of her confidence. Camilla returned her smile with equal diffidence.

"You're very brave to make this trip with a baby," Katy said.

"He's a good baby," Camilla replied. Her expression relaxed a bit at Katy's obvious interest in the child. "Very easy to care for."

Katy sat down beside her. "How old is he?"

"Two months tomorrow. His name is Liam."

"Good Irish name."

"He is named after Patrick's father. I hope he will grow up to be as strong and good a man."

Camilla laid the infant across her lap and rubbed his back. In a few moments, a man-sized burp erupted from the fat little body. The women both laughed. "May I hold him?" Katy asked.

"Yes, of course. He is very outgoing, and loves to meet new people."

Katy took the baby from Camilla as if the tiny, pudgy body were made of the most fragile china. As he dangled from her hands, the infant regarded Katy with round blue eyes. They were nearly the same color as Jonah Armstrong's eyes, Katy noted, but lacked the roguish twinkle. Tiny blond lashes fringed the baby's eyelids and a thin fuzz of reddish blond hair stood up from his head in whorls and cowlicks. He waved chubby arms and kicked his feet as if he, too, could dance to the Irish tunes that came from his father's fiddle. Then he burped again. A stream of watery milk bubbled from his mouth as he gave Katy a delighted smile.

"Oh dear!" Camilla exclaimed.

"Oh my!" Katy echoed. "Is he sick?"

Camilla laughed. "No, of course not. Babies always spit up a bit."

Katy flushed at her ignorance. Competence with infants was one of those woman things with which most females seemed naturally endowed, but not Katy. Olivia had given birth to a baby boy several years after she had married Katy's pa, and Ellen had delighted in helping their stepma take care of little David. Katy had contented herself with admiring her new half brother from a safe distance, however. She felt much more at home chopping wood than changing baby didies.

"Let me have him," Camilla said. "I'll clean him up." She wiped Liam's face and chest, then handed him back to Katy with instructions. "Babies like to be held next to you, cuddled like so." She made a cradle of her arms and hugged an imaginary infant against her ample bosom.

Katy couldn't match Camilla in the bosom department, but she valiantly gave the cuddling a try. Young Liam gurgled with content, spit up a bit more, then gurgled again. The gurgling drew Hunter's attention, and the wolf pranced over to investigate, big triangular ears pricked forward, face intent with curiosity. Camilla immediately tensed and reached for Liam.

"Don't worry about Hunter," Katy assured her as she handed her the squirming baby. "He's very gentle."

Camilla smiled weakly. "He's a very big dog."

"Actually, he's a wolf." Camilla paled, and Katy quickly added: "An old, fat wolf. Very tame. He's been with me since I was a kid, and he likes babies. I have a baby brother. Or at least, I had. He's five now, so I guess I can't call him a baby any longer."

Patrick laughed. "Calm down, Camilla." He stretched a fearless hand toward Hunter, who responded with a politely friendly sniff. "The lady says he's tame. Don't be such a mouse."

Katy wondered about Patrick Burke's lack of regard for his wife's fears. The woman was certainly not a mouse, not if she had the guts to hazard the trip to Dawson with a two-month-old infant. But Camilla gave her husband an apologetic smile. "This is a strange place, this Alaska," she said softly. "Some things that look fierce are harmless, and other things that seem innocent can kill you."

"That's very true," Katy agreed. "I've lived in places like this for a lot of my life. If you need any help along the trail just let me know."

"Thank you so much," Camilla said with a gentle smile. Patrick didn't answer. He was once again busy playing his fiddle.

They covered only three more miles that day. On her own, Katy could have traveled twice the distance they made, and she suspected that Jonah could have done as well. The pack train slowed them, however. The laden horses were in no condition to sustain more than a very slow walk up the trail, though Jack Decker shouted at them and cursed their laziness while his assistant employed a switch from behind. Katy noted that the boy almost never touched horsehide with his whip; he used it mostly to wave in the air over their rumps and urge them to greater speed. Even though the animals were not impressed by the show, the boy didn't beat them. If he had, Katy would have removed the switch from his possession, forcibly if she'd had to. And if she hadn't, she suspected Jonah would have. From the moment Jack Decker had shown up with his ill-conditioned horses, Jonah had been giving the pack train and its handler dark looks. Katy had thought she'd seen Jonah's anger, but the fury that simmered in the glances he gave those poor horses was a different flavor entirely than the vexation he'd loosed on her a time or two.

Not that any of the other pack animals they saw on the trail were in much better condition than Decker's. Most had ribs and hipbones jutting into ridges and peaks beneath their skin, eyes that looked out upon the world with the dullness of near starvation, and skin that suffered open sores rubbed by ill-fitting pack saddles and halters. The fact that all the other packers on the trail abused their animals equally didn't excuse Jack Decker in Katy's eyes. It only made her madder. Her options were limited, however. The five horses in their train belonged to him, not her, and as long as he delivered the services she had paid him for, Katy had very little room to object.

Jonah, however, being a greenhorn, was less indoctrinated with the Westerners' code of live and let live. When they stopped to make camp that first night—just before the log toll bridge leading into the canyon of the Taiya River, the matter came to a head. The sun was high enough above the horizon to give them time before sunset to make camp, but not high enough for them to make it to Camp Pleasant, the little settlement just above the canyon. Several other parties had decided to stop as well, and cookfires were making the air pungent with their smoke.

They chose a clearing well off the trail to set up the tent. The spot showed the scars of other parties that had been there—a smoke-blackened ring of stones, a square of logs set around the fireplace as benches, a too hastily dug latrine, and several patches of flattened weeds and wildflowers where tents had sat. Katy gratefully shed her pack and propped it against one of the logs. Then she went to help unload the pack train so the animals could eat and rest. Jonah was already in frowning discussion with Jack Decker.

"This is my pack train," Decker was saying to Jonah, "and

I'll run it as I see fit. No pissant ignorant dandy is gonna tell me what to do with my nags."

"And no sonofabitch is going to abuse animals this way while taking my pay!"

"You pay me to haul your goods, mister. I'm haulin' 'em. End of story."

"It'll be the end of your story unless you—"

"What's going on here?" Katy interrupted. The look on Decker's face made her nervous. The look on Jonah's face was downright scary.

"He's not going to unload the horses," Jonah told her. "And he's not going to feed them."

"They can graze," Decker said, and spit a wad of tobacco onto the ground.

What grass had once grown at this popular camping spot had long since been grazed off by other horses and mules. Only a few weeds remained to poke through the needles of spruce and fir that covered the ground.

"There's not much fodder here," Katy pointed out.

"There's enough. I don't see no reason to waste freight space carryin' feed along. And I'm not gonna unload 'em, neither. We'll take off what we need for the night, but the rest of the stuff stays on their backs. You want to waste time in the morning loading 'em again?"

"They need the rest," Katy said. "Unload them."

"I need the rest a helluva lot more than they do," Decker declared. "If you unload 'em, missy, you'll load 'em back up in the morning. Ain't part of my job to waste time and effort because some softhearted female's got her corset in a knot."

Jonah growled a warning. "Watch your mouth, Decker."

"Jesus Christ!" Decker groaned. "You damned uppity know-nothing city boys don't have the brains to take your pants down before you shit. Who're you to be telling Jack Decker what he can say and what he hasta do?"

"You're fired, Decker," Jonah said in a voice hard as steel. "I'll buy your goddamned horses."

"Like hell you will!" Decker laughed and threw the first punch. Jonah threw the second, which landed precisely in the center of Decker's nose.

Katy's hands curled into fists as she groaned. Jack Decker was going to pummel Jonah to a bruised and bleeding pulp. She knew he was. "Remember what I taught you!" she shouted into the fray.

She doubted that Jonah heard her, for he was busy defending himself against Decker's fists and landing a few blows himself. Decker was bloodier than Jonah, but the packer didn't seem to notice. The grin on his face showed his enjoyment of the brawl.

Decker's assistant scuttled over to stand beside Katy. His bony arms delivered punches to the air in sympathy with the fight.

"It's about time someone took on that sonofabitch!" he said.

Since the boy hadn't know Jonah long enough to think he was a sonofabitch, Katy concluded he referred to Decker.

"Git 'im in the balls!" he shouted to Jonah. "Shove his eyes down his throat!"

The boy was a fighter after Katy's own heart. She shouted her own encouragement. "The throat, Jonah! Remember the throat!"

The fight ended before much of an audience had a chance to gather. Decker was big, powerful, and his body odor alone could stagger a bull. Jonah was also big, however. He was fast, and, more important, he was deadly angry. He had absorbed what Katy had taught him about 'act-as-if-your-life-depended-upon-it' fighting. After his first blow caught Decker in the nose, he danced away from the infuriated retaliation until Decker left himself open out of sheer frustration. Then Jonah pounded the man's paunchy gut. When Decker bent over, gasping for air, Jonah sent a fist directly to his jaw. The big packer flew back and skidded into the dirt. He moaned, but he didn't get up.

Jonah took a roll of bills from his shirt, counted out a few, and dropped them onto Decker's heaving chest. "There's your fee through today." He peeled off a few more. "There's for your horses, though the poor creatures aren't worth half that. As I said before, you're fired. Get out of here."

Decker didn't argue. He heaved himself to his feet, grabbed the money, and, keeping a cautious eye on Jonah, scuttled away.

Katy felt a ridiculous sense of pride in her pupil. "Not bad," she conceded with an impish smile. "For a man who claims not to fight at the first cross word, you get into a good number of battles."

Jonah wiped a hand over his face as if to clear away the anger that still stiffened his features. "There's a few things in the world worth fighting for," he said softly.

She had been worth fighting for, Katy remembered. And horses were worth fighting for also. Katy admired his priorities.

"Besides." His face relaxed into a smile. "Decker and I were long past the first cross word."

Katy chuckled. "Jonah, you should have been born in Montana. You're wasted on being an Easterner."

"I am, am I, sister mine?"

"You are, brother. Come on. Let's get the horses unloaded. Then I'll see if anyone else camped around here has some grain they can spare."

They were untying the canvas that covered the packs when the boy tapped her on the shoulder. Katy had almost forgotten about Decker's young assistant.

"I could do that for you, ma'am," the boy said.

Katy looked at Jonah, who looked back uncertainly. Apparently he had forgotten about the kid also.

"I can do a lot of things to help," the boy said. "And I ain't no trouble. I'm good with the horses, and I don't eat much. I'd 'preciate it if you'd keep me on, even though you fired Mr. Decker."

Hunter, who'd been watching with lupine interest, walked

over to the boy and nudged his hand. The boy instinctively scratched the plush gray fur between the wolf's ears. The simple gesture made it almost impossible for Katy to refuse the boy. In a way that was almost painful, the kid reminded her of herself not too many years back. Besides, he had been cheering for Jonah in the fight.

"What's your name, boy?"

"Andy."

"Do you have a last name?"

"Reese."

"All right, Andy Reese. You can start by going around to the other camps to see if you can buy some grain. Jonah, give him a dollar. No one's going to part with feed for cheap."

Jonah watched the boy doubtfully as he ran from camp with a greenback clutched in his grubby hand. Then he turned his eyes on Katy, one brow raised.

She arched a brow right back at him. "Decker would've taken it out on him, and we can use the help. Loading and unloading five packhorses is no snap of the fingers."

"I didn't say anything," Jonah denied.

"You were thinking I should have sent him off with his boss."

Jonah smiled. "No, Katy. I wasn't thinking that. I was simply admiring your gentle heart. You should have been born Back East. You're wasted on being a Wild Westerner."

Katy hid her flush behind a grimace. "Yeah. Right."

CHAPTER 8

The Burkes were among the people who stopped before the toll bridge to set up camp for the night. Katy caught glimpses of them as she helped Jonah unload the horses and set up their tent. Camilla looked even more tired than she had at Finnigan's Point, three miles back, but she had no sooner taken off her pack and found a safe resting place for Liam than she was helping Patrick unload from their cart the things they would need for the night. Then, with no fuss or bother, she dumped flour and salt into a bowl and began to mix a batch of biscuits. Katy remembered the heavenly biscuits her sister Ellen could make. Her mouth started to water, and she was struck with sudden inspiration. Leaving Jonah to finish staking down their tent, she wandered over to Camilla's fire.

"Howdy," she said.

Camilla looked up with a welcoming smile. "Hello, Miss O'Connell."

"Call me Katy. Look's like a dandy batch of biscuits there."

"Patrick thinks he cannot live without biscuits for dinner and biscuits for breakfast." She cast a fond look toward her husband, who had abandoned the task of putting up their tent and was swapping stories with the men of the neighboring campsite.

"Have you ever had fresh roasted hare?" Katy asked.

"Do you mean rabbit?" Camilla laughed quietly. "Patrick and I are both from the city. In the part of Boston where we lived, the only wildlife one sees are rats. I'm not sure I would recognize a rabbit if I saw one." She greased the inside of a heavy cast iron Dutch oven with lard and started to roll balls of biscuit dough in her hands. "Patrick is not a huntsman, so we brought lots of salt pork, dried beef, and bacon, as the pamphlets said we should."

"There's no sense eating that stuff before you have to," Katy said. Those biscuits of Camilla's were going to be light and fluffy and delicious. She could almost feel one melting in her mouth. In boasting to Jonah of her cooking along with her other myriad talents, Katy had stretched the truth a bit. At home, she preferred to chop the wood for the stove and let Olivia and Ellen prepare the food.

"I'm going out with Hunter to bring in some rabbits," she told Camilla. "Why don't you and Patrick join us for some fresh meat roasted over the fire?"

"You are very gracious," Camilla said. "But we couldn't impose."

"We'd be glad of the company. Besides, there'll be plenty. You could . . . uh . . . bring the biscuits. It'll give us a chance to get to know each other. After all, we're fellow Irishers. At least, I'm half an Irisher. And Jonah, too, of course, 'cause he's my brother."

"Yes. Of course." The twinkle in Camilla's eyes said that she didn't for one moment believe Katy was Jonah's sister, but her smile was warm, and it made her face look much younger. "You are very kind. I will ask my husband, and I think he will like the idea."

"We'll see you both a little later, then."

Back at camp, Jonah was scribbling in his notebook by the last light of dusk. In the fireplace was a blaze that would soon burn down to a good cooking fire. The greenhorn learned fast. Building a good fire was an art. Andy fussed with the horses, brushing the caked mud from their coats while they munched the grain he'd scrounged for them. Katy looked on approvingly. Mud on a horse's coat ground into the skin and produced sores when it was caught beneath a cinch, saddle, halter, or harness.

"Hunter and I are going after dinner," she announced. She half hoped Jonah would come. She wouldn't have minded showing off her skill with her rock sling. But he only looked up from his writing and smiled.

"If you're going to the market, would you get some fresh greens and a loaf of bread?"

Katy chuckled. "The only market I'm going to is the nearest rabbit hole. Why don't you whittle me a spit, and while you're at it, take out the best china and polish the silver. I invited the neighbors to dinner."

"Yes, sister dear," he teased.

The Burkes arrived in camp just as Katy and Hunter returned with dinner. Katy had sent Hunter in one direction, and she had gone in the opposite. The skirt she wore made moving noiselessly through the brush impossible, and she cursed the awkward thing. She didn't know why she was still wearing such impractical clothing, except that she wasn't quite ready yet to give up her pretense of being a lady. The role she'd played back in Skaguay seemed to cling to her, somehow. Noisy skirts regardless, she bagged two hares with her sling, and Hunter brought in one. No doubt it was the second to fall to his powerful jaws, and the first had continued on down to his stomach. Expecting him to donate everything to the pack would have been unreasonable.

The little impromptu dinner party went well. Camilla was not disgusted when Katy taught her how to clean, skin, and prepare the rabbits as a rather green-tinged Jonah looked on. The Irishwoman marveled aloud at Katy's competence and heartily praised the results when she tasted her first bite of roast hare. Patrick opened a bottle of good Irish whiskey. Katy found it hard to believe that even an Irishman would be so dedicated to whiskey that he would carry it over Chilkoot Pass, but apparently this one was. He took out his fiddle after they were through eating and played softly while the rest of them gabbed. They talked of the Klondike, what they hoped to find there, the tales they'd heard about the journey ahead. Camilla talked a bit about growing up a poor Irish girl in the slums of Boston, which made Katy more grateful than ever that she had so far in her life avoided living in a city. Patrick urged Jonah to relate some of his experiences as a newspaper correspondent, a calling that Katy would have thought quite tame. His stories showed her to be wrong, though—unless Jonah was simply spinning yarns. As a writer, he should be quite talented at that, Katy mused.

Liam was as good as a little angel all through the evening. Jonah was quite taken with the infant, which Katy thought rather strange, given his gender. Most men seemed to regard babies as carriers of some dread disease. They feared getting too close, and they certainly took great pains not to be exposed to any fluid that might leak from noses or mouths or less savory places. When Camilla handed Liam to Jonah, however, he seemed perfectly comfortable holding the baby in his arms—much more comfortable than Katy had been. Unlike Katy, he didn't have to be told to hold the baby close. He didn't mind when the kid spit up on him. In fact, he laughed. And when little Liam felt asleep in his arms, he continued to cradle him, as if the cradling were second nature to him.

Katy was surprised and a little envious. She could understand fathers being good with their own babies, but women were the ones who supposedly had the talent for dealing with infants in general. That was a womanly attribute—one among many—that Katy lacked. She had the equipment to be a mother, but not the instinct. The few babies she had known, including her own half brother, had seemed like little beings from another world—mysterious, fragile, unpredictable. They didn't take to her, either. She was moved and not a little fascinated by the sight of little Liam in Jonah's arms: the baby's smooth, pudgy little hand lying against the hard muscle of the arm that cradled him; unblemished, almost-translucent baby skin contrasting with the sun-browned hairiness of Jonah's masculine hide. For some reason the sharp disparities brought a flush to Katy's face.

"Your brother has a very gentle touch," Camilla said to Katy. "Such a shame he does not have a wife and children of his own."

"Some woman will run him down someday," Katy answered. She was a bit jealous of the woman who would do it. Jonah Armstrong might be someone worth running after—for a woman who was interested in that sort of thing, which, Katy reminded herself, she wasn't.

The Burkes retired to their own camp shortly after Liam fell asleep. Tomorrow they would be on the trail before the sun rose, and bodies weary from the day's journey demanded sleep. Andy refused Katy's offer to make him a bed in the tent and went into the woods with a blanket and a canvas tarp to find his own private sleeping place. Hunter was stretched out, fast asleep with feet twitching in pursuit of dream rabbits, against one of the log benches near the fire. Katy and Jonah were left with only each other's company.

"Are you tired?" Katy asked.

Jonah rolled his shoulders and grimaced. "Sore is more like it. I'm not used to carrying a pack. You?"

"I'm all right." Not for the world would Katy admit that she was a bit sore as well. "You'll get used to it."

He chuckled. "I'd better. It's a long haul to the top."

Katy got up and stood behind him. She placed her hands on his shoulders and started to knead the knotted muscles. He grunted in pleasure as she dug into his hard flesh. "That feels great."

"It's the least a devoted sister can do for her brother."

"Tell my sister Daphne that if you ever meet her. She's more likely to cause knots than massage them away."

Katy chuckled. "I used to do this for my pa after he'd spent a long day in the mine."

Surprisingly, Jonah's shoulders were every bit as wide as her father's. She wondered where in his citified life he'd gotten such muscles.

"Pa had a silver mine in the mountains above Elkhorn—that's a little town in Montana. A boomtown, I guess you'd call it, though it's not booming much since the price of silver dropped. Anyway," she continued as her hand worked at his shoulders, "he had this mine for a while and worked it with just a pick and shovel. It was a one-man operation, but he got a lot of silver out of it. I helped him in the tunnel sometimes. Once the thing caved in and I thought he was a goner for sure, but we got him out, my stepma and me."

"Sounds like a hard life for a young girl."

"Oh no. It was a good life. The best."

"You must miss your parents."

"I do." Not quite in the way he thought, for they weren't gone forever. But she did miss them.

He flexed his shoulders, and muscles rolled beneath her hands. The air was cool, but his firm flesh was warm where she touched him. Massaging Jonah's shoulders certainly produced different sensations in her than massaging her father's, Katy mused.

"I feel better," Jonah declared. "And I'll return the favor."

"No thanks. I'm fine."

"Uh-huh," he said unbelievingly. "Sit down."

His tone brooked no argument, so Katy sat. She jumped slightly when his warm hands landed upon her shoulders, but soon relaxed under the spell of his ministrations. He was strong, but he knew how to temper the force he used. His thumbs separated the muscles while powerful fingers worked them until they softened. The process hurt, but it felt good at the same time. Blood started to flow freely into her arms again; she felt it as a warm flood from her shoulders to the tips of her fingers.

"That does feel good," she admitted.

"Yes. It does."

The magic hands moved to her neck. His fingers rested lightly at her throat while the thumbs worked up and down the sore muscles that held her head upright. She flinched at first, then let her head roll forward as the muscles seemed to turn to water.

"Not sore, huh?"

"Well, maybe a little."

"It's no wonder if your neck aches. Look at all this weight you're carrying around on your head. I don't think I've ever seen such thick hair."

One of his hands continued to massage her neck while the other worked at the pins that held her braids coiled atop her head. Once he had removed the pins, he freed the braids themselves by threading his fingers through the strands. It felt so good that Katy couldn't protest. She was so relaxed, so weary, that she probably couldn't have protested if a volcano had erupted beneath her.

"That better?" Jonah asked.

"Mmm."

"I thought so."

He pushed the thick veil of hair forward over her shoulders and continued to massage her back, shoulders, and neck. No knot or sore spot escaped his attention. He had an uncanny ability to find every place that dared to ache. But his attentions started an ache in the core of her belly that had nothing to do with sore or strained muscles.

Feeling ridiculously safe with the fire at her front and Jonah at her back, Katy let herself slip into a contented, sensuous haze. The sensation of her defenses melting was unexpectedly enjoyable. Her blood simmered pleasantly. Her muscles turned smooth and buttery. Her eyes surrendered their focus, seeing only the shimmering orange blur of the fire surrounded by velvet black night. She could not have moved for anything short of an earthquake.

"A bit weary are we, Katy?" rumbled Jonah's voice.

Katy felt herself lifted from the log. She didn't protest. When he carried her into the tent, the canvas blocked the warmth from the fire, but she scarcely had time to shiver before he covered her with the blankets of her bedroll. Even the hard ground didn't diminish her relaxation. Yet as mellow and tired as she felt, something inside her coiled tightly in unfamiliar need. When Jonah's hand brushed her cheek as he brought the blanket around her shoulders, it coiled even tighter.

"Sleep tight," he said, as if he were tucking a child into bed. "And remember,"—his fingers brushed her cheek, this time not by accident—"you asked for it."

Katy heard him settle into his own bedroll. Hunter padded in, sniffed her face, and curled himself in the bend of her knees. Warm, comfortable, and vaguely dissatisfied, she fell asleep wondering just what it was she had asked for.

Dawn arrived under a cloak of scudding gray clouds that shrouded the mountains and misted the valley with a cold drizzle. Andy was already packing the horses by the time Katy and Jonah stumbled from the tent. Katy had trouble greeting the morning with her usual bright energy. She had slept too deeply the night before, and dreamed deeply as well. Clear memory of the dreams had fled moments after she woke, but the disturbance they created remained. She felt restless and distracted, and fought an urge to dive back into her bedroll and return to those dreams, whatever they were. When Jonah patted her shoulder and inquired how she had slept, uncharacteristic diffidence gripped her. The sight of him tousled and unshaven brought an unexpected flush to her face. Katy couldn't imagine what was wrong with her. Last night was not the first night she'd slept in the same tent with Jonah. She'd seen him tousled, combed, yawning, angry, laughing, sleepy, sour-faced, and smiling. She'd even seen him half-dressed and thought nothing of it. Or not much, at least. She wondered if she was getting sick.

They ate a breakfast of cold, greasy hare and the biscuits that Camilla had generously left for their morning meal, then hefted their own packs and joined the traffic already tramping across the toll bridge.

Andy was as good as his word about being a hard worker. He handled the pack train well, but the horses' skittishness on the muddy, slippery trail made minding them more than a one-man job. Katy was about to step in and help when Jonah beat her to it. She watched with interest as he helped Andy settle the animals to their work. The greenhorn had an instinct with horses as well as babies. Anyone watching him wouldn't guess that he'd been a citified dandy only a few weeks before. He even looked the part of a Westerner now. His skin was bronzed from the sun and wind, and weathered laugh lines added character to his face. He wasn't wearing his hat—his pack kept knocking it off, he said—and his thick brown hair was plastered to his head by the rain. The wet didn't seem to bother him. Neither did the mud nor the cold wind nor the horses whose hooves danced so dangerously close to his feet.

Katy led the way up the trail. Once across the toll bridge, the traffic spread out. The trail followed the Taiya River for only a short distance beyond the bridge. In a steep-walled canyon, it left the river to climb slowly up the more gentle side of the valley. Where yesterday Katy had lamented the lack of challenge, today she couldn't complain about the ease of their passage. The going was steep, the footing bad, alternating between sucking mud and slippery rocks that gave boots and hooves very little purchase. A hundred yards ahead of them were three men having considerable difficulty. Bent under impossibly heavy packs, they slipped, stumbled, and panted. One finally lost his balance where the path sloped precariously in the direction of the river. He and his pack tumbled down the slope about ten feet before they came to rest against a stubby, prickly spruce. His companions, winded and red-faced, simply sat down beside the trail, apparently too tired to help him extricate himself. When Katy reached the trail above him, he was still cursing.

Jonah left the pack train in Andy's capable hands and came to stand beside her. Together, they peered down at the unlikely argonaut who struggled to right himself, pack and all, like a heavy-shelled turtle trying to flip onto its feet after being turned over on its back.

"I don't suppose it would occur to him to take the pack off," Jonah commented.

"I don't suppose it would," Katy sighed. If they stopped to help everyone who faltered along the trail, they would never get to Dawson, but it went against the grain to simply walk away and leave the poor man. His partners weren't going to be much help to him.

As if reading her mind, Jonah went back to the pack train and took a coiled rope from one of the packsaddles. He tossed one end to the man below and fastened the other to the trunk of a sturdy spruce tree. Inspired by Jonah's Good Samaritan efforts, the man's companions roused themselves to help by looking over the trail and shouting instructions.

When the man finally got himself and his pack back on the trail, with the help of Jonah's rope, the only thanks he gave Katy and Jonah were envious glances at the pack train. "Could I buy one of them horses?" he asked.

"Sorry," Jonah said. "We can't spare any."

"We couldn't find a single horse in town. Seems unfair, you folks havin' five and us havin' none."

"Life's like that," Jonah philosophized.

By now the Burkes, who'd still been packing their cart when Katy and Jonah left camp, caught up with them.

"Trouble?" Patrick asked hopefully. The affable Irishman's eyes sparkled in anticipation of a fight.

"No trouble," Jonah replied.

The man they had helped, along with his companions, watched them resentfully as they got the pack train in motion once again and made their way up the trail.

"Interesting attitude," Jonah observed from behind Katy as she took up the trudge once again.

"That's what gold does to people," she said. "My pa told me once that gold was a disease that turned men's blood to molten greed."

"Your pa was a philosopher."

"Naw. He had a silver mine. That's almost as bad as gold."

In company with the Burkes, they passed several other parties who were struggling with their packs, or the mud, or the steepness of the climb through the canyon. One man's packhorse had stepped into a quagmire of mud beside the trail. They helped the man lighten the poor beast's load so it could free itself. Unlike the recipients of their earlier good deed, this man was effusively grateful. Katy didn't embarrass him by a warning to keep his horse strictly to the trail. If he hadn't known that basic rule of handling a packhorse when he started this morning, he certainly knew it now.

On the whole, Katy observed, the Klondikers were a sorry lot to be challenging the Alaskan and Canadian wilderness. Some of the men on the trail looked as if they spent their entire lives behind a desk, or clerking at a store. Others were woefully ignorant of what they faced—as was the pair who were struggling to ride bicycles up the rocky trail. The cyclists gave up before the morning was half-gone. Katy and Jonah met them walking their bicycles down the trail. How many others would turn around before they reached the summit of Chilkoot Pass? Katy wondered. Already they had passed several weary men, their faces sagging with defeat, who were headed down the trail instead of up. How many others would find that their strength was not sufficient to meet the demands of the trail, their courage not equal to the wild country beyond the pass?

As for themselves, Katy had no doubt that they would be

among the few who would make it to Dawson. Compared to many of the others along the trail, Jonah was a tower of strength and competence. He might have even made it without her, Katy admitted to herself. Probably not, but he might have.

They nooned with the Burkes. Dark smudges shadowed Camilla's eyes. Her husband, who reveled in every small adventure along the trail, seemed not to notice. Katy offered to help with little Liam and drew Camilla's laughter when she tied the baby into a diaper with only one leg hole.

"It takes some practice," Camilla assured her as she re-pinned the soft cloth. "Before I had Liam, I didn't know anything about babies either."

Back on the trail, Katy let Jonah lead the way, with Patrick Burke and his cart following close behind. The rain had stopped, and the sun ducked in and out of the clouds, warming the afternoon with a bit of sunshine. Camilla walked beside her husband, or directly behind him in spots where the trail was too narrow for them both. He was having difficulty with the cart. It sank into the mud or stuck its wheels between rocks, inspiring Patrick to exhaust his repertoire of Irish curses. But he was determined to get the load to Sheep Camp, several miles ahead, where he could hire Indian packers to carry the load over the summit and down the other side to Lake Bennett—the head of navigation for the upper Yukon River.

Katy brought up the rear of their combined parties with Andy and the pack train. One day of decent treatment could not change the horses from what they were—broken-down nags each with one hoof in an equine grave. They were slow and stumbling, but they were better than nothing. Katy and company got more than one envious look from parties that passed them on the trail, for those who had not been able to find horses would be required to make numerous trips to Lake Bennett and back to haul their supplies—or hire Indian packers, who were as expensive as horses and could carry a good deal less.

"They're tryin' hard," Andy told Katy as she urged the horses along. "Ol' Decker didn't give 'em much to eat, even when they was in the stable. No days of rest, neither. Last trip we made, one of the horses went down on his knees and all the tuggin' in the world wouldn't make 'im git up. Decker just left 'im there to starve. Didn't even bother to shoot 'im. Wouldn't waste a bullet, he said."

"Somebody ought to treat Decker the way he treats his horses," Katy growled.

"Yes'm. That's what I thought. He whupped me once 'cause I gave 'em too much to eat—least to his way o' thinkin' it was too much. I wouldn't want'cha thinkin' that I was working' for Decker 'cause I liked 'im."

"Why did you work for him?" Katy asked.

"He's the only one would hire me, 'cause I'm small, you know, an' everyone figgered I couldn't handle these nags on the trail. But I can, and I need to earn the money to get to Dawson."

"You're kind of young to be prospecting for gold."

At Katy's smiling comment, Andy drew himself up to his full scrawny height, which wasn't very impressive. "Gold don't care for young or old. Don't make no difference. And young folks can like bein' rich just as much as old folks."

The second horse in line balked as Hunter dashed across the trail in pursuit of some small rodent. Andy swished his switch above the nag's rump. It laid back its ears in annoyance, then lurched forward after the lead horse.

"That's a mighty fine-lookin' dog you got," Andy said.

"He's a wolf, not a dog. He just acts like a dog."

"A wolf?" Clearly the boy was impressed. "That's why the horses don't like 'im."

"He won't hurt them." Hunter dashed out of the brush beside the trail, tucked himself neatly into a sitting position in front of Katy, and presented her with a dead mouse.

"Look at that!" Andy exclaimed.

"Thank you, Hunter. Good boy." Katy took the mouse without a qualm. Hunter had presented her with things far worse. Holding the offering by the tip of its little tail, she tossed it back to the tongue-lolling wolf. "Yours," she told him as he caught it. In one gulp, the mouse was gone.

"I had a dog once," Andy confided. "She died having puppies."

"That's too bad. When was that?"

"A long time ago."

"Andy, how old are you?"

"Uh . . . sixteen."

Katy knew a lie when she heard one. The kid was twelve, she guessed, or a small thirteen.

"Do you have parents?"

"Oh sure. My ma's a whore in Seattle. She ain't real good at it, I guess, 'cause we were dirt-poor all the time I lived with 'er. I was kinda helpin' out by, you know, stealin' things here and there, but Ma said I should go before I got my ass locked into jail. So I lit out. And when I heard about the gold strike I figgered that was for me. I just hope there's gold still left in that river when I manage to earn my way to Dawson."

"Just don't decide to steal someone's grubstake to get there," Katy warned. "You're likely to find yourself buried in the ground instead of digging in it."

"Naw. I've turned honest. My stealin' days are over."

They trudged on. Andy entertained Katy with anecdotes from the stews and bordellos of Seattle, and Katy told Andy tales from her wild days running with her fugitive father. Andy was suitably impressed, especially when Katy related how she'd shot a hanging rope from around her father's neck when she was only ten.

The terrain finally broadened out after the long climb. In the midafternoon they reached Camp Pleasant, which straddled the trail at the very top of the canyon. The place was crowded with argonauts taking advantage of the abundant water and timber for the night's camp. They passed it by, heading for Sheep Camp a mile and a half farther up the trail. According to all the maps Katy had studied, Sheep Camp was the last timbered place to camp below the summit.

Beyond Camp Pleasant they climbed steadily toward timberline. The spruce and aspen got more sparse and smaller. The terrain was rugged. Hanging valleys notched the steep slopes that rose on either side of the trail. Some had glaciers snaking their frozen way down the axis of the valley. In others, the arm of the glacier had receded, leaving behind a scoured trail.

The sun had sunk below the mountaintops by the time they reached Sheep Camp. The place boasted two restaurants and a saloon, all of which were doing a booming business. The available camping spots were also crowded.

"We could go on to Stone House with the Burkes," Katy told Jonah. Patrick had decided he could get his cart to Stone House, a landmark gigantic boulder which was a mile farther up the trail, and hire his Indian packers there.

"There're a few camping spots left here," Jonah said. "I need to work on my notes. We'll stop."

Katy made a face.

"Don't be so impatient, sister mine." He grinned mockingly "We'll make it over the summit tomorrow whether we stop here or at Stone House. If I don't get something written, my editor will come after me with a stick."

"We'll see you at the top." Patrick waved a jaunty farewell. Still whistling, he leaned energetically into the harness that strapped him to his cart. Camilla smiled wanly, adjusted Liam in the sling that rested against her chest, and followed after her husband.

Katy and Jonah chose a campsite down the hill from Sheep Camp's busy enterprises. There was nothing peaceful or wilderness-like about the crowded place. Cookfires smudged the air. Conversation and laughter echoed off the once-silent mountains. A few minutes passed before Katy realized that the loudest laughter and conversation came from the campsite next to theirs, and the voices making all the noise were feminine.

She peered through the trees in the direction that Jonah and Andy were already gazing with marked interest. It appeared that they had walked two full days over rocks and through mud and rain to camp directly next to a passel of whores.

CHAPTER 9

Jonah sat with his back against a tree. The lantern hanging from the branch above him shone sufficiently bright for him to see clearly the blank page in front of him, but it didn't cast a similar brightness into his weary brain. Never before had he experienced so much difficulty putting his thoughts onto paper. He had written while dodging cinders from Milwaukee's great fire in 1892; he had written in the middle of the 1894 miners' riot in Pennsylvania that left eleven people dead; he had written while huddled in a bombed-out school during Cuba's revolt against Spain in 1895; he had written while accompanying William McKinley's presidential campaign just a year ago in 1896. Now, in the great gold rush of 1897, he had reached the point where he couldn't write while comfortably seated under a tree, safe under a peaceful and starry sky.

The task of concentrating was made no easier by the noise coming from the neighboring campsite, which was growing more raucous as the evening wore on. The ladies next door were doing a rousing business—not surprising given the circumstances. Still, noise and confusion rarely could distract Jonah when he wrote. The shouts and laughter that disturbed the night were not the real problem—the real problem had black hair, almond green eyes, and a smile like a mischievous elf's. Katy O'Connell was a distraction who could have kept Tolstoi from writing *War and Peace*. She led Jonah's mind astray by her mere presence. Just now she sat on a log not twenty feet away, mending the cheekstrap of one of the pack train's halters. On some other female her plain garments would not have been fetching, but on Katy they were. She wore a vest of some sort of hide, a soft cambric shirt with a missing top button, and a skirt which, in the absence of the usual feminine multitude of petticoats, draped over her lap in an enticing outline of her thighs. White, ruffly bloomers peeked from beneath the hem of her skirt.

Ruffly bloomers and missing buttons—Jonah was a journalist; journalists noticed such details.

Journalists also learned to follow their instincts, and Jonah's instinct told him he was not going to finish the piece about Andy tonight. Instead, he would work on another article about Katy. That should be easy enough, since she insisted on flaunting herself by sitting across the campsite from him. He could write an account of the poker game—the *Record* readers would eat up the story of how she had taken his hundred dollars and gambled it into a small fortune. She had looked incredible in that red dress. He searched for the words that would describe the wild energy she'd had about her. The emerald eyes had been alive with animation, the inviting curve of her mouth had combined seduction with just a hint of shyness. Even her skin had glowed with vitality. Beautiful, yes, but beautiful was inadequate. So was stunning. She had glowed brighter than the lanterns in that saloon. Every man there had been panting for the chance to play cards with her, and whatever more intimate games they could persuade her to play, no doubt. He should have been repelled by such behavior, Jonah reflected, but he couldn't be anything but entranced. The much-vaunted charm of feminine diffidence and innocence paled before Katy's bolder appeal.

Jonah surreptitiously examined his subject as she was now, dressed in wrinkled cambric and deerhide. The red dress had not been the source of that extraordinary glow that night, he admitted. Katy shone from every pore, even hauling a pack train through rain and mud or skinning rabbits for their dinner. Even sitting quietly on a log fiddling with a mule's dirty halter.

"Helloooo!" warbled a feminine voice. A redheaded, scarlet-gowned ambassador from the neighboring campsite sauntered out of the trees. Two of her professional sisters followed close behind. "Hello there! We saw you sitting over here all by yourself, and you looked very lonely."

"Maudie said maybe you was too shy to join the party," another said. Her gown was purple silk. Feathers of the same color adorned her black, black hair—hair black as Katy's, but without the glimmer and shine.

"So we thought we'd take a little break from the crowd and be neighborly," a silver-blond nymph giggled. She was petite, but her curves were anything but diminutive. Jonah couldn't help but stare at the breasts that swelled above her corset. They remained confined surely in defiance of every law of physics. "I'm Maude," she giggled again. "And this is Cecily and Rhona. Are you going to Dawson, too?"

Jonah controlled the impulse to quip that no, he wasn't going to Dawson; he was headed to South America by way of the Klondike. Andy had paused in brushing one of the pack-horses and was giving the women a cold stare. Across the campsite, looking like a bastion of propriety in comparison to the three colorful visitors, Katy scowled darkly.

The scowl was all the inspiration Jonah needed. He smiled wickedly. "Welcome, ladies. Have a seat. Andy, break out the whiskey that Patrick left with us last night."

Katy's scowl grew even darker, and Jonah's grin widened. Katy was always entertaining when she was irked. Jonah got to his feet and made a gentlemanly bow, as if he were in a ballroom in Chicago instead of in an alpine meadow on an Alaskan mountainside. He gestured in Katy's direction.

"Ladies, this is my sister Katy. And I'm Jonah. We're very pleased to make your acquaintance."

"Your sister?" Maude giggled. It appeared that the woman couldn't open her mouth without giggling. "Really?"

Cecily and Rhona sized up Katy like cats eyeing another feline who had strayed into their territory. Katy eyed them right back. A slow smile spread across her face that might have scared Jonah if he had been its target.

Rhona placed a hand on a seductively cocked, generously proportioned hip. Her eyes flashed a challenge toward Katy. "Travelin' along with your brother, are ya, honey? Better keep close watch on him, or some lonely lady will simply swoop down and carry him off—a delicious hunk of man like him." She turned toward Jonah, her hips rotating as she moved. "Speaking of lonely, handsome. Must be downright dreary on the trail with just a sister for company. You should come over to our camp and get acquainted."

"Yeah," Maude breathed. "Come over later, when it's not so crowded." She insinuated herself between Rhona and her prey. "A gent like you deserves special, special attention, you know?" Giggling, she brushed against him, in one brief, efficient moment stroking him with every inch of the merchandise from her breasts to her hips. Andy chose that moment to break in, Patrick's bottle of Irish whiskey in his hands.

"We've only got two cups," the boy announced tersely.

"Oh look!" Cecily exclaimed. "Isn't he cute! Who're you, sweetie?"

"How old are you, sweetcheeks?" Maude tittered.

Andy's brows lowered as he backed away.

"I'll bet he's old enough," Rhona crooned.

Cecily and Maude cut off poor Andy's retreat and fluttered around him like perfumed butterflies. Rhona stayed draped over Jonah as though she couldn't stand on her feet without his support. The heavy musk of her perfume rose in waves on the warmth of her body. The odor polluted the fresh night air. Jonah had second thoughts about inviting the attention of these female predators when he saw Katy rise to her feet with the grace of a cobra about to strike.

"Leave Andy alone." Her voice was low, but it cut through the women's cooing and giggling like a knife.

"Andy?" Cecily purred to the boy. "Is that your name, love? Andy?"

Andy twisted out of the arms that tried to entice him.

"Leave him alone," Katy warned.

She bristled like a kitten, Jonah noted with appreciation. A lion kitten. There was nothing tame or domestic about the look she shot him. "You can get your claws out of that one, too," she told Rhona. "The kid's too young, and that one's too ignorant to know any better."

Ignorant, was he? Jonah had been about to send the professional ladies on their way when Katy had made that scathing comment. He decided to let the bossy little curmudgeon fight it out on her own.

"Ease off, sister girl." Rhona slid Katy a feline glance. "Maybe the gents here are in the market for a little entertainment." She gave a velvety laugh. "Better they get it from us than start looking at you for it, eh?"

"They're not in the market for what you *ladies* are selling!" Katy marched over to Rhona and peeled her off her prey. "You have enough jackasses in your camp without raiding mine for more."

"Well I don't expect you have your brand on these particular jackasses, honey." Rhona smiled and arched a painted brow. "But I'd be willing to check this one's rump, just to be sure."

Jonah tried hard not to laugh at the expression on Katy's face. A flash of her eyes let him know he was in deep trouble. "If this jackass wants to drop his pants for you, he's a lot greener than I thought. But leave the boy alone. He's too young to get his pocket picked while getting a dose of the pox."

"Not from me he wouldn't get the pox!" Maude said, then giggled.

"And if I put my hand in a man's pocket, sister girl, it's not to get at his wallet." Rhona swaggered toward Katy with swaying hips and a lethally contemptuous expression.

Katy met her with a look every bit as dire. "Why don't you and your friends just take your high-toned bustles back to your own camp."

Jonah almost laughed at Katy's ferocity. She obviously was a pro in this kind of catfight.

Andy had managed to squirm out of the tender grasp of Cecily and Maude. "Don't trouble on my account, Miss Katy. I . . . I can take care of myself."

"You see?" Rhona purred. "The boy wants to make up his own mind. And the man . . . ?" She turned toward Jonah and appealed to him with a dramatic lift of her shoulder. "You let your sister ride herd on you, handsome?"

Jonah just smiled. "Sister Katy cracks a mean whip. I wouldn't cross her if I were you."

"Well then," Rhona sighed, "we'll leave you to your sister's lively company." Her eyes traveled up and down his body. "Don't forget the invite if you get lonely."

Maude blew a kiss toward Andy, who, if possible, blushed an even brighter red, and then smacked loudly in Jonah's direction. Cecily pouted her lips into a long-distance kiss and waved to Jonah sorrowfully. Jonah almost regretted them going. Katy was entertaining to watch when she was annoyed. He nearly laughed as she looked him up and down in the same manner Rhona had, as if trying to discover what the sporting woman had seen in him.

"I can't believe you let that trollop hang all over you like some kind of hungry suckerfish!" she hissed. "Don't you city boys know anything about whores?"

"I've had my share of lessons," Jonah said with a smile, "for an ignorant jackass, that is."

"Well it didn't teach you much, did it? Don't you know what those women wanted?"

Jonah shrugged innocently. "They wanted me?"

"Hah! Men! Always ready to believe that women are ready to swoon at their feet for the sake of your smile!"

"Well," Jonah said ingenuously, "I did get the impression they were after more than a smile."

"You bet they were, greenhorn. They were after anything they could steal, and I don't mean your precious reputation! And you!" She whirled on Andy, who jumped back at her sudden attack. "You of all people ought to know to stay away from those women. They'll feed you liquor and who knows what else and get your mind so twisted around you won't know if you're coming or going."

Andy studied the ground. "Yes'm. I don't cotton much to whores. My ma was one, and I run with the pack when I was a kid, but I ain't never had 'em come at me like turkey buzzards at a dead mouse."

"As long as you're working for us, you keep away from that flock of turkey buzzards."

"Yes'm. You want this whiskey now?" He held out the bottle he'd been sent to fetch.

"Put it back in the tent."

"Yes'm. G'night then."

"Good-night."

When Andy had taken his blankets into the woods, Jonah crossed his arms and leaned against a tree trunk. "A bit hard on the boy, aren't you? He's just a kid, you know, and kids his age get curious about such things."

"His ma was a whore, so he probably knows more about trollops than you do. It's a good thing you have me to look after you, or you'd get stolen blind before you got halfway to Dawson."

"Your faith in my innate intelligence is always uplifting. Maybe the ladies were just after a little pleasant company."

Katy sniffed. "You think your handsome face was what

brought them over here? Think again. Believe me. They were more interested in kissing your greenbacks than anything else you might have that's worth kissing."

Jonah heard a tinge of the green in Katy's voice. He grinned. The possibility of her being jealous was intriguing. Could his little Daniel Boone in skirts be suffering the same impossible attraction that he felt for her?

"Of course, you know all about whores and what they want," he goaded.

"I've known enough of them to know how they operate."

"And you know all about men, too, I suppose, and whatever it is they have that's not as enjoyable to kiss as a wad of greenbacks."

Katy gave him an arch look. "I know enough, believe me! Most men overestimate their power over women."

"Is that so?"

"That's so."

"When I kissed you in Missoula, I suppose that wasn't anything that could make a whore forget her preoccupation with greenbacks and pocket picking."

"*I'm* not a whore," Katy replied with a sniff. "So I couldn't really say. But it certainly didn't have *me* swinging in the clouds."

"You seemed ready enough to kiss me in Skaguay," Jonah reminded her wickedly.

"That was for luck." She shrugged and smiled with superior unconcern. "I've kissed my share of men, and more besides. I could kiss you all day and get only sore lips from the experience."

"Really?"

"Really! Not every female turns into a limp noodle when you pucker up, Jonah Armstrong."

Jonah grinned, unable to resist the challenge, especially when it presented itself in the guise of Katy's sweetly curved mouth and flashing eyes. "Are you all words, Katy girl, or do you have the guts to back up that claim with money?"

"What do you mean?"

"You're a gambling woman. Put your money where your mouth is. Or maybe I should say put your mouth where your mouth is."

Katy blinked. "You're joking."

"Hell no, I'm not joking. I'm so eminently resistible to women. Prove it. Kiss me."

"That's ridiculous."

"Hah! I thought so. Katy O'Connell talks big, but when it's time to put up or shut up, she's not quite so cocky. You're afraid of me."

Fists balled on her hips, Katy sneered. "Afraid of you? When pigs fly. Like I said. I could kiss you all day and not feel a thing!"

"Be my guest."

"All right. I will. Two bucks says I can plant one right on your mouth and walk away without even breaking a sweat."

"Two bucks isn't much."

"You want to lose more?" she taunted.

"All right." He pushed away from the tree and reached for her.

Katy jumped back. "Wait a minute. I'm supposed to kiss you."

"Oh no. That's stacking the deck in your favor. You could just give me some little maidenly peck that wouldn't melt soft butter. *I* get to kiss *you*."

He enjoyed the flash of uncertainty that crossed her face. Then she gathered her courage and faced him squarely. "Do your worst!"

Jonah thought his best was called for, not his worst. From their first meeting, Katy had alternately bullied him and mothered him. She treated him as though he were a wet-behind-the-ears kid who didn't have enough sense to come in out of the rain, ridiculing his skills, his strength, his talents, and now his virility. He had a powerful need to render Katy O'Connell flustered, disoriented, helpless, and completely at his manly mercy. The problem was, the moment Jonah touched his lips to hers, he discovered that he had other powerful needs as well.

For her part, Katy wasn't sure just how she'd been stupid enough to get herself into the current predicament. Gambling with a pair of lips was much more dangerous than gambling with mere money—and she didn't know the game nearly as well. The touch of Jonah's mouth was temptingly intimate. His day's growth of whiskers scraped pleasantly across her cheek. The scent of him—woodsmoke and clean male sweat—enveloped her like a warm blanket.

His mouth nibbled. His tongue played at the seam of her lips, which she stubbornly kept closed, in spite of a weak-kneed instinct to open to him.

"Open your mouth," he whispered against her cheek.

"No," she whispered back.

"That's part of being kissed. Are you a welcher, Katy O'Connell?"

Hesitantly, she cracked her mouth open. With tickling caresses of his tongue, he persuaded her to let him explore farther. He deepened the kiss, and that liquid surrender that Katy wanted to deny started simmering in her veins. She couldn't help molding herself to his hard, warm body. It was all she could do to not lift one leg and wrap it around his as his hands pressed her hips against his.

Suddenly he broke off. They both gasped for breath. Katy figured she could win the bet simply by backing out of his arms and making some casual remark to show how unaffected she was. But she couldn't. She could no more move away from Jonah at that moment than she could move out of her own skin. His eyes wouldn't let her go. She didn't know that blue could be a warm color, but in Jonah's eyes, it was. She was hypnotized by the heat of his gaze. Her senses whirled in a dizzy spiral, and when Jonah once again lowered his mouth to hers she met him with unreserved gusto, moved by a sudden need to show him that she could be just as much a woman as those bosomy, painted whores in the next camp. Instinct took over as she warred playfully with his seeking tongue and pressed her hips against his. She could hear the rapid drumming of his heart—or was it hers? Her body became soft and molten, fitting to every hard plane and curve of masculine muscle. When his hand slid between them and gently squeezed her breast, she thought she would explode from the bolt of aching pleasure that shot from her heart to the most private parts of her body.

"Aw, Katy, dammit!" he whispered against her throat.

Pliable as a willow, she bent back when he urged her. His mouth traveled to the hollow at the base of her throat. She lay against his strong arm as he unbuttoned her shirt and kissed the thin cotton chemise that guarded her breasts. She trembled with unfamiliar need when he pushed the chemise aside and caressed her bare flesh with his lips. Not until his mouth fastened on the hard nub of her nipple did a tingle of alarm rouse her from the lethargy of desire. Passion congealed to shock at both herself and him. She pushed desperately on his shoulders.

"Katy," he murmured against her breast. "You're goddamned beautiful."

"Get away! Let me go!"

He released her instantly. They stared at each other for a moment. Jonah looked almost as dazed as Katy felt. He blinked, as if trying to bring himself back to reality, then reached out and closed Katy's still-gaping blouse.

Katy jumped back. She hadn't even realized she was half-undressed. A fiery flush burned her cheeks. Suddenly she was furious.

"You . . . you . . ." The words to describe him eluded her. "Don't you have something better to do than try to play pattycake with every female in sight? You . . . you randy jackass!"

She fled to the tent. Holding her blouse closed as if it was her damaged dignity she held together instead, she simply stood and stared at the canvas wall. The tent flap opened, and a footstep scraped the tarp-covered floor behind her. Jonah cleared his throat. His breathing sounded like a bellows in the confined tent.

"Katy . . ."

She didn't turn, didn't move.

"Katy . . . goddammit . . ."

She heard him leave, and whatever strength that held her collapsed. Limply, she sank to the blankets of her bedroll. The half-full bottle of Patrick's whiskey sat in the middle of the tent where Andy had left it. Katy reached for it. If any day deserved a swallow or two of whiskey, this one did.

When she finally crawled into her blankets, Hunter had come into the tent, but Jonah had not.

Katy did not sleep. Her clothes were binding and annoying, but they were a sort of armor between herself and shame, and she refused to undress for mere comfort's sake. The near disaster she had invited upon herself whirled through her mind in a confusing eddy of embarrassment, chagrin, and fascination. At the same time that she mentally kicked herself for getting into such a situation, she marveled at the hurricane of sensation that had swept through her—that still lingered in little sparks that seemed to fire randomly in various parts of her body. Her nerves were on edge and her mind was jumbled. One part of her wanted to flatten Jonah Armstrong with her fist, while another part wanted to kiss him again. Still another part fretted over just what Jonah thought. Why had he kissed her like he wanted to eat her alive? Had he been trying to prove his point? Had he been making fun of her? Had he shared in the hurricane of sensation or simply created it? She wished Jonah was in the tent so she could ask him. She was glad he was gone so she didn't have to face him. She was totally confused.

Damn those prancing whores, anyway! What had happened was all their fault! Katy was not prim or straitlaced, but when those perfumed and gussied-up giggling knotheads had started hanging all over Jonah, she'd wanted to rip some fancy satin dresses and pull some artfully curled hair. Defending poor Andy had just been an excuse for her temper. The boy could take care of himself with trollops, Katy figured, but Jackass Jonah obviously could not.

Katy yanked the blankets up around her shoulders. Now she was angry again. Let Jonah stay out in the rain that was pattering on the tent canvas. Maybe it would cool him off. Maybe he could crawl under Andy's tarp and the two of them could compare notes on whores.

She finally got to sleep after what seemed like hours of tossing and turning. Hunter woke her once or twice by whining and pacing the tent. The wolf's behavior should have told her something was wrong, but Katy was so dog tired that she simply told him to lie back down. Therefore, when the earth beneath the tent began to rumble, she was unprepared.

She woke to enveloping sound: rattling combined with an all-encompassing roar. A voice shouted over the noise. Someone screamed. Katy came full awake with the certainty that something was terribly wrong. Then the tent flap jerked back and Jonah, dripping wet, his shirt plastered to his chest and his hair curling wildly from wind and water, stared in at her.

"Katy, you here?" he said into the darkness.

"Yes."

"Well get out! There's been a mudslide up valley, and it's flooding down here. The water's rising fast. We've got to get to higher ground."

"I'm coming!"

Jonah disappeared as Katy untangled herself from the blankets and pulled on her boots. Still woozy from sleep, she lit the lantern and started to roll up the blankets to be tied. Hunter dashed out of the tent as she stuffed her extra stockings and gloves into her valise and snapped it shut. Valise and bedroll under one arm, lantern in the other hand, she headed for the door when something struck the tent. Water rushed in to cover the tarp floor. The spruce boughs she had slept upon floated around her ankles and were rising toward her knees.

"Omigod!" Katy muttered. "He wasn't kidding!"

She pushed the tent flap aside. Cold driving rain hit her in the face. Here and there lanterns bobbed in the darkness. Voices shouted over the tumult of rain and roaring flood. The water swirled above her calves, and her heavy twill skirt tugged her along with the flow. She fought against it. In the darkness, with the water whirling dizzily around her, upslope was impossible to discern from downslope, and she had slept in so many campsites over the last few days that she didn't remember which direction was uphill.

"Jonah! Where are you?"

The roar of water drowned out her call. She slogged in the direction she thought was uphill. Suddenly Hunter bounded out of the darkness, spraying water with every bound. He whined once and turned. Katy followed. The water rose past her knees. Hunter stopped bounding and started swimming. Katy felt a hint of fear squeeze her stomach.

"Jonah!"

No answer. She could only hope that he had gotten Andy and the horses to safety. Debris swirled past them—branches, a wooden box, a stool. The water had risen to midthigh when someone's tent came barreling along on the swift current. Katy was not able to get out of its way. It hit her square on and engulfed her in a tangle of poles and canvas. She dropped the lantern, and the world became dark. The tent seemed alive as she struggled with it. It rose above her, tugging her along as it was tossed by the flood. Her feet went out from under her. She flailed, went under, clawed her way to the surface, and finally freed herself from the tent's deadly embrace. By now she had been carried out into the current. Everything was dark. A branch swept by and clubbed her so hard she saw stars burst before her eyes. She gasped and got gritty water in her mouth instead of air.

"Jonah!"

Her feet couldn't reach the bottom. Around and around the current twisted her, until up, down, back, and forward had no meaning. Choking on mud and water, gasping with weariness, she was so cold that she scarcely felt the logjam that scraped by her and took some skin from her back.

"Help! Jonah!"

She had no strength left to call, no strength to keep her head above the swirling water.

"Jonah!"

Where was that damned greenhorn now that she was the one who needed rescuing for a change?

CHAPTER 10

"Katy!"

Jonah's voice was scarcely audible above the chaos of rain and flood, but it was there, calling her name, and it gave Katy strength.

"Katy! Catch the rope!"

What rope? How am I supposed to see a damned rope in the dark?

A swish and splat nearby inspired Katy to reach out. She touched rough hemp, but the current swirled it away from her.

"Catch the rope!" Jonah's faint voice insisted.

Two more throws didn't even come close enough for her to hear the rope landing in the water. Then there came another swish and splat directly behind her. She twisted, exploring the water frantically. The rope brushed against her and she grabbed, this time capturing it before the current could jerk it away. As soon as she tied it around her, it tightened.

By the time her feet touched bottom, Katy felt as if she'd been in the cold, rushing water forever. She didn't feel the rope where it cut into her beneath her arms; she couldn't feel her hands where they still convulsively clutched her lifeline. When Jonah and Andy reached out to grab her, she couldn't walk. They had to drag her to dry land like a waterlogged sack of flour. Andy unfastened the rope from where it was tied around a tree while Jonah pumped the water out of her.

Spilling a gutful of dirty water onto the mud was not how Katy would have chosen to begin the new day, but she was grateful for every uncomfortable heave. Every twinge and discomfort meant she was still alive, a condition which only moments ago had seemed an unlikely proposition. Even Jonah's scolding sounded like sweet music compared to the heavenly harps she might have been hearing.

"Katy, goddammit to hell, why didn't you follow right behind me, you little contrary, addlepated twit?" Jonah continued the physical pounding along with the verbal abuse, and more water came up. "Always do things your own way, don't you? Never listen to anybody else. Didn't believe me when I told you to hightail it out of there fast."

Katy wanted to tell him that were many possible interpretations of the word 'fast,' but she was too weary. All that came out of her throat was a groan.

The pounding stopped. Jonah's arms circled her, cradling her against his chest, which right then seemed the strongest, solidest thing in a suddenly uncertain world.

"Christ, Katy, I thought you were gone." His breath in her hair was like a caress. His arms were a circle of warmth. "It was a miracle I heard you, a damned miracle the rope landed in the right place."

They lay in the mud together without moving. Katy was content to lie in the rain with Jonah's arms wrapped protectively around her. Scarcely able to believe she was alive, she burrowed more securely into his muddy embrace. She could have stayed there forever.

Forever wasn't granted her, however. A sudden explosion of shouting and footsteps pounding past them made Katy suddenly aware of how they must look. She reluctantly disentangled herself. As they got to their feet, Jonah caught her hands in his. "Are you all right?"

"Oh sure," she sighed. The beginnings of a smile twitched

a corner of her mouth. "It takes more than a flood to stop Katy O'Connell—if there's someone nearby who's willing to pull her out. Have you seen Hunter?"

"He's all right. He practically sank his teeth into my hand to let me know you were out there. I couldn't see a damned thing. It was only when he made me listen that I heard you calling."

"If you couldn't see me, how did you know where to throw the rope?"

He grinned. "I didn't. Dumb luck it reached you."

Katy felt death's breath in an icy whisper against her skin. She shivered. Dumb luck. She should be dead. With a sudden nameless fear, she reached for Jonah, but before she could move into the comfort of his arms, Andy pelted up to them and breathlessly panted out the news that someone was caught on a logjam down valley.

"Bring the rope," Jonah told Andy with a tired sigh.

Several lanterns bobbed around one end of a dead tree that projected into the flood. A tangle of debris traveling downstream had caught on the tree and extended far beyond the limit of the lantern light. Screams and sobs that came out of the darkness bore witness that a woman was part of the trapped debris.

"We could try throwing the rope again," Katy said.

Jonah shook his head. "It would likely get tangled, and if our pulling broke any part of the dam loose, the whole thing might go and carry whoever it is with it."

They learned who it was when Rhona ran up to them, wildeyed and disheveled. Water had eroded valleys in her face paint, and black stripes of mascara gave her the appearance of a tragic clown. "It's Maude out there!" she told them. "Poor little Maudie. She can't swim, and she'll drown for sure when that tangle of stuff breaks up."

"Why can't she just climb along all that junk and come in that way?" Andy asked.

"She's probably too scared," Katy said.

"No one's willing to go after her," Rhona wailed. "They're afraid of the jam breaking loose and carrying them away."

Katy grimaced. "I'll go get her."

"No, you won't," Jonah said.

"Yes, I will. I'm light and agile."

"And I'm telling you that you won't. Andy, take hold of Katy and don't let her go."

"Yessir."

"And give me the rope. I'll go after Maude." He tied the rope around his waist and gave the other end to Katy. "Tie this around something sturdy. I don't want to become part of the flotsam rushing down the valley toward Dyea."

"You should let me do it."

"Yeah. I know. I'm a greenhorn fool. You've told me often enough."

Katy didn't want him to go. He was obviously cold and tired, his strength nearly exhausted. Then she thought of giggly, plump Maude, and remembered how it felt to be sucked into the flood. Jonah was serious about not letting her go out on that debris dam, and no one else would go after the whore. No one else was half as foolish as her quixotic greenhorn.

"Jonah. Be careful, please."

He grinned. "Make sure that rope's anchored well. I don't want my obituary to be the concluding piece to this series I'm writing."

Katy tied the rope around a sturdy spruce. By the time she turned around, Jonah had disappeared into the darkness beyond the small circle of lantern light. Maude's cries continued. Katy's hands fisted at her sides. Her nails dug into her palms. She relaxed only slightly when Jonah's strong voice instructed Maude to keep talking so that he could find her.

"He should have taken the lantern with him," Rhona said.

"No," Katy replied. "He'll need both hands for balance on that mess of branches and brush."

"Poor Maudie! Poor baby."

Maude's cries were replaced by a loud shriek followed by a faint splash.

"Haul us in!" Jonah shouted. "Slowly!"

Katy and Andy both grabbed the rope. A few minutes later Jonah waded from the water with a piteously moaning woman wrapped around him as tightly as a bloodsucking leech. Jonah climbed out of the rope that tied them together and gently tried to peel the weeping girl off him.

"No!" she shrieked. "No!"

"You're all right now, honey," Rhona told her.

"Don't let me go! Please!" Maude begged. Her arms circled Jonah's neck; her legs climbed his hips in a manner that made Jonah flush with a high color that was obvious even in the poor lantern light. Katy folded her arms scornfully as Maude latched onto his lips as if she would suck the breath right out of him. In an excess of gratitude she squirmed against him like a fish swimming up the current of his chest.

Katy resisted reaching out and pulling the woman back by her hair only by remembering that she had wanted to do something very similar when she had emerged from the flood. She would have gladly lain there in the mud with Jonah until dawn—and Jonah had only thrown her a rope; he hadn't risked life and limb to climb out on a precarious pile of floating debris to fetch her.

The difference was, Katy reminded herself resentfully, that Jonah Armstrong was *her* greenhorn, not Maude's, and she didn't appreciate the little giggly idiot staking a claim in her territory.

"That's enough!" Katy muttered. With Jonah's help, she managed to peel Maude away from him.

As Rhona took the sobbing girl in hand and gently led her away, she tossed Jonah a look full of promise over her friend's shoulder. "Anytime, handsome. Just wander our way. For you, it's free. As many times as you want."

Jonah sent Katy a crooked smile and shrugged helplessly.

"My hero!" she sighed with soupy sarcasm, then walked sinuously away in a fair imitation of Rhona's hip-weaving exit.

The morning was a muddy one. The rain had stopped, but the sky was still a sullen gray. Though the flood had diminished to a mere trickle, what the day before had been a green alpine valley was now a sea of mud. Trees, uprooted stumps, packing boxes, and boards stuck up from the mess like half-buried skeletons. The carcass of a horse lay in the mire not far from where Jonah had climbed across the debris dam to rescue Maude.

Andy and Jonah had gotten the horses and some of the provisions onto high ground, but the tent, most of their clothing, and many of the supplies purchased with Katy's poker winnings were buried somewhere in the mud. They spent the day searching the devastation around their campsite and several miles downstream. Katy found a packing box of flour, sugar, and saleratus wedged into the fork of a branch half a mile downstream. The box had broken open, of course, and the contents were ruined. Jonah recovered his extra pair of boots, which could be cleaned and dried, and Katy's fur-lined parka. Andy came up with a sack of canned goods that had been dented and muddied, but not otherwise damaged. When the three of them met in the midafternoon to compare what they had found, it was clear that over half their supplies had been swept away or ruined. They were left with scarcely enough to get them to Lake Bennett, much less to Dawson and the goldfields.

Others had lost much more. A German man had seen his son swept away by the water and had been unable to help him. The body was found at midmorning, two miles downstream. The arm of another man had been crushed between heavy packing boxes as he had attempted to move them out of the way of the flood. Among the lucky ones whose campsites had survived, many had lost heart if not their provisions. As the day wore on, more people headed down valley, back to Dyea and civilization, than continued the trudge to the summit.

Katy couldn't be stopped by a mere flood, however, and she was not surprised to learn that Jonah also was willing to continue the trek. City boy he might be, but Katy had to admit Jonah had grit and heart. Her own heart was fairly giddy after the previous night's brush with death, and when Jonah was close to her it got giddier. She kept remembering the sound of his voice when he'd said he thought her gone, the feel of his arms holding her close.

There was too much to be done for Katy to allow herself the luxury of such distraction, however. They still had funds from her poker winnings, and they managed to replace most of their foodstuffs with supplies being sold by people turning back to Dyea. Clothing, also, was on the market. A woman who had been traveling with her brother—her real brother, from the looks of them—sold Katy a pair of rubber boots, gloves, two woolen skirts, and an assortment of underclothing. A boy not much older than Andy provided her with an oilskin coat, three shirts, a heavy wool sweater, and a broad-brimmed hat. Jonah was able to scrounge a similar wardrobe, motley but usable. Andy ended up benefiting from the flood, for he'd started the trip with only the clothes on his back, and Katy purchased him a change of clothing, a parka, and extra set of boots, socks, and heavy woolen gloves.

That night they camped far above the highest reaches of the flood, all three crowded under a single tarp. A used tent was tucked among the other provisions they had acquired, but the task of putting it up seemed too much effort. Camped close by were Rhona and Maude and the rest of the bedraggled, damp birds of paradise. No laughter or loud invitations issued from their camp tonight, however. Katy had seen them searching the debris and scrounging supplies throughout the day. Those profit-minded ladies weren't about to give up their venture just because of a little hardship, she guessed. She had to admire their guts. The memory of Maude wrapped around Jonah like a clinging vine made Katy grimace, but even that thought could not keep her from sleep.

Next morning, as dawn lightened the sky above the mountains, they packed the horses and began the trudge toward Stone House. The going was difficult, for in places the trail was obliterated by mud and debris. Trees and boulders had tumbled down the valley along with mud and water and sometimes made the way all but impassable for horses, if not people. One treacherous tangle of brush, mud, and an uprooted tree almost cost them one of the horses, who panicked when he slid off the slippery and precarious path around the obstacle. The creature managed to wedge one leg dangerously between two unstable logs and almost broke the bone before the three of them working together were able to free him.

It was that incident that allowed the flock of soiled doves to catch up with them. Maude, gowned in a dress that might have been modest if it hadn't been screaming yellow and a size too tight, strayed from the flock as it struggled over the path that had been the packhorse's downfall. The curvaceous little entrepreneur latched onto Jonah with a vengeance, gushing her gratitude for his heroism in saving her life.

Andy whispered a comment to Katy. "She's gonna be climbing him like a bear climbs a tree in less than a minute. Wanna bet?"

Katy eyed the spectacle with narrowed eyes. She could hardly begrudge the girl's gratitude. Jonah had saved the slut's life, after all. But he'd saved Katy's life too, in a manner of speaking, and you didn't see *her* making an out-and-out fool of herself, climbing all over the poor man and gushing over him like some weepy, useless heroine in a bad melodrama. The sight fairly made Katy's stomach churn, and the suspicion that Jonah was enjoying Maude's silly little act made the churning even worse.

Katy interrupted the tender scene with a sharp reminder. "We've got to get moving, Jonah. The way things are going, we'll be lucky to make Stone House by tonight."

"Sure thing."

Katy noted irritably that he wasn't very quick about disentangling himself from the worshipful Maude.

"Don't let me hold you up," Maude said with a giggle and an adoring smile. "I'll just walk right along with you."

The little whore carried out her threat. Katy supposed there was no hope of Maude trying to catch up with her own group, for her pert body, with its top-heavy shape and soft, generous curves, was made for something other than trudging through mud and climbing over treacherous rocks. Even at their slow pace, she had trouble keeping up. Katy observed to Andy that the girl might have an easier time walking if she didn't waste so much breath in ceaseless chatter, and Jonah might have an easier time if the helpless floozy wasn't constantly grabbing his arm—or any other convenient part of his anatomy—to help her over the trail.

"Last night was a turning point in my life, you know?" Maude said with a dramatic, breath-wasting sigh. "I thought I was a goner for sure, and I reckoned I was goin' straight to hell for, you know, being what the preachin' men call a fallen woman." Despite her subject being hell and damnation, she giggled and slanted Jonah a coy look. "Not that I think pleasuring a man is sin, you know. Pleasin' a man is what I do best. The boys back in Anchorage called me the Northern Star. They said my tits was purtier'n any they'd seen—bigger, too."

Behind Jonah and his full-figured admirer, Katy gave an inelegant snort. Maude threw her an arch look over her shoulder.

"It's true, you know," Maude continued. "There wasn't a night in Anchorage when I didn't make at least ten bucks. You gotta have talent to do that!"

Jonah cleared his throat and kept his eyes strictly forward. "I'm sure you're very talented, Miss Maude."

"You bet I am." Feigning a stumble, Maude clutched at Jonah's arm. As if by accident, she pressed his hand against the fullness of one breast. Katy had never seen such a deliberate bit of foolery. The girl's stupid giggle when she did it was a dead giveaway. Katy fantasized pricking those oversize bosoms with a pin and seeing them deflate like balloons.

Jonah quickly reclaimed his hand, but Maude seemed not to notice. She chattered gaily about how the close brush with death had made her realize it was time to change professions and get morals, no matter how good a whore she was. She was going to change her ways for the better and stick to one man—or at least one man at a time, and since Jonah had so heroically saved her life, he was the man she was going to stick to for now.

"I'm all yours, honey," she said with an expansive smile. "Leastwise till we get to Dawson. I figure you deserve a reward for savin' my life, and I'm it."

A flush crawled up the back of Jonah's neck. "You don't need to do that, Miss Maude. Really you don't."

"Sure I do," she declared with a little giggle. "Don't you be shy, now. L'il Maudie knows what a man needs. You deserve the best"—she shot a look of triumph over her shoulder at Katy—"and you're gonna get it."

He's going to get it, all right, fumed Katy, *if he doesn't get rid of that whore before nightfall!*

When they stopped for a noon break, Stone House was still a good way up the trail. Maude might be donating her company to Jonah free of charge, but she didn't hesitate to eat heartily from their supplies of beans and jerked beef. The girl consumed enough food to sustain those plush hips and pillowy breasts, Katy reflected sourly. The woman looked like an overstuffed couch.

Katy had little sympathy for Jonah, who spent his lunch break trying tactfully to extricate himself from Maude's plans for his immediate future. If he were being pestered by a mosquito, Katy reflected morosely, he would have swatted it. One good swat ought to send Maude up the trail in search of the comrades of her "former" profession. Jonah simply wasn't trying hard enough.

After lunch Jonah took Katy's place with the pack train and Katy led the way. Jonah had little time for Maude's shenanigans while dealing with the skittish horses, so the girl walked beside Katy and showed herself perfectly capable of negotiating the trail without grabbing for parts of someone else's body every minute or so. Her hips swung enticingly as she walked. No doubt, Katy mused, Maude was taking this opportunity to present Jonah with the charms of her ample backside. The trollop also made clear to Katy that she didn't for one minute swallow the story about Katy being Jonah's sister. While Jonah was treated to the tempting view of her undulating hips, Katy got the full benefit of her sharp claws.

"Who taught you the trade, sister girl?" Maude asked scathingly. "Didn't they ever tell you that men prefer ladies with a little meat covering their bones?"

"I'm not *in* the trade, Maudie girl. And if you cross me, you're not going to have much to offer a customer after I whittle you down a bit."

"Do tell?" Maude lifted a painted brow.

Katy wondered how the girl managed to carry so much paint on her face without her skin sagging.

"You talk tough, sister girl. You look tough as well—like a piece of meat that's been left in the sun, sunken and dried up, you know?"

"I'm surprised you're acquainted with the sun," Katy replied. "I figure you haven't seen it much before this. Lucky for you that most of your business is at night. Women look younger in moonlight, *you know*?" She finished with a mimic of Maude's favorite phrase.

Maude pouted her lips. "At least some of us look good in moonlight. Others don't look good in any light at all."

The rest of the afternoon followed a similar script. Jonah stayed with Andy and the pack train, keeping well clear of the catfight in front of him. How a man could spit in death's eye as Jonah had done the previous night and run like a yellow dog from a sorry creature like Maude was beyond Katy's understanding. Maybe he didn't want to run. Maybe he liked this pathetic excuse for a woman. Maybe she wasn't a pathetic excuse for a woman. Katy hadn't given much thought to what a woman should really be. She'd had very little interest in the subject until she'd met Jonah.

Their total progress that day was the short distance to Stone House, and they were grateful to make that landmark before dark. They had climbed above the tree line, and here the landscape consisted of hummocky alpine grasses and jumbled rocks. The stark, rocky summit loomed above the gigantic boulder that gave Stone House its name. Glaciers crawled down several of the side valleys, one with its crevassed snout not far from where they camped for the night.

They set up the tent in the grassiest spot they could find. Knowing there would be no timber for a fire, they had carried some with them from Sheep Camp. While Jonah and Andy unloaded the horses for the last time—beyond this point pack animals were unable to go—Katy started the beans heating. There was little game in this rocky meadow for her or Hunter to bag for supper, so she had to dig into their provisions. She contemplated the possibilities of making a batch of biscuits that were edible, then discarded the notion.

While everyone else worked, Maude arranged herself artfully on a slab of granite and watched. She showed no interest in removing herself to the sporting ladies' camp, which was up the trail and on the other side of the landmark boulder.

"I'm going to wander around and try to find someone to buy the horses," Jonah told Katy. He wiped his muddy hands on his trousers. Katy noted that Maude's eyes followed his every movement. No doubt she wished those were her hands instead of his rubbing over the hard muscle of his thighs.

"Are you all right?" Jonah asked Katy. "You look flushed."

"I'm fine," she snapped.

"I'll go with you," Maude purred, rising elegantly and sinuously from her seat. "There's nobody better than me at haggling and selling."

"I'll bet," Katy agreed.

Jonah arched an amused brow in Katy's direction. She sent him back a look that spelled out jackass as plainly as if she'd shouted it.

"Come ahead then, Maudie. You're welcome to stay for dinner before you go back to your camp."

"Stay for dinner? Oh you silly boy. I'm staying for much more than that."

Jonah grimaced as Maude took his arm. "Now, Maude," he cautioned as they walked away together, "don't you think that . . ." The rest was beyond hearing.

Damn Jonah and his polite city manners, Katy thought. Didn't he know that the only way to get rid of someone like Maude was to apply a boot to that well-upholstered backside?

Andy plunked himself down on a rock beside the fire and sniffed at the simmering beans. "You want me to mix up some biscuits to go with that?"

Spit! Even the kid was a better cook than she was.

"No thanks. You'd better go brush out those horses if we're to sell them."

"Yes'm." He made no move to go, however. As the dusk deepened, he continued to sit and stare into the fire. "Uh . . . Miss Katy? You gonna hire some Indian packers to get all this stuff to Lake Bennett?"

"Yep."

"I know some good packers that hire out of here. Ones that won't cheat you at the Scales."

Nine hundred vertical feet above Stone House was a plateau and a set of large scales, where hired packers reweighed their loads and adjusted the prices. Katy had heard stories of them adjusting the prices drastically in their favor.

"I could hire you some fine, honest packers. And I could be a lot of help on the trail, and the river, too. I'm handy at about anything."

Katy saw the longing in the boy's expression. She felt a pang of sympathy.

"Miss Katy. I stand on my own two feet, and I don't like askin' folks for help, but I sure would be grateful if you didn't make me go back with the horses. There ain't nuthin' for me in Dyea, and now I don't even have a job with Decker. I got to get to Dawson."

Katy's own longing to be somebody, to do something special, to seek adventure and independence were mirrored in Andy's pleading brown eyes. She wished she could grant his plea, but she couldn't.

"Andy, we don't have enough provisions to take on another person."

"I don't eat much! Honest! And me and Hunter could bring in game, just like you was doin' down in the woods. You could teach me how to use that little rock sling of yours. I'd learn real fast."

"Andy . . ."

"And you wouldn't have to worry about me once I got to Dawson. I could find a job there and make enough to stake a claim and get me through the winter. Please, Miss Katy . . ."

Just then Jonah and Maude returned. "Ah, beans!" Jonah said, rubbing his hands together with gusto. "Smells good." He looked pleased with himself. Katy wondered if he'd gotten a good deal on the horses or a good deal with Maude. Her stomach soured.

"Beans again?" Maude commented. "Goodness! Didn't we have beans for lunch?"

Katy ignored her. "Did you sell the horses?" she asked Jonah.

"Got twenty-five dollars for them, which is probably more than they're worth. A trio of three fellows headed down to Dyea said they could use them. Said they'd take good care of them." The smile he sent Katy was gently teasing for her worry about the horses—teasing, but understanding, too. The trail from Camp Pleasant to Stone House was littered with the carcasses of pack animals that had been turned loose to fend for themselves after their usefulness was finished. She should have known that Jonah would place the horses with someone who would do well by them. He cared about such things.

"Twenty-five bucks ain't much," Maude said. "You coulda got more from those Injuns who wanted 'em for meat. Those fellas been makin' good money up here packin' goods back and forth. Rhona and me hired our Injuns in Dyea. Figgered they'd be cheaper there."

"These men came from Dawson," Jonah continued. "They said all those rumors we've been hearing about no more claims to be staked on the Klondike aren't true—yet—but the good ground is going fast. There is a concern about Dawson having enough supplies to get everyone through the winter. You were right to insist we bring so much with us."

Katy smiled, her heart swelling ridiculously at such a small compliment. "Of course I was right. Have I steered you wrong yet?"

Miffed at being ignored, Maude insinuated herself between them just as Jonah was reaching out to—to do what, Katy would never know, because an intruding, formidable bosom came between them.

"She steered you wrong on those beans," Maude said with a giggle. "Cain't you smell 'em burning?"

"Omigod!" Katy rushed to the cookfire to rescue dinner.

"That's all right, honey," Maude said. "I have to get my stuff from Rhona anyway, and I'll bring over some of the best baked beans and bacon you ever tasted."

Jonah rolled his eyes heavenward—out of gratitude or frustration Katy couldn't tell. "Maude, you don't need—"

"Jonah, sweetie!" Her voice suddenly turning pleading. "I'm a woman tryin' to redeem myself. You wouldn't turn away from me after pulling me from that flood, would you?"

"I really think that—"

"You come along and help me get my stuff."

"I . . . I have to work on an article. Maude, I think you should—"

"Ta-ta, then. Work away. I'll be back soon."

Jonah shook his head in bewilderment. "Lord above. A freight train would be easier to stop than that woman once she sets her mind on something." Still shaking his head, he ambled toward the little creek of glacial runoff to wash.

Andy slid his eyes cautiously toward Jonah, then sidled over to the fire. Katy wasn't sure if the firelight was playing tricks with the boy's eyes, or if the light of mischief gave them their devilish sparkle.

"What would you give for Maude to go back to her own camp for good?" he asked Katy quietly.

A slow smile spread across Katy's face. "A lot," she said. "I'd probably be so grateful that I'd offer someone a job for my entire stay in the Yukon."

Andy's brows twitched upward. "You would, huh?"

"I'd manage it somehow."

"You got yourself a hired hand, Miss Katy. You just wait and see."

From the look in Andy's eyes, Katy could almost feel sorry for Maudie-the-Northern-Star. Almost, but not quite. Jonah Armstrong was going to be rescued from the clutches of that buxom, blond she-devil, whether he liked it or not.

CHAPTER 11

"This whole trunk is yours?" Andy fingered the bright dresses, hats, and petticoats with rapt appreciation. The satin was bright as gold. Flimsy feathers dyed to colors no bird had ever dreamed of trimmed sleeves, hems, and saucy little hats. Andy's mother Gloria—Glory, she liked to be called—had once had nice things, soft and colorful and trimmed with feathers and sequins, but as she'd grown older and lost her looks, her clothes had gotten more meager. The food had gotten meager, too. Cheap liquor had been the main course of every meal, and between meals as well. By the time Andy had left, Glory had all but forgotten she had a kid.

Maude slapped at Andy's hands. "Get your grubby little fingers off that. And yes! These are all mine. What do you think I am? Some kind of pauper?"

"No, ma'am!"

"I do right well for myself."

"Yes, ma'am. You sure do."

"Not that the work's easy, mind you. But it's one way for a girl to get ahead in the world. Now I seen the light, though, boy. I'm gonna get morals—and a man to go with 'em. A permanent man."

"Mr. Jonah?"

Maude laughed. "Naw. Your Mr. Jonah ain't nearly rich enough, sonny boy. I owe him is all, and he's a good looking sonofabitch, ain't he?"

Andy considered. "I guess."

"Jonah gets the prize until we get to Dawson and I can find me a rich gold king."

"Rich is mighty important," Andy agreed. "I'm gonna be rich once I find gold in the Klondike, and then I'm gonna tell the world to go to hell."

Maude's eyes twinkled. "Well then, maybe I oughta latch onto you, boy. You're not as well growed as Jonah Armstrong, but in a few years, you might be quite a prize."

Maude might be surprised at just what kind of a prize, Andy reflected wryly. "I don't go in fer girls."

"That'll change with you grow a man-sized set of balls, honey." She sent a robe, satin slippers, and a pair of boots sailing in Andy's direction. "Put those in that bag. I'll leave the trunk for the packers here. I'm helping to pay them, so they can damned well continue to haul my stuff, you know?" She pulled a dress from an untidy pile on the floor of the tent, then a wrinkled skirt and blouse, a petticoat, corset, and flimsy chemise. "This trail may be a sonofabitch, but I'll be damned if I'll start looking more like a man than a woman—like that drab little bitch who calls herself Jonah's sister."

"You don't think Miss Katy is Jonah's sister?"

"In a pig's eye! If she's Jonah's sister, then I'm the Queen of Sheba. And I ain't. I'm not worried none, though. A little brown stick-girl like her ain't exactly competition for the Northern Star, now, is she?"

Andy guessed Maude hadn't seen the way Jonah looked at Miss Katy. If that wasn't brotherly affection in his eyes, then the poor sod was well on the road to being smitten. "I guess there's competition and then there's . . . uh . . . competition."

Maude scowled. "You gonna help here, or just stand around yammerin'?"

Andy helped Maude gather up the things she indicated. A polished wooden hairbrush and comb set. Hairpins, face creams, a lace-bedecked corset, bloomers that sported ruffles from waist to ankles. The silky material of a lacy pink chemise snagged on cracked and dirty fingers. "This is sure pretty."

"Thank you," Maude said, rescuing the chemise from Andy's hands. "If you're really, really nice to me, I might let you see me in it someday."

"No, thanks. I seen plenty of ladies in stuff like that. Don't do a thing for me."

Maude propped a hand on one generous hip, the chemise dangling from her fingers. "You're a cool one, ain't ya, boy?"

Andy shrugged. "So's you. You're all right, Maudie. I do admire a lady with guts. Guts and looks, too. It's no wonder you done so well in the world."

Maude dropped a pair of boots into the bag they were packing. "Yeah. I done well enough." She shot Andy a suspicious look. "What do you mean, guts?"

Andy puttered casually with a box of hairpins. "Ain't every woman who'll latch onto a man with Jonah's temper. Especially a woman who's been makin' good money off of her looks. You wouldn't want that face of yours to get messed up."

"Get outta here! Jonah Armstrong's a gentleman if I've ever met one."

"He sure is, most of the time."

"Shit, kid. Every man's got a temper. Goes with the balls, you know? Well, no, you probably don't know. You're not old enough yet. But trust me, I know. Most men is just naturally mean as snakes."

"No kiddin'?"

"No kiddin. Besides, Jonah Armstrong's a goddamned hero. He saved my life. How much of an asshole could he be?"

"Yeah. You're probably right," Andy agreed with just a slight grimace. "You owe him, and I do admire a person who pays up what's owed. Hope he's nice to ya."

Maude threw a hand mirror in the bag, hesitated a moment, then pulled it out and held it up. She pouted prettily while examining first one side of her face, then the other. "He's really got a temper, huh?"

"I reckon it ain't any worse than others, if'n ya say all men is such mean devils. Leastwise he's a nice-lookin' gent who don't spit in front of ladies. I guess hittin' ain't as bad manners as spittin'.'"

"Hittin'?"

"Hell yes! He's got a punch you just gotta admire. You shoulda' seen the one he threw at Miss Katy a couple'a weeks ago. You know how she looks so crochety all the time? Well, let me tell you . . ."

"What the hell is keeping them?" Jonah went to the edge of the firelight for the tenth time and peered through the darkness in the direction of the sporting ladies' campsite. "They've been gone for an hour and a half."

"Maybe Maude's packing the whole camp to bring over here," Katy speculated sourly.

Jonah returned to the fireside and smiled ruefully. He dished up a plateful of the beans that he'd refused earlier. "She's a persistent little devil, isn't she?"

"So is a snake. When I was a kid I once spent hours watching a snake swallow a mouse. You wouldn't have thought it could get that furry body down its gullet, but it surely did. Ate it whole."

Jonah pushed the beans around on his plate. "That's an appetizing picture."

"Yep. That old snake just kept working at it and working at it." She lifted a brow in his direction. "You might take a lesson from that poor mouse."

His eyes reflected the fire's orange blaze, or was that glint part of the amused smile he gave her. "Thanks for the warning, sis."

Katy expelled a frustrated breath. "Men have got no taste!"

Jonah laughed. "What? Do you think I'm lusting after Maudie? I haven't been deprived of a woman's company that long!"

Katy's temper instantly flared. Deprived of a woman's company, was he? What did he think she was? And if she wasn't a woman, just who had he kissed not so long ago—kissed deep enough to suck the lungs out of her chest? He *had* been making fun of her.

"I don't give a fig who you lust after," she snapped. "It's nothing to me. She's a bother, that's all. She'll slow us up."

"Probably. She'd make colorful reading in the *Record*, though. Likely a bit too colorful for my editor."

Katy merely huffed her disgust. She agreed with Jonah's editor.

Jonah took a bite of beans and swallowed with a grimace. He speared another couple and nibbled at them cautiously. "They've been gone too long," he complained, glancing into the darkness.

"Don't worry about Andy. That kid can take care of himself. He can take care of Maude, too," she said. A smile twitched at the corner of her mouth. At least she hoped Andy could take care of Maude—with something short of murder.

"He's just a kid."

"Like you said, kids his age are curious about these things."

"I'd better go see what the problem is." He set his plate on the ground for Hunter to finish—a task the wolf accomplished with a few enthusiastic gulps. "I'll be back soon."

Katy watched Jonah's lantern bob in the darkness until it disappeared behind the mass of Stone House. Not for a minute did she believe Jonah was heading toward the whore's den to see what was keeping Andy. The kid could take care of himself, and Jonah knew it as well as she did. Katy set her plate on the ground and sighed. Just what was it those floozies had that she didn't?

"Dumb question," she told herself, looking down at her sturdy, sensible clothes and resisting a silly urge to unplait the thick braid that held her hair. "Dammit!" She kicked at her plate. Hunter shot her an uncertain look. "Go ahead," she told him. "Finish it off. I'm not hungry anyway." She ran her hand fondly through the gray coat as he gulped down the last of her supper. "Why do I care, anyway?" she asked the wolf. "I don't want to wear face paint and walk as if my hips are out of joint."

Licking his greasy chops, Hunter seemed to be in agreement.

"If Jonah Armstrong likes that sort of thing, he can have it. What do I care what he thinks?"

The wolf lost interest in the conversation and started to sniff around the fireside for dropped morsels he might have missed. Katy hunkered down and stared into the flames. What Jonah thought did matter, she admitted reluctantly. She'd never before had such feelings of inadequacy. All her life she'd been a rough-and-tumble scamp. Knowing how to skin a hare had been more important than knowing how to sew the hare's skins into a hat. Bringing home the game had been more important than knowing how to cook it. She wore dresses and tried to learn manners to please Olivia and her pa, but her heart was always dressed in trousers and boots.

Only since meeting Jonah had she wished to be different. He made her want to curl her hair, wear frills and lace and ruffly petticoats that swirled and swayed and cunningly peeked out around her ankles whenever she lifted her skirt to walk.

"Dumb!" she told Hunter. "I am really being dumb."

Hunter raised his nose from its quest and padded over to lie beside her, as if understanding her need for something warm and familiar. She glided her fingers through his fur. "Love you, you old wolf you."

But she certainly didn't love Jonah Armstrong, in spite of all the feminine silliness that afflicted her. The notion was preposterous. He was not at all the type of man she admired. He enjoyed paved streets, tall buildings, and crowds of people; he scarcely knew the butt of a pistol from its barrel; he would rather fight with words than fists.

Yet he'd fought for her on the steamer from Seattle, and he'd fought Jack Decker for the sake of those poor horses. He'd risked his life to save a strumpet when everyone else was willing to let her drown. And though he might be accustomed to paved streets and soft beds, he didn't complain about the mud of the trail nor the hard earth that they slept upon at night—nor about a sky that either blasted them with the sun's furnace or drenched them with cold rain.

Jonah had a nice laugh, Katy decided. She liked his face, with its clean planes and strong chin. She liked the laugh lines around those devilish blue eyes. She liked the way his hair grew in springy curls that he couldn't quite tame. Sometimes she longed to touch the wisps of hair that curled every which way at his nape. His voice made her shiver inside—a pleasurable sort of a shiver. The long, strong line of his back made her shiver too, and his legs. Jonah had nice legs. A nice backside as well.

Katy hid her heated face against her drawn-up knees. Shame on her for being such an idiot. She wanted the old familiar Katy back—the one who didn't care what men looked like any more than she cared what she looked like. Damn Jonah Armstrong for making her feel this way. She would make him sorry he preferred the whores' company to hers. She would show him that a girl didn't need perfume and bosoms the size of a cow's udder to be a woman.

Jonah's humor was high as he and Andy walked back toward their own camp. His worry about the boy had been groundless. He'd found him in the ladies' tent, a veritable palace strewn with silken pillows and scented with heavy perfume. A customer or two was being entertained among the pillows, but most of the ladies were gathered around Andy, who regaled them with anecdotes from his mother's unsavory life in Seattle. The kid showed little interest in the erotic spectacles that were being played out in front of him—Jonah assumed that he'd seen plenty of the like before. And the girls seemed to take a motherly rather than a salacious interest in the boy, a virtuous attitude that didn't apply to the attention they showered upon Jonah when he walked in.

While Jonah had tried to politely fend off the flock of debauched lovelies, Andy had not helped the situation by offering to return to camp with the explanation that Jonah would be spending the night with Maude's friends. The boy's eyes had sparkled with the devil's own light.

Jonah had scarcely escaped the tent with his clothing and virtue intact, but one good thing had come of it all: Maude had suffered a change of heart about lavishing him with her attention. She wasn't ready to become a one-man woman, she'd told him. The way she'd jumped like a skittish filly when he'd entered the tent made Jonah suspect she was a bit off her rocker. Not two hours past she'd been hanging on him like moss on a magnolia, and now she acted as if he'd grown horns.

Good thing, too. Katy had been simmering ever since Maude had swaggered into their camp. Jonah didn't mind little Miss Daniel Boone finding out that not every woman considered him a piece of useless baggage. Some women found him attractive, even if he didn't have an overdeveloped trigger finger and smell like the rear end of a cow. On the other hand, an annoyed Katy was something akin to a stick of dynamite with a lit fuse. One didn't want to let the situation go on too long.

Katy's simmer appeared to have reached a boil by the time Jonah and Andy got back to the campsite.

"Nice party over there?"

"Ask Andy," Jonah said. "He was the center of attention."

She cocked a brow toward Andy. He shrugged and smiled.

"Where's Maude?"

"Maude's had a change of heart," Jonah told her. "Seems

her friends convinced her there's more future in high-stepping than walking the straight and narrow."

"I wouldn't exactly call anything about Maude straight and narrow," Katy quipped. She had an impish smile for Andy that belied her tart tone, however, and Andy puffed himself up like an overproud sparrow.

"I'll just be goin' to sleep now," Andy said. "Tomorrow I'll find us some packers. We'll be on the trail by noon." Grinning from ear to ear, the scamp grabbed his blankets and tarp and went to find a sleeping place.

"What was all that about?" Jonah asked suspiciously.

"I told him earlier he could come with us to Dawson. I figured you wouldn't mind. You seem to collect colorful characters like some men collect notches on their pistols. You can write about him for one of your stories about the wild and woolly West."

Jonah was getting a bit tired of the Wild West and the wild women it nurtured. He recalled the Chinese curse of wishing a man the misfortune of living in interesting times. The curse could more effectively wish a man to become involved with an interesting woman.

"This has something to do with Maude, doesn't it?" he ventured.

Katy smiled with silky satisfaction.

"All right, Katy. Maude was my fault. I admit it. I should have hustled her out of here the minute she showed up. But let me tell you something about men and their little weaknesses—"

"I know a lot about men and their weaknesses," Katy declared archly.

"Well, it's damned near impossible for a mortal man to be real diligent about getting rid of a female who makes him feel as if he's God's gift to women."

"So men like to be drooled over like some kind of juicy steak?"

"Well . . ." Jonah could feel himself getting into hot water. "On occasion."

"And Maude was one of those occasions?"

Maude had been an excuse to get a rise out of Katy—an excuse that had gotten out of hand. "Maude was . . . a bit of stupidity on my part. Satisfied?"

Katy snorted indelicately.

"How long are you going to carry a grudge?"

"I'm not carrying a grudge," she corrected with a feline grin. "I was just watching out for your virtue. After all, you were the one so concerned about reputation."

"Reputation and virtue are two separate things—especially for a man."

"Well you ought to know!"

She kicked dirt onto the fire with unnecessary violence. Jonah wasn't sure if the subsequent hissing came from the buried coals or from an indignant Katy. She turned and marched into the tent. Jonah followed. The little devil was not going to have the last word!

"Katy, you're acting like a child. In fact, you're beginning to act like a real sister."

"I'm not your goddamned sister!"

"I should hope not."

"I'm just your guide. What do I care if you drag every two-bit whore with you on the trail to Dawson. If you have such a need to be drooled over, don't let me stand in your way."

Katy smiled suddenly in a manner that made Jonah very uneasy. It also sent a jolt of pure lust arrowing to his groin. It was the same smile she'd turned loose on those hapless fools in the Skaguay saloon, and it glowed with a heat that would make Venus herself envious.

"Just what do men find so entertaining about those women, anyway?" she purred. "Is it the way they walk?"

"Katy . . ."

She turned and slowly took three paces that were the length of the tent, her hips swaying with a graceful lilt that would have turned Maude green. A coy peep over her shoulder made Jonah's temperature rise a notch farther.

"Is that the way they do it?"

"Katy, what are you doing?" He could feel the sweat break out on his brow. His appetites were in no condition to withstand such bombardment. He'd spent the last two weeks coming to a boil over Katy, and Maude's every touch, every subtle hip thrust, every heated glance, had sharpened his hunger, not for the whore, but for the girl who'd stood by watching with her face in a high flush and her eyes shooting fireworks.

"I'm just curious," she claimed with exaggerated innocence.

"Be curious about something else. Behave yourself."

"Why? I thought men liked it when the ladies made them feel like—what was it—God's gift to women?"

"Don't be ridiculous."

She glided toward him again, reached out, and flicked a finger against his chin the way Maude had done a time or two. The gesture had been annoying when Maude had done it. When Katy's finger touched him, though, she might as well have been wielding one of those hot branding irons that had become a symbol of the Old West. He jumped back before he gave in to the temptation to catch her hand and pull her against him.

Her eyes glinted up at him, bright with equal parts of mischief and malice. "Don't be so cranky, Jonah. Maybe it's not the walk that you like. Maybe it's the way all that hair swishes around their faces." She pulled the pins from her coiled braids and swiftly ran her fingers through the thick ropes of shining black. Jonah's groin clenched as she artfully spread the curtains of hair over her shoulders and around her face. "How's that?" she crooned. "It's not red or silver-blond, but maybe in a pinch it would do?"

"Don't, Katy." Jonah's voice was hoarse.

"Don't what? Don't you think I can be a woman? Just because I looked like a boy when you first saw me, you think I'm some kind of kid who doesn't know she's female."

"I know you're a woman, Katy. I don't have one god-damned doubt about it." Jonah was nearly undone by the scent of her. She smelled of pine and woodsmoke and woman, which proved to be a headier perfume than any potion Maude and her companions bathed themselves in.

"Well," she twirled lightly away from him. "Good for you." She tilted her head in a pose of exaggerated reflection. "Maybe it's the flirty eyes that men like." She batted her eyelashes and smiled seductively. "What do you think?"

Her eyes, flashing emerald green in the lantern light, were suddenly all Jonah could see. They glittered like jewels in the lush black forest of her lashes. Then her lips intruded. Rosy without the aid of artifice, softly sculpted into a perfect bow, they were moist and slightly parted in an inviting smile. A flash of anger added to the heat that already made him sweat. Little Katy was getting revenge in the world's most ancient way. No doubt she had entertained enough men in her adventurous young life to know exactly what she was doing to him—and doing very effectively. That the buttons of his trousers hadn't given way from the painful pressure of his arousal was a miracle.

"Don't you like the eye thing?" she inquired with a final bat of her lashes. "And you didn't like this either." She swayed toward him, imitating Maude's hip-thrusting walk. "What else does a woman do to entertain a man? Oh, yes. Now I remember. They ōoooh and aahhh over what a hero he is, and then hang all over him like they can't stand on their own feet without his awesome strength to help them."

Her fingers brushed his arm with a butterfly touch. Jonah went hot and cold at the same time as her hand slid up his arm to his shoulder.

"Don't do this, Katy."

"Do what?" she purred in a fair imitation of Maude's breathy voice.

"Goddamn it!" He grasped her shoulders to hold her still. "You've pushed me far enough."

Katy felt her body go limp in his grasp; he didn't need the vise of his hands to hold her motionless, for at that moment she couldn't have moved if Stone House itself had tumbled onto their tent. Her skin went hot then cold, then hot again. Inside that deep blue-eyed gaze was a man she'd only glimpsed—still Jonah Armstrong, but with the banter, refinement, and patience burned away. Her spiteful little act had suddenly become very serious indeed.

"Jonah . . ." Katy didn't know if she meant his name as a warning or an invitation. Perhaps it was a call to the old Jonah—the one she'd met in Willow Bend and pestered until he'd allowed her to stay with him, the one who met her most outrageous behavior with a chuckle and a shake of his head, the one who had such a ready smile and buoyant laugh. He wasn't smiling now, though. The muscle at the hinge of his strong jaw jerked with tension, and the lines of his face were rigid. He was, she guessed, about as mad as a porcupine who'd sat on his own spiny tail.

An eternity seemed to pass while they stood there with gazes locked. Hunter poked his head inside the tent flap, gave them both a brief stare, then hastily backed out. Slowly Jonah's grip relaxed. He let her go, but she couldn't move away. His eyes burned with a blaze that made her giddy with a delicious, wild, madness. As if spellbound, she reached out her hand and laid it gently upon his chest.

"Don't! For God's sake!" His arm jerked up to sweep away her hand and accidently caught her shoulder with a solid blow. Katy staggered back. Groggy, as if she had just awakened from a dream, she lost her balance and fell back onto the spread blankets of her bedroll.

Jonah was instantly beside her. "Katy! Jesus! I'm sorry! Are you hurt?"

"No." In fact she could feel nothing but his hand gripping her arm, see nothing but his serious face. The tent and its contents faded to a pale blur as she reached up to touch the face that hovered above hers.

"Jonah . . ."

Surrender softened his eyes the instant before he kissed her. His mouth worshiped hers as he stretched out beside her. Giving in to her natural instincts, Katy tangled her legs with his, arched into his hard body, met his seeking tongue with her own. Panting, he broke away and looked down at her. His eyes were warm with a light that sent a thrill of anticipation shivering through her.

"Katydid. My beautiful Katy. What have you done to me?"

CHAPTER 12

A great stillness settled over Katy's spirit. She was suddenly very certain of what she was doing. No more playing at silly games; no more battering herself with uncertainties. Lying entangled with Jonah seemed natural and right. She could hear his heart beat and feel the rhythm of life surge through his body where his hard flesh was pressed against her. Their breath mingled, and for a moment their very souls seemed to entwine.

"Katy . . . My Katy."

Katy closed her eyes as his mouth once more drowned her in sensual possession. His lips moved over hers with a confidence that lacked the desperation of their last kiss. She met the thrusts of his tongue in an eager duel, then willingly let him explore the recesses of her mouth. He tasted of coffee and burned beans, smelled of woodsmoke, clean male sweat, and warm, musky lust. Unafraid, Katy allowed her senses to be overwhelmed by the sheer maleness of him, of his hard compared to her soft, his strength pressed against her newly discovered delicacy, his size looming over her smallness. She wanted him so much she could scarcely breathe. With every heartbeat the fire inside her grew hotter.

"Jonah please . . . Please don't stop."

"Hush," he breathed against her neck. His tongue traced the ridge of her collarbone in the open vee of her shirt. "No chance of me stopping. Another damned mudslide couldn't make me stop."

He slid his hand over her breast, and Katy groaned with pleasure as he gently kneaded the tender flesh. Desperate for the sensation of his hand on her bare flesh, she fumbled at the buttons of her shirt. With a quiet chuckle, he helped.

"Impatient, are you?"

Impatient was not the word. There were no words to describe what she felt when his warm hand cupped her naked breast, or when—paradise on earth!—he took her hardened nipple into his mouth and nursed upon her full flesh like a suckling babe. Warm rivers of pleasure spread from her nipple in every direction, racing through her body to finally pool between her legs, where a liquid ache grew to outright pain. Even the pain was ecstasy.

She called his name aloud, more of a panting whisper than a word, but he refused to be hurried in his exploration. Baring her other breast, he treated it to the same tender worship he'd given the first one. By slow degrees he peeled away her chemise and tasted each inch of flesh that was bared. When her hands tore at his shirt, he willingly shrugged it off and pulled his long-sleeved undershirt over his head.

Katy wanted to look at him forever, to drink in the beauty of supple muscle and broad shoulders, of hard, flat stomach and lean ribs, but her own desires clamored for satisfaction. The thick wiry hair that forested his chest drew her fingers as hard, puckered male nipples invited her mouth. She touched her lips to him, then her teeth. His soft groan of pleasure echoed in his chest, and Katy's spirit soared in a surge of power. She tangled her tongue in his chest hair, darting in to count coup on his flesh. She nipped at his ribs and nibbled his breastbone, but before she could feast further, he pushed her down onto the blankets and captured her exploring hands.

"Not so fast, you little cannibal." His smile was wicked. "It's my turn at the table, and I have a different feast in mind."

He kissed her breasts, each in its turn, and paid hard and thorough homage to her mouth. Gentleness had fled. She didn't need it any longer. His sweet ravaging met its match in her hungry response. Eagerly he rucked her skirt and petticoat up around her waist and ran his hand along a leg protected only by the thin cotton of ankle-length bloomers.

"Women wear too damned much underwear," he muttered against her mouth. He didn't let the bloomers spoil his sport, though, and boldly settled his hand between her legs. The tingle of shock Katy suffered as he kneaded that most private flesh couldn't compete with the aching need his caress inspired. She gasped for breath as he deftly found the center of erotic ache, a place she hadn't known existed. A warm moistness greeted his gently seeking fingers. Katy wanted to rip away the bloomers that separated his hand from that most tender flesh. She squirmed in frustration, pressing herself into his hand with a little cry of need.

"Hush, Katydid. I'm going to give you what you want. Hush now."

The few seconds he took to peel away her bloomers felt like an eternity of frustration. Her need was so great that the moment his fingers returned to brush against her heated, naked flesh, her body convulsed in climax. Jonah egged her on, sliding his fingers inside to demand another tribute to his sensual power, and her body obeyed. Katy's senses tumbled in a maelstrom that swept the last shred of control from her grasp. At her cry of ecstatic release, Jonah clamped his hand over her mouth.

"Easy, my love. You don't want the whole Chilkoot Trail looking in on us."

His other hand soothed and caressed, teasing the swollen flesh between her legs. She lay in exhausted bliss as he continued to touch and tantalize. Unbelievably, her sated body began once again to contract inward around a center of pure desire.

Katy could only lie in a needful haze as Jonah struggled hastily out of his trousers. The sight of him springing free of restraint, hard and huge, sent a spurt of liquid fire through her veins. When Jonah settled himself eagerly between her thighs, she wrapped her legs around him in welcome.

"Katy." He kissed her breasts, then her mouth. "Beautiful Katydid," he whispered against her lips.

His erection prodded at the moist, swollen flesh between her legs, seeking entrance. Then he was inside her, pressing gently into her only a little way, then withdrawing, then forward again in tender exploration. Panting, he touched her brow with his. His skin was moist with sweat, hot with the fire he struggled to control.

Katy closed her eyes and thrust her hips upward, forcing him more deeply inside. He expelled a breathy groan, stilled her with a strong grip on her hips, and thrust boldly to the hilt. The pain caught Katy unprepared. She yiped softly but didn't struggle to escape the relentless invasion. Jonah froze.

"Good God!" He glared down at her, his eyes blazing with accusation as well as desire.

"It's all right, Jonah." The pain was fading. Katy moved beneath him, gently experimenting with this strange feeling of having him so much a part of her. She prayed he wouldn't stop now. If she could have her way, he would never stop. She wanted him inside her forever.

His head thrown back on the strong column of his neck, he remained still as she moved. Gradually his face softened. He began to move with her, slowly at first, then taking control of their rhythm and driving faster, harder. Katy willingly surrendered to his lead. She wrapped her legs tightly around his hips as he thrust into her. Her nails dug into his shoulders, her breathing panted in time with his. The fire that burned through every fiber of her body put her earlier passion to shame. Huge as he was, deeply as he rammed into her, she couldn't get enough of him—until he clamped her hips in his hands and pulled her up to meet his final searing tribute. Sealed to him, melting around him, her body convulsed in a shock wave of rapture. She welcomed the hot spurt of his offering with primitive glee, watched in barbaric satisfaction as his glistening body spasmed in completion. Spent, breathing slowly and deeply, Jonah lowered his mouth to hers for one more devouring kiss. If the remnants of passion drove him to try to suck the very air from her body, Katy didn't care. If Jonah had wanted at that moment to eat her alive, she would have offered herself willingly.

While Katy retreated into exhausted sleep, Jonah lay awake beside her and stared into the dark. The frustration that had built into such a thick, choking cloud over the last week had been swept away by the flood of his passion. Their passion. His hadn't been the only spark that had started the combustion in this tent. The fuse on that stick of feminine dynamite had refused to be doused, and the resulting explosion was a kind he had not imagined.

Jonah raised himself on one elbow and looked down upon Katy's sleeping form. She was a blur in the darkness—curved, smooth lines stirred by almost-imperceptible breathing. Her face was a pale oval against the inky black of her hair—hair darker even than the black night. Jonah reached out and gently brushed a knuckle against her cheek. So smooth. So soft. He felt himself start to grow hard yet again.

"Jesus!" he muttered. "Enough is enough!"

He rose stiffly from the blankets. Cold air produced goose bumps on his naked skin. He stifled the urge to crawl back into the blankets and wake Katy with the hard thrust of himself between her beautiful legs. He'd once read a book that claimed overindulgence in carnal sport could lead a man to mental degeneration and eventually insanity. Overindulgence had never been a problem with Jonah. One time was generally enough for him. If all women were as tempting as Katy, however, the nation's mental institutions would certainly see a sharp increase in business.

Jonah groped the darkness for his clothing. The wrinkled, cold garments smelled of sweat and passion, but then, so did he. He donned his parka and took refuge in the cold air outside the tent. On this treeless stretch of grass and rock below the Chilkoot summit, the night carried more than just a promise of arctic chill. The breeze had winter's bite, and the few hummocks of grass that grew among the rocks were stiff and frozen. He exhumed a few winking coals from the remains of the fire and added several sticks of wood. Hunter, who was curled in a grassy pocket between rocks with his tail covering his nose, stirred and raised his head. His eyes glowed red in the faint light of the revived fire.

"Party's over," Jonah told him. "You can go in now if you want."

Hunter's jaws opened in a lupine grin. He got up and padded toward Jonah for a scratch on the head, then nosed his way into the tent.

Jonah sat on a flat boulder and threw a larger stick on the fire. Tonight was certainly a night for surprises. Katy the temptress. Virgin temptress. Damn! Who in his right mind would have thought such a bold, adventuresome, cussing, poker-playing, gun-toting, fistfighting female would be an innocent?

Jonah dropped his head into his hands. *He* should have, Jonah admitted. He should have known from the clear innocence of those crystal green eyes, despite the bold manner, seductive smile, and absolute lack of maidenly sensibilities. He should have known. Not that it would have made any difference in the end. Ever since she'd sat down next to him on the train from Willow Bend, disguised as a proper miss in her straw bonnet and primly coiled braids, he'd been a fish hooked on Katy's line, fighting like hell not to be landed, but still being pulled steadily toward an inevitable end. She lit a fire in him that no other woman had ever matched.

That was because Katy had no match, Jonah thought with a smile. She shattered every rule, broke every convention, danced around society's dicta as though they were conceived only for her amusement. Yet she had kept herself untouched and innocent. She had allowed no man to taste so deeply of her beauty until Jonah Armstrong had come into her life. How could he help but love her?

The thought took him by surprise. Love Katy? What else could it be, this maddening, confusing, frustrating, exhilarating emotion? So much more complex than simple lust, it was, encompassing affection, need, worry, respect, and a certain amount of fearfulness. The lust was still there, too, he acknowledged with a grin.

Love Katy. The notion wasn't quite as frightening once it took hold. He could get used to it, Jonah decided. He could spend a lifetime exploring it. Loving Katy.

Jonah got up, stretched, sighed, and looked toward the tent. He did love Katy, and a good thing, too, for he'd have to marry her. A man of conscience didn't take a young woman's maidenhead without paying the price. It would serve his straitlaced mother right. After years of nagging him to marry, she'd get a daughter-in-law who would probably carry a pistol stuck through the sash of her wedding gown and run a poker game at the reception. And likely she'd have a wolf join the wedding party.

Jonah smiled, finding that the picture didn't displease him all that much. His chief objection to marriage was his reluctance to settle down and care for a wife. Katy probably wouldn't settle down unless someone tied her down with chains, and she certainly didn't need to be doted over and pampered. In fact, he realized, Katy O'Connell would make him a perfect wife. Marry Katy. The perfect solution.

Conscience eased, Katy's future decided, Jonah banked the fire and returned to the tent. Nudging Hunter aside, he joined Katy beneath her blankets. She murmured in her sleep and cozied herself against him as though they were made to fit together. Jonah relaxed and enjoyed the expectation of many, many nights with Katy in his arms. He fell asleep imagining the delight on her face when he proposed.

"You want to do what?" Katy asked incredulously.

Jonah stayed on bended knee, from where he'd made his proposal. "I said I want to marry you." His smile faded from confident to a bit uncertain. "Don't look as though I asked you to jump over a cliff!"

"You want to marry me?" Katy laughed and pulled the blankets more closely around her shoulders. "Jonah! Don't be ridiculous! Get up. You're going to hurt your knees on the rocks beneath this tent."

"So much for the traditional approach." He got up from the ludicrous position. Katy's heart flip-flopped as he stood. Broad shoulders, powerful arms, slim hips, strong, straight legs. He had to be the handsomest man she knew, and on this morning after the night before, there was a new depth to her appreciation. A flush rose to her cheeks. She wanted to invite him to sit back down upon the blankets they'd shared the night before. Her hand itched to smooth the pucker from his brow and ease the serious line of his mouth.

"Katy, I'm serious." He frowned. "And you shouldn't laugh at a man when he's proposing. It's bad manners."

"All right," she agreed. "I'm not laughing. You're very nice to ask," she said primly. "But I don't want to marry you."

"You don't mean it."

"I do mean it. I don't want to marry you."

It was partly a lie. Something inside her warmed to the thought of spending the days and nights of her life in Jonah's company. But another part of her, a smarter part, warned her that she was not wife material. At least, she wasn't wife material for a man who lived in Chicago and thought women were born to be protected.

"I don't believe you." Jonah dropped down beside her on the blankets, looking at her as though he might find evidence of fever or some other malady. His inspection made Katy feel the awkwardness of her disarray. She was tangled in a chaos of blankets and clothing. Her skirt was twisted around her waist, baring an expanse of leg and hip that should have given her a chill in the cold morning air, but the exposure made her flush with heat instead. Her bloomers lay in a pitiful pile of cotton in one corner of the tent. Her shirtwaist hung open, and her arms had escaped the straps of her chemise, which clung precariously to her breasts.

He grinned wickedly as she tried to rearrange her jumbled clothing into a more modest covering. "A bit late for that, don't you think?"

Katy glared, refusing to acknowledge embarrassment. "You could leave and let me get dressed."

"Not until you say you'll marry me."

"No!" she shouted, suddenly impatient. "I will not marry you. I don't want to marry you. So dust off your knees and save your pretty proposal for someone else."

He didn't get up. In fact, he moved closer—just what she didn't want—took her jaw in his hand and forced her to meet his eyes. "Katy, what is this? After last night, I could've sworn that you loved me."

His eyes seemed more blue than ever. Deep, clear blue, and endlessly compelling. She felt once again the power that had turned her into a vulnerable mass of jelly the night before. He'd driven her to delirious heights, lifted her to a peak of emotion where she was beyond control. Katy did not like being out of control. The memory of ecstasy and intense desire drove her close to losing control once again and doing something stupid.

"Let me go," she demanded in a quiet, intense voice.

He complied, and instantly she was sorry. She liked his touch. She liked looking into those wonderful blue eyes. He was right. She did love him.

"Did I hurt you very badly last night?" he asked quietly.

"Jonah, you didn't hurt me at all."

"You should have told me you hadn't been with a man before."

"Oh yeah? When was I supposed to bring that up? When we were hauling the horses through the mud, or maybe when Miss Maudie the Northern Star was telling you how lucky you were she'd decided to latch on to you? 'By the way, greenhorn—and anyone else who might be listening—I've never taken a man to my bed before. Is it fun?'"

He lifted one brow, then laughed softly. She loved his laugh. She loved the way his eyes brightened with his smile. "You're right," he admitted.

"Of course I'm right."

"But you're still going to marry me."

"You are the most muleheaded man I've ever met. No. I won't marry you, and that's that."

"Katy, a man simply doesn't seduce an innocent girl and not marry her."

Now she understood the reason behind his proposal. The understanding hurt a bit. "You want to marry me because you feel guilty!"

"That's not true."

"Well, you don't need to feel guilty, Jonah, because you didn't seduce me. I seduced you!"

"Did you think when you began that silly game last night that you'd end up with me making love to you?"

"Well, no. But—"

"Then I seduced you, dammit!"

"All right!" she shouted back. "You damn well seduced me! Are you satisfied? Knock yourself over the head a few times with a rock if that will make you feel better, but don't expect me to marry you. I'm going to find gold in the Klondike and run my own life, make my own rules, and the hell with what anybody thinks!"

"Coward! You're too chicken to marry me!"

Those were fighting words. No one called Katy O'Connell chicken!

"Get out!" she demanded.

He made no move to comply as she scrambled out of her blankets and kicked them aside. With violent, jerky motions she tore off her skirt and shirtwaist, wadded them up and threw them heedlessly into a pile in the corner where her bloomers were already dead and buried. Trying hard to ignore him, she dived into her valise to find her trousers and heavy denim shirt. To hell with dressing like a woman! Just look what it had gotten her. Confusion. Chaos. Disaster.

His eyes never left her. Their weight was an unbearable pressure.

"What are you staring at?"

"Someone who ought to grow up. The world isn't a kind one for a woman alone, Katy, even a woman with mountains of gold."

She yanked on her trousers. "Well thank you so much for offering to save me."

His irrepressible grin returned. "You're welcome. It would definitely be my pleasure."

"That's what you think." She pulled on her boots, tucked the denim shirt into her pants, and shoved her old familiar slouch hat onto her head. All the while his gaze followed her with hungry, unnerving intensity.

"Think about it, Katy. Just think about it."

Katy stalked out of the tent without answering. If he wouldn't leave, she would. A sour taste in her mouth and a leaden weight in her stomach made breakfast an unwelcome prospect, even though Andy had beans and coffee simmering on the fire.

"Let's go find some packers," she told the boy.

"Already got some," he said with a grin. "All friends of mine. Injuns. Four of 'em. They'll make as many trips as they need to get all your stuff to Lake Bennett, and they won't cheat ya, which is more than I can say for some of the others."

"You're mighty efficient this morning," Katy observed tartly.

"Found 'em while you and Mr. Jonah was palaverin' in the tent."

If she and Jonah had been merely palavering in the tent, then the Little Bighorn had been just a friendly chat. Her stomach clenched. "Yeah. Okay. Let's get this stuff packed, then."

"Yes'm."

Katy didn't acknowledge Jonah when he came out of the tent. The more she looked at him, the stronger was the urge to give in to the giddy warmth that he inspired and do something stupid. Along that path lay disaster. Love wasn't the only consideration in marriage. She could just see herself in Chicago sipping tea, pinky raised, lips pursed. She'd putter in a garden, gossip with the other proper matrons, and do whatever her husband told her to do, staying home like a well-behaved little lady while Jonah traveled about on his adventures. How long would love last living in a hell like that?

Of course, marriage didn't have to be that way. Olivia didn't always do what Katy's pa told her to do. In fact, her pa knew better than to push his luck by assuming the role of husbandly dictator. But that was wild Montana, not citified Chicago, and Katy's pa, unlike Jonah Armstrong, didn't think much of rules and conventions. It would never work, Katy told herself. Never in a million years.

Yet it was still there, floating in her mind—the magic of Jonah's kiss, the warm rumble of his laughter, the quickness of his smile. Jonah Armstrong was an invitation to trouble, and Katy had never been one to resist the lure of trouble. How she wished the gentlemanly jackass of a greenhorn had not proposed.

As Katy greeted the cold morning at Stone House in Alaska, her father, William Gabriel Danaher O'Connell, reined his wagon team to a halt on the rise overlooking Thunder Creek Ranch outside of Willow Bend, Montana. Beside him on the wagon seat, Olivia Baron O'Connell sighed with weary gratitude.

"It's good to be home again." Olivia's hand sought her husband's. He took her small hand into his much larger one and squeezed gently.

"I believe this journey of ours was your idea," he reminded her with a lift of one brow.

"And a good idea it was. I'm sure Ellen appreciated having us to help her get settled at Cornell. And after eight years of marriage, it was time you passed my father's inspection."

Gabe grimaced. "Your father makes a lynch mob look like a friendly church social."

Olivia gave him a dimpled smile. "I think you held your own in that quarter."

"Surviving a lynch mob or surviving your father?"

"Both," she said with a chuckle. Her eyes surveyed the vista below—the neat log ranch house and outbuildings, the cattle that were dark brown dots against the green sweep of the valley. In the clear, cool morning air, everything looked almost unnaturally sharp and clean. "It was good to go," she mused aloud, "but it's better to be back."

"You got that right," Gabe agreed. He slapped the reins along the horses' back. "Git up there, you nags. My stomach's growling, and I'm hoping that Katy didn't eat all the breakfast."

"Just hope that Katy didn't cook the breakfast," Olivia commented with a fond grin.

As the wagon rumbled down the slope, the blankets piled in the back with the luggage stirred and groaned. "Are we there yet?" Five year old David O'Connell emerged from the blankets, auburn curls springing up every which way from his head and sleepy green eyes cast pleadingly toward his parents.

"Almost, sweetie," Olivia answered. "Want to come up here and see?"

Davie scrambled into his father's lap, placed chubby hands on Gabe's brawny arms, and bounced up and down as if the activity would make the horses pick up their pace.

"There's the ranch! I c'n see it!"

"That's it all right," Gabe agreed.

"We're comin', Katy; we're comin', Hunter; we're comin', Katy," the boy chanted all the way down the wagon track until they stopped in front of the barn. "Where's Katy?" he asked when he didn't immediately see his older sister.

Olivia wasn't worried when Katy didn't greet them in the yard. If her stepdaughter was working the cattle, she'd probably seen the wagon and would come in soon. "Katy will be here," she promised Davie.

"Where's Hunter?" Davie cried impatiently as his father swung him down from the wagon. "I want Hunter!"

"You don't need to shout to the mountains about it," Gabe chided. "Hunter's probably with your sister."

"Yeah," came a new voice. "I'd guess that he is."

"Clem!" Olivia greeted the ranch manager with a smile.

"Howdy, Olivia, Gabriel. Got your letter. Glad to see you got in okay."

"Where's Katy?" Gabe asked as he shook the older man's hand.

Clem Jenkins took off his battered felt hat and scratched his balding pate with one finger. "Well, now, that's a purty good question, Gabe."

Gabe's eyes narrowed. "What do you mean?" His face instantly transformed from open and pleasant to a countenance no one would want to face behind the barrel of a gun. Olivia knew that for a fact, because she'd been there—facing that grim expression over the business end of a pistol.

She placed a calming hand on her husband's arm. "Clem, what are you saying?"

The ranch manager handed Gabe a piece of notepaper. "Found this one morning back in late July. It was addressed to you, but I read it anyways."

Gabe scanned the lines on the page. With every word he read, his scowl grew darker. "I'm going to wallop her little behind until she can't sit for a month," he finally growled.

Olivia felt a tingle of alarm. "What is it?"

He gave her the note to read. "Oh my!" she exclaimed. Then she smiled wryly. "That's Katy."

"Why the hell didn't you telegraph us?"

"I did," Jenkins said. "You'd left New York for Paris, and I couldn't find the name of that friend of Olivia's where you were staying."

"Damnation! What possessed the little idiot? Running off on a wild-goose chase for gold—alone, to the Klondike of all places?"

Jenkins looked at the ground, shifted his scrawny weight from one foot to the other, and cleared his throat. "Well now, Gabriel, she ain't exactly alone."

"Did Katy take Hunter?" Davie demanded indignantly.

"Yes. Yes, she did," Jenkins said. "And though Katy didn't say anything about it in that note of hers, ol' Myrna up at the saloon said she weaseled her way into guidin' some tender-foot newspaper writer up to Dawson."

"Newspaper writer?" Gabe repeated ominously. "A man?"

Jenkins squirmed. "Well . . . yeah."

"Katy's gone to the Klondike with a man." Gabe's voice was quiet, as though he were trying the idea on for size, but Olivia knew the signs—the twitch at the hinge of his jaw, the narrowing of his eyes, the flare of his nostrils.

She squeezed his arm. "Gabe, let's talk about this inside. Davie, would you help Clem put the team away, please? Come on, Gabriel, let's go inside."

"I'll kill him," Gabe said quietly as Olivia pulled him toward the log ranch house. "And I'll break every bone in his body before I put him out of his goddamned misery."

"Now Gabe . . ."

He grabbed the first thing at hand when they entered the house and sent it crashing across the kitchen. Fortunately, the milk pail was unbreakable, and the dent it put in the wooden cabinet just added a bit of rustic atmosphere to the kitchen.

Olivia sighed. Her husband had many virtues, but an even temper was not one of them. "Gabriel, sit down. You're acting just like a typical father!"

"I am a father! I'm an outraged father! Goddamn it to hell, what the hell kind of burr does she have under her blanket to go and do something like this?"

"Sit down. Let me get you a cool drink."

He thumped himself down on the bench that ran the length of the kitchen table. "Stop treating me like one of your patients."

"I will when you stop behaving like a grizzly with a bee sting on its butt. Do you recall how my father acts whenever he sees you?"

Gabe just growled.

"That's exactly how you're acting. Gabriel, Katy is a grown woman capable of making her own decisions. She was very restless here. We both knew it. She needs to find a place for herself and choose her own life."

"In the goddamned Klondike? Olivia, do you have any idea what it's like up in that country?"

Olivia propped her hands on her hips. "You think it's something Katy can't handle? When she was ten she rescued you from a lynch mob. When she was twelve she saved us both from Ace Candliss by riding down a mountain and fetching Crooked Stick and his band. Really, Gabriel, I don't think Katy needs a nursemaid." She filled a glass of cool water from the pump in the sink and set it on the table in front of him.

Gabe took a swallow and scowled. "Katy might not need a nursemaid, but she sure as hell doesn't need to be playing nursemaid to some slick city Don Juan."

"Don't jump to conclusions." Olivia sat down beside her husband and patted his knee. "For all we know this poor fellow might be sixty years old, stand four and a half feet tall, and have no hair on his head. Besides, Katy's old enough to protect herself from a man."

"Olivia, you were twenty-six when I met you, and you weren't old enough to protect yourself from me."

"Mmm," she said with a smile. "But if I'd been as capable as Katy, I probably would have shot out both your knees when you dragged me up that mountain."

Gabe turned a simmering look on her. "That's not what you would have shot out, and you know it."

She lifted a brow. "That's probably so."

"According to your father, you should have."

She smiled. "It would have put a crimp in your style."

In a lightning move, he kissed her. Without releasing her mouth, he stood and scooped her off the bench into his arms. "You know what getting mad does to me," he whispered against her lips.

"My love, getting mad has nothing to do with it. Everything does that to you."

He chuckled and headed toward their bedroom. "Only when I'm with you."

"Gabriel," Olivia said as he deposited her on their bed, "I'm glad that I didn't shoot your knees out when you dragged me up that mountain." She grinned wickedly. "Or anything else."

"So am I." He lowered himself beside her, nuzzled her neck, and started to work on the buttons of her bodice. "But if that tenderfoot is doing anything like this to Katy, I'll kill him."

CHAPTER 13

Katy and Jonah were on the trail by midmorning with the Indian packers that Andy had procured. The climb was a grim one. Just above Stone House, the trail crossed a vast snowfield with its treacherous broken ice and slippery footing. The sun blazed off the snow in a blinding brilliance that hid pitfalls and dangerous irregularities. A man ahead of them lost a toehold on the slope and slid down the icy incline to the sharp rocks below. He lay there until someone reached him by climbing over the boulder field above Stone House. His rescuers waved to his comrades above that he was alive, but he had a broken leg. His trek to the goldfields, for the time being at least, was over.

Above the snowfield, the trail all but disappeared. Flags, cairns, and splashes of paint on boulders marked the way, and in places rough handrails had been erected to help the struggling hikers pull themselves up the steep ascent. The landscape was a jumble of boulders, some bigger than a house, others small and ready to roll and shift under unwary feet. The Klondikers scrambled, crawled, or leapt precariously from boulder to boulder—however they could manage the task. Progress was slow and irksome.

During the first hour of climbing, Katy conceived a healthy

respect for the professional packers who labored over this trail again and again to haul goods for the hopeful gold kings. A wire-rope tramway intended to lift people and goods over the summit was in the initial stages of construction, but until it was finished, the only way to conquer this most formidable barrier between the seacoast and the goldfields was sweat and muscle. The packers put a good amount of both into every trip they made. Any fee, no matter how steep, was paltry considering what they had to endure.

The climb was grim, however, for reasons other than the difficulty of the trail. Jonah was dour and silent—very unlike him. Katy was equally morose. She spent most of the morning telling herself that if Jonah was stupid enough to propose, then he deserved the setdown she'd given him. A little humility would do him good. Then she spent the afternoon telling herself she had made the right decision. She could have jumped into Jonah's arms and told her better judgment to go to hell. That was the way she usually did things, Katy admitted, and it had gotten her a pantload of trouble more than once. She should be congratulated for showing some good sense this once in her life.

Nine hundred vertical feet above Stone House they reached the plateau known as the "Scales." Katy rested against one of the boulders that littered the brittle, hummocky grass while the packers took their turn reweighing their packs. Caches of goods were piled here and there under tarps that were weighted down with stones. Klondikers who shuttled their provisions across the pass in numerous trips often stored their goods at the Scales and hoped they would stay there undisturbed.

Exhausted and sore, Katy couldn't imagine having to make this terrible climb more than once. Even gold could not tempt her to such agony. As her breath slowly returned, she cast a surreptitious look at Jonah, who sat resting against one of the covered caches, his head tilted back against the tarp, his eyes squinted shut in the bright sunlight. Katy felt free to admire the column of muscle in his throat, the strong line of his jaw, the sunburned height of his wide brow. He'd made the climb so far without complaint. In fact, he'd even shared a joke or two with Andy and their packers. How had she ever believed him to be a weak dandy just because he was from east of the Mississippi?

Suddenly his eyes opened and focused onto her as if, even with closed eyes, he'd known she was looking at him. He lifted his hand in a casual salute—mocking or real, Katy couldn't decide—before he dropped his head back onto its rough pillow and stared at the sky.

Six hundred more vertical feet of climb earned them the summit of Chilkoot Pass, 3550 feet above where they had started the trek at Dyea. Exhausted, heads swimming from shortness of breath, dry-mouthed, and aching, they dropped their backpacks and collapsed against them. Even the professional packers were staggering by now. Ten full minutes passed before Katy noted the crowds, the tents, the Royal Mounties' tent that guarded the border between Alaska and Canada. The summit was a hive of activity—more so than she would have imagined. Not far from the Mountie station, a group of men indulged in a fest of backslapping and laughter. How did they find the energy? Katy wondered wearily. How did they even find the breath to laugh after that climb?

"Would you look at that?" Jonah smiled crookedly as he struggled to his feet. "Look at what's going on over there."

One of those parka-clad figures was a woman, Katy noted. The woman's mittened hand was clasped firmly in a man's grip, and they stood before a fellow who, with stiff and serious mien, flipped through the pages of a book he held open before him. Katy closed her eyes and collapsed back onto her pack, grimacing with the irony of it. Just what she needed right now—a wedding!

"Mr. Armstrong! Katy! I'm so glad to see you here!"

Camilla's voice forced Katy to open her eyes. The young Irishwoman was bundled in parka and headscarf. Little Liam was tucked beneath the parka, but one wool-clad little foot had kicked its way free and thumped erratically against his mother's ribs.

"I was so afraid that you'd been carried away in that dreadful flood. I wanted to go back to Sheep Camp to find you, but"—she shrugged in apology—"Patrick is very anxious to get to the goldfields."

Jonah touched the brim of the battered hat that he'd purchased after the flood. "Kind of you to worry about us, Mrs. Burke, but we came through just fine. How's that little boy of yours?"

Camilla laughed wearily. "Fussy. Always tired. But I might say the same about myself," she admitted with a self-deprecating smile. "Patrick is the strong one."

Katy didn't think so, but she kept her thoughts to herself.

Camilla eyed Katy's attire with hesitation. "My poor Katy! Did the floor carry away your clothing?"

Katy looked down at her trousers, then met Camilla's sympathetic gaze. "Yeah. Sort of."

"Well, we will find you something to wear. Never fear. And look! You arrived just in time to see the big event," Camilla told them. "Mr. Roy Parker and Miss Elizabeth Wright. Isn't it sweet? They met in Juneau. She was traveling with her father and brother. Mr. Parker proposed at Pleasant Camp—you know, that little settlement on the trail just above the Canyon. After the flood at Sheep Camp, Miss Wright's father and brother decided to go back, but Mr. Parker convinced her to climb with him to the summit and marry him here. It's so romantic."

Jonah was already scribbling notes, but he paused long enough to look Katy's way and raise one brow. Katy grimaced and looked away. What was it with marriage and weddings? Once mentioned, they appeared everywhere.

"I guess we might as well watch," Katy said with ill grace.

"Wouldn't miss it." Jonah grinned.

They joined the curious crowd who watched the ceremony. Roy Parker towered above his diminutive bride. His bulky sweater and parka emphasized his bull-like build, and he topped most of the men present by half a head. His face had a week's worth of scraggly beard, and his hair stuck out from beneath a stocking cap in irregular spikes. He smiled down at the woman with unmistakable adoration, though. Elizabeth Wright, her shape and almost everything else about her hidden beneath layers of clothing, returned his adoration in the tenderness of her smile.

As the preacher prepared to get underway, the groom bent down and gave the bride a sound and thorough kiss.

"None of that now!" came a jovial shout from somewhere in the crowd. "Not till the words have been said!"

The kiss continued while Roy brushed the teasing off with a wave of his hand. A few enthusiastic cheers rose from the crowd. Katy could feel Jonah beside her, even though she didn't dare look his way. Her body tingled. Her lips grew hot, until she was tempted to lick them to cool the fire. She wondered how long she would remember the way Jonah kissed. One of his kisses could make a girl forget every lick of good sense she possessed.

"Ahem!" The preacher cleared his throat loudly.

Roy released his bride, tenderly straightened her headscarf, and grinned. "You can start now," he told the preacher.

The couple were so absorbed in each other, Katy doubted they heard the words said over them. Katy heard them though. Love, honor, and cherish. Through thick and thin. During youth, middle age, and doddering decline. Katy didn't look sidewise to where Jonah stood beside her, but she could picture him in her mind, his teasing smile, blue eyes, the well-weathered laugh lines that creased his skin. She could hear the bantering of his voice—bantering that could turn deadly serious if something he really cared about was at stake. A woman could make such promises to a man like Jonah and look forward to keeping them.

Standing nearby, Camilla sniffled. "Oh my. Weddings always make me cry. And this one is so romantic, isn't it?"

"Yeah," Katy mumbled. "I suppose so."

She thought of her pa's wedding to Olivia, and the memory inspired a twinge of homesickness. Her pa and Olivia weren't like most married folks. They gave a whole new meaning to love and cherish, and they weren't ashamed to show it. Folks said her pa was lucky to have Olivia, and Katy conceded that might be true. Olivia was the really lucky one, though, for Gabriel O'Connell had rescued her from the fate of living out her life in New York.

If Katy were foolish enough to marry Jonah, folks would surely comment that a girl like Katy was lucky to get such a polished gent, just as they commented on Gabe and Olivia. That was where the analogy ended, though. While her pa had come to realize that Olivia had her own mission in life separate from him, Jonah thought women should be coddled and protected in a cocoon of safe domesticity. While Gabriel O'Connell had offered Olivia a life in wonderful, wild Montana, Jonah made his home in a land of crowded streets, smoky air, and the stifling confines of civilization. Katy looked out at the grand vista afforded by the summit they had struggled so hard to reach. In every direction lay a jumble of wild mountains. In the crystal-clear air, ridges looked as sharp as knives, glacier-carved peaks thrust upward in silent majesty, valleys flowed between the treeless heights like rivers of verdant green. Above it all stretched a brilliant deep blue sky.

What would happen to someone who had spent her life in such country if she tried to squeeze herself into the confines of narrow streets and dark buildings? What would happen to someone who longed for independence if she tried to bind herself with the shackles of wifely obedience? What would happen to the hoyden who tried to play the lady for keeps instead of just a game? What would happen? She would die. That's what would happen.

"I remember my wedding," Camilla said with a sigh.

"I'll bet it wasn't on top of a mountain," Katy said tartly.

"It was in Saint Patrick's Cathedral in Boston. No one but

our families were there, of course, so the church was nearly empty. It was grand, though. Poor Patrick. He'd celebrated so much the night before that he could scarcely stand."

Katy wondered why any woman as sensitive and gentle as Camilla would promise to love and obey an irresponsible, overgrown boy like Patrick Burke.

"How old were you?"

"Seventeen," Camilla said, smiling. "Patrick was twenty-three, and he was the handsomest, most charming man I'd ever met. When he proposed I'd thought he must be talking to someone else."

Camilla hadn't thought past handsome and charming, and look where it had landed her.

"When you were growing up," Katy asked, "did you even think about not marrying?"

"Live as a spinster? No children, no husband? Oh no. I could never do without Patrick." She turned a gentle smile on Katy. "I need someone to care for, someone to lean upon."

Well, Katy sure as hell didn't, especially not in some fusty house in Chicago sipping tea with her pinky in the air. Not Katy O'Connell. She was going to find gold, be independent, and make her own rules. Love was forged from chains meant to hold a woman down. Her heartstrings might hum when she looked at Jonah Armstrong, but she would get over this foolishness, just as she'd gotten over the diphtheria when she was twelve.

Jonah listened as the preacher embellished the wedding service with a few comments on the serious nature of marriage. His audience listened more raptly than any righteous, go-to-church-every-Sunday congregation would have, because it touched a subject close to the heart of almost every man on that summit. Women. Family. Many of the Klondikers had left wives and children at home to seek their fortune. Others had no family to remember, only a lonely existence that seemed even lonelier when watching two people join their lives together for mutual comfort and companionship. Every man in the crowd, Jonah observed with a touch of amusement, was mush-faced with romanticism. Probably himself as well. Once he'd been immune, but no more.

Man and woman must cleave together, the preacher declared. Only together are they whole. Apart they are incomplete. Nothing. Crippled.

Before he'd met Katy, Jonah would have laughed at the man. Some men were meant to be free, he would have told the preacher. Some men didn't have the time to spend on a luxury like marriage. Then Katy had swaggered into his life. Now he realized that when the right woman came along, marriage was no longer a luxury; it was a necessity.

"Woman is man's moral anchor!" the preaching man shouted, stabbing at the sky with a finger.

Fine moral anchor Katy would be, Jonah mused with a smile. She cussed, gambled, wore trousers, and probably, when no one was looking, spit.

"Man is woman's strength and protection!" the reverend declared.

Katy had strength of her own, and so far, she'd protected Jonah more than he had protected her. Who, though, would protect her from that trusting innocence she didn't even realize she possessed? Who if not Jonah Armstrong?

Jonah had spent the hike to the summit nursing the sting of Katy's rejection, telling himself he was lucky to escape the trap he'd almost fallen into, convincing himself that he didn't really want to marry. He'd been shocked by Katy's virginity and felt guilty for his misunderstanding of her character. With every painful step toward the top he told himself that he had proposed out of obligation. He was lucky the little termagant had said no.

But that was a load of shit. He hadn't mistaken Katy's character—not really. Somewhere inside him he'd known exactly what he was doing. And his proposal had been more of a plea than a placation. He wanted Katy. Frightening as the thought was, he loved the swaggering, bossy little imp. She was a breath of fresh air in a world growing stuffier by the day, a bright flame of passion in a life where the embers of excitement were growing cold.

"If anyone here knows a good reason why these two shouldn't be married, let him speak now," the preacher invited the crowd.

Up until recently, Jonah Armstrong had a list as long as his arms why a man like him shouldn't marry. Now he couldn't think of one. He slid a glance toward Katy where she stood with Camilla a few feet away. She leaned her head toward Camilla and smiled at something the other woman said. Perhaps she also had been thinking on her way up the trail. Perhaps she had merely been frightened and shocked this early morning when she'd refused him. She watched the bridal couple with a strange light in her eyes. She might be thinking right now that marriage to Jonah Armstrong was a good idea after all.

"I now pronounce you, Roy Matthew Parker, and you, Elizabeth Mary Wright, man and wife," the preacher droned. "What God has joined together, let not man put asunder. Amen."

An enthusiastic chorus of amens rose from the crowd. Roy took his cue and kissed Elizabeth once again—a long, thorough kiss. Katy pressed her lips together and clamped them between her teeth. Jonah could almost see her squirm. It wasn't Roy Parker she was thinking about; it was Jonah Armstrong. She loved him. She wanted him. Jonah could feel it.

The crowd dispersed. Katy wandered off with Camilla. Andy was with the packers, and a long line stretched in front of them before they could weigh in and pay the fees to cross the border into Canada. Jonah was left with no company but his own, so he introduced himself to the bride and groom and asked their permission to write their story for the *Record*. Roy was eager to talk about their plans for the future. Elizabeth blushed charmingly and let her new husband do the talking.

Jonah couldn't help compare her to Katy—two women following the same trail but different as a wild rose and a pampered pansy. Clinging to her groom's brawny arm, Elizabeth was all blushes and feminine adoration, content to put her life in her husband's hands. Katy, on the other hand, was untamed beauty studded with thorns. She would never be content to have her future rest with anyone but herself.

Why couldn't he have been smart like Roy Parker? Jonah asked himself. Why couldn't he have fallen in love with a woman like Elizabeth Wright? Life would have been so much easier. And so much duller, he reminded himself.

Jonah left Roy and Elizabeth to their newlywed billing and cooing and went in search of Katy. He found her with Andy setting up the tent. Her glance slid off him uneasily as she explained that they wouldn't get through the border until morning. Besides which, the Burkes had been delayed by the desertion of three of their packers, and Andy had offered to help them hire others.

"Fine," Jonah said. "I'm in no hurry."

He helped set up the tent and start a fire, taking satisfied notice that he was getting good at such things. He was also becoming accustomed to some of Katy's outlandish ideas of what sort of game animals were suitable to go in the dinner pot. A case in point was some small limp creature that Hunter held between his jaws as he trotted up to Katy.

"Do I dare ask what that is?"

"It's a pica," Katy said. "Hunter's brought in enough of them for a stew, I think."

Hunter dropped his victim at Katy's feet. It was the size of a small chipmunk—or a medium size rat, Jonah thought with distaste.

"They live among the rocks above the tree line," Katy continued. "Some of those indignant squeaks we've been hearing are these guys telling us to get out of their territory."

"I'd be squeaking too if a wolf decided to collect me for the stewpot."

"We need to conserve our provisions," Katy said sharply. "The nearest grocer is a few days' hike away."

Jonah raised his arms in surrender. "What did I say? Pica sounds delicious. Mmmm!" He could picture Katy serving pica stew to his mother when his family came to visit for Sunday dinner. That was something he would love to see. He truly would.

"I'll skin and clean 'em," Andy offered.

"All right," Katy said. "Give one of them to Hunter, and give him the innards of the rest."

"Yes'm."

Now that was an appetizing picture indeed, Jonah reflected as Hunter trotted after Andy. He wondered if his mother would be able to teach Katy to cook.

"I saw your friend Maude and her group a while ago," Katy said, her back to him and her face hidden.

She bent over and picked up a piece of firewood to throw onto their little fire, and Jonah couldn't help but notice the way her trousers stretched tight over her small rounded bottom. His reaction was instant and uncomfortable. If trousers ever became accepted fashion for women, he mused, the men of the world were doomed.

"They got through the border and are headed down the other side," she continued.

"Huh? Oh . . . yeah. Good. Uh . . . listen, Katy."

"Listen to what?"

"Have you . . . seen the view over here?"

Katy looked at him as though he were some kind of idiot. He *was* an idiot.

"Yes. I've seen the view."

Just leap right into the subject and get it over with, Jonah told himself. Then again, why not give her time to think about what a mistake she'd made in refusing his offer. They had at least another five weeks before reaching Dawson. Plenty of time for her to realize what a good catch he was.

He wandered over to a high point that afforded a spectacular vista of the surrounding wilderness. She followed and sat beside him on a large, flat boulder. That was a good sign. Maybe the wedding had put her in a receptive, romantic mood.

"If you look real hard down this way, you can see the Lynn Canal," he said.

Katy squinted in the indicated direction, then smiled. "Sort of reminds me of the mountains above my pa's mine." The sharpness had left her face. Her expression was soft, her smile a gentle reflection of fond memories. "Sometimes I'd climb up to Thunder Ridge, high above our cabin, and look out over all the mountains and valleys. It was a lot like this."

"It's really something," Jonah admitted. "Almost another world. Unsullied. Untamed. Wild and clean and free."

Katy sighed. "My world."

"Beautiful." His eyes were on her, not on the view. The soft curve of her cheek, the delicate arch of her brow, the stubborn lift of her chin—that beauty drew his eye more surely than anything this wilderness could offer. "Katy," he said quietly. "This is only one world. There are others just as beautiful. I'd like to show you mine."

She frowned slightly.

"Don't jump to saying no," he warned. "Last night was special, Katy. Sometimes a man and a woman want each other and—" her lifted brow made him hesitate, but he plunged on. "And they lie together and do the things we did, and it doesn't mean anything, really, except that they scratch an itch."

Color was crawling up Katy's face, but Jonah kept on. He figured that anyone who could face down the Hacketts, thumb her nose at angry gamblers, and eat pica stew should be able to talk about sex without turning purple.

"That's not what we did, Katy. We made love. It was special, and it means we're special. We're special together. I love you. I really do want to marry you. Katy, I think you love me, too. I'm hoping that watching that wedding might have gotten you thinking in that direction, thinking about me."

His hopes sank as he saw her almost visibly draw her armor of cocky nonchalance about her. "If it did, I was thinking how to feed your face for dinner without burning another batch of beans. Stop bothering me with all this marriage nonsense, Jonah. You've done the noble thing and proposed, but I keep telling you that I don't care what other people think."

"I love you, Katy."

Her color grew deeper. "You shouldn't. You don't even know me. If you knew me, you'd know I can't marry you."

"Goddamn it, you bullheaded little idiot! What is your problem?"

"You're the one with the problem!" she snapped. "You're the one feeling guilty!"

If one rejection stung, then double the dose felt like a cat-o'-nine-tails snapped across Jonah's exposed feelings. "I'm not guilty of anything but getting softheaded over a female. You're the one who prances around in trousers, gambles like some kind of fancy cardsharp, and bellies up to the bar like a . . . like a tart."

"I am not a tart! I like to wear trousers. Just try wearing all those skirts and a corset and see how comfortable you are! And I like to ride, shoot, gamble, and cuss. How could you want to marry me if you don't like who I am? That's who I am, and that's who I'll always be!"

"Damned little fool! That's not who you are."

"Yes, it is."

"No, it isn't! I'll tell you who you are, Katy O'Connell."

She turned her face away, but he was having none of that. Taking her stubborn chin in a firm grasp, he forced her to look at him. I'll tell you who you are. You're a pair of the most beautiful green eyes I've ever seen, the most gorgeous hair, the smoothest skin. But that doesn't even begin to define who you are. You're a butterfly just crawling out of her cocoon, with a spirit like the wind. There's not an ounce of artifice in you. You're strong, smart, and brave—about everything but your heart. You're not afraid of passion. You're not really afraid of Chicago—hell! You'd take the city by storm if you wanted to. I'll tell you what you're afraid of, Katy O'Connell—you chicken. You're afraid of me, because with me you feel like a woman."

"Bullshit!"

"Bullshit yourself, you little fiend." He bent forward and kissed her hard. Her lips were stiff and cold. He felt rather than saw her hand ball into a fist against his chest. Katy being what she was, she could have decked him with that fist if she'd truly wanted to. She didn't, though. Her lips softened and opened beneath his. He took the invitation and scoured her mouth with his own, wanting to cure her of this foolishness by the force of his own passion.

Regrettably, he eventually had to surface for breath. The pause gave Katy time to regroup. She sucked a deep breath into her lungs and pushed him away. "You're not acting very brotherly, brother dear!"

"To hell with that act! I'm past caring what people think. You love me, Katy. I know you do. And you're going to marry me sooner or later."

He reached for her again, but she retreated. "No! This is not going to happen again."

Jonah grinned. "You don't think so?"

"It is not. This has gone all wrong. You get to Dawson yourself, Mr. Know-it-all. You and Andy. You always claimed you could do just fine without me." She scrambled to her feet.

"Katy wait! This is ridiculous!"

"I'll take a couple of the packers and leave you the rest. You can have the tent."

"You're serious about this, aren't you?" he said in amazement as he followed her back to their camp.

"I don't want your company any longer, Jonah. Go write your goddamned stories and bother somebody else!"

"Coward!"

She stopped and whirled to face him. "I am not a coward, you randy horned toad!"

"You're afraid to stay with me. Afraid you'll give in. Afraid you might have to grow up!"

For a moment Jonah thought she might hit him. Her hands curled into fists at her sides. Her eyes narrowed into bright slits of green fire. He almost wished she would hit him. His temper was high enough that he just might take a swing back. But in the end she merely ground her teeth, growled, and stomped away, leaving him with a fireball of frustration eating at his gut.

"Way to go, Romeo," he mocked himself. "You'll have her eating out of your hand in no time."

CHAPTER 14

Katy couldn't decide which was more difficult, the up or the down. Climbing to the summit of Chilkoot Pass had been exhausting, but scrambling down the other side just plain hurt. Her knees and back ached, the muscles of her legs quivered, her hands stung from bracing herself on rough boulders and falling on patches of loose gravel that slid from beneath her feet.

Downhill, she decided. Downhill was definitely worse than up—not only because gravity tried constantly to send her down the mountain much faster than she wanted to go. Climbing up to the summit she'd had Jonah to watch, spar with, dream about—yes, she admitted that she'd done a bit of foolish dreaming, never suspecting the trouble it would get her into. Going down from the summit she had only Patrick Burke's stupid whistling to listen to, along with Liam's fussing.

Katy stopped for a moment—a tricky feat going down a trail this steep. Her calves were demanding a rest in no uncertain terms. Camilla stopped behind her by putting a hand on Katy's shoulder to momentarily steady herself.

"Would you like me to carry Liam for a while?" Camilla offered.

"No. We're fine." Katy figured the weight of the baby in his sling against her chest balanced the weight of the pack on her back. Still, she didn't envy Camilla for carrying the kid all the way from Dyea to the summit. He was a load, and a noisy one at that.

"Really, Katy, it's very nice of you to spell me, but I don't mind carrying him. You look tired."

"Nah. I'm strong as a horse."

"Yes, dear. You're amazingly strong. But sometimes an emotional upset—like your disagreement with your brother— can drain a person's energy."

Patrick had stopped whistling. He leaned on his walking stick and called to them from down the trail. "What's the delay back there?"

"We're coming," Camilla called back.

"Let's go!" Patrick shouted. "Time's a burning."

"Jackass," Katy muttered under her breath. Patrick Burke was a living, breathing advertisement for spinsterhood. He had the constitution and strength of an ox, and it never occurred to him that Camilla, frailer than he and burdened with the care of their infant, might not be able to maintain the pace he set. Impatience with his wife often broke through his whistling good humor.

"I don't understand men," Katy sighed as they started down the trail again.

"Best not to try," Camilla warned.

"And I don't understand why we let men make all the rules."

"You're brooding about your brother. You had a row about some rules, dear?"

Katy hesitated only a moment. "Jonah's not my brother."

"Ah," Camilla said with a smile. She didn't seem at all shocked.

"We say I'm his sister because he thinks people will get the wrong idea. I'm his guide. He hired me to take care of him on the way to Dawson."

"My goodness. Jonah seems to me like a man who can quite well take care of himself."

Katy sighed. "Well, I'll admit he does pretty well for himself. I badgered him just a bit to hire me on."

"Really?"

"Maybe more than a bit."

"Indeed! What a surprise." Camilla chuckled. "Just what rules did you and Jonah disagree about?"

"All of them! If you're a woman, you have to do this. If you're a man you have to do that. And if you step over the line"—Katy puffed her cheeks out in exasperation—"you've gotta pay the price. Hmph! He wants to marry me!"

Camilla grabbed the side of a boulder and braced herself to a stop. One corner of her mouth twitched upward. "Does he really? How very thoughtless of him!"

Katy had to laugh at the twinkle in Camilla's brown eyes.

"You don't like Jonah?" Camilla asked.

"I like him. I like him fine."

"You don't love him, then."

Katy blinked. Her face grew warm. "Maybe I love him." Images from the night before flashed through her mind. Her body began to tingle at the memory of Jonah's touch, the feel of his warm breath on her skin, the infinitely tender care he took of every part of her. Equally clear were the memories of how easily he laughed, the light in his eyes when he teased her, his dead serious, no-nonsense determination when he'd stopped her from going into the flood after Maude and insisted on going himself. "I . . . I love him," she admitted cautiously. The revelation was both daunting and unexpected. Jonah wasn't the sort of man she had thought to fall in love with. If the truth be known, she hadn't really expected to fall in love—ever. Katy wondered if love was curable, like a disease or a rash. "Love can certainly muddle a girl's mind," she sighed morosely.

At Patrick's impatient backward glance, they started down the trail again.

"You're very right," Camilla told Katy. "Love does muddle a woman's mind, and a good thing it is. Elsewise most of us would never be content with our husbands."

"Well, I'll just wait for my mind to clear. I'm going to be independent and make my own rules. I don't want to follow any man's lead. I'll lead myself, thank you."

Camilla laughed quietly. "Katy dear. Women were meant to follow a man's lead. A man without a wife is like a boat without an anchor. And a woman without a man . . ." She thought a moment, then smiled. "A woman without a man is like an empty vessel waiting to be filled."

Katy's cheeks grew hotter. If she told Camilla that her vessel had been good and filled just the night before, what would the gentle Irishwoman think? "I can live without being filled," she said almost pugnaciously. "I'm going to be independent."

"Independence will not keep you warm at night nor give you children," Camilla reminded her gently.

A good crackling campfire would do for warmth, Katy told herself, and as for children—well, if little Liam was an example, then she'd been away shooting squirrels when God parceled out the maternal instinct, because the poor little tyke had been squirming and fussing ever since she'd taken him.

As if in full agreement with her assessment, Liam suddenly signaled his dissatisfaction with a louder than normal wail.

"I'd better take him," Camilla said. "Poor baby. Poor boy." She transferred the sling to herself and cuddled the infant. "Where's Mama's sweet angel, eh?"

Liam quieted from frantic to merely fussy. Momentarily, Katy pictured herself with Jonah Armstrong's child in her arms—a child conceived with Jonah's body fused to hers, a child born of tender kisses, intimate laughter, loving words, a child with Jonah's wicked smile and Katy's green eyes.

Katy sighed, then scolded herself. That was the road to trouble.

Secure against his mother's breast, little Liam produced a noise that sounded remarkably like a raspberry. Katy laughed, and Camilla joined in. *Out of the mouths of babes* . . . Katy mused with a strange sadness.

They climbed down through the windswept, treeless valley that led from Chilkoot Pass. The packers carrying the Burkes' outfit and the two that Katy had taken accompanied them at their own pace, some behind, some ahead. Camilla and Katy took turns carrying Liam, and even Patrick once assumed the burden of his son, though when the baby messed, he promptly landed back in his mother's custody.

The trail was crowded, though not as packed as on the other side of the pass. Slowed by Liam and a tiring Camilla, they often were passed by faster parties, much to Patrick's freely expressed disgust. One of the parties that went around them on the trail was Jonah and Andy. Andy skipped and waved. Jonah touched the brim of his hat, but his mouth was set and grim, his eyes hooded beneath lowered brows.

A knife twisted in Katy's gut. What had she expected? she asked herself—a hug and a kiss?

At the midday break they were entertained by watching the daring few who sped their trip down the trail by sliding down the snowfields that formed dirty white chutes on the steep slopes. Everything from boards to oilskin slickers were used as sleds for both prospectors and goods. Amid whoops, hollers, and shrieks, many made fast and successful trips to a point far below where they could have walked in several hours. A few came to grief on the rocks at the foot of the snowfields.

"Fools," Camilla remarked.

Patrick gave Camilla a look that made Katy suspect that if not for his wife and infant child, Patrick would be taking his chances on the snow with the rest of the fools.

The first night down from the pass they camped at Crater Lake, which sat like a jewel in the cup of an ancient glacial basin and reflected with perfect clarity the rocky heights that rose above them. Katy tended Liam while Camilla fixed supper. Patrick coaxed a lilting Irish folk tune out of his fiddle and filled the little valley with music. People in camps all around the lake clapped and whooped in approval.

Crater Lake was the first in a string of lakes and waterfalls that cascaded downslope toward Lake Bennett. The high mountain valleys through which the Klondikers trekked were the birthplace of the mighty Yukon River. Katy marveled that the place still seemed so wild and untouched even with a parade of goldseekers trampling its dignity. More than once her eyes caught the graceful soar of an eagle overhead. Marmots sat atop rocks and squeaked their loud indignation. Picas occasionally added their comments to the chorus. Hunter brought Katy two of the rodents who weren't fast enough to duck into their holes when he passed by. She took them with proper thanks, then tossed them back into his jaws for him to snack upon. She doubted very much if Patrick and Camilla Burke would appreciate a pot of pica stew.

Midafternoon of the second day from the summit they saw trees for the first time since leaving Sheep Camp. At Lake Lindeman, a long, narrow finger of water that stretched for several miles above Lake Bennett, scraggly spruce struggled to survive the arcticlike environment. Klondikers impatient to take to the water chose Lake Lindeman to stop and build the boats that would transport them down the Yukon to Dawson, but most hiked on to Lake Bennett, where the timber grew taller and thicker and a sawmill sat on the lakeshore to provide lumber.

Katy and the Burkes planned to go on to Lake Bennett, but Katy surreptitiously inspected every tent they passed on the shore of Lake Lindeman to discover if Jonah and Andy might have stopped. Their familiar tent was nowhere to be seen, however.

They reached Lake Bennett and the little tent town that had sprouted along its shore with almost an hour of daylight to spare. Anxious to make arrangements for continuing the journey, Patrick left to negotiate for a boat at the sawmill as soon as they'd chosen a campsite. Katy made Camilla sit down with the baby while she pitched the tent, built the fire, and started beans and salt pork to heating.

Patrick returned with bad news.

"The sawmill isn't taking any more contracts for boats," he told them. With an impatient grimace, he poured himself a mug of coffee from the pot heating over the fire. "I'll have to build one."

"Oh, Patrick," Camilla said with a sigh. "What do you know about boat building?"

He grinned and raised his cup to her in salute. "I'll learn, my love. How hard could it be? After all, we're simply floating down a river, not crossing the briny deep. Be a good lass, now, and shovel me up a plate of those beans."

Patrick had talked with Messrs. Markus and Rocco, the carpenters who owned the sawmill, and arranged to cut timber in exchange for a portion of the trees being sawed into lumber. He was optimistic about the length of time required to earn enough lumber for a boat. They had to wait for the rest of their outfit to be packed over the pass from the Scales in any case, for Patrick had not been able to replace the Indian packers who had deserted him, leaving them with only two. Katy wasn't surprised that more packers had refused to hire on with the Irishman, for he treated the Indians more like horses or mules than people. Katy wouldn't have treated a horse with the casual contempt Patrick reserved for the packers. His attitude had earned him a delay at Lake Bennett while the two packers who had stuck with him shuttled their goods across the pass in three or four trips. Even had the sawmill been able to give them lumber right away, they could not have left until all their outfit had arrived.

Musing on Patrick's deficiencies brought to mind Jonah's contrasting behavior, for he had gotten on surprisingly well with the Indian men and women who had hired on to carry their provisions to Lake Bennett. She wondered how he would react to her uncle, Crooked Stick, the Blackfoot warrior who refused to stay on the reservation when there were more interesting things to do and see elsewhere, or to her grandmother Squirrel Woman, who was a very powerful medicine woman. He would never meet them, Katy reminded herself sharply, so she would never know.

If the mill was accepting no more contracts for boats, then Jonah was subject to the same delay that she and the Burkes were, Katy realized. She wondered what the greenhorn knew of boat building. Probably nothing, and Katy would have been little help to him in that if she'd been with him, for she'd been a landlubber all her life.

Patrick and Jonah were not the only amateurs who would be building their own boats. Exploring the tent town with Hunter by the evening's last light, Katy saw many a boat-building operation going on. Most of the Klondikers followed the same design. Some whipsawed their own lumber. Others had purchased lumber from the mill in exchange for labor in cutting trees. The knotty green spruce boards were hardly the ideal sort of material to make into a boat, Katy guessed, but the goldseekers weren't about to let that stand in their way. The shoreline resembled a shipyard with boats in all stages of completion—sharp pointed little vessels with wide sterns and flat bottoms to negotiate the shallows of the river. The boats were caulked with oakum and heavily pitched—some not nearly enough, as Katy discovered when she watched the maiden launch of a just-completed boat. The boat wasted no time in sinking. The sodden captain swam back to shore, warming himself and all the campsites within earshot with his curses.

When darkness fell, Katy was loath to return to the Burkes' camp, Liam's constant fussing, and Patrick's sharp mood, for in spite of the Irishman's rationalization that they would soon be on their way, he still chafed with the necessary delay. She wandered randomly around the tent town, looking at boats, saying hello to a few acquaintances from the trail. Before much time passed she found herself looking at a battered tent that was as familiar as the Thunder Creek ranch house back home—Jonah's tent.

Heart beating rapidly, she slipped into concealment behind a spruce tree and hissed for Hunter to join her. Andy squatted beside the campfire, drinking from a tin mug. The smell of coffee was pungent in the cold air. No sound or movement revealed Jonah's presence. He wasn't there.

Katy's heart slowed a bit. She told herself it was from relief. She had nothing to say to Jonah, after all. Nothing at all. But a quick hello to Andy would only be polite.

"Andy," she greeted him as she left the cover of the tree. "Hi there."

"Miss Katy!"

"How's it going?"

"Good! Hey, I caught some fish for dinner. There's some left over. Want some?"

"Sure."

Andy presented her with a plate of whitefish and beans.

"What did you catch them with?" Katy asked.

"Bacon. It was easy. Some of the folks around here are putting out gill nets, though. I'm going to try that."

"I'll show you how to smoke fish so you won't have to waste the leftovers."

"Gee, thanks. Jonah should be back in a while."

Katy was almost afraid to ask where he was. She'd passed Maude's group doing a good business two hundred yards down the shore, and those ladies weren't the only band of entrepreneurial sporting women who were camped at the lake.

"Jonah's up talking to the sawmill owners," Andy said without Katy asking.

"About lumber for a boat?"

"No. Well, maybe that, too. But he's writing about them for his paper. You know, everyone Mr. Jonah talks to is hell-bent to get written about for that paper of his. You'd think it was some big honor, or something."

Katy grinned. "Keeps him busy and out of trouble."

"Yeah."

"Things going okay with you two?"

Andy gave Katy a speculative look. "I guess. But Jonah's about as cranky as an ol' bear who's had his balls shot off."

Katy suffered a pang of guilt. Jonah would get over it, she told herself. And, of course, she didn't have anything to get over.

"You ain't really Jonah's sister, are you?"

"Hell no." She had told Jonah that that particular dodge would never work.

"Yeah. I figured. A fellow don't act like someone's twisted his trousers over a fight with his sister."

"We didn't fight. Not exactly."

"Yeah. Right." He looked at her from under his lashes with an expression that might have been envy. "So, you gonna go to Dawson alone?"

"I'm tagging along with the Burkes—helping Mrs. Burke a bit."

"Gonna dig for gold on your own?"

"Yeah."

Andy sighed. "Me too." He grinned. "We're both gonna be rich, I guess."

"More'n likely." Something moved behind the tent, and Katy jumped. She didn't want Jonah to find her here. It wasn't as if she was checking up on him, after all. She'd just wandered over to this familiar tent by accident. "Gotta go, Andy. Thanks for the fish. Me and the Burkes are camped over in that little bay. Come by and I'll show you how to smoke the fish."

"But don't bring Jonah, right?"

She gave the grinning boy a quelling look. "Jonah can do whatever he wants. You take care, now."

Cheeky little devil, Katy mused to herself as she left. He reminded her of herself a few years back.

At the Burkes' camp, Patrick was playing his fiddle and relaxing with a bottle of whiskey. He offered Katy a cup of the brew when she sat down by the fire.

"No thanks," she said. The whiskey was a temptation after the last few days, but she wouldn't be fit to spit in the morning.

"Katy, is that you?" called Camilla from inside the tent. Her voice was sharp with worry.

"Liam's still fussing," Patrick explained. "Kid ain't a good traveler."

Katy got to her feet and went into the tent. Camilla was sitting among the bedrolls and spare blankets, cuddling the baby to her breast. Her face was pinched and weary in the harsh lantern light.

"He won't nurse," Camilla told Katy.

She couldn't help there, Katy mused. "Maybe he's too tired. You look all done in yourself, Camilla. Why don't you let me hold him for a while and you can lie down and rest?"

Camilla looked doubtfully at Katy, then at the fussing baby. Sighing, she gave Liam to Katy. "Lord forgive me, but sometimes I wish Patrick had never heard of the Klondike gold. Our little rooms back in Boston weren't much, but they were cosy and warm. They weren't made from canvas that flapped and billowed in the wind, and I could walk down to the market and buy fresh greens and fruit. My mother lived just half a block away. She had nine children and never lost a one of them to sickness or puniness. I wish she were here now so I could ask her if Liam's sick."

Katy thought the baby did look a bit puny, but then, what did she know about babies? "He's just tired, I'm sure," she said inadequately. "You lie down. Maybe you can sleep."

Camilla wrapped herself in a blanket and lay still, but she didn't sleep. Katy settled back against one of the bedrolls, rocked back and forth, and quietly sang a little ditty she remembered her father singing to her and Ellen when they were small. The song was not a lullaby, exactly. It was a cattlemen's song, a tune to lull restless cattle on long nights in the saddle standing watch over a herd. Katy and Ellen had always fallen asleep before the second verse, but Liam was not nearly as cooperative. If anything, he grew fussier. He squirmed and waved his fists, drooled profusely on Katy's flannel shirt, and grew red in the face. Before too much time passed, Katy realized that the flushed skin and the heat radiating from the little baby was not the result of crying. She felt Liam's face, his feet, his stomach—everywhere she touched the baby burned. The fussing had become more a wheeze than a cry.

"Camilla," Katy called.

Camilla jumped, jolted from a light doze. "What? What is it?"

"Come look at Liam. Maybe he is sick."

In the blink of an eye Camilla knelt beside Katy and took the baby from her arms. "Oh my dear Lord!" she cried as she brushed his face with gentle fingers. "God have mercy! My poor baby!"

The sickness wasted no time in tightening its grip on poor Liam and revealing its dread nature. Diphtheria was a familiar killer. Katy and her sister had suffered and almost died from it when they were twelve. Olivia had saved them; the illness had been the catalyst that had brought Gabriel O'Connell and Dr. Olivia Baron together. But Olivia was not here to save Liam, and though an antitoxin had recently been developed to fight the disease, it certainly was not available in the Alaskan wilderness on the shores of Lake Bennett.

That night was a cold, dark slice of hell. Word traveled quickly in the small tent-town community. Nearly every woman in the little settlement came by to offer suggestions and sympathy. One told Camilla to hang the baby upside down and tickle his throat with a feather—her grandmother's tried-and-true treatment. Another recommended a thimbleful of warm whiskey every hour. Camilla had enough sense, however, to know that the only treatment possible was constant and patient nursing.

Jonah and Andy came and stayed. Andy fixed hot coffee and tea for Camilla and Katy while Jonah kept a frantically pacing and quite drunk Patrick out of the women's way.

Camilla and Katy both worked to keep the infant wiped down with cool cloths, but the fever climbed higher. Liam spit out or drooled out every drop of lukewarm water that Camilla dripped into his mouth. The disease raced along its course. One so young and fragile had no defense against it, no reserves to fall back upon, no strength to call up. By midnight, the characteristic thick rubbery membrane had formed at the back of Liam's throat. He wheezed for breath and labored to swallow his own saliva, until his crying became no more than piteous gasping. By two hours past midnight, he was dead.

Camilla didn't cry. Not right away. She stared at Liam's lifeless little body with a face grim and cold as stone. She took no notice of Katy's hand on her shoulder, but rose and marched from the tent. For a moment she simply stared at Patrick, who sat by the fire, his head in his hands, his body weaving slightly from the effects of a bottle and a half of whiskey.

"Come look what you have done," Camilla said quietly, her voice cold and sharp as an icicle. "Come look what you have done, you and your damned gold fever, Patrick Burke."

When he didn't move, she grabbed his arm and yanked him to his feet with a strength that belied her small frame. "Get up, you no-good, drunken, wandering Irishman! Come look what you have done!"

"Cammie . . . " Patrick groaned.

"No!" She screamed the denial and covered her ears. "I will not listen to your excuses. You killed my baby as sure as if you had taken a shovel to his head! You have no thought for anyone but yourself, and now you've killed my baby!"

Patrick staggered to his feet. "Cammie . . . sweetheart, you're talking crazy. Just settle down."

Camilla went for him, flailing like a madwoman. Her fists hammered his head, shoulders, and chest, and her feet kicked at his shins. When he instinctively drew his arm back to return a blow, Jonah grabbed him.

"Don't even think about it," Jonah warned.

Meanwhile, Katy managed to pull Camilla away from her

husband. Her fit of violence over, the Irishwoman collapsed against Katy, weeping so desperately she could scarcely catch a breath. Patrick twisted away from Jonah and went into the tent. He came out a moment later, his face chalky, his hands shaking. If he could have beaten on himself, Katy guessed, he would have done it, but he merely shook his head and went searching for a bottle.

Katy sat with Camilla the rest of the night while Jonah dealt with the little body and made arrangements for a burial the next morning. With the aid of a healthy dose of Patrick's whiskey, Camilla finally succumbed to uneasy sleep. Katy stayed awake, sitting on the tent floor beside Camilla's bedroll, in case the Irishwoman should wake and need her. Not that she could have slept anyway. The unfairness of Liam's death ran restless circles in her mind. She had known the infant a very short time, but the little one had wormed his way into her heart all the same. Babies were like that, she reflected. Nature made them irresistibly endearing. Otherwise, with all their spitting up, crying, and messing, babies would be the last thing any woman in her right mind would want to put up with.

In the dark silence of the night, Katy remembered Liam's gurgling smiles, his little fists flailing in an infant tantrum, his wide-eyed fascination at the funny noises Jonah sometimes made for him. Jonah—who had assumed the sad tasks that should have been Patrick's. All the times Katy had seen Jonah with Liam flashed through her mind—holding him, playing with him, rocking him to sleep as if caring for a baby was second nature to him. The memories focused her sadness and made it sharper. Resting her head upon her drawn-up knees, she gave in to tears, crying silently for Liam's loss, for the ache in her heart that encompassed the baby, Camilla, and Patrick, and for a loneliness that she was loath to acknowledge, a loneliness that wore Jonah Armstrong's face.

CHAPTER 15

Almost every person at Lake Bennett was in attendance early the next morning as little Liam Burke was laid to rest in a peaceful clearing a few minutes walk from the lakeshore. Few in the crowd were acquainted with Camilla and Patrick, but the death of an infant touched everyone. The few women in the tent town closed around Camilla in a circle of comfort, decent women and whores alike. Where babies were concerned, women were simply women, and no lines were drawn between the virtuous and the fallen. They shared stories of their own babies, some of them so sad that Katy wondered how women could bear to have children at all—such fragile things babies were, and so entwined in a woman's heart that the loss tore at the soul as nothing else could.

Katy stood a bit apart and listened to the women talk, feeling out of place—like a child looking on at an adult gathering. These women far surpassed her in both experience and courage, Katy reflected. She might be able to shoot the eye from a squirrel at a hundred paces, fight like hell, outsharp cardsharps, and ride circles around most cowpokes she knew, but these women who closed ranks around Camilla possessed a less flamboyant courage that was deep and firm as the very roots of the earth. They seldom received credit for it. Katy herself had scoffed at womanly accomplishments time and time again as she was growing up.

"Katy, are you all right?"

The unexpected concern came complete with a comforting hand on her shoulder. Katy looked up into Jonah's dark blue eyes, and her heart jolted. "Of course I'm all right."

Jonah regarded her with a slight smile and shook his head. "I don't think I've ever seen you look quite so done in."

Katy made an effort to straighten her shoulders and raise her chin, then decided the attempt was hopeless. "I'll miss Liam. I feel really sad for Camilla. I can't imagine birthing a baby, nursing and caring for it night and day, and then losing it. Why do women ever take the risk of having children?"

"Because they have a lot more courage than men do," Jonah answered. "The Good Lord knew if he gave men the job of birthing kids, this old world wouldn't go anywhere."

Katy heard no hint of teasing in his voice. Tears blurred her eyes—tears for Liam, for Camilla, and for her own suddenly obvious inadequacy.

"Come on." Jonah led her to a moss-covered log that offered a bench at the edge of the trees. "Sit down. Everything seems worse when you're tired."

"I'm sorry," she said as the tears overflowed. "This is stupid."

"Crying for a baby is stupid?" Jonah took a scarf from one pocket of his trousers and dabbed at her cheeks.

"I should be helping Camilla."

"Camilla has plenty of help. Maybe a good gullywasher of a cry would make you feel better."

She stubbornly sniffed back her tears.

"Don't you ever let yourself cry?" Jonah asked gently.

"No."

He smiled. "Only us sissy greenhorns get to cry, huh?"

A soft chuckle bubbled through Katy's tears. "You're not a sissy, Jonah Armstrong. Not much of a greenhorn anymore, either." She let herself look at him for a moment. Even blurred by her tears, his strong features seemed sharper than they had been when they'd parted. His hair was an uncombed tousle. The line that cut from nose to mouth was more deeply etched. The fan of creases at the corners of his eyes looked more like tired lines than laugh lines.

"You were great last night, Jonah. I don't know what we would have done without you."

"You were great yourself."

Inexplicably, the affectionate tenor of his words brought more tears to Katy's eyes. "Do you mind if I go ahead and have that cry?"

"Be my guest."

He held her during the storm of weeping, his fingers combing gently through her hair and stroking her back. Katy soaked his shirt with her tears, crying until she no longer knew what she cried about. The thud of Jonah's heart beat a steady, comforting rhythm next to her cheek. His hard chest was a rock that anchored her against the chaotic pull of her emotions. His arms wrapped her in a cocoon of warm affection that she couldn't resist. When the storm had finally passed, she left the safe harbor he provided with great reluctance.

"Now I really feel stupid," she admitted, pushing back from his embrace.

Jonah smiled. "You look like someone dumped you in the creek and wrung you out to dry."

"Thanks."

"Don't mention it."

They were alone now. During Katy's bout of weeping everyone had headed back to the lake, leaving little Liam to the peace of the forest. The clearing was indeed peaceful. Birds whistled down at them from their perches in the trees. A breeze sighed sadly through the spruce needles, sounding like the very breath of the earth. A surprising sense of quietude soothed Katy's soul. Jonah was right. A good gully-washer of a cry did make the world seem brighter.

She sniffed and wiped her nose on the scarf Jonah handed her. "My sister Ellen sometimes cries at the drop of a hat," Katy said with a small smile. "I always teased her for it."

"You have a sister?" Jonah slipped to the ground and sat with his back propped against the log.

"A twin sister."

Jonah rolled his eyes toward the blue sky. "There're two of you in the world."

Katy laughed. "Ellen is nothing like me. She's very quiet, but you have to watch out for her. When you're least expecting it, she'll slip something by that you never saw coming. She's going to medical school to become a doctor."

Jonah raised a brow.

Katy guiltily studied the ground. "My . . . uh . . . parents took her out to Cornell a few months ago."

The brow arched higher. "Are these the same parents who're so sadly dead and gone."

"Yeah. Well, I lied a bit."

"Just a bit?"

"I said they were gone," Katy reminded him. "I never said they were dead."

Jonah laughed. "Katy O'Connell, you are a devil. Not that I believed you in the first place."

"You didn't?"

"Hell no. You can't outslick a city slicker." His blue eyes twinkled up at her. "Is Katy O'Connell your real name?"

"Yeah. Although I've used others."

"Why doesn't that surprise me?" Jonah wondered aloud.

"When my pa was running from the law, we used his mother's name—Danaher. And then, there's the name my mother's uncle gave me when I was born. White Horse Woman. He named me after his favorite horse."

"His horse?"

"Among the Blackfoot, such a name is an honor," Katy informed him. She'd always been proud of her Indian name.

"Your mother's people were Blackfoot?"

"My real mother. Her name was Many Horses Woman." Katy looked Jonah in the eye, almost challenging, and awaited his reaction. She was proud of her Blackfoot heritage, but she'd been taunted with the name "half-breed" often enough to know that not everyone shared her respect for her mother's people.

Jonah's gaze didn't waver. "Your mother must have been the prettiest woman between here and the Mississippi."

A constriction Katy hadn't known was there loosened around her heart. "That's what my pa always said."

"This would be the pa who was running from the law?" he asked, one brow cocked.

"Yeah," Katy said proudly. "A mob was going to hang him, but I shot the rope in two and made off with him. That was when I was ten."

"They were going to hang him," Jonah repeated slowly. "Why?" He looked as if he didn't really want to know.

"Murder," Katy said matter-of-factly.

Jonah leaned his head back and contemplated the brilliant morning sky. "Murder. Great. I seduced the daughter of a murderer. I wonder how long I have to live."

"Pa's not a murderer," she replied indignantly. "He killed a man who hurt my mother."

"He only kills people who mess with his family. That's a comfort." The look on Jonah's face made Katy laugh in spite of the dark memories of that violent time in her young life. Jonah's eyes caught hers, and the laughter faded away, leaving a glow in the pit of her stomach.

"I like to hear you laugh, Katydid."

Her mind was suddenly muddled, roiled by the sudden intensity of his dark blue gaze. She labored to drag the conversation back to the light tenor of before. "Pa always says I'm too serious."

"Does he?"

She grinned. "Yeah. He does. Don't worry about Pa coming after you, Jonah. After all, you aren't the one who did the seducing, are you?"

"Wasn't I?"

The conversation hung on a precipice. Katy swallowed hard. A new warmth was blooming between them, and she discovered that she wanted more than anything to have Jonah as a friend again. Perhaps for that to happen, some of the clutter of the last few days needed to be swept away.

"No, you weren't." She met his eyes, and found that simple act took more guts than facing a grizzly. "I . . . I acted like a fool, prancing around and sniping at you because Maude had gotten me riled. Then things just sort of got away from me. You shouldn't feel guilty at all."

Jonah covered her hand where it rested on the log. "You weren't any more of a fool than I was, Katy, and I should have known better." A brow twitched, and a smile played around his mouth. "But I have to admit truthfully that I don't regret one minute of it."

Katy's face heated. His fingers played with hers. She understood now that if she didn't watch herself, she could very easily be a fool again.

"Katy O'Connell," Jonah said softly, "if I were your father, I would take a shotgun to me."

"The shotgun in the family belongs to me. My pa uses pistols."

His eyes twinkled. "Pistols. That makes me feel a lot safer."

Katy chuckled. "Don't worry. Pa's in Paris with Olivia— she's my stepma—visiting some of her friends there. Even if he were here, my pa knows I can take care of myself."

"Do you want to always take care of yourself, Katydid?"

Jonah's hand closed around hers. The blue fire in his eyes threatened to burn a hole in the strongest of her resolutions. She snatched her hand away.

"I do," she breathed.

Jonah merely smiled.

"Sheee-it!" Jud Hackett spit a brown gob of mucus into the dust at his feet. "That piss-yaller no-good cheatin' sonofabitch newspaper scribbler from Back East? Sure I remember 'im. 'Member 'im plain as day."

Gabriel O'Connell's eyes narrowed slightly. He didn't care much for either of the Hackett brothers, but neither did he care for some man luring his daughter into a wild-goose chase for Canadian gold.

"So yer Katy up and ran off with the fancy man, did she?" Jud chortled. "Ain't that jest like a woman? Fallin' fer a pretty face and sweet-talkin' ways instead of lookin' fer a man who gits dirty with a bit o' work. Thought yer Katy had more sense, though."

Gabriel glanced across Willow Bend's main street to the two-story frame house that was Willow Bend's hospital—Olivia's hospital, really, though she claimed it was Willow Bend's. In a moment or two, his wife would appear at the door looking for him. They were going to dinner at Millie Perkins's restaurant. Olivia would have seen him drive into town, and she'd be wondering what was keeping him. Gabe had seen Jud loitering by the door of the Watering Hole Liquor Emporium, however, and he couldn't resist asking a question or two.

"Tell me about the man," Gabe growled.

Jud grinned. "He was purty, all right. Slicker 'n a skunk that's been in the goose grease. Suckered me'n' Jacob into a game of cards—and you know we ain't easy to sucker. Let us win a few hands to get us hooked, then started some fancy stuff with the cards. When I calls 'im on it, yer girl took it in her mind to butt in. Guess he suckered her as well as he did me and my brother."

Gabe's eyes narrowed even more. "Young?"

"Young 'n' snortin' as a green stud horse jest turned out o' the barn."

"Good-looking?"

Jud blew a breath through the gap in his front teeth. "Real ladies' man, from what I could see. Kinda' surprised he took up with Katy. Seems ta me that curvy singer over at the Strand or even that pretty widder woman who runs the hotel would be more his style."

Gabe gave Jud a black look that made the grin fade from the man's face. Unreasoning anger welled up to choke him. Anger and fear—a combination not conducive to levelheaded thinking, but at the moment, Gabe didn't care about level-headed. A man could think and ruminate and cogitate all the day long on a problem and not move a single step toward solving the damned thing. Action was what he needed. To hell with level heads.

"Thanks, Jud."

Jud regarded him cautiously. "Anytime, Gabe. If'n you see the greenhorn skunk, tell 'im he owes me."

As Gabe had predicted, Olivia appeared at the door of the hospital. When she saw him leave Hackett's company, her head tilted in curiosity. She greeted him with one raised brow, but he didn't give her a chance to speak.

"I'm going to Dawson," he declared.

Olivia sighed. "Myrna said—"

"Yeah, I know Myrna said this Armstrong was some sort of church school teacher—"

"That's not exactly what she said. She described him as a nice, innocuous fellow who wouldn't hurt a fly."

"That tipped her hand right there," Gabe insisted. He took Olivia's arm and led her into the hospital. The sharp pungency of disinfectant leaked into the reception area from the adjoining surgery, but after being married to a physician for eight years, Gabe scarcely noticed the odor. He associated the scent with Olivia as another man might recognize his wife's favorite perfume. "No man who drinks and plays cards with the likes of Jud and Jacob Hackett is that innocent. Myrna's got a soft heart, and she's just trying to keep Katy out of trouble."

Olivia sat down in one of the chairs along the wall. She picked at an imaginary flaw in her white apron. "I can see you've made up your mind."

Gabe sat down beside her. The look she gave him was more

amused than annoyed. "I've been doing some reading on the Klondike," he said.

"Of course you have."

"The fastest way to get there is to take a steamer from Seattle to the mouth of the Yukon and then go up the river on a steamer to Dawson." Now that he'd made up his mind to go, Gabe felt the stir of adventure in his blood. New York and Paris had been all right because Olivia had been with him, but the Klondike was really more to his taste. For a moment he understood why Katy had gone. She was more like Gabe than a daughter should be. Not that she wasn't in a load of trouble for running off with some slick-talking, card-cheating no-account. The thought made him angry all over again.

"Gabe," Olivia said. "I want you to promise to keep a cool head where this young man is concerned. If you were anyone but her father, you'd know that Katy can very well take care of herself."

Gabe leaned back in his chair and folded his arms across his broad chest. "Katy can take care of herself with a bear or an ornery horse—but a man?" He scowled. "Jud Hackett says this Armstrong's a young, good-looking, cocky sonofabitch. A man like that has mostly one thing on his mind."

Olivia smiled wryly. "You ought to know."

Gabe's glare was only halfhearted. "I should have married a nice, meek Irish girl like my mother wanted me to."

"And I should have married my father's junior banking partner in New York." The dance of light in Olivia's eyes belied her Hippocratic dignity. "We seldom do what we really ought to do. Remember that when you catch up with Katy and this young man."

Katy could scarcely refrain from jumping up and down like an eager child. "We have a boat! I don't believe it!"

"Big enough for all five of us," Jonah said proudly as Andy and Patrick joined Katy at the campfire. "Hunter, too." He picked a piece of cold squirrel meat from the congealed leftovers of the night's supper and tossed it to the wolf. "Can't leave our best hunter behind."

"How the hell did you do it?" Patrick demanded. "I must have talked my tongue off at those boys up at the sawmill, and all they could say was they weren't takin' no more contracts."

Jonah gave them all a roguish grin. "You've gotta have the touch. Those poor lambs are out of their league dealing with a big city wolf like me."

Patrick returned his grin. "You part Irish, Armstrong?"

"Not a bit. Pure cussed Chicagoan. It's just as bad."

The dark night beyond the campfire suddenly seemed brighter as Katy contemplated being on their way once again. The promise of progress toward the goldfields made her heart beat and her toes tingle with the urge to dance. Traveling with Jonah once again had nothing to do with her excitement, Katy assured herself. Over the last few days, they had begun to build a friendship on the ruins of what had gone before. Nothing more than friendship, safe, undemanding friendship between two people who were sharing an adventure.

"How soon do we get our boat?" she asked.

Jonah's eyes twinkled at her. "Start packing your gear, Katydid. And fork over some coin. The boat's ours as soon as Mr. Rocco sees the color of our money."

Katy's heart warmed at the silly name he'd begun calling her. She'd told him huffily that she wasn't a bug, and he'd replied with an easy smile that it was no worse than being named after someone's horse. All the same, the nickname made her smile.

When morning dawned they got their first good look at the craft that would ferry them down the treacherous headwaters of the Yukon River. "I'm glad I know how to swim," Katy commented.

"It's not too bad," Patrick said.

Camilla, still sunk in the lethargy of grief, said nothing at all. Patrick put a cautious arm around her. "What do you think, lass? Our chariot to gold, eh? When we're rich, I'll buy you the fanciest house in Boston, and you'll have so many silk dresses that you'll wear one once and toss it in the ragbin. What do you think?"

Camilla shook her head sadly, her mouth a tight line.

The boat didn't look like much, but neither did any of the other flat-bottomed craft that daily started the journey downriver. Plenty large enough to take the five of them along with their gear, the boat had a sharply pointed bow and a wide, unwieldy-looking stern. It needed a final sealing with pitch, so despite Jonah's optimistic words, they couldn't leave that morning. In a few days time they would be on their way, though, which was a much more favorable prospect than the few weeks it would have taken them to build a boat from a share of lumber that Patrick and Jonah cut for the mill. A good thing it was, too, for an extended stay at Lake Bennett would not only have increased the risk of winter blowing through the pass and trapping them somewhere on the Yukon, but it also would have meant buying more food. The price of flour in the tent town was $140 per barrel, compared to $4 per barrel in Dyea. Other foodstuffs sold at similarly inflated rates. Understandably, nobody wanted to go grocery shopping.

After Liam's burial, the Armstrong and Burke parties had joined their camps in unspoken and mutual assent. Jonah's help during the crisis had bound them into a family of sorts, and his offer to share his precious boat solidified the union. They worked together to get the boat ready for its journey, and on the third morning they set sail just as the first golden rays of the sun touched the wooded slopes of the St. Elias Mountains, which rose steeply from either side of Lake Bennett. It was a glorious sunrise, a gorgeous day with a clean blue sky arching above them and just a hint of a breeze rippling the lake. Sitting in the bow with Camilla, one arm draped around Hunter while they watched the golden sunlight crawl down the mountain slopes, Katy took the day's beauty as a sign that from this time forward, the trip was going to progress without a hitch. What more could happen, after all?

So far she had been mistaken for a boy, unjustly fired from her first real job, attacked on the decks of a filthy, crowded little steamer, rained on until moss grew between her toes, nearly drowned in a flood, upstaged by a whore, and shown in a very hands-on demonstration just exactly what married ladies whispered about behind their hands. Worse than all that rolled into one, she'd had to watch a baby die.

No, Katy decided. The trip couldn't get any harder than it had already been. If she managed to get to Dawson in one piece, she would deserve every ounce of that fortune in gold she intended to find.

"Katy!" Jonah hollered from the stern, where he tended the rudder. "Quit staring at empty sky and raise the sail. There's a nice breeze coming up."

"Aye, aye," she said cheerfully.

Their makeshift sail, however, was not as easily handled as Katy had imagined, especially with that "nice breeze" making the heavy canvas billow and snap in her hands. Katy felt rather than saw the amusement in Jonah's eyes as he watched her struggle. Finally he turned the rudder over to Patrick and joined her at the mast.

"Sailing isn't one of your accomplishments?" he asked innocently.

"Sails are of little use in Montana," she snapped.

"Temper, Katydid. Don't let a piece of canvas get the best of you. Let me show you how."

"I suppose you can do it better?"

"Chicago's on a lake, Katy. A very big lake, with lots of sailboats. I've been boating since I was a kid."

"Oh."

"Let me demonstrate."

Katy wondered if it were really necessary for Jonah to trap her in the circle of his arms while he showed her how to raise and secure the sail. She should have told him in no uncertain terms to back off, sail or no sail. If they were to be friends, they should stay a friendly distance from each other. The heart palpitations that came from feeling his breath in her hair, his hard chest pressing into her back, his arms brushing along her ribs and sometimes—accidentally, Katy was sure—brushing the sides of her breasts: All that went far beyond friendship.

Katy couldn't quite get a sharp objection out of her mouth. The laughter in Jonah's eyes told her that her pretense at ignoring him was as transparent as glass. When the little session of instruction was over, Katy realized that she hadn't paid a bit of heed to his tips on sail handling.

A favorable wind pushed them that day almost to the limits of the twenty-six-mile-long lake. They camped that night just two miles above where Lake Bennett emptied into the channel known as Caribou Crossing. Wearied by the sun and wind and by the constant struggle to control the boat, they retired early to their tents—Patrick and Jonah to one, Camilla and Katy to the other. As was his habit, Andy took a blanket and made himself a bed beside the open fire.

"I likes ta sleep without other gents snorin' in my ear," he announced when Camilla expressed concern. "Don't you worry none, ma'am. I could sleep on a block of ice if'n I had to, and if it rains, it don't bother me none. I'm a good sleeper."

Accustomed to Andy's peculiar ways, Jonah and Katy knew better than to argue.

"Is the boy always so stubborn?" Camilla asked Katy in the privacy of their tent.

"This is nothing," Katy told her. "On the way up the pass he went off into the woods to sleep. He doesn't like crowds, I guess."

A brief, dry chuckle escaped Camilla's lips. "I guess he's been doing the same since we've been camped together, and I didn't notice."

"You've had other things on your mind," Katy said quietly.

"Yes, I have."

Camilla had new lines in her face. Her eyes seemed more sunken, her cheeks more hollow. But she never mentioned Liam's name, and her rage against Patrick was past. Tonight, however, was the first sign of Camilla noticing anything in the world other than her grief.

"He's a nice boy, is that Andy, but wild as a wolf cub." Camilla smiled slightly. "Someone needs to take him in hand, don't you think?"

The light of a maternal crusade brightened some of the shadows around Camilla's eyes. Katy was glad the Irishwoman was showing some interest in life again, and could only be glad she had set her sights upon poor Andy and not her.

Her gratitude, however, came a bit too early.

CHAPTER 16

By the time they had sailed through the two-mile channel of Caribou Crossing and into Lake Tagish the next morning, Camilla had expanded her crusade to include Katy. It had started before breakfast when Andy, with instincts honed no doubt by practice avoiding his own mother's attention, deftly dodged Camilla's insistence that she should mend his clothing.

"No time right now, Miz Burke," he'd said with false regret. "Got to catch us some fish for breakfast."

"I'll go with you," Katy offered quickly, but Camilla's gentle hand on her arm made escape impossible.

"Katy, dear, why don't we start to work on some proper clothing for you? Wouldn't you like to wear something besides those terrible trousers?"

Katy watched a grinning Andy escape to the lakeshore with a fishing pole. "I . . . uh . . . no," she said with a sigh. "To tell the truth, Camilla, I got mad and threw my dresses away after those stupid skirts nearly drowned me at Sheep Camp."

Not quite the truth. Trousers seemed a talisman of protection after what had happened at Stone House. If she didn't dress like a woman, then she needn't worry about her woman's heart and woman's foolishness. Trousers were more practical than skirt and petticoats anyway. She didn't know why she had ever set out on this journey in bothersome women's garb.

"An understandable reaction, dear." Camilla regarded her with an understanding that was all too piercing. "You are a woman, though, and women are expected to bear with these little inconveniences. We'll simply make you something more proper to wear."

Katy sighed. She was lucky there were no yard goods stores in the Yukon wilderness.

By the time they'd breakfasted on the whitefish and grayling that Andy caught, Camilla had solved that problem by deciding to alter a couple of her own skirts to fit Katy. The Irishwoman still had her eye on Andy, though, surveying with disapproval the wild reddish hair that stuck out from beneath the boy's cap, the baggy, dirty flannel shirt, and the threadbare knees of his britches. While Patrick and Jonah watched in amusement, Andy stayed as far away from Camilla as he could manage.

Once they were on the water, Katy didn't have much to do besides watch Jonah, for Lake Tagish was a nineteen-mile stretch of calm water that required little attention to the boat or sail. There were things other than Jonah to watch, of course. On either side of their watery highway, mountains climbed toward the sky in spectacular ruggedness. Hawks circled on rising currents of air, and in the late morning a solitary eagle swept over the valley in silent majesty. Flotillas of wild ducks quacked at them from beyond Andy's stone-throwing range. Fish jumped. Clouds played chase with the sun, creating shadows that raced through the valley and over the mountains.

In spite of nature's entertaining show, Katy's eyes kept returning to Jonah—Jonah helping Andy set the sail, or talking to Patrick, both men hunkered on their heels at the rudder and laughing at something that doubtless only men would find amusing. The onetime tenderfoot had grown as rugged-looking as the mountains around them—tanned, his jaw darkened with a thick, short growth of beard he no longer bothered to shave. The warmth of the Indian summer sun had prompted him to shed his jacket, and beneath his shirt hard muscle rolled and stretched with every movement.

Not that Katy was moved by all that masculinity. Well, maybe she was moved a little, she admitted to herself. At Stone House she'd proved her susceptibility in no uncertain terms.

That night they dined on duck spitted over the fire—thanks to Katy's rock sling and Patrick's willingness to wade into the lake to retrieve the duck.

"If we had a good hunting dog along," Jonah commented with a waggle of his brow toward Hunter, "Patrick wouldn't have to get wet."

Hunter pricked his ears at Jonah's words, then curled comfortably on the warm sand of the shore with an aloof indolence that communicated better than words that wolves were far above that sort of thing.

The evening passed peacefully. Hopes were beginning to edge upward again, dissipating the dark mood that had gripped all of them since Liam's death. Patrick tried to teach Jonah to play the fiddle, without much success. Andy practiced with Katy's rock sling while Hunter watched, and Camilla busied herself altering one of her skirts and petticoats to preserve Katy's propriety. Katy was suddenly homesick—something she thought she would never be. She wondered if her pa, Olivia, and little David were back from Paris yet, and what they thought of her leaving on her great adventure.

"Hey, Katydid. Why the long face?" Jonah sat down beside her on the driftwood log she had dragged to the fire to serve as a bench.

"What long face?"

He placed a fingertip at the corner of her mouth and tugged it downward. "That long face. You look as if someone told you there was no more gold to be had in the Klondike."

Katy tried not to shiver at his touch, but the feel of him—just the tip of his finger, even—sent a ribbon of warmth curling through her, the kind of warmth that made a person shiver instead of sweat.

"No long face," she denied. "I'm happy as can be. At least I am until Camilla finishes that stupid skirt and petticoat and steals my britches."

"Good for Camilla," Jonah said. He slipped off the log and settled his buttocks into the sand, stretched his arms above his head and yawned. "You're too old to be running around in trousers, you know."

There was that insidious curl of heat again, starting between her legs and shooting upward through her stomach to her heart. That yawny stretch of Jonah's must have showcased every damned manly muscle in his arms and chest.

"I like trousers," she argued. "You try running around in skirts and see how much you like it."

He let his eyes wander over her legs and hips in a manner that made her want to squirm. "I think I like you in trousers better than I would like me in skirts."

Katy had to laugh at the image of his hairy ankles peeking from beneath a frilly hem. He laughed with her. Suddenly she wanted to reach out and feel the texture of his beard, but she didn't. Such a gesture would be expected of a lover, or a wife, but not a friend, and she had made her choice. He was doing his part by treating her like the sister Patrick Burke still believed she was—unless Camilla had filled him in on their little deception. Still, Katy was suspicious of all the times in the last few days that Jonah had brushed close by her with seeming innocence, the opportunities he took for small touches, his comments and smiles that might have been innocently spoken to a true sister but had double, seductive meanings for one who wasn't. Katy wondered what Olivia would tell her to do about Jonah. Would her pa like him? Probably not. In many ways, Jonah was like her pa—ways that Gabe O'Connell probably wouldn't appreciate.

Jonah got to his feet and brushed the sand from his trousers. "Gonna go check the nets," he said. "Maybe a nice trout or salmon decided to sacrifice itself for tomorrow's breakfast. You coming?"

"Sure," Katy said.

He put his arm around her when they left the heat of the fire. Katy felt the effect of his touch from her shoulders to her toes. In the moonlight, Jonah's grin looked wicked and knowing. Her imagination was playing games with her, Katy told herself. Or maybe the one playing games was Jonah.

Jonah had been called a variety of uncomplimentary names in his life, but no one had ever called him a quitter. On the contrary, in journalistic and political circles in Chicago, he had a reputation as a bulldog—once he got hold of something he seldom let go.

Unfortunately, he frequently had the finesse of a bulldog as well. He'd certainly done a fair job of spooking Katy with his charge into the subject of marriage—not once, but twice. His mistake was in assuming she was like almost every other young woman in having marriage at the top of her priorities. He should have known better. Katy was like no other woman he'd ever met. That was part of her allure. But in spite of her skittishness, he had no intention of giving up, and the more he watched her, the more certain he was that Katy was worth fighting for.

Watching Katy had become Jonah's favorite pastime. As they sailed through the dawn pinks and roses that painted the quiet waters of Lake Tagish, Katy sat in the bow with Camilla, enduring the woman's instruction in needlework. Jonah watched them, his mouth curling in amusement. Katy had no use for sewing or other such feminine pursuits; she'd told him often enough. But she was kind enough to let Camilla assuage her maternal needs with Katy as victim. When they stopped for the noon meal, he watched her practicing the rock sling with Andy. The two of them together looked like kids out for a lark. Katy could out-imp the boy who was king of the imps. Sometimes she looked like a boy herself in her britches and loose-fitting shirt. Other times she looked so much like a woman that Jonah could scarcely catch his breath. She sang through his blood and smiled at him in his dreams—the woman whose innocent ardor had been a flame in the night, whose guileless passion had touched off a chord of response that still hummed through every fiber of his body.

The sailed out of Lake Tagish and over six miles of river into Lake Marsh without incident. Days marched by as the miles fell behind them. Mornings were cold and misty, and in the early hours a scum of ice covered rain puddles and the camp wash water, a reminder that the arctic winter was breathing down their necks. Generally, though, the weather was kind. Morning clouds and fog gave way to blue skies and sunshine by noon. Heavily laden though it was with five people, a wolf, and two tons of supplies, the boat proved a worthy craft with no leaks and a comfortable steadiness under sail. Fish were plentiful and easily caught, and the shores were rich with cranberries, blueberries, pineberries, and wild currants.

They were not alone in enjoying the Indian summer. Usually they had at least one other boat in sight, and the last night on lake Marsh, Jonah counted five campfires winking from the lakeshore. At times the mountains and the cold night air would play tricks with sound, and conversations or singing from other camps would drift to his ears. All the Klondikers seemed in high spirits. Jonah made note of it in his journal.

The majestic beauty of the mountains and river is enough to lift the spirits of the most cynical and mercenary of goldseekers, he wrote. *Like beads strung on a necklace, the glassy smooth lakes follow one after another with short sections of peaceful river between them. The journey has mellowed. Where we fought rain, mud,*

and crowds to struggle to the summit of Chilkoot Pass,
on the headwaters of the Yukon we struggle not at all.
The river and the woods feed us; the sun and blue skies
pamper us., Here there are no crowds, for many who
struggled toward the pass turned around in discourage-
ment or still labor to build their boats at Lake Bennett.
We are the lucky ones who sail down this beautiful river
toward Dawson while winter prepares to close the doors
to the goldfields behind us.

All in all, Jonah thought as he closed his notebook, the hazards of this part of the trip to Dawson had been greatly exaggerated in stories and rumors. He continued in that thinking
until they sailed out of Lake Marsh and into the stretch of the
Yukon River known as Miles Canyon.

The three-quarter-mile canyon was the first set of real
rapids they encountered. They beached the boat a short distance above the rough water and climbed the bank to examine
the challenge before them. The rapids didn't look too bad,
Jonah thought. Perhaps he didn't find them frightening because of his long experience sailing. Or perhaps, he thought
some while later, he was so blasé because he was an arrogant,
stupid fool, for once they eased the boat down the chute of
fast water that led to the rapids, he found himself battling the
rudder for all of their lives. The boat that had proved so steady
on the lakes dropped sickeningly into troughs so deep they
could see the rocks of the river bottom through the rushing
green water. For a few tense seconds, the boat would wallow,
then lift as the current carried them into a foam-flecked standing wave. The rudder jerked violently in his hands as the boat
tried to turn its side to the wave and capsize. Water broke over
the boat, pounding them like a huge freezing hammer. They
shot out of the wave, bow pointed toward the sky, then
dropped once more, and the terrifying cycle began again.

They were drenched in seconds. Everything that wasn't
tied down went overboard. Katy had insisted that a rope be

strung from bow to stern for the passengers to cling to. She sat in the bow, the most vulnerable spot in the boat, Jonah realized as he saw the front of the boat lift to plow through another wave. With one hand she grasped the rope. Her other arm was wrapped around Hunter in a secure vise. Even fighting the boat, the current, the foaming white water, and his own unexpected, gut-wrenching fear, Jonah found one part of his attention riveted on Katy. Of all of them, she was the only one not screaming with fear. Her shout carried above the crash and roar of the water, but it was a shout of exhilaration, not terror. She met each plunge into a trough with a whoop of joy and each hammering wave with a smile of glee, riding the bucking, tossing boat as a bronc rider might ride his wild mount. Hair streaming water, eyes alight, she glowed, and the glow infected Jonah with some of the same foolish, fervent courage that let her see the wild ride as adventure, not terror. He smiled. He cursed the rudder that tried to jump from his grip and the boat that wanted to wallow sideways into the next wave, but with the curse came a wild grin. Katy turned her head briefly to glance at him. She smiled widely and laughed. Jonah laughed with her.

After sixty seconds of chewing them up, the river spit them out the bottom of the rapids, where the water subsided into innocent, smooth green ripples as if it had never transformed itself into a raging monster. They beached the boat to check for loss and damage. Jonah succumbed to the need to engulf Katy in a hug.

She hugged him back. Her delicate brows lifted playfully. "Fun, huh?"

The warmth that softened his heart had nothing to do with desire or sex. Jonah had only thought he was living before he met Katy. If he lost her, her leaving would rip out the core of his heart.

Their boat had come through the rapids with no damage, and, thanks to Katy's insistence that they tie everything down, little had been lost overboard. Nearly sixty miles of river lay ahead of them before reaching the little town of Whitehorse and a short distance beyond Lake Laberge. A much greater distance lay between them and Dawson, and the distance included more stretches of white water whose names and reputations had drifted back over the trail from those who had gone before them. After enduring Miles Canyon, Jonah figured he should have been downright scared at the prospect. If he had any sense he would have been. Instead, he felt as though someone had pumped the fresh juice of life into his veins.

From Miles Canyon, the Yukon gathered momentum as it rushed on its way, gathering the water of side streams and rivulets along its way. It tossed them about in riffles and choppy water, but nothing as challenging as the Canyon. Every night Jonah chronicled the day's events in his journal, and in rereading his own words, recognized his own growing fascination and affection for this wild and rugged land. He purged his impatience to actively pursue Katy—and perhaps once again frighten her away—by adding to the character sketch he'd written of her. It would never be published, Jonah acknowledged to himself. When he'd started to write it, he'd had every intention of sending it to his editor, but now he realized that the picture of Katy on those sheets of paper was for him to savor, not share. No matter how brilliantly he might write, however, words on paper would never have the same glow as Katy in the flesh.

"Trout's done," Andy called from where he squatted by the fire. Jonah had always liked fish, but they'd eaten so much of it lately he thought he might grow fins.

Katy gave a little yip of joy as she helped Camilla lift the cast-iron Dutch oven out of the coals. The Irishwoman had wrought a miracle in baking a blueberry cobbler for dessert. "Would you just look at that?" Katy chortled. She looked like a hungry urchin eyeing the goods in a bakeshop window. "If I could cook something like that, it might be worthwhile to learn how to cook."

"Katy dear, it's not that difficult."

Jonah had to smile. Camilla would never give up. She had badgered Andy into washing his face—even to the extent of his ears—before every meal, and she had convinced Katy to don feminine attire once again, if only during evenings in camp. Jonah missed the trousers. If Camilla could convince Katy to take up cooking, though, he certainly wouldn't object to that. He had ambitions for Katy that would make her knowing how to cook a welcome skill.

Later that evening, stomachs contentedly full with trout and blueberry cobbler, Katy lingered beside the fire after Camilla, Patrick, and Andy had retired to their respective beds. Jonah joined her in the late-night vigil, and she didn't object. Without the intrusion of human voices, the night was unbelievably peaceful. Stars lit the sky in a glorious blaze, and newfallen snow on the high peaks glowed in the stars' gaudy light. The silence was broken only by the hushed whisper of the river and small sounds of life that burrowed and skittered in the forest. Hunter sat beside Katy, his ears moving like furry antennae to gather in every sound of the night.

Drinking in the peacefulness, Jonah could feel a contentment radiating from Katy that was similar to his own. All her brashness had quieted to peace. Her verve, drive, and sparkle slowed from a boil to a warm, comfortable simmer.

Katy sighed and drew her knees up to her chest. One of Camilla's shawls draped her shoulders, and she tightened it around her to keep out the night's chill. "Mountains like these remind me of the story my grandmother Squirrel Woman used to tell me and my sister on summer nights we spent in her lodge."

"What was the story?" Jonah asked.

"It was about the Old Man who created the world and everything in it. His name was Napi, and he walked over the earth piling up rocks into mountains and carving out the beds of rivers and seas and lakes. He made all the plants and animals and people and told each how they should live."

"Big job," Jonah said wryly. "Did he do it alone?"

"No. Eventually he made himself a wife. Old Woman. She agreed that Old Man should have the first say in everything, as long as she got the second say."

"Hm. The origin of women's suffrage."

"What?"

"Never mind."

Katy's tempting little mouth curved upward in an impish smile. "Squirrel Woman says Old Man only thought he had first say."

Jonah chuckled. "If Napi was anything like men today, then Squirrel Woman was right. What happened to poor old Napi?"

"After he was done creating the world, he went to live in a mountain in Alberta. I've never seen the mountain, though my uncle Crooked Stick has. I'd think it looks a lot like that mountain over there." Her chin pointed toward a glowing white peak that dwarfed the others around it. Lesser mountains clustered about its slope like acolytes sitting at the feet of a master.

"Not a bad place to spend retirement, if one were the creator of all this," Jonah commented.

Katy cut him a suspicious look. "You're making fun of me."

"No. The longer I stay in these mountains, the more they awe me. Sometimes, looking at these peaks, I feel like I could open my mouth and speak directly to God."

Katy nodded her head. "I suppose you don't have mountains in Chicago."

"Hardly even an anthill."

"Like the plains in eastern Montana?"

"Not exactly. The country around Chicago has a lot of rivers, and everything that hasn't been cleared for farming is thick with trees. Nothing is sharp there like it is here. Even on a clear day, the moisture in the air seems to soften the edges of everything you see. The horizon, the trees, buildings, the clouds in the sky—everything looks just a bit blurred. The air feels soft, like a caress on your skin. The country there is beautiful, but it's a tamer, more serene beauty than what we see here." He could see her musing upon the picture he drew. "Wouldn't you like to see other parts of the world someday, Katy?"

She nodded thoughtfully. "After I make my fortune. But just to visit and see what there is to see. I'd always have to come back home to the mountains. They're my roots."

Jonah was tempted to tell her that letting herself love him would give her stronger roots than burying herself in the mountains, but he was beginning to understand the spell the West could cast on a person's heart. Fighting the West and its mystique was worse in some ways than fighting a flesh-and-blood rival—except, Jonah thought with some confidence—he had some weapons at his disposal that the mountains, rivers, and clear air didn't have, and he wasn't ashamed to use them.

They sat for a while longer in silence before Katy said good-night. "Will you bank the fire when you leave?" Katy asked.

"Sure. I've gotten good at banking fires."

She wound the shawl more tightly around herself and started to rise from the log that was their bench, but Jonah stopped her with a gentle touch on her arm. "Sleep well," he said, and cautiously pressed his lips to hers in a kiss. She didn't move away, but tentatively put her hands on his upper arms. As he deepened the kiss, her fingers dug into his biceps. The scent of her—wild forest and woman—made his nostrils flare in sensual pleasure; the pliable softness of her lips inspired a predictable reaction at his groin, but he didn't yield to the temptation to fold her against him and show her just how much he wanted her. Until she realized that she wanted him just as much, he would be patient.

When he let her go, her breath puffed into the air in frosty little gasps. He raised one brow at her and smiled. "More fun tomorrow," he reminded her.

She looked dazed. "What?"

"Another wild ride." Even in the ruddy firelight, he could see high color flood her face. "More rapids," he reminded her.

Katy gusted out a breath into the cold air. "Rapids. Right. Whitehorse Rapids."

"Maybe your Blackfoot name will keep us safe riding through them, White Horse Woman."

She stood up, putting distance between them. "Yeah. That's what Squirrel Woman would say." She smiled tentatively. "She'd say the rapids and I, we have the same spirit looking after us. You've got an Indian turn of mind, Jonah Armstrong."

"Is that good?"

"I think so." For a moment she stood gazing at him as if she might want to kiss him again, but in the end she turned away toward the tent.

"Good-night, Katydid."

She flashed him a smile over her shoulder, then was swallowed by the darkness. He heard the rustle of the tent flap. Hunter stayed by the fire, sitting placidly on his haunches, head cocked mockingly as if he could read Jonah's mind.

"Well, go on," Jonah urged the animal. "Go keep her company, since I can't."

The wolf got up and trotted in the direction of the tent. Jonah scratched at his new beard and gazed morosely into the fire. "Keep the spot beside her warm, wolf," he whispered. "I'll be there one of these days soon."

Five boats had pulled ashore above Whitehorse Rapids to preview the churning water they would soon ride. The rapids had a nasty reputation, and Klondikers usually waited for several boats to gather before anyone made an attempt to shoot the white water—just in case something went wrong and a rescue was needed. Stories of disasters in Whitehorse Rapids floated regularly up the river to meet the Klondikers making their way downstream. Katy had dismissed many of the stories as rumors designed to encourage the fainthearted to turn back, therefore leaving more gold for those with the guts to continue. But standing on a rock that overlooked the channel of churning white water, she gave more credit to the stories' truth. The toll the rapids had taken decorated the banks on either side of the river—scrap wood that had once been boats, barrels, and boxes that had once held miners' provisions, clothing, cook pots, and unidentifiable bits of flotsam that had once been bound for Dawson.

Beside her, Camilla put a hand to her mouth. "Oh my."

"We'll be fine," Patrick assured her blithely. "Look. There's the first boat going through right now."

The boat was a three-man craft. One man steered the boat with the rudder and the other two aided the steering by paddling according to the rudderman's orders. They slipped down the chute—the smooth tongue of water that rushed from the upper lip of the rapids—and into the white water.

"That man at the rudder knows what he's doing," Jonah commented.

The little craft deftly dodged rocks and a dead tree that reached out into the current like a skeletal arm reaching for passing boats.

"Hell," Patrick said. "The run isn't that hard. They're getting through just fine."

Katy was silent. She couldn't share Patrick's casual attitude about the torrent. The roar of the water seemed to shake the very walls of the valley.

"They're in trouble," Camilla gasped.

The boat plunged toward a huge hole in the river created by the downthrust of water over a submerged rock. Katy could see the rudderman shout as he attempted to veer away. Caught in an eddy of current, the boat spun in a circle. The oarsmen paddled frantically. The boat stopped spinning, then plunged into the hole stern first. For endless moments it disappeared from view. Katy heard the collective intake of breath of all those on the bank watching. Fully a dozen Klondikers waited for something to reappear—a boat or splinters of a boat. After what seemed an eternity the game little craft shot out of the hole, bow pointed toward the sky. It flew clear of the water and for a breathless moment hovered in the air. Then the water reached out and grabbed it. The oarsmen put their muscles into their paddling. The boat straightened and surged forward, heading toward calmer water. Katy watched them until they disappeared downstream amid the spray and foam. They had perhaps another half mile of rough water to endure, but for them, the worst was over. They would pull to shore downstream and wait for the other boats, standing guard over the mouth of the rapids to snatch people and goods from the river if the need arose.

The second boat negotiated the rapids without excitement or incident. The third bounced off a rock or two, but held together and was still upright when it disappeared downstream.

Camilla gripped Katy's hand when it came their turn to brave the passage. "It'll be fine," Katy told her, hoping it was true. The other rapids they had bounced through had been fun, not frightening; the other rapids had been mere riffles compared to Whitehorse.

Patrick was at the rudder as they drifted toward the drop-off that was the chute into the rapid. With the roar of the water deafening her ears and uneasiness clutching her stomach, Katy would have felt more confident with Jonah steering, but it was Patrick's turn, and the Irishman was loudly confident of his ability to get them through safely. Jonah sat in the bow, oar in hand, and Andy sat opposite him. Camilla and Katy crouched amidships, hands gripping the tie-down ropes, arms linked. Camilla was as pale as ash, and Andy didn't look much better. Jonah's face was impassive except for the ever so slight wink he sent in Katy's direction—or was that simply her imagination.

Hunter had declined to join them in the adventure. He trotted along the bank as they floated downstream, then, when the gently sloping valley tightened to a steep-walled gorge, he easily loped to the top of the cliffs and watched their passage as they had watched others.

Katy had a bad feeling about Hunter's temporary desertion. Maybe the wolf had more sense than they did. She gripped Camilla tightly as the boat rushed down the chute, suddenly wishing that she had given in to the urge to kiss Jonah one more time the night before. All night long her dreams had been haunted by that step she hadn't taken, that one step where her courage had failed her. Suddenly, as the roar of the water and the cold slap of the river in her face drowned all other sensations, that one missed kiss seemed very important.

Their run started well. Patrick deftly avoided the hole that had captured the first boat. Their boat bucked, plunged, and wallowed, but it remained under control with its bow pointed downstream. Then an errant twist of current sent them against a rock. They merely nudged it and bounced off, but the nudge slapped the rudder from Patrick's hands. Before the Irishman could regain control, their one effective steering device was split and splintered. Jonah lurched to the stern to use his oar as a rudder, but the river had them and wouldn't let go. Katy screamed as the boat upended. The river reached up and grabbed her.

CHAPTER 17

Hunter's warm tongue persuaded Katy to regain her senses. It slithered wetly over her cheek and ear. A cold nose snuffled through her hair, and then the tongue returned, licking insistently. She slitted her eyes open to see a very close-up view of river sand and small bits of waterworn driftwood.

The cold nose landed on the nape of her neck.

"Aaaargh! Enough!"

She rolled into a little ball, shivering. Gradually she became aware that the roar battering her ears was the river. Dim memories of being in the water teased her groggy mind. The fight to stay afloat. The gritty taste of the water, the quick numbing of her body. She'd scarcely felt the pain of being pummeled upon the rocks like a piece of tough steak being pounded by a butcher. Someone had grabbed at her—Jonah? They had clung together for only a moment before the current ripped them apart. Jonah. Where was he?

Panic shot a bolt of energy through her quaking limbs. She sprang up, only to land on her backside once again as a wave of dizziness swamped her. "Jonah!" she groaned.

Hunter growled softly, then trotted a few paces upstream. Katy turned painfully to look. Twenty feet away, a body was draped loosely over the sand and cobbles. Katy crawled on hands and knees toward it, terrified. She recognized the khaki-colored parka that covered those broad shoulders. She recognized the rich brown hair plastered to the back of that head.

With great effort she turned him over. His face was full of sand. A gash over his eye spilled crimson down his cheek.

"Jonah! Don't you dare be dead, you ignorant, miserable greenhorn!" She shook him, slapped his face. He breathed out a liquid gurgle. Katy pushed and shoved until he lay on his belly, then pounded on his broad back until he coughed up what seemed a bucketful of water. He arched up beneath her pounding and groaned.

"Goddamn!" He spewed up another fountain of water, then succumbed to another bout of coughing.

"Jonah!"

"Katy!" He rolled over and caught her by the arms. "Katy!" Gasping for breath, he dug his fingers into her arms as if to keep the river from snatching them apart once again.

Katy surrendered to her dizziness and bent over until her head rested on his chest. He threaded his fingers through her hair.

"Goddamn!" he croaked. "If it isn't one thing, it's another."

She half giggled, half wept into the soggy front of his shirt. Her head pounded, every muscle screamed in pain, and she felt as though she had swallowed half the stinking Yukon River.

Hunter stuck his nose against Katy's face and huffed.

"You knew, you old wolf you," Jonah said. "You had better sense than all of us." He massaged Katy's neck, her shoulders, her back, pressing her into the solid comfort of his chest. "Are you all right, Katydid?"

"Yeah." She reluctantly pushed herself away from him. "You?"

"Unnnh!" He groaned as he sat up, flexed his arms, moved his legs. "Everything seems in working order, more or less. The others?"

"I don't know."

When she had come to her senses, Katy's mind had been filled with Jonah, but now the rest of the world impinged on her awareness. Other Klondikers were scrambling down the steep cliffs toward them. Not far from where the river had spit Katy out upon the sand were two wooden boxes. One had splintered and spewed its contents of cooking utensils upon the ground; the other was intact. Of the boat there was no sign, nor of the other three passengers. An awful dread closed its cold hand around Katy's stomach.

"There's Camilla!" Jonah pointed toward the opposite bank, where a man was helping a sodden woman to her feet. Katy squinted for a closer look, but the man didn't look like Patrick. He had to be a rescuer from one of the other boats. The man waved his arm at them, signaling that Camilla was all right.

They searched for ten minutes before coming upon Andy. He was wedged between two rocks in the shallow water, limply hanging there with his legs and hips submerged in the freezing river. Jonah waded out to fetch the boy in.

"He's alive," he called back, then hesitated. "What the hell?"

"What's wrong?" Katy yelled.

"Well goddamn me for a stupid blind idiot." Jonah gave a great bark of laughter. "Twice fooled in as many months!"

"What?"

Jonah hefted Andy over one shoulder and waded back to shore.

"Is he all right?" Katy demanded. She saw nothing in the situation humorous enough to merit Jonah's intermittent chuckles.

"Bruised. Waterlogged. Scraped. That finger looks broken," he said as he laid Andy out upon the sand.

Katy saw immediately what inspired Jonah's strange behavior. Andy's parka had been torn from his body by the current, and his shirt clung soddenly to a pair of budding, adolescent breasts. Andy was not a he, but a she, and a clever she at that, having fooled them all during many days of living together in rather intimate circumstances.

"Well I'll be damned," Katy said, shaking her head in chagrin.

Jonah grinned. "Now you know how I felt on the train that day."

Just then Andy opened her eyes and groaned. Katy knelt beside her and brushed aside the scraggly red hair the river had plastered over her face. Andy rolled over and coughed up river water. "Am I dead?" she groaned.

"Not yet," Jonah answered wryly. "But you're gonna be."

Andy's explanations had to wait, however, for Patrick was still missing. Katy and Jonah scoured the riverbank on one side while two men from another party searched the other bank. Camilla, who had been transported across the river in the calm water above the rapids, was put in Andy's charge near a fire the rescuers had built.

Searchers found Patrick in the midafternoon, half a mile beyond the mouth of the rapids. His battered body was tangled in a little jetty of dead branches that sieved the calm water near the shore. The boyish face was a ghastly bluish white, and the merry Irish eyes stared sightlessly at the sky. Patrick Burke would never see the goldfields of the Klondike.

Camilla took the news too calmly. She stood like a stone throughout Patrick's burial, shedding not a tear as a stranger read from the Bible over the freshly turned earth of her husband's grave. When Katy escorted her to the tent that had been loaned to them, Camilla allowed herself to be led along like a child. Katy didn't know what to say in comfort. The Irishwoman had lost her baby son and now her husband. How much could a woman bear in one lifetime?

Katy got Camilla into dry clothes—donated trousers and a wool shirt that came down to her knees—and wrapped her in a blanket. Camilla hiccoughed out a tentative sob as Katy pulled the blanket around her. "He died . . . he died without

me telling him that I forgive him." Tears welled in her eyes.
"He'll never know. Now he'll never know. I shouldn't have
blamed him for Liam's death. I shouldn't have said those hor-
rible things to him."

Katy patted her arm. "You had every right to be angry with
him, Camilla. And he does know. I'm sure he does."

Camilla let loose a miserable sigh and seemed to draw into
the blanket as a turtle might retreat into its shell. Katy finally
persuaded her to sleep with the help of a quarter of a bottle of
fine Scotch whiskey. She left her snoring gently. Some of the
color had returned to the Irishwoman's face, and her arms
clutched a wad of the blanket as if it were a baby.

Jonah and Andy sat disconsolately by the fire. Jonah raised
his head as Katy sat on the ground beside him. "Camilla
sleeping?"

"Like a mule kicked her in the head. The whiskey helped."

Jonah rubbed his brow with one hand. "I could use a shot
of whiskey myself."

"I could get the bottle. Camilla doesn't need it anymore."

"No." He sighed. "A hangover would just make things
worse." He eyed Andy, who sat cross-legged on the other side
of the fire. She looked every bit the boy again, hat jammed
crookedly upon her head, red hair sticking out from beneath
at odd angles, shapeless clothing hiding the least hint of her
form. "It's been a hell of a day," Jonah said.

Katy looked around the camp at the few scattered items
from their outfit that the river had tossed up. Jonah's note-
books were intact, along with a few items of Jonah's underwear, an extra pair of boots, and a scarf. They'd also rescued
a sodden sack of flour, three blankets, a single mitten, and
Jonah's baby-sized pistol. Camilla had lost everything, including her husband. Andy had lost her false identity, and
Katy felt as though she'd lost all the starch in her spirit.

"I'm goin' to bed," Andy said, pushing herself off her
haunches.

"That's what you think," Jonah replied sternly. "Sit down, you little imp of the devil."

Andy gusted out a rebellious breath and sat. "I suppose you're riled."

"I'm getting tired of not knowing whether the people I hire, travel with, eat with, and sleep with are male or female. Annoying is what it is."

Katy detected a bit of reprimand in his statement for her as well as Andy. "Now, Jonah . . . "

"You be quiet, Katy. I'm thinking you two are pretty much birds of a feather."

The same thing had occurred to Katy. She couldn't help but feel some kinship with the little scamp.

"Now. Andy. You're going to come clean, or you're going to find yourself without employment. Not"—Jonah gestured to the paucity of their camp—"that we have much left to employ you with."

Andy gave them both a resentful look and folded her arms and legs in upon herself.

"What's your real name. It couldn't be Andy."

"Alexandra." She drew out the syllables in a mockery of hauteur. "A grand name, ain't it, for a whore's kid? Sounds like some sorta pissin' princess. I like Andy better. It fits me."

"Why didn't you tell us you were a girl?"

Andy laughed sharply. "You think a girl would've gotten a job mindin' Jack Decker's horses? Decker might hire a female to do something in his stable, but it wouldn't be cleanin' up horse crap and slingin' hay. You think that *you* would've hired me if'n you'd known I squatted to piss instead of standin' up?"

Jonah cleared his throat. Katy was tempted to laugh. "She's right, Jonah."

"You would be on her side!"

"Somebody has to!"

"I seen what happens to girls who ain't got no folks or money," Andy declared. "My ma was a whore, and I got around the streets and the sportin' houses and saw gals younger'n me workin' on their backs 'cause they had no place to go. Not me, though. I'm gonna find gold in the Klondike, and I'm gonna have all the money I need. I swore I would if it took me years of working myself to the bone to get there. I shoveled coal in a steamer to get to Alaska, and I spent three months shovelin' horse crap in Jack Decker's stable before you tossed the sonofabitch on his ass and fired him. And now here I am, almost there, and a damned river spoils it all! Hell! What a time for my stupid tits to start sproutin'!"

Jonah shook his head and lowered it into his hands, from which a muffled, choking sound that might have been suppressed laughter issued.

"I guess I'm on my own from here on out, huh?" Andy muttered.

"I don't think this is any time to split up the team," Katy said.

"What about him?"

Katy grinned. "Oh, we'll let Jonah come with us, too."

A slow smile lit up Andy's face. The kid was really quite pretty beneath that wild mop of hair and under all the scratches, bug bites, and dirt. Katy was amazed she hadn't realized before that Andy was a girl.

"You're really not going to fire me?"

"I promised you a job for as long as I stay in the Yukon," Katy said. "I don't break my word."

Andy looked ready to spring at Katy and give her a hug, but she confined herself to leaping to her feet and executing a couple of jumps that proved she still had the heart of a child, despite the tough exterior. "You're a hell of a sport, Miss Katy! You really are!"

"Yeah. I really am," Katy said as Andy bounced off to find a sleeping place. She stared into the fire for a moment, feeling her spirits slip now that she didn't have to put on a bold face for Andy. When she looked up it was into Jonah's eyes, which seemed more black than blue in the shadows that darkened his face.

"Well, sport. How're you doing?" he asked.

"You weren't really going to fire her."

"Did you think I was?"

"Naw. You've got a soft spot mushier than a rotten apple."

"Kind of you to say so."

Katy sighed and let her shoulders slump.

"Your clothes are still wet," Jonah noted.

Katy plucked at her damp shirt. She wore a coat around her shoulders, and that was damp also. She'd been cold from the inside out for so many hours that it didn't seem to matter any more.

"You'd better get into something dry."

"I gave what we had to Camilla. Mine will dry if I sit by the fire long enough."

Jonah grunted noncommittally, got up, disappeared for a moment, then came back to the fire with a blanket. "Get out of those things and wrap this around you. We'll lay out your clothes by the fire to dry."

Katy sighed. Depression was making her almost numb to the cold.

"Hop to, Katydid. Do as I say."

"I'm fine! Just leave me be."

"You're going to get sick, and then I'll have to take care of you. Get out of those wet clothes."

"Oh all right! Give me the blanket." She doffed her wet coat and started to fumble with the buttons to her shirt.

"Not here," Jonah said. "Come with me."

He led her to a little shelter made from brush, spruce boughs, and saplings. The floor was carpeted with dry leaves, boughs, and blankets.

"You built this?" Katy asked.

"With my own two hands."

"You're getting to be a real frontiersman."

"That's me. Mountain Man Jonah Armstrong, at your service."

Katy managed a weak smile, then shivered. Jonah handed her the blanket. "There's plenty of dry blankets. Everyone camped here must have brought over at least two."

Katy fumbled with her shirt buttons. Her fingers were stiff and awkward with cold.

"You're going to take all night like that," Jonah told her. "Let me do it."

She slapped his hands away out of pure instinct.

"Shy, Katy? There's no part of you that I haven't already seen." His eyes caught at hers, and a shiver traveled down her spine that had nothing to do with the cold. "Seen, and touched, and kissed. Now, let me help you."

His deft fingers made short work of her buttons, and with seeming detachment he helped her pull off the soggy boots that had tightened upon her feet and worm out of the damp britches that clung to her hips and legs. When she was dry and naked, wrapped in a warm blanket like a butterfly in its cocoon, she finally began to feel a hint of warmth relieve the iciness that cut to bone.

"We should share this shelter with Andy," she murmured sleepily.

Jonah chuckled. "Since when has Andy slept anywhere but exactly where she wants to sleep? That kid's wild as a little wolf cub."

"Mmm."

While Jonah took her wet clothing away to lay out by the fire, Katy surrendered to weariness as warmth relaxed her body. She gathered more blankets around her and curled up on the floor of springy, pungent spruce boughs. Hunter wandered in and curled at her feet.

Jonah had done a very good job in constructing the little shelter, she thought as she drifted into a doze.

Katy had scarcely closed her eyes before she was roused by a warm body burrowing into the blankets beside hers.

"Jonah," she whispered groggily.

"Go to sleep," he advised. His breath was warm in her ear. She came fully awake then. "Jonah! What are you doing?"

His arm clamped around her bare middle in comfortable possession as he fitted their bodies together spoon fashion. "The least you can do after I built this dandy shelter is to help keep me warm in it. Be still, Katy. All I'm after is a little warmth and a few hours' sleep."

She believed him, partly because she was too tired and discouraged to argue. For some perverse reason, the thought that Jonah wanted nothing more than her body heat to warm his sleep sent her spirits sliding into the final downhill tumble. She turned her face into the blanket beneath her. Lordy but she'd never cried as much in her life as she'd cried since meeting Jonah Armstrong.

"Katy, are you all right?" His voice was soft and low, and Katy felt it reverberating in his chest as much as heard it with her ears.

"Of course I'm all right."

His arm tightened around her middle, drawing her back more closely against him. "You're crying."

"Hell yes, I'm crying! Why shouldn't I cry? Patrick Burke drowned. Camilla's lost her entire family. We've lost everything but the clothes that are scorching by the fire, and we're miles from where we want to be with no boat, no food, and very little money. The only thing we have left is a sack of soggy flour, your spare underwear, and a couple of cooking pots."

"That's not all we have, Katy."

The warmth in his voice made her cry even harder. It was a vicious circle. She hated women who cried, but the madder at herself she grew, the harder she cried.

"Katydid . . . "

She expected him to do the manly thing by telling her not to cry, but he didn't. He shifted her so that she could bury her face against his chest and flood his forest of chest hair with her tears.

"Go ahead and cry, Katydid. Cry all you want. You've got more than one good cry owed to you."

Katy took him up on it with a vengeance. Strangely enough, she felt safe crying within the circle of his arms with his big, hard hands moving in slow caresses up and down her back. Crying kept her so busy that she didn't think so much about their predicament; it took the last morsel of her energy and drained her of the will to do anything but sleep. She scarcely knew it when she stopped crying and snuggled against Jonah to absorb his warmth and strength, and then slipped quietly into slumber.

Katy woke to see the dawn backlighting the mountains and painting wispy, high-flying clouds in a rosy tint. For a moment she lay still and inhaled Jonah's warm scent. The ever-present roar of Whitehorse Rapids seemed more muted in the still morning air. Above the rumble she heard the whistle of an early-rising bird and a distant shout of someone in another camp. At least five campfires had burned last night on the riverbanks above the rapids. After Patrick had drowned and all the rest in their party had lost everything but their lives, the Klondikers had shown very little enthusiasm for making a try at the rapids themselves. The new day would bring renewed courage and bolstered determination. Most likely everyone would make it through the white water today, Katy mused. The rapid had taken its sacrifice for the week. What would the remnants of their little party do when those who had stayed and donated food, blankets, and comfort headed downriver?

Katy pushed the dismal thought aside and disentangled herself from Jonah. What she needed was a brisk bath to scrub away grime and depression. Wrapped in a blanket, she gingerly made her way barefoot to the fire and gathered up her clothes. Breath puffing in icy clouds, she pulled on her boots, wrapped the blanket more securely about her, and headed upstream toward the deep, quiet part of the river that was dammed behind the rapids. Far enough from the campsites that she was safe from intruding eyes, she shed boots and blankets and slipped into the cold water—as if she hadn't gotten enough of the river the day before, Katy reflected grimly. The water was frigid, almost numbing, but the load of depression and anxiety lifted as she dived into the green depths and let the water wash away the stickiness of sweat and the pungent odor of woodsmoke. The cobwebs that clung to her spirit washed away with the grime. She surfaced, sputtered and spit, stroked against the icy, sluggish current, and knew that whatever the odds, she would get to the Klondike, and so would Jonah and Andy, and they would take care of Camilla on the way.

When she turned for the shore, she saw Jonah standing on the bank.

"What're you doing here?" she asked.

"I followed you. The blankets got cold after you left."

With no concern for modesty, he shed his blanket and dived into the quiet river. Seconds later he shot out of the water like a Fourth of July rocket. He practically walked on the surface in his haste to regain the shore. Katy's laugh came soaring up from her belly and cleared the last cobweb from her spirit.

"That water's like ice!" Jonah wheezed, hunkering naked on the bank and trying to get his breath back. "What are you, a penguin?"

"Come on, greenhorn! Out here there aren't any big brass tubs and water heated over the fire. If you want to get clean, you've got to toughen up a bit!"

"Toughen up, my foot. Freeze your ass off is more like it!"

Katy tut-tutted and dived again. She surfaced suddenly near the shore, like a killer whale surprising its prey, splatted the water with both hands, and sent a stream of cold water in Jonah's direction. Her aim was perfect; he yelped.

"You little miscreant! I'll get you for that!"

She stuck her thumbs in her ears and waggled her fingers at

him tauntingly. Then it was her turn to yelp as he dived into the water after her. Before she could leap away, his big hands closed around her waist and pulled her down into the cold green depths. She struggled mightily, succeeding only in getting her bare legs tangled with his—a not unpleasant sensation if she hadn't been three feet underwater with his hand firmly upon her head.

Just as spots began to swim before her eyes, he let her up. She bobbed to the surface with a fierce growl and tried to dunk him in turn.

"Huh-uh!" he said, laughing. "Don't try it, Katydid, unless you want another turn under the water. I'm bigger than you."

She dived, came up behind him, and pushed him under. When he surfaced in a sputtering fountain of water, she grinned wickedly. "And I'm sneakier than you."

"Typical of a woman. Come here and keep me warm."

"Horsefeathers! If you want to get warm, go back to the fire. I'm here to get clean."

They fetched the soap she'd left on the bank and managed to work up enough lather to scrub both of them as their faces turned from the rosy red of their battle to an icy blue. When they were through with their wash, Jonah wrapped Katy in a cocoon of blankets and carried her to a spot beneath the trees where a soft, dry carpet of needles made a fragrant bed. When he wormed his way into the cocoon with her, Katy couldn't help but giggle at his contortions.

"What are you doing?"

"I'm going to get warm."

"You can have one of the blankets."

"I'd rather get warm with you to keep me company."

She gasped as his leg slipped between hers. A surprised jolt of desire set her heart to pumping at twice its normal rate. "I don't think this is a good idea."

"Sure it is. It's a great idea."

He grinned down at her, his eyes the same dark blue as the morning sky. The short beard that curled around the strong line of his jaw gave him the look of a pirate or gunslinger. Katy couldn't suppress the answering smile that curved her lips. "You look absolutely nothing like a city boy from Chicago."

"Us city boys have a lot of surprises up our sleeves."

"You certainly do."

His muscular thigh rose to press against the already-throbbing flesh between her legs. She closed her eyes, wanting him so badly that the wanting was almost pain. Somehow in the last few days, logic and common sense had slipped away. She couldn't quite recall the reasons that she couldn't be with Jonah. The reasons were still there, she was sure, but they melted in the heat of desire awakened by blue eyes and a wicked grin, by the knowing pressure of Jonah's hard thigh against her tender flesh.

"Jonah," she managed to say. "What are you doing?" As if she didn't know.

He answered with lips pressed warmly against her ear. "I know an excellent way to get warm."

"We shouldn't," she objected against the crying need of her heart.

"Yes. We should. I won't hurt you, Katydid. I want to love you."

His lips moved down her throat, left a warm trail over her collarbone, and forayed onto the upper swells of her breast.

"Ooooh!" Katy half laughed, half shrieked as cold air invaded their blankets. "That's freezing!"

"Now who's the sissy?"

Somehow he managed to preserve the integrity of their warm cocoon as he worked his way down her body. His teeth gently grazed her nipple, which was already pebbled hard with desire. His tongue laved the lower curves of her breasts, and his breath tickled her ribs.

"I could eat you alive," he said when he surfaced for air.

"I thought that's what you were doing."

He chuckled low in his throat. "Sweet, innocent Katy. If I

did to you what I really wanted to do, you'd wake every
Klondiker in ten square miles with your yelling, and you
wouldn't be yelling from pain, sweetheart."

The glitter of his eyes made her insides turn to warm syrup,
and that syrup slowly trickled downward and pooled between
her legs. She closed her eyes to shut out the sight of him looking down at her, half-afraid of the feelings he stoked. "I'm not
nearly as innocent as you think."

"My love, you're as innocent as spring grass is green. You
just don't know it." With his finger he traced circles around
her nipple, then drew a fiery line to her navel, and lower, until
he tickled the soft nest of curls between her thighs. "Someday
I'm going to take you to a warm island in the Caribbean.
We're going to spread a blanket on the sand where no one can
see, and with the hot sun beating down on us and the waves
pounding on the sand just beyond our toes, I'm going to show
you just how much you don't know about what men and
women can do together. And I'm going to show you just how
much I love you." His finger slipped inside her and stroked
gently, deeper and deeper in a steady rhythm that made her
body grow as taut as the string of a drawn bow.

She fought to free her hands from the restraint of the blanket. A hunger raged in her—to touch him, stroke him, feel
supple muscle and sinew beneath her hands. She ached to take
his erection in her hands and glory in his size and hardness,
knowing that it was she who inspired his need. He gasped
when she brushed her fingers against a flat male nipple and
stroked her palms along the breadth of his shoulders.

"Katy . . . " he half whispered, half groaned.

She discovered his trim buttocks and kneaded the muscle
there with admiring hands, then slipped around his hips to let
her fingers walk the length of his erect penis.

"Christ Almighty, woman!" he breathed. "What are you
doing to me?"

"I don't know," Katy admitted honestly in a husky, confused voice.

He kissed her, all the while rearranging blankets, legs, hips, and torsos so that they fit neatly together with him pressed between her open thighs. Katy felt his need in the pounding of his heart. His kiss was wild and devouring, mouth slanting across hers in eager possession, tongue stroking deeply, tasting her fully and leaving the tang of himself in her mouth. The hard tip of his erection parted her, and she wanted to surge upward, impale herself, suck him inside her and drain him until she was full.

"What's wrong with me?" she moaned softly.

Slowly he sank into her. The raw pleasure of it made her eyes open wide and her breath stop in her throat.

"Nothing's wrong with you," he promised. "You're just in love."

"No," she breathed as he drew himself out, then thrust again.

"Yes, Katy. You love me." His voice was honey pouring into her, smooth and sweet as the deep, slow strokes that he courted her with. "You love me," he told her softly. "How else would we be doing this?" His penetration deepened as Katy strained to open fully to his loving. Soft, silky words echoed in her mind in time with the rhythmic beat of their bodies. "You love me. Love me. Love me." *I love him, love him, love him.*

The tightly wrapped blanket held her captive as Jonah thrust into her. Finally she managed to wrap her legs around him, taking him deeper, moving with him, clenching herself around the hard, thick flesh that she wanted to hold prisoner within her.

"Christ!" he groaned. "Oh lord, Katy, I love you." With a fierce final thrust and a low growl he spent himself within her. Katy's whole body tightened around him, drawing him with her into a warm explosion that had every nerve in her body singing. For a moment she felt so relaxed and content she could scarcely bother to breathe. Then her heart started again, her lungs filled with air and released a sigh of joyous contentment.

The blue sky above them, the crunch of spruce needles beneath them, the distant roar of Whitehorse Rapids, and the smell of drifting woodsmoke slowly made their impressions on Katy's returning senses, reminding her of their whereabouts. She closed her eyes with a wry smile. "I really am a shameless fool."

He laughed, sending himself slipping out of her. He didn't move from his intimate position between her legs, however. "You can't say that about my future wife, Katy O'Connell."

"Oh, Jonah. Jonah. I didn't say I'd marry you."

"You'll marry me, someday."

She shook her head, grasping for logic and good sense. The feel of him pressing against her most private, feminine flesh almost drove those things beyond reach. Even now she could feel her body ache in need of him. "You don't have to be a gentleman," she whispered feebly.

"I'm not a gentleman." He kissed the tip of her nose. "As you well know."

"Jonah! I mean you don't have to marry me."

"I never thought I did."

"I mean . . . dammit, Jonah! Do you know how hard it is to talk with you . . . with you . . . you know!"

He chuckled, tightened his arms about her, and rolled them over, blankets and all, so that Katy rested atop him. "There, my love. Do you enjoy looking down instead of up?"

Her legs still encompassed him, and the constricting cocoon made shifting to a more modest position impossible. "I can take care of myself." Her breathing quickened as he moved slightly beneath her.

"I know you can."

"You don't want me as a wife."

His hand stroked her back, teased her buttocks, slipped between her legs to softly caress her love-swollen flesh.

"You don't want a wife at all." She gasped as he found that most tender of spots. "You told me so back in Willow Bend."

He teased and stroked and touched. She closed her eyes as the warmth of his touch melted her.

"Needs change." His voice was thick with desire. He was growing thick and hard again. "Wants change. I want you."

"No," she gasped, knowing there was a reason why, but not able to remember it right now. She could feel the hot swell of him between their bodies.

"You can't live without me," he assured her with a slow grin.

She shook her head.

"You just don't realize it yet."

"We're friends," she reminded him. "Good friends."

"The very best friends," he agreed.

He shifted her slightly and fitted himself into her, pressing her down until she took all of him. "No, sweetheart, don't move," he warned, cradling her against him. "This is rather precarious at best."

He rocked them together. The slight movement fired an acute need through every part of her. She moaned against his bare, warm shoulder.

"I know, my love," he crooned. "I know."

Jonah worked his hand between them and found the tender hub of her desire. With gentle expertise he sent her climbing rapidly toward the stars, the rocking of his hips a magic carpet carrying her to the sky. Precarious as their tangle of bodies was, the ride was swift, the climax hard and hot.

"Best friends," Jonah whispered as they drifted back to earth. "Very, very best friends."

CHAPTER 18

That dawn loving was the only good-bye Katy got, for as the sun rose brightly on the morning after the disaster, the Klondikers who had been reluctant to brave Whitehorse Rapids on the same day it had taken a man's life were ready to move again. A trio of brothers, ex-lumbermen from Portland, made room for Jonah on their boat for the trip downriver to Dawson, but they had room for only one. A minister and his son took Camilla into their care, and Katy, Andy, and Hunter were taken on by a grizzled prospector who looked old enough to have dug gold in the rush of '49. By a careless swat of fate, Katy and Jonah were yanked apart to go their separate ways.

Camilla accepted the minister's guardianship with apathetic placidness, but the blood drained from her face when she realized she would have to ride once again through the dangerous chaos of Whitehorse Rapids. The understanding minister suggested the new widow hike around the rapids and meet the boats at the smooth water below. Katy hiked the two mile trail up the cliffs and back down to the river with her, as did Andy, whose gender was once again indistinguishable.

Katy was glad to have an excuse not to ride the rapids again, but the necessity for quickly gathering what little gear she had and hitting the trail left no time for long good-byes with Jonah. As she stood high above the river and watched the lumberjacks' boat carry Jonah through the white water, her heart pounded so hard she thought it might hammer its way right out of her chest. When they were safely through the worst of the rough water and rounded the bend out of sight, she waved good-bye, even though Jonah couldn't see her. The emptiness inside her had little to do with her missed breakfast.

John Stanley Sanders—"call me Stewpot," the old prospector had told Katy and Andy when they first stepped onto his boat below Whitehorse Rapids—was skilled at the business of handling a boat on a treacherous river. They made good time. The fish Andy and Katy caught and the rabbits and squirrels run down by Hunter, who was jubilant to be in an area of plentiful game once again, added enough to the old man's supplies so that his provisions didn't suffer from the addition of two people and one wolf. The prospector himself certainly didn't suffer. He talked their ears off, filling the long days and weary evenings with stories of gold camps and frontier towns, famous badmen and lawmen that Katy doubted he'd really met.

Jonah should have made the acquaintance of Stewpot Sanders, Katy thought more than once. He could have filled his big-city newspaper first page to last with the blarney tales the old man spun.

Jonah. His absence seemed to make the wind colder, the rain wetter, the mud stickier. Evenings around the fire were empty without him, and memories of their time together waited around every bend of the river.

Sailing Lake Laberge, just downriver from Whitehorse, Katy recalled the long, lazy drift across lakes Bennett and Tagish, the sound of Jonah's laughter as he'd minded the rudder with Patrick at his elbow. The rough, rocky stretch of river beyond Lake Laberge, known as Thirty Mile River, called to mind their first experience with white water in Miles Canyon, how Jonah had caught her eye and laughed just as she'd concluded he was so scared he'd pop his suspenders.

Nighttime always brought memories of the quiet stargaze she had shared with Jonah while talking about Napi and Old Woman, the mountains, and the dubious wonders of his Chicago. Frosty mornings made her think of the goose-bumps on Jonah's skin when they bathed together in the frigid river—and of his sweet, determined seduction. She wondered if she would ever again be completely warm without his arms around her.

Below Thirty Mile River, the Yukon gained volume and momentum as it gathered the waters of the Tahkeena, Hootalinqua, Big Salmon, and Little Salmon rivers. The Teslin River joined the Yukon with such a load of silt that the stuff hissed against the side of the boat as if they sailed through sand, not water. The Teslin also deposited a load of Klondikers onto the river, for this was the point at which goldseekers who'd followed the Stikine River trail from Canada joined the headwaters of the Yukon.

Though the Yukon swelled with the waters of tributaries as it approached its confluence with the Klondike, it became tamer as it grew deeper and wider. Once past the Hootalinqua River, only two stretches of white water stood between the Klondikers and their goal: Rink Rapids and Five Fingers. With Katy and Andy helping out with oars, Stewpot guided his boat through the rough water without so much as a single tense moment. Finally, twenty-two days after setting sail on the headwaters of the Yukon at Lake Bennett, on a gloomy, wet day with winter blowing down their necks from the valley behind, Katy sighted Moosehide, the huge scar of an ancient landslide that marred the mountainside above Dawson. A short time later, the town itself came into view. Dawson, gateway to the new El Dorado: the goal of thousands who had set out from Seattle and Portland to sail up the lower Yukon, from Skaguay and Dyea to endure Chilkoot and White Pass, from Edmonton on the long overland trails. Dawson: the end of the rainbow vouchsafed for only a few to attain. She had made it. Katy O'Connell. One of the few. Katy thought that her father would be proud of her for making it to the gold-fields.

"Damn that girl for an imp of the devil!" Gabe muttered as he stood shivering in the cold wind on the docks alongside the Yukon River not far from where it joined the cold arctic sea, just west of St. Michael and just south of Nome. Some fathers might need to stand guard at their front door to keep overeager suitors at bay. Others might wear their parlor carpets thin, pacing and worrying about what the little dears were doing or thinking. But Gabe was willing to bet he was the only father forced to chase his daughter through the wilds of Alaska and Canada.

He could only hope that Katy was having an easier trip than he was. The weather had been miserable—cold, damp, and windy. Every man and his brother were trying to reach Dawson before winter, or so it seemed, for when Gabe had arrived in Seattle, there wasn't a northbound ship not full to the scuppers. He had been reduced to winning a berth in a poker game, a task which had taken him longer than it would have some years ago. The settled, quiet life was taking its toll on his seedier talents. It also seemed to have reduced his patience with sleeping in the rain, food that tasted like pig slop, and companions whose body odor was more powerful than their intellect.

Now, at the mouth of the Yukon River, all the river steamers that were due to leave the docks in the next two weeks were fully booked, and after two weeks were up, the chance of anything steaming up the miles between here and Dawson without getting frozen in was slim at best.

"Damned little idiot." Gabe stamped his feet against the cold and stuck his gloved hands into his armpits to keep them warm. "I should have stayed home and let her deal with the Klondike—and Mr. Jonah Armstrong—alone."

"You are talking to yourself, Gabriel O'Connell?" The inquiry came from Mrs. Delilah Von Stratton. Mrs. Von Stratton, young widow of a German industrialist, had made Gabe's acquaintance on the steamer from Seattle. Adventurous as well as rich, she had decided to include in her tour of America a visit to the fabulous Klondike that had everyone's ears pricked and mouths buzzing. With her traveled two maids, a genteel companion, a bodyguard, and a huge mastiff named Guntar which made the bodyguard superfluous.

As Mrs. Von Stratton slid her arm through Gabe's, Guntar the mastiff circled behind and came at him from the other flank, sniffing up and down his leg. Gabe hoped the beast hadn't mistaken him for a tree.

"Come now, Gabriel. Why do you scowl so? I do not approve of such a scowl. I insist that everyone around me enjoy himself. Such a ferocious face does put a damper on our grand adventure."

"Well now, ma'am, I didn't mean to put a damper on your adventure."

"There now. That is much better. You must join me in my cabin once we board and we will warm ourselves with a glass of fine schnapps."

"I'm afraid I don't have a berth on your boat, Mrs. Von Stratton."

"Oh." She sounded truly disappointed.

Gabriel didn't have any illusions about the rich widow having designs on him. They'd whiled away several evenings on the steamer from Seattle—playing cards and talking. She had put out a few feelers—Gabe guessed that she was a woman who did that with any man who still possessed all his limbs and teeth—and he had filled her ears with stories of Olivia and his children. From then on they'd become friends of a sort. Mrs. Von Stratton found American ways, especially the ways of the West, to be as entertaining as a comic opera, or so she'd told him. She listened raptly to stories about Olivia, Katy, and Ellen, or about the Blackfoot relatives of his first wife, and Gabe enjoyed telling them to her. He missed Montana. He missed Olivia, little David, and the ranch. Somehow adventuring didn't have the appeal it once had.

"You are staying at this miserable place to wait for the boat that will leave in three days?"

"Well, to tell the truth, I don't have a berth on that one either."

She looked at him askance. "You are perhaps going to walk these long, cold miles to the land of gold?"

Gabe laughed. "I'll find a berth one way or another. These feet of mine don't take kindly to walking."

"Ah, Gabriel." She tugged him along as she strolled along the dock, her arm tucked securely within his. Guntar ambled behind, herding him like a sheepdog herded a sheep. "I do so admire you American men. You are so spontaneous. So impulsive. You spring to action and leave the thinking for later. Very refreshing."

Olivia wouldn't call it refreshing, Gabe reflected. Olivia would call it idiotic. Feeling the arctic winter breathe down his collar and lacking a way to get the rest of the way to Dawson, Gabe would have to agree with her.

"And like cats who jump off of heights without looking, you always land on your feet, you Americans."

Guntar gave Gabe a look that made him suspect the cat analogy might not be wise.

"This time I will be your benefactor, eh?"

"I beg your pardon?" Gabe said.

"You will come on the boat with me. As my guest."

"I . . . uh . . . appreciate the thought, ma'am, but the captain's already told me the boat's full up."

"Nonsense. He wouldn't dare say no to me. I booked passage weeks ago for my entire traveling party. I'll simply tell him you're my second bodyguard. We have become friends, and it is the least I can do."

Olivia would likely take a scalpel to him if she found out. She was a sensible woman, his little doctoress, but when she got riled, she could make a she-puma look like somebody's tame house cat.

"Come now, Gabriel. I would miss your stories. And think of your poor daughter, who is probably in Dawson by now. You cannot abandon her." Her eyes twinkled merrily. "I promise I will not attempt to take advantage of you, my friend."

"You're a generous lady, Mrs. Von Stratton. Only a fool would say no."

"Excellent! I look forward to meeting this remarkable daughter of yours."

"So do I," Gabe said as he scowled upriver. Katy could get him into trouble when she was miles away, the little imp—her and that newspaper man, on whom he aimed to beat until the scoundrel's stuffings busted their seams. He wondered apprehensively how Katy had survived the hazardous trip to Dawson, and with a certain amount of wry realism, he wondered if Jonah Armstrong had survived the hazards of being with Katy. Could be that the man wouldn't have any stuffings left for Gabe to beat out of him.

"This town is a piss-poor excuse for the end of the rainbow, let me tell you!" Otar Johnson spit a gob of brown tobacco juice into the spittoon in the corner of the cabin, and Jonah wondered for the umpteenth time how the lumberjack could be so dead-eye accurate.

"Give it time," Jonah told him. "The town's only a year old."

Otar spit again. "I'll be glad to get the hell outta here and up to where the gold is. Shit. Ain't nothin' in Dawson but bog and dog dirt. The whiskey in the saloon tastes like horse piss, and the whores don't wanna go with no cheechakos, no newcomers. They all wanna tickle the dicks of them what's already proved a claim."

"Well, they are businesswomen, after all."

"Shee-it! They are that. By the by, lad, little Maudie said to tell ya hey. She gave me a free tumble jest 'cause I was a friend of yours."

"Decent of her," Jonah said blandly. Maude and her companions had arrived in Dawson a week ago, about the same time Jonah and his lumberjack benefactors had beached their boat on the narrow ledge of summer bog upon which perched the town of Dawson. Here where the Klondike River emptied into the Yukon, saloons and dance halls prospered along with all of the other businesses hastily erected to serve the gold-seekers. Maudie and her friends were doing a roaring business mining the miners for their gold.

Jonah set aside the piece he'd been writing and added a stick of wood to the sheet iron cabin stove. The stove had cost him a pretty penny at the Alaska Commercial Company store, but it did a good job of keeping the cabin warm, even with a cold wind sneaking in beneath the door and around the windows.

"Two more days," Otar sighed. "Me and Buck and Sven will be digging real gold up on Hunker Creek. We got noses for gold, my brothers'n' me, and a good thing, too, for I've been hearin' that the Brits are gonna start takin' a cut pretty soon."

"A royalty." Jonah closed the stove door and went to look out the window at the dreary, rainy town. "I heard that, too. People up here aren't too happy about it. They're also going to cut down the allowed size of the claims and reserve every other parcel along the creeks for the government."

"Yah. My brothers an' me, we're lucky to file our claim so fast. We work hard and get rich before the government gets their greedy fingers into the pot. You should do the same, my friend."

Jonah smiled and tapped the papers on the table where he'd been working. "This is why I'm here. Not gold, but tales of the gold diggers."

Otar snorted his contempt for that notion. He lumbered to the door and shrugged on an oilskin. "I hear whiskey calling. This rain, it has me cold to my bones. I need more than a stove to warm them." He hitched a blond brow at Jonah. "Will you come?"

"Thanks, but I have work to do."

Jonah watched Otar walk through the mud toward town, his shoulders hunched as the rain beat down upon him. The lumberjack was right. Dawson was a piss-poor excuse for the end of the rainbow. The first two days he was here, he'd walked the town from end to boggy end, stuck his head in every one of the thirty saloons, got a haircut in one of the town's two barbershops and a shave in the other. He'd absorbed the town's atmosphere, breathed in its stink, let its numerous roaming dogs sniff at his heels, listened to the town drunks, and watched the newly rich throw gold dust around like it was sawdust.

All so he could write an account of what an end-of-the-trail gold rush town is really like. Not the El Dorado of people's dreams, but a bog-ridden hellhole that catered to men's lust and greed, a town that most men came to and got out of as fast as they could—to go to the diggings, or to give up and go home.

Above and beyond the journalistic curiosity in his explorings, however, was Jonah's search for Katy. When he hadn't found her the first day, he'd worried. The second day he'd been nearly frantic. The third day in town he'd spotted her with Andy in tow, looking around the town like Dawson was her own personal Pearly Gates into Heaven. He'd wanted to run to her, pick her up, and crush her in his arms, but he hadn't. Even since he realized he loved Katy, he'd been pushing her, and she'd raised her stubborn little hackles and pushed right back. Now was the time to give her some line. He recalled his father's advice on a fishing trip they'd taken when he was a kid. Jonah had hooked a trout that had fought so hard the line had almost snapped. Let the fish run, his father had advised. Let it wear itself out. If the hook was properly set, he could reel it in easily when it tired.

In the trout's case, the hook had been barbed steel. For Katy, the hook was love. Only time would tell if it was properly set.

Jonah stood up straighter and squinted through the rain. There she was, the little bedraggled imp, headed toward Dawson's meat market with a brace of rabbits in her hand and Hunter trotting at her heels. Every day since she'd come, Katy had brought in game to sell or trade. In a town where everyone wanted to spend their time getting rich, where gold dust was more common than greenbacks, where people were getting nervous over a threatening food shortage and soon-to-be-impassable river, fresh meat was a precious commodity.

Jonah waited for Katy to come out of the meat market and make her daily tour of town—looking for a job, Jonah figured, and unlikely to find one. Katy didn't have the skills necessary to support a lone woman in Dawson. Quite a few seamstresses took in a good bit of business. Camilla was already doing very nicely in that trade. Several laundry businesses run by women were booming, and the Great Northern Hotel employed several female cooks and a couple of girls to serve tables. Katy didn't have these domestic skills, however, and the only other positions open to a woman was flat on her back in one of the whorehouses or dancing in a dance hall.

An ornery part of Jonah almost enjoyed Katy's predicament. He'd done enough investigation to assure himself that she was all right, for the time being at least. But little Miss Independent was not doing all that well on her own, living in a tent at the edge of town with Andy and Hunter, bartering game for flour and bacon, cruising the town for a job and finding only closed doors and invitations to take herself elsewhere. He did feel a bit sorry for her, and perhaps a bit proud of her persistence, but damned if it didn't feel good to see that she might actually need his shoulder to lean upon for a change.

She came out of the meat market, pulled her hat farther down on her head to keep off the rain, and looked down the muddy street. The stubborn little scrapper never gave up, Jonah mused, expecting her to march off on her usual tour of the town. To his surprise, though, she struck out in a different direction—straight toward his cabin.

This was it, Katy told herself as she slogged through the mud toward Jonah's lair. For three days, ever since she had learned that Jonah was staying in the snug little log cabin just east of town, Katy had debated confronting him. But hell! Why should she go looking for him? He was the one who'd been so hot to tie the knot. He'd been the one so confident that she couldn't live without him. He'd been the one spouting all that nonsense about love and marriage until he had her almost liking the idea. Good thing she'd not taken his cajoling seriously, for now that Jonah was back in civilization—or at least what passed for civilization up here—his burning desire to make her his wife had cooled mighty quickly.

And that was just fine with her, Katy told herself. She didn't itch to see him. He didn't fill her dreams at night. She didn't turn her head at every tall, broad-shouldered fellow she met on the street to discover if it was Jonah. Nope. Pigs would sing before Katy O'Connell spent time mooning over a man. She was going to pay a call to do him a favor. For old times' sake. He might not realize it, but he still needed her know-how.

Just as she lifted her fist to knock, the door swung open. Jonah smiled down at her.

"Well look who's here! If it isn't Katy O'Connell!"

For a moment Katy was dumbstruck. The last time she'd been alone with that face it had been covered with a coarse brown beard and was red from an icy plunge in the Yukon River. It had also hovered scant inches above hers while the rest of his body, bound tightly to hers by blankets, had managed to make her lose control of her senses. Something in Jonah's grin told her that the same scene was running through his mind as well.

"Hi, Jonah." The rain and cold made her voice shake, Katy told herself. Nothing else. "You shaved."

"It itched."

"I liked the beard." What a stupid thing to say. This was not going the way she had planned. Her heart was racing in her chest, and her mind was at a standstill, able to come up with only inane, stilted comments. Where was her courage? Where was her grit? "Uh . . . can I come in?"

"Please do. Hunter, too. You both look like drowned rats."

"Yeah. Well, this whole town is a drowned rathole." Katy wiped her soggy boots before stepping onto the clean-swept plank floor. Hunter didn't bother. He slipped into the cabin behind her and gave a mighty shake, spraying mud and water in a cold fountain that hissed on the stove and spattered against the log walls.

Jonah laughed. "Thanks, Hunter. Make yourself at home."

Katy had forgotten Jonah was so tall, that he filled a room so with his presence.

"I wondered when you would get around to visiting," Jonah said.

"Really?" His confident tone got Katy's back up. Did he think she had nothing to think about but him, nothing to do but search him out? "I've been sort of busy. I see you've been busy, too. You've got yourself nicely set up here." She looked around at the camp stove, the cots, the pinewood table with its stacked tins of flour, sugar, and salt. In the corner was a container of lamp oil—a truly precious commodity that was in short supply in Dawson. "A very nice place."

"It's not the Waldorf, but it's comfortable enough."

"Considering almost half of the folks around here are still living in tents, I'd say it's a miracle you could get this place."

"Another journalist—a fellow from the *San Francisco Chronicle,* was leaving just as I got into town. He offered it to me cheap. So I moved in along with the Bunyan brothers—"

"Who?"

"The three lumberjacks who gave me a ride down the river."

"They're brothers?"

"In profession as well as blood. Haven't you heard of Paul Bunyan?"

"Of course I've heard of . . . oh. You were being funny."

"Apparently not."

"You look like you inherited more than a cabin." She glanced at the new parka that hung on a peg by the door and gave an approving once-over to his wool trousers and heavy flannel shirt—all new. What was there about flannel shirts that made a man's shoulders seen so broad, his chest so inviting a spot to rest her head? Maybe it wasn't the flannel. Maybe it was just Jonah. To curb the temptation, Katy took off her hat, sailed it to catch upon a peg by the door, took off her coat, and plunked herself down on a wooden stool by the stove. "Last time I saw you we didn't have a nickel between us and your knees were showing through your britches."

Jonah swung a stool under his backside and sat down beside her. "Hell, Katy, of all people, you ought to know that being broke is only a temporary state. I'm surprised you haven't cleaned out some poor sucker's pockets in a poker game yet."

She sniffed indignantly. "I don't clean out suckers. Besides, you can't even get into a game in this town without a pouch full of gold dust."

"So you did try!" he concluded with a grin. "That's my Katy."

Lordy he was annoying when he wanted to be! *His* Katy indeed! Still, the possessive tone in his voice gave her a curious satisfaction she didn't want to admit. "How did *you* get money?" she asked, almost resentfully.

"Easy." He grinned wickedly. "You trailblazers of the Old West might know how to snare a rabbit and follow the dirty end of a cow, but there's nobody beats a big-city slicker at wrangling money."

"Is that so? What'd you do? Rob the bank?"

"Close. I just flashed my credentials and the bank gave me a loan on an IOU from the *Record*.

Katy sighed. "Not nearly as exciting as winning big in a poker game."

"Not nearly," he agreed.

"Not nearly as exciting as making a big strike out there in the gold diggings."

A slow smile curved his mouth. "That's probably true."

Katy tried to keep her eyes off the curled corner of his lips. They were firm and masculine, mobile, molded cleanly enough to belong to a woman. No man should have lips like that. It was immoral.

"But then," he continued, "maybe my idea of treasure is different than those who dig it out of the ground." His eyes glittered with warmth as he looked at her. "Katydid, you look like you could use some hot coffee."

"What I need is money." She was tired of the preliminaries. Katy had never been one to dance around a point. "And you well know it, Jonah Armstrong."

"Ah." He leaned forward, rested his elbows on his knees, and interlaced his fingers. "Money."

Katy's pride stung. She was doing him a favor, she reminded herself. It wasn't a handout she wanted. "Yeah. I need money. And since we're . . . well, you know . . . friends, I thought I'd give you an opportunity to make an investment in the goldfields."

"I'm honored."

She ignored his smug tone and plunged ahead. "I need fifteen dollars for the filing fee and maybe fifty dollars for provisions while Andy and I are settling on a claim. Just until the gold starts coming in. Then we can support ourselves. For that measly amount of cash I'll give you . . . say . . . five percent of the claim."

"An investment, eh?" He sounded doubtful.

"It's a sure thing, Jonah. You'll get your money back and a bunch more. Didn't I deliver when I took your stake in Skaguay? Did I lead you wrong then?"

He looked at her and grinned. "You delivered, Katydid."

The glitter in his eyes brought a rush of heat to her face. "Don't be snide, Jonah. Sixty-five dollars is what I need from you. That's all. If you're not interested in a share of the claim, then make it a loan. I'll pay you back with interest in a few weeks."

The smile slowly curving his mouth had a cat-that-ate-the-cream look that made Katy feel as if she was somehow walking into a trap.

"If there's one thing you learn from life in the big city," Jonah told her, "it's that personal loans aren't a good idea. Especially between friends. Fastest way in the world to spoil a nice, amiable friendship."

"Jonah!"

"It's true. I loaned fifty dollars once to my second cousin, Wilbur. He sold shoes—went all up and down the Eastern seaboard for a big company in Chicago. Never saw him or my fifty dollars again."

Katy made a rude sound.

"And five percent—that's hardly worth the trouble."

"This is ridiculous!" Katy marched toward the door and grabbed her hat from the peg. "Come on, Hunter!"

"I might consider a full partnership, though."

Jonah's words stopped Katy with her hand on the door latch.

"This gold fever is contagious," he admitted. "Like a plague."

"A partnership? For sixty-five measly dollars?"

"Not for sixty-five dollars. I finance the whole claim. You work it."

"Andy and I work the claim."

"All right. You and Andy work the claim. You ladies get half, and I get half."

Katy smiled at the image of her and Andy as ladies.

"Are we partners?" Jonah asked with a lift of his brow.

"Partners!"

He stuck out his hand for a handshake. Katy grasped it, and a current ran through her at his touch. From the glint in his eyes, Katy thought Jonah was not going to settle for a mere handshake. They stood there, hands clasped, eyes locked, for much longer than necessary to seal such a simple arrangement. When he finally allowed her hand to slide out of his grip, she was perversely disappointed.

Shakily, she jammed her hat upon her head and backed toward the door. "Got to go. A lot to do. Stuff to buy. People to talk to."

"Keep me posted on what you need."

"Yeah. Sure." She retreated out the door, then stuck her face back into the cabin. "Jonah, you won't regret it. I'm glad you've finally wised up about digging for gold."

Jonah stood for a moment after the door closed behind her, smiling like a fox who's found the gate to the henhouse unlatched. "I've wised up, all right," he congratulated himself. "Run, little fish, run. I knew you'd come back to be reeled in."

CHAPTER 19

A person who survived Skookum Gulch didn't owe the devil any time in hell, Katy figured. A week digging for gold in this dog-blasted streambed was enough to pay for a lifetime of sins. Pain needled out from her shoulders as she lifted a shovelful of gravel from the trench and threw it over her shoulder. Her hands were numb with cold—just as well, for if they hadn't been numb, Katy would have felt the sting of blisters and the ache of abused tendons. Her arms were on fire. Her lower back felt as though someone had taken a sledgehammer to it, and her feet—well, she hadn't felt her feet in hours. She assumed they were still attached to her ankles.

"Hey down there—yipe!" Andy had peered into the fifteen-foot-deep trench where Katy worked just in time to get a face-ful of sand from the shovel. "Hey!" She wiped the muck from her face and eyes. "Careful!"

"Warn me before you stick your face in shovel range," Katy snapped. The look on Andy's face made her instantly contrite for her sharp tone. "I'm sorry. It's been a long, useless, hell of a morning."

"The rocker broke," Andy told her.

"Spit! That's just great! Give me a hand out of here."

Katy scrambled up the steep ramp at one end of the trench,

grabbing Andy's hand to attain the last five feet. On numb feet she stumped over to the wooden chute into which Andy had been shoveling gravel. A steady stream of water washed through the chute to separate the lighter quartz and feldspar gravel from the heavier magnetite and gold, which would settle in the wooden riffles that corrugated the bottom of the chute. Normally the chute could be rocked to help separate the gravel—thus the name rocker. Right now, however, it not only didn't move, it canted sideways at an angle that made the bottom riffles next to useless. One of the supports had splintered.

Katy muttered a series of curses that would've made a mule-skinner proud.

"We could maybe splint it together with twine," Andy suggested.

"That'll never last. We'll have to cut another support. Where's the ax?"

"Up by the cabin."

They headed toward the log shack at the edge of the trees. The little cabin had already been here when Katy and Andy had arrived, and a ready-made abode was part of the reason they had decided to work this gulch rather than one of the many others that fed into the Klondike—that and the fact that Katy liked the look of the bedrock that jutted out of the hillsides above the gulch. Enough challenges had faced them without their having to build a cabin. They had to haul all their supplies in on their backs, owing to a shortage of mules and horses in Dawson. Then they'd spent a day laying out the claim—five hundred feet along the stream and wide enough to go from the base of one hillside to the base of the hillside opposite—and diverting the small stream that ran through the gulch. Only then could they set up the rocker and start washing the gravel to separate the gold—if there was gold here.

There would be gold, Katy told herself. They'd dug only the first trench, and she'd excavated just fifteen vertical feet so far. She'd heard reports of thirty feet of gravel on top of the bedrock in some gulches. Most claims had gold in only a thin zone of pay dirt—sometimes right on top of the bedrock, sometimes shallower. Two successful prospectors she'd met in Dawson had hit gold on Bonanza Creek under twenty feet of worthless gravel. The gold would be here, she assured herself. It had to be here.

Andy was in no better mood than Katy as they worked to repair the rocker. Dirt clung to her chin and cheeks, which were red from the cold. Wispy strands of bright red hair escaped her cap and straggled into her face, where they clung, despite Andy's irritated blowing them away or scraping them back with dirty hands. When they finally got the rocker erect again, she searched through the box of tools that sat on the sand beside them.

"Where's a knife, goddammit? Gimme a knife."

Katy handed her the hunting knife she kept on her belt. "What do you need a knife for?"

Andy pulled the grimy cap from her head and let her hair tumble down her back.

"I'm gonna chop off this goddamned dirty ugly mop! That's what I'm gonna do!"

"Andy! Don't!" Tangled, dirty, and pushed under a cap as it always was, Andy's wealth of red hair was hardly her glory, but given a little attention, it could be.

"I'm gonna!" The knife neatly severed a knotted tress. "It's nuthin' but a bother! I don't know why I didn't cut it before." Another thick red strand fell to the ground.

"You're going to look like your hair got caught in a sawmill."

"Don't make no never mind to me." She continued to saw and chop until most of her hair lay in a curling red pile at her feet. What remained on her head looked like a fiery nest built by a drunken bird. It was promptly smashed flat as Andy pulled on her cap. "There! That's better!"

"Now you do look like a boy."

"Good! A body's safer being a boy."

"Well, you can't be a boy forever, Andy. Sooner or later you're going to have to deal with being a girl." Katy grimaced as the irony of her words struck her. She was a fine one to lecture someone on femininity!

"I don't see why!" Andy objected. "You're a female, and you got past it."

"What do you mean?"

"I mean, you don't go simperin' around in no dresses, or curl your hair or paint your face. You don't swing your hips at the men or push up your tits with one of those corsets that make a lady look like she's suckin' in her breath all the time."

"I've never pretended to be anything but what I am," Katy protested. "Besides, there's more to being a woman than those things," she said, somewhat surprised at herself.

"Yeah. Like cookin' and cleanin'."

"Most women enjoy caring for those they love."

"Gigglin' and simperin'."

"There's a lot of women on this earth who've never giggled or simpered in their lives."

"Yeah. Like you and me." Andy gave Katy's back a comradely slap. "I wanna be just like you, so no one can tell I'm a girl unless he gets close enough to feel. And you can bet no one's gonna get that close to me!"

Mood apparently much improved, Andy picked up her shovel and started tossing gravel into the repaired rocker. Katy looked at Andy, then down at herself. There really wasn't that much difference, she acknowledged. She looked no older than Andy, and every bit as disreputable in baggy overalls and a frayed wool sweater. Her arms were covered with scratches and bug bites, her fingernails were ragged and dirty. Bothersome wisps of hair that had escaped her braids blew in her face. Her lips were dry and cracked, and she didn't even want to contemplate what her face looked like.

What would Olivia say if she could see her now, after all her work teaching Katy how to dress and act like a lady? Worse, what would Jonah think?

What did she care what Jonah might think? Katy asked herself. Gold was what she should worry about, not her damned appearance. Gold and independence.

Not an hour passed before a cart drawn by a bony, broken-down bay horse arrived in camp. Climbing out of the trench, Katy recognized the poor piece of crowbait that pulled the cart as one of the two horses let out by the livery in Dawson. The woman perched on the seat was Camilla.

"Hello, Katy!" Camilla greeted her with a happy wave.

"Camilla! What brings you out here?"

"Jonah told me where to find you. Actually, Jonah sent me. The Alaska Commercial Company was selling overalls cheap. Jonah bought some and gave me the commission of cutting them down to fit you two." She glanced around the claim. "Oh my! Isn't this . . . ah . . . picturesque."

"No," Katy replied with a laugh. Only the kindest person would name Skookum Gulch, with its tumbledown shack, piles of gravel, trenches, and diverted stream, anything but ugly. "It's a pit. But it's going to make me and Jonah and Andy rich."

"Have you found gold yet?"

"Not yet," Katy admitted as she helped Camilla from the high wagon seat. "But I will. Uh . . . what's Jonah doing these days other than buying the ACC out of denims?"

"He's writing a long article for his newspaper—all about Dawson and the shortage of food and lamp oil and how so many people are still living in tents with the winter coming on. He says he wants the story to go out before the river freezes and we're cut off for the winter."

"I suppose Jonah will be going out on the same boat that his article does." She glanced up at the bright blue October sky. "He'd better hurry. There's more ice than water in that stream over there. When we woke up this morning, the rocker was frozen solid."

"Yes. I imagine it'll happen soon. The people in Dawson are trading bets on the day." Camilla looked hopefully toward the curl of smoke that rose from the cabin's chimney. "Your cabin looks snug. If we go inside, I can fit these to you."

"Yeah. Sure. Come on, Andy." Katy led Camilla to the shack and watched her lay out the work clothes that Jonah had sent. Hunter curled up contentedly beside the stove, and Andy clattered about warming coffee and biscuits. Camilla talked about her growing business in Dawson. The Irishwoman had five other seamstresses working for her and enough work to keep them all busy.

"Isn't it amazing how quickly the days are growing short?" Camilla said. "It feels very strange to think that we'll be almost completely cut off from the rest of the world once the river freezes."

Katy nodded and commented, scarcely aware of what she heard or said. Her mind was occupied with the picture of the last boat steaming down the Yukon for the north Alaskan coast, and Jonah standing on the deck waving good-bye.

Of course Jonah would go. Why would he stay? He'd held up his part of their bargain and then some. He'd never planned on staying the winter, and unless he took a boat downriver before the Yukon froze, he'd be stuck here. Katy certainly hadn't offered him any incentive to stay.

He wouldn't have stayed if you had offered him the moon, a voice inside her head told her. *He was itching to get back to Chicago, to his city streets and fancy job.*

He would have taken her with him, she reminded herself. He would have married her.

And what the hell would you do in a place like Chicago? the voice chided.

"Andy, quit squirming!" Camilla admonished for the fifth time. "How do you expect me to take these in if—oh my!" She jerked her hands away from where she had been pulling up the overalls to adjust the shoulder straps. "Andy?"

Andy turned crimson as a Klondike sunset. Camilla glanced at Katy, her eyes wide.

"Shit!" Andy commented.

"No cussing," Katy scolded. "There's a lady present. I told you that you couldn't stay a boy forever."

"Andy is a . . . a . . ."

"An Alexandra," Katy finished for her.

"Oh my!" Camilla lowered herself gingerly onto one of the stools by the camp stove. "Alexandra . . ."

"Call me Andy!" Andy shed the overalls and flung them aside. She headed for the cabin door, but on the way Katy plucked the cap off her head and grabbed her arm, turning her back into the cabin.

"An Alexandra with a temper as hot as her hair."

"Oh! You poor child! What have you done to your hair? And why would you want people to believe you're a boy?" Camilla's eyes were beginning to light with interest.

"Girls are sitting ducks unless they got some stupid man to take care of them."

Camilla smiled sadly. "That's what I used to think, but I've been doing very well on my own. And look how well Katy does for herself."

"Katy's got me to help her." Andy's mouth curved downward in a pugnacious bow.

"But you aren't a man, are you?" Camilla insisted gently. "It just goes to show how well we can do when we help each other. Just look at you. Let me get my shears and see what I can do for that awful hair."

Both Andy and Katy were gently bullied into doing exactly what Camilla wanted. Andy sat with only minor squirming while the Irishwoman patiently snipped and brushed her hair, and Katy heated water to wash it after the trimming was done.

"Now look at you!" a satisfied Camilla finally said. Still wet from being washed, Andy's hair crowned her head in soft curls of dark red. The absence of the ever-present stocking cap softened her face, which glowed from the vigorous scrubbing Camilla had given it. "You're as lovely a lass as I've ever seen."

Andy turned almost as red as her hair.

"It's true! Katy, bring a mirror. Let her see what a pretty girl she is."

"We don't have a mirror."

"Well, then, Alexandra, you'll just have to take our word on it."

"No. I want to see!" Andy sprang up, grabbed her parka, and shot out the door.

Katy and Camilla wrapped themselves against the cold and followed Andy to the undiverted portion of the stream, where the girl peered into a quiet pool by the bank.

"Look at me!"

Camilla smiled.

"I really am pretty!" Andy's bright eyes dimmed and her wide grin fell. "I can't go around looking like this!"

"Certainly you can!" Camilla told her. "You're not alone anymore, Alexandra. You have friends. Katy and I would never let anyone take advantage of you."

As the smile slowly came back to Andy's face, Katy suffered a pang of jealousy. Andy had literally come to life under Camilla's gentle hand, and Katy envied her friend's maternal instincts.

Camilla left in time to reach Dawson before dark, taking the overalls with her and promising to return when they were cut down to size. Katy and Andy went back to work. Katy noticed that Andy braved the cold without her hat and paused every once in a while to gingerly finger the curls that capped her head.

That night it snowed. The snow continued into the day, but they worked anyway, wet, cold, and miserable. When the sun came out the following day, the stream trickled through fanciful dams of ice that glinted in the light. Icicles turned the everyday spruce and pine into a fairy forest, and the water in the gravel was frozen so that shoveling was nearly impossible. Katy noted the snow-blanketed fairyland around them no more than she noted the harder work. The cold and ice filled her mind with the certainty that Jonah would leave on the next boat, if he hadn't left already.

Long after Katy should have been asleep that night she lay listening to Andy's soft snores. She could think of no good excuse to delay their work by going to Dawson, but she had to see Jonah again. One more time before he left. Just once more.

Katy blinked at the unfamiliar figure who answered her knock on Jonah's cabin door. He was plump, with a round reddish face chafed by the wind and a fringe of mouse-colored hair around a shining bald pate. He definitely was not Jonah. "Who're you?"

The man cocked his head at her and glanced uneasily at Hunter, who sat attentively at her side. "I might ask the same of you."

"Where's Jonah?" Katy scowled. Manners and patience were not high priorities after a six hour hike through mud, ice, and snow.

"Who?"

"Jonah Armstrong. The newspaper writer."

"Oh. The chap from the *Chicago Record*. Big fellow? Brown hair? Clean-shaven?"

"Yeah. Where is he?"

"Gone."

Katy's heart plummeted. "Gone wnere?"

The man shrugged. "Out of this hellhole would be my guess. He didn't say; I didn't ask. I was glad enough to get this cabin from him. Been living in a tent for a month."

"He didn't leave a message? A letter? Anything?"

The man's eyes softened. "No, lady. I'm sorry. He was in a right hurry, it seemed to me. I guess he had a deadline to meet."

Gone. The word echoed in Katy's heart as she made the rounds of Dawson asking about Jonah's whereabouts. No one had actually seen him get on the steamer that left the day before, but that didn't mean anything. The steamers were always full to overflowing both when they landed and left; he easily could have been missed. At the ACC his account was paid in full. Only one barkeeper knew him, and he said Jonah hadn't been in the saloon in four days at least.

He was gone. In spite of seven thousand people living in tents and cabins, Dawson seemed empty. The whole damned Klondike seemed empty because one damned newspaper writer had finished his job and hightailed it back to Chicago.

"I just can't believe he didn't even say good-bye!" she complained to Camilla. The seamstress shop was the last shop and the last hope, but Camilla didn't know where Jonah was, either.

"I thought he was partners with us," Andy said. She'd come to town with Katy but elected to visit the Irish widow instead of doing the rounds with Katy.

"We are partners. Half the claim is Jonah's. Seems like he wouldn't leave without knowing if he was rich or not."

"I'm sure he trusts you to see that he gets everything that is coming to him," Camilla said.

Katy kicked at the leg of her stool and morosely watched two of Camilla's seamstresses pin a pattern on a tailor's dummy. She'd like to give Jonah what was coming to him, all right. *Men called women fickle! Two proposals! Or was it three? And then, without saying so much as a "see you later," he leaves.* Her stomach churned.

"He did show me the article he wrote about Dawson," Camilla said. "He seemed very glad to have it finished in time to get it back to the States before winter closed in. It was very good. Jonah's a talented writer."

"Yeah. I bet." That wasn't all the skunk was talented at. He could take a perfectly stable, satisfied girl and turn her into a mucky swamp of confused emotions with one goddamned kiss. "Come on, Andy. We've got to get back."

"Aw Katy! Can't we stay the night?"

"You can't think of going back to the claim tonight!"

Camilla said in a horrified voice. "It's almost sunset, and the temperature's already below freezing. You'd be hiking in the dark, and Lord knows what you might come across. Just two days ago a man in Gold Bottom Creek was attacked by a grizzly and half-eaten. You two are staying right here in Dawson tonight! You can put up at my cabin."

Katy didn't have the energy to argue. At the moment, she felt like she could give a grizzly the fight of its miserable life, but she couldn't risk Andy's safety because she was in a foul mood.

It was just as well Jonah was gone, Katy told herself. Now she could concentrate on important things—like finding gold. But it still hurt that he hadn't said good-bye.

The next afternoon, the pungent smell of woodsmoke reached Katy and Andy as they hiked along the wagon road into the head of Skookum Gulch.

"Someone's keeping warm," Andy commented.

"Yeah."

Katy and Andy weren't the only prospectors working Skookum Gulch. There were claims both above and below their claim. The smell of smoke was no cause for concern, but Katy suffered a twinge of uneasiness anyway.

Half an hour later, when they rounded the bend just above their cabin and saw the curl of smoke coming from the stovepipe, alarms clanged in Katy's head. She pushed Andy into cover behind a boulder and squatted down beside her. Hunter crowded in between them, his ears pricked alertly.

"Omigod!" Katy whispered. "Claim jumpers!"

The smoke rose lazily into the cold air, but all else was still. In the fading light of dusk, Katy could see a shovel lying close by the rocker—the very shovel that Katy had scolded Andy for not putting in the cabin before they left. Katy had ended up putting the shovel away herself. Someone had moved it since then.

"Look! Someone started a new trench downstream of the old one," Andy observed.

"Damn! You'd think claim jumpers would wait until a body had found gold before they moved in and tried to take it away!"

"What're we gonna do?"

"Let me think." A shotgun loaded with buckshot rode the top of Katy's backpack, and her hunting knife was on her belt. Andy had a whittling knife and Katy's rock sling. All in all, it was a store of arms more suited for dealing with birds and squirrels than driving off claim jumpers.

A swell of rage rose in Katy's chest. After all she had gone through to get to the Klondike, some low-down, lazy, greedy, worthless skunk thought he could just move in and benefit from her hard work. For all she knew, the piece of horseshit had already found gold in her claim.

"Do you think there's just one of them?" Andy asked.

"Doesn't matter. There could be a whole damned army down there, and I'd still find a way to get back what's ours. You see that tall pine by the side of the cabin?"

"Yup."

"Think you could shinny up that tree, lean out, and stuff something down the stovepipe without falling or getting yourself burned?"

Andy grinned wickedly. "You bet."

"Then do it. Go up the hill a ways and come down from where you can't be seen if someone comes out the front." She slung her pack to the ground and dug through it hurriedly, extracting a woolen scarf. "Take this for the pipe. Hurry before the light goes completely, and I can't see. And give me the rock sling."

"You gonna pop 'em with a rock when they come out?"

"I've got only one load of buckshot in the shotgun, but there're enough rocks around here for me to fell an army."

An army of squirrels or sparrows, Katy amended silently as

Andy slipped away. Unless very precisely aimed, a rock sling wasn't likely to do much more than annoy a man.

The wait for Andy to appear seemed endless. The light faded fast, helped along by clouds that were creeping across the sky from the west. They hadn't left Dawson until mid-morning, having indulged the luxury of going to breakfast with Camilla at a restaurant that reputedly served the best flapjacks in the Klondike. Then Camilla had insisted they take the time to try on the overalls she had altered for them—the overalls that Jonah had bought from the ACC.

Jonah. The thought of him sent a pang through Katy's chest. She damned well was not going to let some jackass jump the claim that belonged to her and Jonah. Her and Jonah together.

Andy appeared as if by magic at the tree by the cabin. Agile as a monkey she clambered up, holding Katy's scarf in her mouth. Katy held her breath as the girl came even with the top of the stovepipe and leaned outward. Clinging with one hand to the tree, she stuffed the scarf beneath the tin rain shield that topped the pipe.

"Attagirl," Katy whispered.

Only a moment passed before smoke started leaking out between the inadequately caulked logs of the cabin. A man inside cursed, choking as he did so. The door banged open and out walked their claim jumper.

"Shit!" Katy whispered to herself. "He's got a damned rifle with him."

In the dusky light, Katy saw him turn and look at the cabin's roof, at the stovepipe where one end of the sooty scarf dangled. Andy pressed herself close to the tree trunk, but he was bound to see her. He was going to shoot, dammit!

Panic clawed at Katy's chest. No time for the sling. She aimed the shotgun and fired. The man yiped as a spray of buckshot bit into him.

"Take that, you weasel!"

No one else appeared at the door, so Katy concluded the man was alone. He had dropped to one knee and looked frantically about. But he didn't drop his rifle. Katy could almost hear him grit his teeth as he pumped the handle to cock it.

"Oh damn!" No time to load the shotgun. Katy fitted a stone to the sling, praying that her aim was true. She had brought down squirrels and birds with one shot, but then her hands hadn't shook, and a twelve-year-old girl hadn't hung in the balance. Why did things never go as planned?

The man still searched for a target in the near darkness. Katy let fly, and he dropped to the sand like a limp sack of grain.

Andy whooped. Katy gusted out a breath of relief and galloped down the side of the gulch. "Tie him up before he comes to!" she called to Andy.

As Andy went in search of rope, Katy turned her victim over with her foot and bent down to take the rifle from his hand.

"Oh spit!" Every cuss word she knew came to her lips. The claim jumper wasn't a claim jumper. He was Jonah.

CHAPTER 20

"Ouch! Goddammit! Put a knife in your hand and you become the Marquis de Sade! Not to mention what you do with a shotgun! Yow!"

"Hold still!" Katy demanded of Jonah. "Andy, move the lantern higher." Katy guided Andy's hand until the lantern light shone more fully upon Jonah, who lay prone upon the cot, his trousers and long johns around his knees, his backside exposed to Katy's knife.

"Crazy woman," Jonah muttered, then groaned as Katy pried another piece of shot from his buttocks.

"I thought you were a claim jumper."

"You think some brigand is going to bother with a claim full of useless gravel?"

Katy sniffed indignantly. "Any prospector worth his salt can look at this gulch and know there's gold here. Brace yourself. This one's deep."

"Yowch! God Almighty! They're all deep, dammit!"

Katy chuckled mercilessly. "What a disappointment. I'd begun to think you'd toughened up, Jonah, but now I see you're just a sissy at heart."

Jonah gritted his teeth as the knife pricked once again. "Claim jumper, my ass! You're enjoying this!"

She dabbed the blood away with a cool wet cloth. "It *was* your ass. And a fine one it is, too, don't you think so, Andy?"

"Best I've ever seen," Andy agreed.

"Ow!" Jonah growled into the mattress of the cot. "I'm going to get you both for this."

"It was your own fault," Katy said.

"How does even twisted—ouch!—female reasoning come up with that?"

"Any fool knows better than to sneak onto another prospector's claim."

"Half of it's my claim, dammit!"

"Yes, but I thought you'd gone back Stateside. Everybody in Dawson said you'd gone. Besides, it looked like you were going to shoot Andy."

"I wasn't goddamned going to shoot anyone! You're the one who did all the shooting. Not to mention nearly suffocating me with smoke and cracking my skull with a rock."

"And you thought we ladies couldn't take care of ourselves!"

"Shit! You're both a menace!"

"Quit grousing," Katy scolded. "You'll survive."

That he had survived Katy so far was nothing less than a miracle, Jonah reflected painfully as she worked assiduously on his smarting behind. If he had the sense God gave a sparrow, he'd give up, return to Chicago, and wallow in well-earned praise for the series of articles he'd sent back to the *Record*. If he'd done that, his backside wouldn't have gotten peppered with buckshot, his head wouldn't feel as though someone had it clamped in a vise, and two imps straight from the devil's harem wouldn't be trading comments over his bare arse.

He couldn't leave, though. He'd told Katy he was going to marry her, and he'd be damned if a load of buckshot would stand in the way. Life without her might be calmer, safer, and longer, but he didn't want calm and safe; calm and safe were dull. He didn't want to live until he was a doddering 105: he'd rather die riding a wild river with Katy, or perish of a heart attack making love to her when he was eighty.

"Katy?" he said through a grimace.

"Hold on, Jonah. Almost through."

"You really thought I'd leave you without saying goodbye?"

Silence reigned for a moment, punctuated by the careful forays of her knife.

"Did you?" he insisted.

"Well . . ."

She had, he heard in her voice. And she hadn't been happy about it.

"You thought I'd abandon this . . . this . . . " He waved an arm to indicate the tumbledown cabin, the lonely gulch, the waterlogged trenches and rocker full of useless quartz and feldspar gravel. ". . . this beautiful piece of freezing, windblown, useless streambed?"

"I'll admit it was hard to believe."

He heard the wry smile in her words.

"Why didn't you tell me you were going to come out?" she asked.

"I wanted to surprise you."

Andy chuckled. "Surprising Miss Katy ain't a smart move."

"Andy!" Katy scolded. "Quit laughing. You're making the light move. Go get that bottle of whiskey on the shelf."

"You have whiskey out here?" Jonah asked hopefully.

"Whoever built this shack left the dregs of a bottle. I hope it's not the good stuff, because it's going to get poured over your backside."

"I'd rather drink it."

The whiskey would have felt much better pouring down his throat than over his buckshot-cratered rump, and Jonah did not endure in silence. He could be stoic as the Sphinx if the situation called for it, but at this moment he didn't care if every grizzly bear in the Klondike heard him.

Katy merely patted his shoulder and pulled a blanket over his bare parts. "You're done," she announced.

"Done in is more like it," Jonah said with a groan. He allowed himself to drift to sleep on the thought that Katy gave a new meaning to the term shotgun wedding.

Katy ran her hand along the riffles of the rocker. Her fingers came away coated with tiny grains of black, shiny magnetite and a few dark fragments of some other mineral she couldn't identify. No golden flakes relieved the dark color.

"Where the hell is that gold? I know it's here."

Andy emptied another shovelful of gravel into the rocker, and the stream of water began bouncing rounded pebbles down the chute.

"How long have we been digging?" Katy asked, disgusted. "A week at least. Three trenches."

The first had threatened to collapse at twenty-five feet and had never reached bedrock. The second, dug mostly by Jonah, had actually collapsed at thirty feet, nearly burying Katy in a flood of sand and gravel. Only Jonah's quick grab for her and determined strength in pulling her free of the sand had saved her. The third trench they were digging wider to improve stability. It was down to fifteen feet, and still there were no shows of gold.

Katy wondered if she should start making contingency plans for not being rich.

In the trench, however, Jonah did not look equally discouraged. Katy nearly got a faceful of flying gravel as she peered over the edge.

"Watch out!" he called up to her, grinning.

"Anything new?"

"Got a layer down here I haven't seen before. The gravel's coarser."

"There's lenses and pods of that stuff all through here. I've seen it." She allowed herself the tiniest bit of hope. "See anything in it?"

"Gravel. Dirt. Sand. More gravel." He chuckled. "What a surprise."

How could he sound like he was having a good time? Katy wondered. She paused at the lip of the trench to watch him work, unable to take her eyes from the play of muscles in his shoulders and back as he plied the shovel. Cold as it was, he'd discarded his parka and flannel shirt and worked in only his long-sleeved undershirt, which hugged the contours of his back and arms as muscle bunched and rolled in effort. He'd tied the straps of his overalls around his waist. The loose garment was the only clothing Jonah could tolerate on his healing wounds besides a very soft and worn set of long johns.

The more Katy watched him, the more the old longing stirred—that foolish coil of admiration, liking, and desire that had been fueled by the long days and nights together on the trail. She couldn't help but wonder if he still wanted to marry her. Now that they were together again, she'd expected him to renew his pursuit. She'd expected him to tease her, reason with her, persuade her, seduce her. Andy's presence made things a bit awkward, but Jonah had managed to woo her—or had she wooed him?—on a trail in company with a thousand Klondikers.

Give in, a voice in her head urged. *Marry the man and discover if happily ever after really exists.*

Happily ever after in Chicago? she scoffed silently. Not likely. Besides, Jonah seemed very content to leave things as they were. Now he pursued gold rather than her. Where before he'd been content to write about gold, now he blistered his hands and dripped with sweat in search of it.

"Do you want something to eat?" she asked him.

He threw a shovelful of sand and gravel onto the pile. "What has Hunter brought us for supper?"

"Hunter's been lying by the stove all morning, staying warm."

Jonah chuckled and dug his shovel into the floor of the trench. "Smart wolf. Smarter than us."

"There's beans, smoked trout, and biscuits from break-fast—"

"The ones I made?"

"Yes. There's strawberry preserves I got in Dawson, and some cans of beef."

"Feast fit for a gold king." He tossed his shovel out of the trench. Katy reached down to help him up the steep ramp. He gripped her forearm, his hand closing all the way around it. "Pull," he urged. "I'm a cripple, you know. Some crazy woman shot me."

"Your legs aren't what I shot." She pulled. He surged forward, and Katy landed on her back on the damp gravel with him on top. Clear blue eyes twinkled down at her, and a sudden blaze of desire left her breathless. His chest flattened her parka-covered breasts, and against her thigh rose the evidence of his state of male attention.

Her eyes narrowed, shooting daggers up at him. "A bit a revenge for your sore ass?"

"Me?" His smile was innocent as a child's. "You underestimate me, Katydid. When I take revenge, there won't be any question or subtlety about it."

"Oh my!" It was Camilla's voice. Jonah and Katy had been so absorbed in each other that they'd missed the clatter of her cart descending into the gulch. "Katy! Jonah!" She sounded mortally embarrassed.

Jonah laughed and got to his feet, pulling Katy up beside him. "It's all right, Camilla. Katy was just helping me out of the trench and I was a bit too much for her."

"Too much for me?" Katy whispered out of the side of her mouth. "That'll be the day."

Jonah merely smiled. "You're just in time for supper," he said to Camilla. "Light and rest a while."

"Jonah! I thought you went back to the States!"

"And let Katy and Andy have all my gold?" he said with a laugh.

"You found gold?"

"Not a trace," Katy told her. "Yet."

"Well," Camilla said. "If anyone can find it, you can, Katy. I brought a few things for Alexandra—and you too, Katy. I know you lost everything in the Sheep Camp flood, then again at Whitehorse." She could refer to that tragedy now without flinching. Katy was reminded again of how much she admired Camilla's courage. Making one's own way in the world by choice was all very well and good, but to be alone because your loved ones were lost—that was something entirely different.

Camilla tugged a bundle from the back of the cart. "Alexandra needs some feminine things, and there were a couple of dresses someone ordered from me and never picked up."

"Dresses?" Andy asked suspiciously.

"Yes, Alexandra," Camilla answered firmly. "Dresses. How old are you?"

"Dunno. Maybe twelve or thirteen. I don't keep track."

"From the looks of you, you're plenty old enough to wear proper clothes."

"I got proper clothes! These are nice and warm."

"You won't be digging for gold forever. Soon you'll be a rich young lady. Do you want to look like a scarecrow, and a poorly dressed scarecrow at that?"

"Yes'm."

Katy wanted to laugh. Too well she remembered the day that Olivia had first decked her out in female fripperies in the cabin above Elkhorn, Montana. She'd been so embarrassed that she'd had to be dragged down to greet her father when he came in from working the mine. She must have looked very much like Andy, she thought. A glance downward showed her that she didn't look much different even now, eight years later.

Jonah relieved Camilla of the bundle as they walked toward the cabin. Andy and Katy fell in behind.

"Don't want no dresses!" Andy hissed quietly into Katy's ear.

"Just try them on," Katy advised. "Make her happy. Camilla has a good heart, and she's being very kind to both of us."

Andy expressed her doubt in a soft growl as they walked through the door of the cabin.

They warmed themselves with coffee while Camilla told them the latest from Dawson. A couple of prospectors had brought in a big strike on Hunker Creek. George Digby at the North American Trading and Transportation Company had come down with the influenza and died. Rumor had it that a steamer on the Yukon had gotten itself wedged between some ice floes halfway between Dawson and the coast. Camilla had heard that there was some rich foreign lady on the boat with a monster dog. The woman had offered a reward to anyone who could get the steamer free, and a party of men had left Dawson to help dig the boat out. If the steamer made it to Dawson, it would doubtless be the last one that made the trip until spring.

Camilla accepted a second cup of steaming coffee. "Andy," she said, "you are going to adore the way you look in these dresses. I think the fit will be good, but if it's not, I'll simply alter them to your size." She unwrapped the bundle and held up a long-sleeved blue polka-dotted gingham trimmed with lace around the collar and the cuffs.

"This is too good to wear every day, but for special occasions like church, or . . . well, going out, this is perfect."

She tossed the first dress to Andy and shook out another, a brown wool serge with a vee waist and sleeves that were full and puffed from shoulder to elbow and tightly fitted from elbow to wrist. "This looks a bit old and sedate for you, but I could add a flounce and do something with the sleeves. Hm?"

She threw it on Andy's lap with the other.

"And here is the best." She took out a green, ruffly garment that was exactly designed for a little girl blossoming into young womanhood. "Isn't this sweet?"

Andy made a choking sound before a lethal look from Katy silenced her.

"And now we ladies will retire behind the screen over there and transform Alexandra into a proper lass."

"Why don't you ladies use the whole cabin?" Jonah offered. "I hear a shovel calling me back to work."

Andy looked longingly at the door as Jonah escaped, but before she could protest Camilla took her by the hand and started measuring with her eyes. "Let's see what we have here."

By the time an hour had passed, poor Andy had been tucked, pinned, flounced, hemmed, and trimmed. Her hair had been dampened, wound into short red curls around Camilla's fingers, and set next to the stove to dry, along with the rest of her. Her face had been washed and her fingernails scrubbed. All the garments expect the green dress and two petticoats needed altering, and now she stood in the ruffly and very feminine little green gown and looked embarrassed as a dog in cat clothing.

"I can't work in this," she protested.

"You can do women's work, dear, but of course a dress wasn't made for shoveling and such."

"Got to shovel to find gold," Andy growled.

"Of course you do. These clothes are for coming into town and celebrating once you've found it."

Somewhat mollified, Andy looked down at herself suspiciously.

"You're a very pretty girl," Camilla told her. "In a few years, the boys are going to be on you like flies on honey."

"Yeah, I bet." Andy didn't sound happy about that idea, and Katy sympathized, considering the girl had narrowly escaped being trapped in her mother's sordid profession.

"Men do have their uses, Andy," Katy reminded her. She thought of her father and how tender he was with Olivia. She thought of Jonah. "Not all men are like those who came to your mother."

"Oh? Andy? Your mother is still alive?" Camilla asked.

"My mother's a whore," Andy answered belligerently. "I got raised in a whorehouse, with all the men flockin' around me. They was like flies, all right."

"Oh my! Then my remark was certainly ill considered. I meant no harm."

Camilla looked truly stricken. Andy took her hand. "I know you didn't mean no harm. I like the dresses. Really. I'll wear 'em next time we come to town."

Camilla had her eyes cast downward and couldn't see the grimace on Andy's face, but Katy could. She was surprised at the girl's concession.

"You really do look beautiful in that green," Camilla said softly. "Let's call Jonah and see what he thinks."

Andy rolled her eyes as Camilla went to the door and called out.

Jonah and Camilla spent the waning afternoon making such a fuss over Andy's new duds that by suppertime, Andy herself began to preen. Her face took on a warm glow and her manner became almost shy.

Camilla agreed to spend the night. In fact, she seemed eager to. When Andy, dressed once again in warm woolen trousers and a parka, left the cabin to fill the water buckets from the stream, Camilla broached an unexpected subject.

"A school is starting up in Dawson," she told Katy and Jonah.

"Good!" Jonah approved. "Where there's people, there's kids."

"Education is very important to a person these days," Camilla said. "The world is changing, you know. Days when a person could build a future with just hard work and a piece of land won't be around much longer. You can't get by in the world without reading and writing and numbers—more even. Women are going to college, getting the vote, and becoming as educated as men."

"My stepma's a doctor," Katy said.

"How admirable! Just my point exactly! I dream of the things I could do if I had more of an education."

Camilla had come a long way from the obedient wife who had followed in blind devotion while her husband led the way to disaster, Katy thought.

"That's why I . . . well . . ." She glanced anxiously at the door, as if fearing Andy's return. ". . . I was hoping you might let Andy stay with me in town and start attending school. She's such a wild little thing, but she has so much potential."

An unexpected bolt of panic shot through Katy. "But I promised Andy a share of the claim."

"She could help you on weekends and holidays," Camilla countered. "Besides, surely you won't be able to work once winter sets in for real."

"There are ways to work even when the ground is frozen solid," Katy protested. "You light a fire and melt the gravel—"

"But now Jonah is here to help."

Jonah was looking at Katy with an expectancy that reminded her of the looks her father used to give her when she was being childish, which was frequent.

"Andy would want to stay on the claim," Katy insisted, feeling selfish even as she said it. Almost without Katy being aware of it, the kid had slipped into her heart. She was a companion and a little sister. The thought of losing her made her heart sink.

"She'll probably want to stay," Jonah agreed, still looking at Katy. "But you could talk her into going with Camilla."

Katy's rebellious silence was broken as Andy banged the door open and stumped in carrying two brimming buckets. "Not enough for baths," she announced cheerfully. "Stream's practically frozen over."

Jonah's stool scraped the floor as he got abruptly to his feet. "Andy, stay here and entertain Camilla for a while. Katy and I have some chores to do outside."

"What chores?" Andy asked. "It's dark."

"Chores," Jonah replied tersely.

"It's mighty cold," Andy warned.

Jonah threw a parka at Katy. The steel determination in his eyes brooked no argument.

Once they were away from the cabin, Jonah stopped and propped his fists upon his hips. His voice had as much steel as his eyes. "You're going to convince Andy to go with Camilla," he said confidently.

"She won't listen to me."

"You're the only one she'll listen to."

"I promised I'd give her a job for as long as I'm in the Klondike."

"This has gone way beyond a job, and you know it."

Katy answered with silence. She scraped the toe of her boot across the gravel and refused to look up into Jonah's moon-silvered face. That he cared so much about Andy moved her. That he cared nothing for her own needs and feelings hurt, however.

"She'd hate it," Katy finally protested. "She'd probably run away."

"She wouldn't run away from Camilla. Camilla's got a knack with kids, and Andy likes her a lot. Andy will do it if you ask her to."

Katy gusted out a sigh.

Jonah laid a hand on her arm. Even through his glove and her parka the touch tingled on her skin. "Camilla can set her on the right path," he said. "Andy needs to learn to be a girl, and a child. And . . . Camilla needs to be someone's mother."

That was true, Katy acknowledged reluctantly to herself. She saw the glow in Camilla's eyes whenever she looked at Andy. And it was true that Andy showed a bit of softening when she spoke to Camilla.

"I could teach her," Katy said in a small voice. "I'm a woman, too."

Jonah's smile made her heart jump. "I did notice that."

"But I suppose Camilla's better at being a real woman."

"You're as real a woman as anyone could ever want, Katy-did. But I think Camilla needs Andy more than you do right now."

Katy gave a disgusted snort.

Jonah smiled and touched her cheek with a gloved finger. "Everyone needs to grow up sometime, Katy."

As he walked back toward the cabin, leaving her in cold solitude, Katy wondered if he was talking about Andy or her.

Katy huddled in the quilts on her cot and stared into the darkness. A crude screen of blankets partitioned off the area of the cabin that was the "ladies' boudoir," as Katy and Andy had jestingly called it after Jonah had moved into the cabin. For the two nights since Andy had left, Katy had slept behind the blankets with only Hunter as company, and she was not enjoying it. The screen blocked the heat from the stove, and the little cubicle was cold as ice. Andy's presence in the other cot had at least added some body heat, or maybe she had simply added the warmth of companionship. In any case, Katy was so cold she might as well be sitting on the North Pole, and loneliness sapped whatever meager heat was left in her body.

Andy had rebelled at first when they had sprung Camilla's offer upon her. But Katy's assurances that she would still have part of the claim, the enticement of learning how to read and do numbers, and the unspoken need that shone from Camilla's eyes had persuaded her. The next morning she and Camilla had left on the cart, Andy handling the broken-down livery nag much more expertly than Camilla had.

Katy huddled deeper into the quilts and ached for Andy's absence. She didn't like being alone, Katy decided. All her life she'd had loved ones around her—sister, father, mother, stepmother. She'd never thought of how loneliness would feel when she had declared that she would forgo marriage and a family to be an independent woman. Now she was alone, and she didn't like it one bit.

Jonah was here, of course, but somehow his presence only made her loneliness worse, for soon he would go back to his world and leave her to hers. That was the way it had to be. But the thought of it left an emptiness in her heart that was colder than the air outside.

In the night quiet of the cabin, Katy could hear Jonah's soft, relaxed breathing, punctuated every now and again with the snap of burning pine and spruce in the camp stove. How good it would feel to have his arms around her in the dark. He would warm her, make the darkness less oppressive. Would it be so wrong to seek his comfort while he was still here to give it?

It would be wrong, her conscience told her. *It really would.*

Katy was no ignorant child who didn't know the risk of joining Jonah in his bed. But she wanted it just the same.

Maybe, her conscience suggested, *you don't mind the risk because conceiving a child will take the decision out of your cowardly hands.*

Or maybe, Katy answered herself, she was simply a wicked woman. Wicked and lonely, and she loved a man she shouldn't have.

The argument with herself was pointless. She had no energy to resist the compulsion of Jonah's nearness. With a sigh of surrender, she padded to his cot, nightgown gathered tightly around her, icy plank floor biting through the wool of her socks.

"Jonah?" She touched his shoulder.

He woke immediately. "Katy." One hand reached out and took hers. The other lifted his blankets in invitation.

She crawled into the warm haven of his narrow cot and snuggled against him as his arms pulled her close. Through his long johns she felt him hard and ready the moment their bodies touched. She sighed in bliss, kissed his bare chest, and wormed her way upward on the cot to kiss his mouth, which welcomed her with eager passion. Too soon, though, he set her back from him. His hand captured hers as it wandered downward over his chest.

"Katy, no."

"No?"

He kissed the tousled top of her head, his breath warm and comforting in her hair. "No. This is wrong, Katy. You can't decide to accept one facet of love and reject the rest. This is wrong."

"You don't want me?" she asked incredulously.

"Oh, my beautiful Katydid. I want you so badly that I'm likely to burst right out of my skin. But I want all of you, not just the little part you're willing to give."

For a moment she was merely stunned. Embarrassment brought her back to life. She tried to scramble from the cot, but his arms held her prisoner.

"Don't raise your hackles, Katy. Stay here and let me keep you warm."

Indignation battled loneliness and need, and in the end she settled back against him. The hurt of his rejection was a lump in her throat that made words impossible, but the solid strength of his arms around her and the warmth of his body dealt out some comfort. Finally warm, if not satisfied, Katy surrendered to sleep.

Jonah listened to Katy's breathing as it settled into the quiet, steady rhythm of sleep. His body still screamed a protest, and the painful hardness at his groin showed no indication of abating. In sleep, Katy pressed unwittingly against him in a very graphic reminder of what he had so nobly declined.

He smiled wryly into the sweet tangle of her hair. This was certainly a new twist on an old game; usually it was the woman who held back her favors until the man was brought to the altar. But then, Katy was a new twist unto herself—on womanhood, on love, on life itself. None of the tried-and-true rules applied to her.

Tomorrow, he promised himself, they would have a talk. If he had to tie Katy to a chair while he pounded some reason into her stubborn head, he would, by damn, and then they would let the rocker lie idle while they sealed their love in passion.

He woke with morning's first pale light stealing through the window. The cot beside him was empty. From outside, the dull thunk of a shovel told him Katy's whereabouts. He lay for a while planning just what he would say to prove that she had nothing to fear from marriage, or from him, until a shout derailed his train of thought.

He had just flung off the blankets when the cabin door banged open and Katy marched in, her face alight, a wide smile curving her lips.

"Jonah, you lazy slugabed. Look at this!"

She dropped the black, cold mud she carried in her hands onto his bare chest. Freezing water ran into his navel and dripped onto the cot where he lay, and within the black muck a thousand tiny flakes glittered like sequins.

"Gold!" Katy crowed. "We've found gold!"

CHAPTER 21

When Katy celebrated, she celebrated with a passion. The lights that danced in her eyes were brighter by far than the oil lamps that lit the dining room of the Great Northern Hotel. She was just tipsy enough to make her smile a bit lopsided, but not tipsy enough to eschew dancing when the dining room pianist began to pound out a tune.

"Come on, Jonah!" she demanded. "Let's dance!"

Jonah allowed her to pull him away from his steak and beans. She slipped into his arms and tilted her face up to his with a smile that gave his heart a jolt.

"How does it feel to be rich woman?" he asked.

"Like I'm walking on air."

What she was walking on was his feet. Katy still was not a good dancer. Graceful and quick, she couldn't follow his lead, a characteristic he had noted in other aspects of her life as well.

"How does it feel to be a rich man?" she asked, an impish twinkle in her eyes.

"You mean aside from the sore back and blistered hands and frostbitten toes?"

"You don't have frostbitten toes!"

"They feel that way."

"It's worth it, though, isn't it?"

Katy was worth it, Jonah acknowledged. The gold didn't actually seem real yet, though they'd dug far enough into the pay zone to determine the deposit wasn't an isolated lens or pod, and the assayer in Dawson had confirmed the richness of the find.

"Well?" Katy demanded impatiently while mashing one of his toes. "What are you going to do with all the wealth that I made for you?"

"You made for me?"

"I staked the claim."

"With my money."

"I decided where to dig."

"And I did a good part of the digging."

She grinned. "Just finding out if being rich has made you less ornery."

"Me? Ornery? I was a very amiable fellow before I met a certain hell-raiser from Willow Bend, Montana."

"You raise a fair amount of hell yourself," she said, and Jonah imagined he heard a certain fondness in her voice. "Will you buy a big house in Chicago?"

"My family already has a big house in Chicago."

"A yacht to sail on that big lake you told me about?"

"Sorry. We have one."

"Take a trip to Europe?"

"Been there."

Katy's lower lip thrust out in a playful pout. She was having more fun thinking up ways for him to spend a fortune than for herself. Jonah wondered if she realized that, however he spent the money, she was going to be right by his side.

The small dance floor had gotten crowded. They bumped against Andy, who danced with Camilla. Camilla's face glowed with maternal pride, and Andy was scarcely recognizable in her blue polka-dotted dress and bouncy red curls. The lumberjack Johnson brothers had also crowded onto the floor, Otar and Buck danced together like two lumbering bears, and Sven danced with Dawson's schoolmistress. Around the dining room, whooping and stomping to urge the dancers on, sat clerks from the Alaska Commercial Company and North American Trading and Transportation Company, prospectors, and a couple of newspaper reporters—one from Kansas City, another from San Francisco. Folks in Dawson believed in helping to celebrate a golden success story, even if it wasn't theirs.

Jonah guided Katy back to their table. "You've broken every one of my toes," he complained. "I can't dance anymore. I think I'll use part of my fortune to buy you dancing lessons."

"I thought gentlemen were supposed to suffer in silence rather than mention a lady's shortcomings."

Jonah grinned. "I've learned better than to try to be a gentleman around you, Katydid."

"Shame on you, Jonah Armstrong," Camilla joined in as she and Andy took their seats. "If you don't act the gentleman, how do you expect Katy to act the lady?"

"Thank you, Camilla," Katy said, looking down her nose at Jonah in attempted hauteur.

Katy was happy all right. Jonah watched her dance, eat, and dance again, her manner innocently flirtatious and brightly vivacious as she spread her wings in happy triumph. It seemed as if every prospector in Dawson had crowded into the Great Northern Hotel to join the party, and Katy danced with every one of them. Despite the ache in his toes, Jonah envied every man she partnered. Finally she sank into the chair next to him.

"*They* don't think I'm a bad dancer," Katy shot at Jonah with a grin.

"All of them have been dancing with other prospectors who wear size twelve boots. What do you expect?"

"You're mean when you're rich."

A grizzled old man grabbed Katy's shoulder from behind. Katy whipped around in protest, then her eyes widened with delight. "Stewpot!"

"Yup! In the flesh, Katy girl. Hear you made a strike."

"Jonah, you remember Stewpot Sanders, who brought me and Andy down the river."

The two men shook hands, and Stewpot pulled up a chair. "Where be the young'un?" Stewpot asked.

Across the table, Andy's face turned beet red. Stewpot glanced her way, then stared. "Well, I'll be."

"Meet Alexandra," Katy said apologetically.

"Well, I'll be," the old man repeated.

"Did you make a strike yet?" Katy asked, hastening to change the subject.

"Yup. Up Bonanza Creek. Good color fifteen feet down. I'm headed out on the steamer to spend the winter where it's warm and the sun shines. Be back next spring."

"Has the steamer made it in yet?" Jonah asked.

"Nope. But she will. Some boys hiked down the river to get her free of the ice. It'll be her last trip till spring, though, and she's gonna be full to the gills."

Jonah's mood lifted as possibilities suddenly blossomed in his mind.

Midnight had come and gone by the time Jonah handed Katy through the door of her hotel room. She pulled him in behind her, grasped his hands, and whirled them both in a circle of joy. Hunter jumped from the bed and danced around them, joining the silliness.

"We're rich! Do you believe it?" Katy threw her arms around Jonah's neck and grinned at him. "Now aren't you glad I convinced you to look for gold instead of just writing about people who look for gold?"

"I guess I am."

She kissed him, quick and hard, giving him a jolt worthy of lightning, then released him and bounced away in a very Indian-like dance of triumph. Finally she collapsed on the bed with a happy sigh. "My grandmother taught me that victory dance. Her name was Squirrel Woman. Did I ever tell you about her?"

"Yes." He didn't know how long he could resist Katy sitting on that bed, half-child, half-siren. He retreated toward the door. "Good-night."

"Wait!" She sprang from the bed and pulled him back. He smelled the hint of wine on her breath, and the warm scent of roses she had dabbed on mingled with her natural fragrance that Jonah knew so well. "Jonah. Thank you."

"You did it, Katydid."

"Not without you."

She pulled him down for another kiss, and the leash Jonah had kept upon himself snapped. He cupped her head between loving hands and adjusted her to give him better access to her mouth. Her lips opened beneath his; her tongue teased his with playful forays, until he captured it and made it his. She breathed a tiny groan into his mouth as his hands slid down her body and clamped her forcefully against him.

"Katy!" He growled against her throat. He tasted the warm, firm flesh from her chin to her collarbone. He was aroused to the point of pain, and her instinctive movements against him were pushing him past the point of control. He ached to push her down upon the bed, rid her of her clothing, and satisfy himself with a wild abandon he knew she would match.

She sought his mouth again. Her lips captured his, devouring him, flesh and breath and spirit. He felt himself sinking into a state of total animal need.

"No! Katy, goddammit!"

"What?" she cried as he set her back from him.

He panted like a man who had run five miles. His grasp slid down her arm to her hand, which he refused to give up. "Katy. You've got what you came for—gold. I've written—well, not all that should be written about this by a long shot, but all the *Record* readers will stomach. Let's go out on the steamer. The gold we got out of the claim in one day will pay for our fare to Seattle and then some."

"You're crazy! What about the claim?"

"It's duly staked and recorded, and no one would be fool enough to bother it during a Klondike winter. It will be here next spring, and we can spend the whole summer digging gold to your heart's content. If you stay here for the winter, you're going to freeze your little rumpus off. You'll need to melt the gravel with fires. It's a slow and dangerous way to mine. Wait until after the thaw next spring."

"But—"

"Marry me, Katy. We'll honeymoon in San Francisco. We'll have the whole winter to decide what to do with all this gold."

As if she thought he was teasing, Katy laughed, but there was uncertainty in the laughter. "Jonah Armstrong! Shame on you. You want to marry me for my fortune."

"Don't laugh at me, Katy. You know goddamned well that I'm serious."

"I can't marry you! I've told you before!"

"You can't? Or you won't?"

"What's the difference?"

"The difference is that in every other walk of your life there's no such thing as can't. What makes marriage to me the one thing that you *can't* do?"

Her mouth settled into a mutinous line.

"I know you love me, Katy. You can't lie worth a damn, and everything you feel shines in your eyes as bright as the sun. I know you love me."

"I'm half-Blackfoot. I grew up running wild all over Montana. I can just see me sipping tea in Chicago and parading down the streets with a parasol to keep the sun off my face."

"You think that's the life I would ask you to lead?"

"I want to decide the kind of life I'll lead! I'm where I belong!"

"Oh, bullshit!" Thwarted desire turned into impatient anger that swelled in his chest and crackled in his voice. "Stop lying to yourself! You're not afraid of Chicago—or New York or Europe or New Orleans or anyplace else on this whole damned world. You're afraid you can't make it as a woman, as someone's wife. You've been running around wearing britches and skinning squirrels so long that you're convinced that's all there is to you."

"That's not true!"

"Isn't it? Look inside yourself, Katy. How many times have you declared that you can't sew, can't cook, you don't know what to do with babies, and you'd rather muck out a barn than clean a house? Do you think those things constitute being a woman? You think you're going to make a fool of yourself because that's all there is to being a wife?"

"That's not what I think," she growled. "I'm not afraid of marriage."

"No? Then ask yourself this. Why, in all this time I've been pestering you to marry me and all this time you've been turning your nose up at going with me to Chicago, why didn't you once broach the subject of me staying out West?"

She scowled.

"It wasn't because you didn't want to be with me, Katy."

"I . . . well . . . " She eyed him uncertainly.

"It's because you were afraid I'd say yes, you little twit."

"What the hell do you know!"

"More than you do on this subject, Katy my love! You're getting all knotted up about problems that don't exist. Sewing a good seam and making great biscuits don't make a woman, just as hard fists and a fast gun don't make a man. It's the heart that makes a person, Katy, and believe me, your heart is purer gold than anything we could ever dig out of Skookum Gulch. I don't need a woman who wants to spend her life building a nest. I want someone who has a spirit of steel and the courage of a lion, who can laugh at things that make other women gasp. I want someone who makes me feel alive, who lights up my life so that if she left, I'd feel like a bottle after someone's poured out all the wine.

"That's you, Katy. I want you. And I don't give a damn if you never sew a button on a shirt or light an oven."

Her eyes were wide, her face drained of color. Without a word Katy grabbed her parka and fled the room. The door slammed behind her, leaving an empty silence.

Katy kicked at a frozen clod of mud. One of the numerous dogs that roamed the streets of Dawson gave her a wary look and made a wide detour around her. She suddenly longed for Hunter. Hunter knew she wasn't a coward. Hunter knew she wasn't a twit. She could bury her face in Hunter's plush fur and draw comfort from her best friend.

But Hunter, the traitor wolf, had stayed in the room with Jonah. No doubt he was listening to the damned greenhorn spout more lies about her.

"Damn!" She paused in her march down the street to kick at another clod, but this one was frozen to the ground, and she jammed her toe with the force of her own ferocity. She hopped a few steps, caught the hem of her skirt with her heel, and sat down hard in the middle of the dark street. "Damned skirt! Damned ice! Damned *everything*!" This was all his fault, the low-down, arrogant, know-it-all, son of a skunk. Afraid, was she? Lying to herself, was she? What did Jonah know? Nothing! That's what! Absolutely nothing!

Katy got up and marched down the street. Light and music poured from the windows of the saloons and dance halls, and bursts of laughter promised companionship, but she knew better than to seek solace in a saloon, especially gussied up in a dress. She passed the two-story log Alaska Commercial Company store, the blacksmith shop and livery, a whorehouse that leaked music around shuttered windows, and finally arrived at the little log cabin that Camilla had rented.

The cabin was dark and still. Camilla and Andy were asleep. Oh well, Katy thought as she sat on the edge of the porch, she didn't really need to talk to Camilla. She knew almost exactly what the Irish mother hen would say.

Well, Katy? You must think carefully. Is it true that you're afraid? Are you a coward and a two-bit twit who's been lying to yourself about why you refuse to marry Jonah?

Camilla might have used gentler words, Katy suspected, but the message would be the same. And what would Katy's answer be? What was the truth of it?

Does he make you want things you never thought you could have? Does he make you lose a part of yourself in loving him? Does that make you afraid, Katy?

Katy wished the phantom Camilla weren't quite so perceptive.

Does he make you afraid that you'll fail as a wife? Do you fear the pain of losing his love? Is it easier to lose him now, when things have scarcely started between you?

She could almost see the sympathetic tilt of Camilla's head, the motherly concern in her eyes. The Irishwoman would pat her hand, give her hot coffee laced with good Irish whiskey, and lecture her gently that men and women weren't meant to walk the earth alone, that love could conquer all.

Horsefeathers! Katy would say to her. Love didn't conquer all. Look at the mess Camilla had landed in in the name of love!

Jonah Armstrong is ten times the man Patrick Burke was, Camilla would admit sorrowfully.

He only proposed out of gentlemanly duty, Katy would say, grasping at straws.

Camilla would raise a doubting brow. *A man might propose once out of duty. Not three or four times.*

Katy dropped her head into her hands and sighed. Camilla had all the answers, dammit. Jonah was right. Living in Chicago or anywhere else had nothing to do with her refusals to marry him. She was scared as a rabbit with a pack of wolves snapping at its heels. Katy O'Connell, who prided herself on being afraid of nothing, was scared spitless of a thing any other woman would meet with open arms, so scared she was willing to give up the man she loved.

Dear Jonah, with his laughing eyes and irreverent smile. What other man in the world combined such courage with such gentleness? What other man would back down from men trying to steal his poker earnings, yet let fists fly at a scuzzy skunk who abused his packhorses? What other man would give up his last funds to stake a cocky pest of a female who claimed she could win enough money to get them across the Chilkoot? Who else could make her soar like a bird and at the same time make her feel as fragile as a butterfly?

Damn but she loved that man!

Love conquers all, Camilla's imaginary voice reminded her.

Katy thought of her father and stepmother. A high-class lady doctor from New York shouldn't be happy with an Irish longshoreman turned Montana ex-outlaw, an ex-outlaw with two half-breed half-wild kids. Yet Olivia was happy. She loved Gabe O'Connell, and Gabe loved her. How frightened Olivia must have been when she first came to Montana, found herself sucked into the middle of a diphtheria epidemic, and then kidnapped by a gun-toting, hot-tempered fugitive with two sick kids. Yet she had charged ahead. Love conquers all. It certainly had for Katy's stepmother. Maybe it would for her.

Damned if she was going to let her life be ruled by fear—she who had faced grizzly bears and Montana claim jumpers without a twitch of her pigtails. And damned if she would let Jonah Armstrong get away with calling her a coward and a liar.

She'd get back at him. That she would. She would marry the son of a skunk.

Jonah's hotel room was dark when Katy slipped inside. Silently she shut the door behind her and stood with her back against it. Jonah's masculine scent filled the room. His quiet snoring was the only sound.

A floorboard creaked as Hunter got up from where he lay on the floor beside the bed, stretched, and padded over to greet her with a cold nose shoved into the palm of her hand. The wolf had preferred Jonah's company to awaiting Katy's return in her empty room. Katy couldn't blame Hunter too much, since she'd just admitted to herself that she preferred Jonah's company over almost anything else on earth.

Before she could worry about Jonah's reaction to her stealthy visit, Katy slipped out of her clothing and got into the bed. Jonah came instantly and violently awake. Before Katy could so much as squeak he had her pinned to the bed with both wrists in a brutal grasp.

"Jonah!"

"Katy! What the hell?"

"Were you expecting someone else?" She rubbed her wrists where he had grabbed her. "I'm going to have bruises," she complained, then slid a mischievous glance upward. "Now I guess we're even, huh?"

"I doubt that you'll have bruises, and no, we're not even. Sore wrists are hardly in the same league as peppering someone's backside with buckshot."

He hovered over her, still pinning her to the mattress with his body.

"Did you think I was someone trying to steal your money?"

His grin flashed above her in the darkness. "Now that I see who it is, I'd say you're more likely here to steal my virtue."

She made a rude noise in her throat. "What virtue?"

Silence descended, heavy and awkward. Finally, he moved off of her and collapsed onto his back. "Katy, what is this?"

Katy's heart raced in her chest. "I came to find out if . . . well, if you're still in the market for a wife." In the quiet, she imagined she could hear Jonah's heart beating as well as her own.

"Did you have a candidate in mind?" he asked softly.

"Do you still want me, Jonah?"

"I'd say that was an understatement."

"I've acted like a jackass every time you've asked me."

"That's a pretty accurate description."

"And you were right—about a lot of things you said."

"It must be painful for you to admit such a thing," he said with a smile.

She frowned at the sting in his words. "You weren't right about everything, though. I'm not really a coward. At times I can be very brave." She raised herself on one elbow so that she could look down upon his grinning face. "For instance, I'm not afraid to do this." Her hand slipped under the blankets and unerringly grasped a most sensitive part of his naked anatomy.

Jonah jolted. "Jesus, Katy! You could give a man a heart attack!" He was already hard and heavy in her hand, and got larger and harder as she caressed and teased.

"And I'm not afraid to do this." She leaned down to kiss him. As their lips joined, his hand came up behind her head to hold them sealed together. His mouth was hard and demanding, slanting across hers with a hunger that erased any worry she had that he might not still want her.

Still holding her into the kiss, he flipped her onto her back and settled himself on top of her, his hips between her thighs, his chest hair tickling her breasts.

"Do you still want to marry me, Jonah Armstrong?" she asked with a wicked grin.

"Yes. And that's not all I want to do to you, you little menace."

He kissed her again, then tasted her throat, her shoulders, her breasts, devouring her as though she were a feast set before him. Every warm pass of his tongue and pull of his lips fed the need that rose up in her. Her hands clutched at his back, roving over bands of hard muscle, slipping around taut buttocks, and diving between their bodies to caress his eager arousal—velvet over hot steel, moisture pearling at the very tip, moving in her hand like a live and hungry animal. She drew him down to touch her own soft, moist flesh, so ready for him that she almost cried out in her need.

"Katy!" Jonah whispered against her breast. "Say it."

"Say it?"

"Say it. Say you love me."

Katy groaned her frustration, but he wouldn't give her what she wanted until she gave him what he wanted.

"Say it!" he demanded.

"Okay. I love you."

"You haven't convinced me."

It was easier the second time. "I love you!" she said with feeling "I've loved you for days, for weeks, for ages and ages, and I'll love you till I croak. There!" she concluded with a wicked grin. "Good enough?"

"Good enough." His eyes reflected her grin, and his face softened. "I love you, too, Katy O'Connell. And I will until you drive me to an early grave."

Her fingers still held him as he slid inside her, and the feel of his rock-hard erection slipping through her hand and penetrating her warm flesh sent her shooting upward into ecstasy so powerful her body convulsed in immediate climax. Jonah stilled. She felt him fight for his own control, and looked guiltily up at him.

"I wasn't supposed to do that, huh?"

Between gritted teeth, he laughed. "You can do that anytime you want, my love."

He moved within her, and desire began to build again. She purred with pleasure as the rhythm of his thrusts quickened, wrapping her legs around his hips and arching upward to take him deeper inside her. She felt whole at last. Complete. Each powerful thrust seemed to reach her heart as well as her womb. His kiss breathed soul into her, his hands plied her breasts, her buttocks, her belly and seemed to rip away every barrier she had ever put between them. And finally, the light touch of his finger on the tiny nub at the crux of her desire sent her into a spasm of completion just as he buried himself to the hilt and pumped his own hot offering into her body.

A few moments later, Katy smiled as she drifted between weariness and joy. "San Francisco sounds good for a honeymoon."

Jonah nuzzled her neck. "Anywhere you want, Katydid. But wherever it is, I guarantee you're not going to see the outside of our hotel room."

Katy and Jonah were halfway to Skookum Gulch the next morning, anxious to secure the cabin and diggings for the winter, when the *Yukon Princess* tied up at the landing in Dawson. On deck, Gabriel O'Connell stood next to the widow Von Stratton and watched as the boat was secured and men on the shore waved and shouted a rowdy welcome. The widow's mastiff barked in answer to all the noise.

"This is Dawson?" the widow asked, one brow raised skeptically.

"It appears so," Gabe said.

"What a disappointment! How dreary and gray. My goodness, they don't even have boardwalks! In the summer the place must be a sea of mud."

"I expect so."

A pack of dogs had gathered on the landing and were baying at the widow's mastiff. The mastiff answered with a deafening roar.

"Guntar! Quiet!"

"Those dogs look half-wild," Gabe commented. "You might want to leave Guntar on the boat while you explore. You are going back with the steamer, aren't you?"

"Oh, most certainly, Gabriel. The captain has made it very clear that this will be the last boat out for some time. Will I have your company on the return journey?"

"If I can find my stray daughter," he replied. "She's about as wild as those dogs out there."

The widow dimpled. "Like father, like daughter?"

"No, ma'am. I'm as tame as they come."

She clicked her tongue against the roof of her mouth. "Always you are too modest. Someday I will get you to show me that wild side I see burning beneath your so proper manners.

In Europe we are much more accepting of a little playfulness between a man and woman."

"Well, ma'am," Gabe said with a grin. "My wife studied in Paris, but I don't believe much of that European attitude rubbed off on her."

The widow sent him a sparkling smile. "Very well, my friend. Find your little Katy and hurry back, or you might be spending the winter with hibernating bears and prospectors instead of that lovely wife of yours."

From his vantage point on the deck of the steamer, Gabe looked out at the dreary little town. Every building and tent boasted a smoking stovepipe, and the smoke rose to join with low, gray clouds that threatened snow. This was certainly not where he wanted to spend the winter, but he wouldn't go back without seeing Katy and settling a score with a certain newspaper reporter.

He hoped he found them soon, because after this hell of a trip, he could use an excuse to blow off some steam.

CHAPTER 22

Katy picked up a holey wool sock and tossed it onto the pile to be burned. A hat that was dirty and battered beyond saving followed the sock. The amount of trash she had produced during her short time at the claim was amazing. Of course, Andy and Jonah had helped. She pulled a torn shirt of Andy's from beneath the girl's cot, considered whether or not the garment could be mended, then threw it onto the pile with the rest of the trash. Andy seemed content to let Camilla dress her in skirts and pinafores. She wouldn't need a threadbare flannel shirt in Dawson, and by the time she came out to the claim next summer, she would have outgrown the shirt, anyway.

Andy had been overjoyed to learn that Katy and Jonah were closing down the claim for the winter.

"Promise I can help next summer," she'd begged when they stopped by Camilla's cabin to break the news.

"You'd better help," Katy had said. "You've got to earn your part of the gold."

"School will be out," Camilla had told Andy, "and you can live at the claim all summer if Katy and Jonah don't object."

Camilla also had been happy at the news of their plans. She'd given Katy a big hug and Jonah a fond kiss on the cheek. "I knew you two would find the way."

"You sure you don't want to come with us back to the States for the winter?" Jonah had asked.

"And let my competitors steal all my business? No indeed. Andy and I will be waiting for you next spring, and you can tell us about your wedding and how you spent your winter."

Jonah had grinned. "Next time we'll take the steamship up from the mouth of the Yukon. One hike over Chilkoot is enough for a whole lifetime."

"Sissy," Katy had teased. "Why would you think that?"

Katy paused in her cleaning to look out the cabin window at Jonah, who was dismantling the rocker. God knew he was anything but a sissy. She recalled the first time she had seen him in Myrna's saloon in Willow Bend, playing poker with the Hackett brothers, looking like he was sitting in some fancy Eastern men's club instead of in a two-bit bar in a dusty cow town. Who could have guessed those fancy clothes had hidden such a man—all that grit, determination, laughter, and strength?

Katy still found it incredible that he loved her. She'd always known how to earn a man's respect, but she'd never thought to earn a man's love. Even now she could scarcely believe it. She expected any moment to awaken from an impossible dream. Yet it wasn't a dream; it was real. Jonah did love her. Katy O'Connell had found a wonderful man who accepted her just the way she was. Who would have believed such a thing could happen?

Katy took the flour, salt, sugar, salertus, rice, and beans from the shelf and packed them into a box for Camilla and Andy. She rolled all the blankets and bundled them into a sturdy tarp that would protect them from mice. Then she turned to the pile of Jonah's papers on the table, stacking them neatly and wrapping a string around them so they could be safely packed in Jonah's backpack.

A scrawled title on top of a page caught her eye. Patrick Burke. Unable to resist, Katy sat down at the table and began to read. Jonah's handwriting was a scrawl; lines were crossed out, others added. Obviously this was a draft of something that he had recopied and sent to his newspaper to print. There was a note above the title to change Patrick's name.

Jonah could have changed the name to Chinese and Katy would have recognized the subject—the jovial, hard-drinking Irishman with an itch for wandering and adventure, never giving a thought to the hardships his adventures forced on others, always ready with a story, a smile, a tune on his fiddle. A man who had never outgrown childhood. Patrick sprang to life from Jonah's words.

Farther down in the pile Katy found notes on brutal Jack Decker and his pathetic horses, Camilla, Andy—even a couple of pages on Maude. She smiled at Jonah's sanitized description of the whores and laughed when she read what Andy had done to get Maude off Jonah's back. How had Jonah pried that information from the little scamp? Katy wondered. Did Jonah know that Katy had been the one who sent Andy to scuttle Maude's ambitions?

She was about to restack the papers when a title near the bottom leapt off the paper and grabbed her. Katy O'Connell. Two exclamation points followed her name. The paper was crinkled and stained from being wet and then dried, and some of the writing was smeared.

The page beckoned. It was a chance to look inside Jonah's mind on a subject that struck to Katy's very heart—the subject of herself. She felt wicked for reading it, but she read it anyway, her face flushed and a smile of anticipation on her lips.

As she read, the color faded from her face along with the smile.

Jonah whistled as he fought with the rocker. The stubborn thing was not coming apart easily, but nothing could ruin his mood today. Not the cold, the lowering clouds, the icy gusts of wind that cut through his parka, nor the sharp cobbles biting into his backside as he sat and struggled with the last of the rocker supports.

Observing the work with a supervisory air, Hunter cocked his head at Jonah's whistling.

"Like that, do you?" Jonah asked, pausing in his effort to remove a nail that joined two sections of the strut. "Friend wolf, that's the sound of a happy man," Jonah confided. "Not only has your stubborn little friend Katy realized at long last that I'm the man for her, but we're getting out of this deep freeze before true winter sets in. For that I am truly grateful."

Hunter swiped his jaws with his tongue.

"Although," Jonah continued jauntily, "on second thought, spending the winter confined to a cozy little log cabin with Katy wouldn't be too bad, now that I think on it. Though this shack would need a lot of work before it could be called cozy."

The sections of the last support parted. "Ah! Finally!" He threw the support on a tarp with the rest of the disassembled rocker that was ready to be dragged to the cabin. There it would be stored for the winter along with the shovels, picks, hatchets, axes, and other tools that needed to be sheltered from the harsh winter. Next summer, he promised himself, he would build a good, tight toolshed for this stuff, and chink the cabin as well, so if they did decide to spend a winter here, they wouldn't spend it freezing.

"Bet you'll be glad to get out of here," he said to Hunter. "Those old wolf bones of yours aren't as springy as they were a few years ago, eh? I suppose if that lady we heard tell about can take some fancy pooch on the steamer, the captain shouldn't object to an honest-to-goodness, true-blue wolf."

Hunter looked toward the cabin and whined.

"I agree. She's taking her time. How long does it take to throw clothes in a bag and supplies in a box?"

Jonah stamped his feet to get the blood flowing and headed toward the cabin. It was some sort of miracle, he thought, that he'd been with Katy since late July, and still his heart lifted in anticipation of seeing her, even though he'd spent the night before making love to her, the entire morning hiking through the mountains with her, making plans, pausing for long, leisurely kisses. If it hadn't been so damned cold, kisses were not all they would have paused for. They were going to be like this forever, he hoped. Katy had a passion that matched her temper and was just as easily sparked. She would make life both precarious and precious.

"The rocker's down," he announced as he walked through the door. "You and Andy put that thing together to last, I'll tell you! I thought it was never going to—" A wooden spoon came flying through the air at him. It was followed by a barrage of socks, a boot, a graniteware coffeepot, and a set of matching cups. "What the—ouch! Katy! What the hell are you—?"

"You low-down, snake-tailed, forked-tongued, son of a horned toad!"

"Whoa! Settle down! All I said was that the rocker was—"

"No!" She slammed her hand down upon the table, scattering a pile of papers. Three pages of what he recognized as his handwriting were separate from the pile. She picked them up as if they were fresh from the latrine. "*This* is what you said."

Recognizing what she held, Jonah winced. He should have burned those particular pages long ago.

"Scruffy little scalawag," she read in an ominous voice. "Rought-cut as a piece of coal."

"Katy, that was when I—"

"More at home in a saloon than a sewing bee," she continued relentlessly. "Could put on a Wild West show rivaling Buffalo Bill Cody's. The gent who tries to tame this filly will need a firm bit and steady seat, or she'll buck him over the moon and laugh as he plummets back to earth." She crumpled the page in her fist and turned to the second.

"That was when I first—" The crumpled page bounced off his nose.

"Surely one of the West's most colorful females," she read in a cold voice. "Pandora, Calamity Jane, and Buffalo Bill contained in one boyishly scruffy package. Even wearing skirts and a cunning straw hat she snaps the world to attention with the forwardness and manner of a man."

The second crumpled page hit him between the eyes. Jonah was grateful Katy didn't have a gun in her hand. "Katy, I wrote that when I first met you."

"Well you got to know me real fast, didn't you?"

"I didn't know you at all!"

"And you decided to let me tag along with you so you could fill in the details for your damned Chicago newspaper."

"That's ridiculous! I fired you."

"And took up with me again when you needed more drivel for your readers Back East."

"I don't write drivel. And you were the one who took up with me!"

"You say you want to marry me? How do I know you don't want to take me back to your stupid Chicago and put me in a cage at the zoo for people to gawk at!"

"Katy! For God's sake!"

"I should have known!" Tears streamed down her face.

Jonah stifled the urge to go to her and fold her in his arms. He didn't live that dangerously. "You should have known what?"

"Why you stuck with me, pursued me, acted like you wanted to marry me!"

"You don't really believe that's true, you little idiot!"

"Now I'm an idiot, am I? As well as a ragamuffin, scalawag, a Wild West side show, and those other clever names you pinned on me."

"Yes, you're an idiot. I wrote that when I first met you, and I was looking for colorful Western characters to entertain my readers. Now you're using it as an excuse to back out of marrying me because, just like before, you're scared."

"Hah!"

"You listen to an ounce of truth about yourself and want to go back where you're safe and don't have to take chances!"

"Truth?" She heaved his pack at him. "You're a newspaper reporter! What do you know about the truth? There's your stuff. Get out!"

"Give me my notes—those that you haven't already thrown at me."

She shoved the sheaf of papers his way.

"Be in town by tomorrow, Katy. We don't know just when that boat is going to leave."

"Maybe I don't want to be on the damned boat!"

"Be there, Katy, or I'll come after you and carry you down the trail over my shoulder! I swear I will! And if reason won't cool you down, we'll see if a dunk in the Yukon will do it."

She shouted after him, "You and whose goddamned army, greenhorn?"

Hunter looked at him inquiringly as the cabin door slammed shut.

"Don't ever get involved with a female," Jonah advised him sourly. Hell, he'd just been thinking that life with Katy was going to be precarious. He hadn't known how soon she would prove him right.

"O'Connell. Hmm." The claims office clerk perused his files and expelled a sibilant stream of air through the space between his two front teeth.

Gabe tapped a finger on the wooden counter and tried to curb his impatience. His little Katy had been with this newspaper fellow for weeks. Another few hours was not going to matter, one way or another. He'd heard stories of the passage over the Chilkoot and White Pass trails. The passengers on the steamer, glad they were traveling to Dawson the easy way, had repeated every grisly horror story about mud, bogs, floods, killer rapids, and mud slides. He hoped like hell that Katy and that jackass reporter had traveled the all water route, as he had done, but he doubted it. Katy hadn't taken enough money with her to afford the passage, and if this reporter wanted to write about the Klondike gold rush, he would want to be in the thick of things. No doubt he'd gone over one of the passes and dragged poor Katy with him.

"Let's see, here's an O'Connell. James. Nope." The clerk scratched a balding pate. "Katy O'Connell, hm. Here's a Kathleen Mary O'Connell. Would that be her?"

Gabe's heart leapt. "That's her!"

"She filed a claim up on Skookum Gulch. Number fourteen."

"Do you have a map?"

"Yes." The little man unrolled a much-used plat of the numerous streams and gulches in the Dawson area. His finger traveled up the Klondike, veered off at Skookum Gulch, and landed on claim number fourteen. "It looks to be about a half day's hike from here. The claim's a joint one. Kathleen O'Connell, Jonah Armstrong, and Alexandra Reese. Now, if you'd given me Mr. Armstrong's name, I would have known who you was talkin' about right off. He's the newspaper fella who comes in here on and off to talk about what's going on. Yessir, he's got the pulse of ever'thin' happenin' in Dawson."

"Is Armstrong in town?" Gabe asked. His hand tightened into a fist.

"He was in just the other day. Saw 'im havin' dinner down at the hotel. Heard he and his partners struck it big. Might still be here. If I see him, I'll tell him you're lookin' for him."

"You do that," Gabe said grimly. "Thanks for your help."

Gabe spent the day searching Dawson, just in case Armstrong was still in town. A couple of bartenders knew him, but didn't know of Katy. A clerk at the Alaska Commercial Company store knew them both.

"Jonah and his wife? Sure," the burly man said. "Good people. They got a strike, I hear."

"His wife?"

Big as he was, the clerk backed away from the menace in Gabe's voice.

"Well, I figured she was. He lets her draw off his account

here. I've seen 'em together at the hotel, and they've been livin' together in a shack up at their claim."

A haze of red misted Gabe's vision.

"She's a right feisty little gal. Gives ol' Jonah a run for his money, I'd say, though she don't even come up to his shoulder."

"She won't be quite so feisty when I get through with her," Gabe growled. "You got a map of this area you can sell me? One with Skookum Gulch on it?"

The midafternoon sunset was blazing crimson across the sky as Gabe marched grimly back to the Great Northern Hotel. He itched to be on his way to Skookum Gulch, but even prospectors who knew these mountains didn't brave the trails after sunset. He began more and more to appreciate how Olivia's father had felt when his bright, sophisticated daughter had run off with a ex-fugitive from Montana.

"Mr. O'Connell!" The clerk at the hotel desk waved Gabe over. "You were asking earlier about Jonah Armstrong, sir?"

"Yes?"

"Well, sir, that's Mr. Armstrong coming down the street just now."

Jonah still seethed. The long hike into town had done little to cool his exasperation. Of all the women his mother had tried to match him with, of all the women he'd met in a career that had taken him around the country, and sometimes exotic places out of the country, why did he have to fall in love with a stubborn, childish, hoydenish, volatile, jackass of a woman like Katy O'Connell? She was ornerier than a mule and flighty as a chipmunk. Damned if he was going to let her do this to him. If she didn't cool off and come to her senses in time to get on that boat with him, he'd march right back up to that cabin and shake her until these stupid notions of hers shook right out of her silly head.

"Jonah Armstrong?"

Jonah looked up. A tall man stood just outside the entrance

to the hotel, his feet planted wide apart, his arms crossed upon his chest. Even allowing for the bulk of his sheepskin jacket, Jonah could see the man was fit and muscular. The way he balanced on the balls of his feet, the set of his broad shoulders, and the glitter in his eyes—all said here was a man set for a fight.

"I'm Armstrong," Jonah admitted, shrugging off his pack.

"I'm Katy O'Connell's father."

"Oh shit!" Jonah muttered.

"I believe you know my daughter."

Jonah sighed. "Unfortunately."

O'Connell stepped closer. His hands were balled into fists. This morning Katy had tried to pelt him to death, and this afternoon her father was going to beat him to a pulp, and Gabriel O'Connell looked like a man who could do it.

"Where is she?" O'Connell demanded.

"Sitting on her high horse up in Skookum Gulch."

"You make a practice of luring innocent young girls from their homes and dragging them halfway across creation, boyo?"

"Innocent young girl?" Jonah had to laugh. His temper had taken just about as much as it could take today. "Ask your stubborn mule of a hotheaded daughter just who lured which innocent into what."

"You can't talk that way about my daughter, friend."

"The hell I can't!"

Gabe lunged, and Jonah stood fast to meet him. Both men were too near the edge of their tempers to have time for explanations or excuses. Gabe's fist caught Jonah on the jaw. Jonah staggered back, then charged forward with fists flying, landing a punch to Gabe's chin and another to his sternum. The air whooshed from Gabe's lungs, but he recovered in time to stick out a foot and trip his adversary on the next charge. They both went down in a tangle of limbs and flying fists.

A small but interested audience gathered. The clerk from

the hotel placed a bet on Jonah. A prospector in town for supplies laid odds on Gabe.

"Saw 'im walking down the street earlier," the prospector explained to the clerk. "Looked ready to kill somebody."

Jonah's head bounced against the frozen mud of the street as Gabe landed a blow. Jonah growled, grabbed at Gabe's throat, and squeezed. Gabe punched him again, then landed a knee in his crotch.

Jonah howled and released him.

Gabe's face was red from Jonah's chokehold, but gleeful just the same. "That one's for my Katy!"

Jonah swung and missed. "Katy can land her own blows," he gritted out. "And has."

Gabe threw a left hook. Jonah ducked, staggered, and nearly lost his balance.

They looked at each other. Painfully bent over, hands braced on their thighs to hold themselves upright, they were both bloodied, bruised, and breathing heavily.

"Are we through yet?" Jonah gasped.

"I don't know. Maybe."

"You're Katy's pa all right. You've got the same left hook."

"I taught it to her," Gabe said, eyes narrowing.

"And she taught it to me. Said I didn't know how to fight worth a damn."

Gabe's mouth twitched. "You do okay."

"Katy's a passable teacher."

They looked at each other a moment longer, Jonah cautious, Gabe considering.

"Let's take a break for a drink," Gabe suggested. "We can finish this later if we have to."

"All right by me," Jonah agreed. "God! Could I use a drink!"

As they stumbled together toward the Palace Saloon, a small figure broke from the audience and ran. A pinafore peeked from beneath her parka, and short red curls bounced beneath its hood.

*   *   *

Katy sat on the cold ground, clutching her parka around her, caught in the awful limbo of indecision. The disassembled rocker, lying on the tarp next to the cabin, had neither moved nor spoken, no matter how long she stared at it. It was being no help at all. Neither was Hunter, who sat on his haunches, looking at her as though she were some sort of strange creature he'd never before seen.

She was a strange creature, Katy reminded herself sourly. She was "Pandora, Calamity Jane, and Buffalo Bill contained in one boyishly scruffy package." To her face Jonah had told her she was a beautiful woman worthy of a man's devotion—his devotion. Behind her back, he'd been writing comments like that for his sophisticated readers in Chicago to laugh at. Why in hell did he want to marry her? So he could write "Calamity Jane Goes to Chicago," or "Pandora Takes on New York"?

She didn't know what to do. All the day before she had walked up and down the gulch or paced the floor of the little cabin, wondering which way to choose in this fork in life's road. Now it was morning and she had no better idea than yesterday.

What she *had* to do, though, was decide whether or not to store the rocker in the cabin for the winter and meet Jonah at the boat, therefore following in the best female tradition of being humble and obedient, or put the damned thing back together and resign herself to a winter alone, melting gravel and fighting frostbite, wondering how Jonah would have explained himself if she had given him a chance. If she let the morning progress much further in this confusing state, time would make the decision for her. The steamer would leave without her, and so would Jonah.

Why did life have to be so dagblamed confusing?

Katy was so absorbed in her dilemma that she didn't hear the horse until it trotted into sight. It was the rawboned bay from the livery, and bouncing along on the horse's back was Andy.

"Katy! Thank goodness you're here! I looked all over town for you, and you weren't anywhere!"

Katy got to her feet and took the horse's reins while Andy jumped from the saddle. "I'm not there," she said, "because I'm here. What are you doing here? Does Camilla know where you are?"

"Yeah. Listen—"

"I see she didn't burn your britches," Katy observed with a smile.

"Skirts ain't good for ridin'. Listen Katy! I come to tell you that yesterday dusk I saw Jonah get the tar beaten out of him in the street in front of the hotel."

"What?"

"'Course, he was givin' as good as he was takin'."

"Omigod! Was he hurt?"

"Dunno. Probably. There was blood all over."

"Who beat him up? Who was it?"

"Some big guy I ain't never seen before. Throws a punch like a mule's kick. He looked pretty tattered himself. They jist about wore each other out, and they were talkin', but I didn't hear what they said. I ran off to find you."

"Did he get robbed?"

"Dunno!"

"Well, damn! I'm going to have to run to his rescue again!" Katy couldn't make the words sound properly disgusted, because her heart was suddenly lighter, in spite of the alarm and anxiety for Jonah. The man simply couldn't get along without her.

CHAPTER 23

Gabe was nursing his fourth cup of coffee in the dining room of the hotel when he saw Katy march into the lobby. She stopped, hands on hips, and looked around her. When she glanced into the dining room and saw him, her eyes widened, her mouth fell open, and she stared. He would have smiled at the expression on her face, but smiling hurt too much.

"Omigod!" she said, and came toward his table, looking every bit like a little girl who's been caught in a flagrant piece of mischief, which, of course, she had. "Pa! Is it really you?"

"In the flesh."

"What are you . . . oh, look at you!" She sat down across from him, her eyes on his face with its purple cheek and gash above the brow. "What happened?" Her eyes grew round with horror as she answered her own question. "You're the one who beat up Jonah!"

"Just who beat up who is a matter for debate," he told her, wincing.

"How could you? What did you do to him? Where is he? You didn't kill him, did you? If you did, I'll . . . I'll . . ."

Miffed by her instant swing of concern from him to Jonah, Gabe scowled. "He's as alive as I am. Probably more so, since he's younger."

"Where he is?"

"How should I know?"

Katy jumped up, but he reached out and grabbed her hand. "Sit down, young woman. We have a few things to talk about."

"Later, Pa. I'm sorry, but I have to find Jonah. He—"

"Sit! Down!"

Her mouth clamped shut, and with a vintage Katy glare that Gabe was all too familiar with, she sat. "I can't believe you took after him, Pa. If you're mad at me, that's one thing, but you ought to be grateful to Jonah. He's done nothing but try to take care of me since we left Willow Bend."

"Yeah. I'll bet! What makes you think your Jonah didn't jump me?"

"He wouldn't do that! He never fights unless he absolutely has to. He's the gentlest, most restrained man I've ever met!"

Gabe gingerly touched a scrape on his jaw. "He is, huh?" Katy's attitude confirmed a father's worst fear: his little girl had learned to love another man. He'd suspected it the evening before while Jonah Armstrong and he had drowned their differences in a bottle of good whiskey. The newspaperman had accused him of siring a daughter who was stubborn, spoiled, reckless, and had a temper like nitroglycerin. The poor man had grown more frustrated and agitated with every fault he'd listed.

Gabe had merely agreed. He'd even expanded a bit on Jonah's list of Katy's irritating qualities and faults. People who love her generally learn to put up with them, Gabe had told the younger man.

With a resigned nod Jonah agreed. She had a heart as soft as goose down, a spirit wild as the mountains, and courage to match, he admitted. Those made up for a lot.

Had Jonah convinced her to marry him yet? Gabe had inquired as the newspaper man had stared morosely into his whiskey.

Jonah had merely groaned, and they'd spent the rest of the evening indulging in the manly pastime of complaining about the irrationality of the female mind.

And here was the troublemaking female in the flesh. Feisty and defiant as ever. Wondering just how attached Katy was to Armstrong, Gabe decided to push a bit.

He finished his coffee, set the cup down, and glared at his daughter across the table. "Do you know how much trouble you've caused? Leaving without telling anyone—"

"I left a note!"

"Skipping off to the Klondike with some greenhorn yahoo who doesn't know his tail from a toadstool."

"Jonah's not like that!"

"Some slick-talking, citified, soft-palmed dandy who figures to get himself a little company on the way to the goldfields by sweet-talking some naive little country girl into going with him."

"That's not the way it was!"

"What kind of belly-crawling vermin would hire a young girl—?"

"I'm not a girl! I'm a woman!"

"—to guide him into a wilderness filled with all sorts of dangers?"

"He didn't know I was a girl!"

Gabe lifted a brow. "Then he's stupid as well."

"He's not stupid!" The more Katy defended Armstrong, the more apparent was her affection for the man. "He'd just never met anyone like me before. He's from Chicago," she said, as if that excused just about anything.

"Chicago, eh?"

"Pa! You have no right barging in here and treating me like some runaway twelve-year-old and treating Jonah like he's some kidnapper holding me for ransom. I'm a grown woman, and if I worried you and Olivia, I'm sorry, but I've got my own life to live, and I'll live it as I please."

"Katy—!"

"No! You listen, Pa. Jonah and I have a good claim that's got a thick pay zone of gold. We're going to be rich. And even if we weren't, we can make our own decisions and live our own lives without—"

"What's this *we*?"

"Jonah and me! We filed the claim together. We're working it together, and—"

"And what else are you doing together?"

"That's our business!"

His Katy had finally grown up, Gabe acknowledged. He had begun to think it wouldn't happen, that she would never outgrow the hoydenish shell of her childhood and emerge as the unique woman he had always known she could be. Here she was, still shaky and wet from her birthing into adulthood, but standing on her own two feet nevertheless. His only regret was that a stranger had brought her to it, not him. Not her father. Yet, Jonah Armstrong wasn't a stranger to Katy. He was obviously more to her than a father ever could be.

Gabe could scarcely keep the smile from his face as he gave his daughter that final push from the nest. "You can forget that fast-talking newspaper man, little girl, because you and he won't be doing anything else together. I went easy on him in the first round, but I've given him until three this afternoon to leave town if he wants to keep his skin in one piece. And he won't be going on the steamer, because you and I are going to be on that boat. You're coming back to Montana, to the ranch. We'll return next summer to work your claim, and then you can do whatever you want with the gold. You can stay on with Olivia and David and me, if you want, or even buy a place of your own and live alone. But if you want a man, find someone who knows which end of the bull has horns."

Katy expelled an indignant huff. "You haven't listened to anything I've said! Don't you touch Jonah, Pa. Don't you dare touch him!"

She grabbed her parka, stuffed her hat onto her head, and

marched indignantly out the door. Gabe shook his head and chuckled. "Katy girl, you're wrong. I listened to everything you said."

Jonah was letting sleep soothe both his injuries and his hangover when Katy exploded into his hotel room, snatched his arm, and tried to drag him out of bed.

"Get up, Jonah! Now! What are you doing sleeping when you've only got till three to get out of town? Up! Get up!"

"What . . . what the hell?" Jonah muttered.

"I just saw my father." Unable to pull him off the bed, she joined him there, kneeling in the tangled sheets and blankets to sorrowfully touch his injuries. "Oh, Jonah! I'm so sorry. Usually Pa isn't this unreasonable."

"Katy! Izzat you?"

"Of course it's me. Look what he did to you! But he could do a lot worse. Dammit, he *will* do a lot worse if you don't get up and get out of here."

"Huh?" Katy's words buzzed around Jonah's aching head like so many persistent flies, and made just about as much sense.

She bounced off the bed and snatched his shirt from the peg on the wall.

"I just came from talking to Pa. I tried to tell him that you're not the villain he thinks you are, but he's got his back up. Believe me, you don't want to mess with Pa when his back is up. If he told you to get out of town by three, then you'd better get of town." She threw his trousers on the bed and rummaged in his pack for underwear. Socks and long johns flew into the air and landed on the bed.

"Three?" he muttered, scratching his bare stomach.

"Jonah!" She plunked herself down on the bed again. "Don't choose this moment to be stubborn and proud. I'll go with you. We'll go to the claim. Pa will be angry when I don't leave with him on the steamer, but I told him I'm a woman who can make my own decisions. He'll leave us alone."

Jonah wondered whether the hint of doubt in her voice was for the fact that her father would leave them alone, or she was a woman who could make her own decisions.

"Uh . . . I have until three to get out of town?" Jonah asked.

"Don't tell me it slipped your mind."

"No." It had never been there to slip. The last he remembered, he and Gabriel O'Connell had spent the evening drinking and complaining about the mysteries and complications of women—a subject that always serves to make men feel superior and comradely. Tongue loosened by whiskey, Jonah had told Gabe the whole story of their adventures—well, not the whole story. The man was Katy's father, after all, and he threw a mean punch. He was also a smart son of a gun, and no doubt he'd filled in the parts Jonah had left out.

"Come on, Jonah! What Pa did to you yesterday is nothing compared to what he'll do if you don't go! Please!" She laid a hand on his bare chest, a gesture that did anything but make him want to leave the bed. "Let's go."

"I'd have thought you'd enjoy seeing me pounded into the ground," Jonah said. "Aren't you the same girl who threw nearly everything in the cabin at me and then tossed me out on my poor buckshot-battered backside?"

Her eyelashes fluttered down over her eyes. "I was riled."

"So I gathered."

The little hand that lay on his chest doubled into a fist and pounded into his sternum. "I had a right!"

"Ooof! Keep pounding like that and there won't be anything left for your father to mangle."

"Then Andy rode up to the claim and told me someone was beating on you. I had to help!"

Bless Katy's heart, wasn't that just like a woman? He remembered Gabe telling him that his wife Olivia might never have married him if she hadn't felt obliged to rescue him from a pack of villains who were gunning for him. Suddenly he understood what Gabe was doing—he hoped.

"I can't run from your father, Katy."

"Why the hell not?"

"Sooner or later a man has to stand up and fight for pride if nothing else."

"Horseshit! Since when have you been so stupid?"

He grinned. "Maybe since I met you."

She pulled on his shoulders, trying to get him off the bed. "You can't fight my father! He'd pound you to a bloody pulp."

"I did all right with him yesterday."

"He was just playing around! Jonah, you're strong and you're fast, but Pa learned to fight on the docks in New York, and then the Blackfeet taught him a few nasty tricks. He'll wipe up the street with you. Please!" She ran her fingers lovingly down his cheek. "I like your face just the way it is."

He put his hands on her waist and drew her closer. "Do you?"

"I'll marry you, Jonah. I'll go anywhere with you. But promise me you won't fight my father."

"Would it be such a sacrifice to marry me?"

She willingly cuddled against him, fitting her body to his. "No. It's not a sacrifice."

"Does it bother you that I can't fight as well as your father, or shoot, or ride, or punch cows? Hell, I don't do any of those things as well as you, much less your pa."

"That doesn't bother me. Jonah, I love you. You're gentle, kind, smart, and you're strong enough and brave enough not to have to swagger around proving to everyone how strong and brave you are."

"I'm that wonderful, am I?"

"Yes."

He turned so that he could bring her closer on the narrow bed. Her hair tickled his lips and smelled of pine and the cold mountain breeze. He wanted to make love to her right then, and spend the rest of the day at that activity as well, but there was an issue that had to be taken care of first. He reached around Katy to his leather-bound journal that lay on the bedside table. "I want you to read something. No, don't move. I like you there. Just read." He handed her the loose pages he'd taken from the journal.

Her eyes scanned the pages rapidly at first, then slowed. She bit her lip. "When did you write this?"

"I've been writing it all along between Skaguay and here."

"The imp of the Old West proves that beauty depends little on high fashion," she read softly, "that femininity lies not in decorum and graciousness, domestic skills, or style. True femininity resides in a courageous spirit and caring heart."

"What you read in the cabin were a few smart-mouth comments I wrote on the train to Seattle." He took the pages from her hand and let them drop onto the floor. "I never sent any of this in to be published. It's too close to my heart."

"Oh," she said in a chastened whisper.

"Katy, don't you see that it doesn't matter?" He rolled so that he loomed above her. In this case he wanted to dominate, he wanted to bully the knowledge into her so forcefully that she would never forget it. "You *are* Pandora, Calamity Jane, and Buffalo Bill wrapped up in one package, and more besides. What's so awful about that? If you can love a smart-mouth tenderfoot who can't set a rabbit snare or catch a fish with his bare hands, why can't I love a boot-stomping, wolf-hugging imp who will never write a homemaking column for *Godey's Ladies' Book*?"

She looked up at him with jewel green eyes that sparkled from pooling tears. "I do love you, Jonah. I have for such a long time."

"And I love you." He grinned wickedly. "You can try to get away from me all you want, Katydid. I'll never let you go. No more pushing me away."

"I promise."

He reached between them and unfastened the buttons of her trousers.

"What are you doing?"

"You have too many clothes on for the climax of this conversation."

"Jonah! We don't have time for this. We have to go over to Andy and Camilla's place to get Hunter, then skedaddle up to the claim before Pa gets wind of what we're up to."

"Ah, ah!" He grinned. "No pushing me away. Remember?"

"But my pa!"

"To hell with him. This is a two-person operation." He managed to get her trousers down around her knees. "Have I ever told you that you wear too much underwear?"

"It's cold out there."

"I think we should settle in a warm climate where you don't have to wear anything at all." His hands slipped under the three layers of shirts. Her breasts were warm, the nipples already hard, anticipating his touch.

"Jonah!"

"Yes?" He had unbuttoned one shirt and pushed up the others to give his mouth access.

"We don't have time." Her voice rang with remarkably little determination as his tongue made lazy circles over each luscious globe.

"Mmm," was his only answer.

"We don't—oh!"

He pushed down her long johns and ran his fingers lightly through the mound of curls between her legs. One finger slipped inside her, then two.

"Oh, Jonah!" Moist and ready, she arched toward his caress.

"You're right. We don't have much time."

She objected with a little gasp of distress as he withdrew. Her hand reached out and firmly grasped what she wanted. "Yes, we do," she said with iron-hard sweetness, bringing him down to where she wanted him.

He almost exploded as her fingers closed around him. They didn't need much time. He thrust, drowning in his need to be inside her, to know in the most primitive way that she was indeed his. She bucked beneath him, limited in taking him deeply enough by the clothing wrapped around her knees.

"Wait," he growled.

"No! Don't leave me!?"

He laughed as he withdrew. "Never. I'll never leave you."

Efficiently he flipped her onto her stomach, lifted her to hands and knees, and thrust home, deep and hard. Each thrust made her gasp with pleasure. Her buttocks pressed firmly into his straining groin, sucking him more deeply inside her until he lost all control and exploded. She cried out and spasmed around him, holding him so firmly inside her he couldn't have escaped had he wanted to.

They collapsed onto the bed, and he held her trapped between his legs. "God, Katy! Life with you might not prove to be long, but it's going to be heaven."

She sighed in answer, then jerked away from him. "Omigod! What time is it? We've got to go!"

Jonah groaned as she leapt from the bed and took her silky warmth with her.

"You're wicked, Jonah!" she said with a half smile. "We should have been out of here long ago."

He rolled out of bed and unhurriedly got dressed. "We do have some business to take care of."

"Jonah! You're not going to fight my pa. Swear to me that—"

A firm knock on the door interrupted her demand. She expelled a panicked breath. "It's him. I know it's him!" She glanced at the tangled bed, breathed in the odor of their lovemaking. "Now he'll really be mad! What have I done?"

Jonah finished buttoning his trousers. "The same thing that most women in love eventually do, but I'd venture you do it better."

She returned his grin with a glare. The knock sounded again.

"Armstrong, I know you're in there."

Katy paled as Jonah opened the door. There was no place to hide. But her father merely raised a brow and smiled when he saw her standing there. She hastily pushed her loosened braids over her shoulder as if hiding the evidence of what they had just done.

"Katy," Gabe greeted her calmly. "Thought I might find you here as well."

"Don't you touch him, Pa. This is all my fault."

"And you should be ashamed of yourself," Gabe commented, leaning casually against the doorframe. "From the looks of him, this man needs some rest."

"You don't look like a spring daisy yourself," Jonah told the older man.

Katy's eyes narrowed as Jonah and Gabe grinned at each other. "What is this?" Understanding dawned upon her face. "You! You never told him to be out of town by three."

"Well," Gabe replied. "The steamer leaves at three-thirty, so he'd better be on his way by three if he's going to catch it."

"You didn't threaten him!"

"Hell, Katy girl. I already beat him nearly to a pulp."

"Not quite," Jonah corrected. "You got as good as you gave."

"True enough. How's the jaw?"

"It'll do. How about your head?"

"Oh, I've had worse."

"You two are friends?" Katy demanded furiously. "This was all an act?"

"Hell no!" Gabe said. He came in and collapsed in a long-legged sprawl on the room's one chair. "I followed you up here foaming at the mouth to drag my little girl back to Montana and pulverize the scoundrel who led her astray, but I found out that Jonah's a good man who can defend himself pretty well and who doesn't turn into a bastard after a few whiskeys—and more important, he loves you. And I found out my Katy isn't a little girl anymore, and more important, you love him."

"So you—you—" She turned to Jonah. "And you—" Katy sputtered, speechless, and then she laughed. "Jonah, you're going to pay for this."

He grinned. "Can it wait until after the honeymoon?"

"I guess it can."

Gabe sprang to his feet. "Come on. With luck, that steamer captain will marry you on the way downriver." He gave the bed a knowing glance. "We'd better get you properly wed, or Olivia will hang me by the ears, which is gentle compared to what she'll do to Jonah."

Jonah picked up his backpack and leaned down to give Katy a kiss. "This is not going to be an ordinary marriage."

"It never is," Gabe said as he closed the door behind them.